'Roger, we've both got to talk to her. She's been given so many advantages—why can't she see that?'

'What advantages? She's never going to be asked to their balls. One day they'll convince themselves they've done the best for her and then she'll be on her own.'

'We don't know that, Roger.'

'Well, of course we do. Their charity extends so far and no further. We're never invited to the hall when they have guests, never for meals, never to social evenings. It's still there, the line your grandfather drew; the little they're doing for Lisa is merely a sop to their conscience, nothing more.'

Inwardly Mary knew Roger was right but some strange feeling of family loyalty wouldn't let her admit it. With a cynical smile he turned away and gave his full attention to the lunch she had set before him.

Later in the day Roger had no doubt that his wife would try to convince their daughter that she should be grateful for the lessons she was receiving, and that she should conform in every way, but Lisa had a mind of her own. He thought grimly to himself that the obstacles in store would be many; Lisa would be her own woman.

Sara Hylton has spent most of her life in local government, working as a personal assistant to a City Treasurer. She enjoys travelling, and the scenes of her travels have featured in her novels.

AN ARRANGED
MARRIAGE

Sara Hylton

M&B

*First published in Great Britain 2004 by Judy Piatkus
(Publishers) Ltd. Paperback edition 2006. This edition 2008
by Harlequin Mills & Boon Limited, Eton House,
18-24 Paradise Road, Richmond, Surrey TW9 1SR*

AN ARRANGED MARRIAGE © Sara Hylton 2004

ISBN: 978 0 263 84979 0

41-0508

*Printed and bound in Spain
by Litografía Rosés S.A., Barcelona*

Book One

CHAPTER ONE

THERE WAS A FROWN ON Anne Walton's face as she looked along the full length of the drive to where it dramatically curved and she lost sight of it. She was annoyed.

For the third time in the week her erring pupil was late for class while the rest of the children sat round the large table behind her, chattering, laughing, unconcerned that their lesson should have started at least half an hour before.

Miss Walton couldn't understand why the girl was coming at all or why her employer Mrs Jarvison-Noelle had even thought of inviting her to join her own daughters in their classroom. It wasn't as though they were related, indeed the girl was the daughter of the Estate Manager and his wife who lived at the house provided for them near the stables. She would really have to speak to her employer and make her annoyance plain.

Miss Helena came to stand beside her, looking up at her with a sympathetic smile. Helena was the eldest of the three girls; the other two were Miss Cora and Miss Sophie, while the one they were waiting for was Miss

Lisa Foreshaw. Anne Walton avoided using the Miss Lisa at every opportunity.

'She's very late,' Helena volunteered.

'Very late; we should really start without her. I'll have to have a word with your mother about her.'

'Here she is,' Helena said with a bright smile and left to return to her sisters.

The girl was not hurrying. Indeed it would seem her feet were intent on finding every puddle along the road as she sauntered carelessly towards the house. Miss Walton would have been amazed how accurately Lisa's thoughts mirrored her own as she plodded up the drive. What was she doing attending the class at all, and why on earth had her mother thought it necessary?

As she neared the house she looked up at the windows to be met with Miss Walton's frown and her hand gesticulating that she should hurry. She didn't, but continued to saunter unconcernedly up the steps and through the front door.

Nor was she in any hurry to reach the schoolroom, it seemed, and when at last she did arrive she was met with an irate teacher looking at her watch and three smiling faces behind her.

'What time do you call this, Lisa Foreshaw?' Miss Walton demanded. 'Our time for school is nine-thirty—it is after ten o'clock now, and I saw no sign of your even trying to hurry along the drive. What excuse do you have?'

She was met by a blank stare from two jade-green eyes in a face she considered unremarkable. Anne Walton failed to see the exquisite bone structure in the girl's pale porcelain face, the unusual eyes fringed with long black lashes and the long blue-black hair that in her eyes was not nearly so attractive as the golden tresses of her other pupils.

'Well,' she demanded, 'what have you to say for yourself?'

Taking her seat with the others at the table, the only thing Lisa said was, 'I didn't realise the time.'

'I shall have to have a word with somebody about you—either Mrs Jarvison-Noelle or your mother. Remember, Lisa, that school begins at nine-thirty, not after ten and I would ask you to show a little consideration and gratitude that you are being allowed this privilege.'

After she had finished speaking Lisa opened her small satchel, took out her books and placed them neatly in front of her, then sat calmly waiting for the lesson to begin.

Sighing with exasperation, Miss Walton felt suddenly inadequate for the morning's work. The lesson proceeded but she had little heart in it. The girls whispered together and received frowns of disapproval from their teacher; only Lisa remained aloof from their giggles, but not, Miss Walton suspected, because she was more interested in her work.

At ten-thirty the door opened and a maid came in carrying glasses of milk and biscuits, and Miss Walton said, 'You can take a break for half an hour then we'll resume with an English lesson.' Then speaking to the maid she said, 'Have you served tea in my room?'

'Yes miss, as usual,' the maid replied.

Miss Walton said, 'Well I need to see Mrs Jarvison-Noelle first. If my tea has gone cold I'll come down to the kitchen and perhaps one of the servants will make me another cup.'

'Yes miss, I'll tell Cook.'

Miss Walton was not popular in the kitchen or with any of the servants. She was neither fish nor fowl. She did not class herself as a servant and they regarded her as something of a nuisance with her likes and dislikes. However, as the maid followed her out of the room and down the stairs she was only too aware of the determined set of Anne Walton's shoulders and the resolute knock on her mistress's door.

Sybil Jarvison-Noelle was sitting at her desk writing letters, something she invariably did in the mornings. The sitting room was charming and the morning sun shone through the window onto her dark hair, caught back from her face by a large tortoiseshell slide. She was a handsome woman in her mid-thirties, the sort of woman who looked both elegant on a horse and in a ballroom, and as the teacher met her long cool glance something of her early determination faded. This was to be the first time she had crossed swords with her formidable employer.

'Well?' her employer commanded.

'I'm sorry to intrude, ma'am, but I do feel you should be made aware of the problems I am having with Lisa Foreshaw. She is invariably late for class and shows no remorse whatsoever. When I admonish her all she does is stare at me defiantly and I am left feeling utterly helpless.'

'What is her work like?'

'Adequate, ma'am, but I have the distinct feeling that she does not wish to be here. I really think she would have been much happier at the village school which she attended before. I can't think why she's been allowed to come here.'

She knew immediately she had said the wrong thing by the haughty frown on her employer's face, and Mrs Jarvison-Noelle said sharply, 'You are employed to teach, Miss Walton, not to select your pupils. I arranged with Lisa's mother that she should come here; it has nothing to do with the fact that her father is the Estate Manager, but stems from the fact that I have known her mother a great many years. Surely as a teacher you can instil some sense of decorum into the child.'

'I have tried, ma'am. I will go on trying, but at the moment I feel I am not succeeding.'

'Does she get along with my daughters?'

'I'm not sure. During lessons they are busy doing their work—I can't decide how friendly they are at other times.'

Mrs Jarvison-Noelle tapped impatiently on the table, then by way of dismissal she said, 'I'll have a word with her mother. I intended to ride in the park this morning, so I'll call in to see her.'

'Thank you, ma'am. I am most grateful.'

After Miss Walton had left the room Sybil sat staring in front of her with every degree of annoyance. Really, these servants took too much on themselves but at the same time she did not wish to antagonise the teacher further. She had come with good references; she was comely without being pretty, was reserved and hardly likely to tittle-tattle with the servants and there was no gentleman friend in the offing.

It really was too bad that Mary Foreshaw's offspring should be causing so much disruption. She would have to speak to her about it, and the sooner the better.

Back in her small sitting room Anne Walton discovered that the tea was cold in the pot and she needed something to cheer her up. Consequently she collected the tray and carried it downstairs to the kitchen in the hope of a replacement.

The servants were sitting round the kitchen table taking their mid-morning break and they each and every one eyed her with unsmiling faces.

Addressing the housekeeper she said, 'I'm sorry to intrude but I was detained with the mistress and my tea has gone cold. Could I possibly have another cup?'

One of the maids rose to her feet to take the tray and another went to the stove to boil the kettle. No words were exchanged and she stood uncertainly just within the door, then, catching Cook's eyes, she half smiled as Cook said, 'I saw that your new pupil was late arrivin' this mornin'.'

'Yes, every morning, I'm afraid.'

'Ay well, she's probably wonderin' what she's doin' 'ere.'

Silently Anne Walton agreed with her; then the maid was handing her the tray and with a brief word of thanks she returned upstairs.

She would have been surprised if she could have heard the comments expressed in the kitchen after she had left.

'I wonder what she said to the mistress,' Cook said. 'She'll get no joy out of it—when madam makes her mind up about anythin' she sticks to it.'

'Why's the girl comin' then?' Betty, the upper house-maid asked. ''er father's the Estate Manager and they never get asked to dos 'ere.'

'She 'as 'er reasons, I'm sure,' Cook replied. 'That stuck-up Miss Walton wants to watch 'erself.'

Miss Walton returned to her duties and saw that the four girls were chatting together quite amicably, although Lisa did not appear to be doing much of the talking.

They resumed their lessons and from the window Anne saw that Mrs Jarvison-Noelle was leaving the house and walking towards the stables. She fervently hoped that what she had to say to Mrs Foreshaw would either result in taking Lisa away or at least produce more enthusiasm.

Sybil was frowning as she cantered down the drive. There had been so much she wanted to do that morning— she had letters to write, the gardener to discuss plans with and later lunch with her cousin, Lucy Hazelmere. Now she had to see Mary Foreshaw who might not take too kindly to what she had to say about her daughter.

Mary watched her arrival from the kitchen window where she was busy bottling jam, and hurriedly taking off her apron and rinsing her hands she went to meet her visitor.

She ushered Sybil into the sitting room and asked if she would like coffee but Sybil said quickly, 'No really, Mary, I had coffee before I left the house; I do need to talk to you about Lisa however.'

Mary didn't answer, but the quick look of alarm was not lost on her visitor.

'Her teacher came to see me this morning—maybe it's a storm in a teacup but I could see that she was annoyed. Lisa is invariably late arriving for her lessons, and Miss Walton doesn't seem able to get through to her at all. Why is she behaving like that?'

'She doesn't see why she has to take lessons at the hall. She was quite happy at the village school.'

'But haven't you explained to her that she is being given chances other girls in the village would die for? Anne Walton came to us with very good credentials. Doesn't she feel she needs to make an effort?'

'She only feels resentment, I'm sorry to say. I'll speak to her again when she gets home. Why bother, Sybil, why not let Lisa go back to the village school? You don't have to do this for her.'

'Mary, I promised you years ago that I'd help you whenever I could. I owe it to you.'

'Well, of course you don't. You've given us this house, given Roger his job on the estate, so surely you've done enough.'

'No, both Lucy and I thought it was terrible that you didn't get any of Grandfather's money. He had three granddaughters and you were the one left out simply because your father married out of his class.'

'Grandfather never forgave him.'

'No, but you were the one who suffered for it. Lucy and I had all the advantages—the balls and parties, the meetings with the right sort of men, everything it seemed. Are you happy with Roger Foreshaw?'

'Well, of course. He's a good man who works hard on the estate. Surely Arthur has no complaints to make about him.'

'No, I'm sure he hasn't, but I am here really to talk about Lisa—she's making things very difficult, Mary.'

'I'll talk to her again, Sybil.'

'Get Roger to talk to her.'

'I don't think that will help as he doesn't see why she's taking lessons at the hall either. He calls it charity.'

'How stupid. Surely he knows why I'm doing it.'

'Yes, we've talked about it, but he doesn't see the need.'

'Well, make him see the need; his daughter's entire future rests on it. The right education, the right connections, the right sort of marriage one day. I have to go now. Mary, I'm lunching with Lucy and there were so many things I wanted to do this morning that I've had to shelve.'

'I'm sorry, Sybil. I will talk to Lisa when she gets home.'

'Yes, well, I would be grateful if you'll do that. I don't want to lose Miss Walton and she does have the right to complain.'

Mary watched her cantering off on her way to her cousin's residence—she could well imagine the subject of their conversation when they got together.

Her two cousins had married well—Lucy to Lord

Hazelmere of Hazelmere Hall, and Sybil to the Hon Jarvison-Noelle, the second son of an earl. Why were either of them bothering to nudge her daughter into the same sort of lifestyle?

She had watched Lisa leave the house that morning, a frown of annoyance on her face, her footsteps lethargic, and she had known she would be late arriving at the house.

Roger had been unsympathetic. 'Why is she even going there?' he had said. 'We don't need their charity. When she's older I'm perfectly capable of seeing that she receives an education suitable for her lifestyle.'

'They feel guilty that they got everything and I got nothing. It didn't matter. I always knew that that was how it would be. It was unfair, but it was inevitable.'

Roger had looked at her long and hard before going out of the house and she knew that never in a thousand years would he understand the pride and disappointment that had poisoned her grandfather's mind. That his second son had turned his back on his family to marry a lowly governess had been sinful in the old man's eyes, and although they elected to live in an old stone house in the village he never called to see them, and drove by in his carriage without favouring them with a second glance.

When she was a little girl she was dismally aware of the carriages driving up to her grandfather's house filled with aristocratic guests, but they were never invited. Money had been scarce. Her father earned a meagre salary working as a clerk in the local solicitor's office while her mother tutored several pupils in the area.

She had been seventeen when she first met her two girl cousins. She listened to their tales of grand balls and garden parties as they walked through the woods on her grandfather's estate. Mary had not been envious, she had loving parents and a good home, but as the time passed Sybil and Lucy both decided that she was their crusade. They had everything, she had nothing so one day they would salve their consciences and do the best they could for her.

When she married Roger, Sybil's new husband was urged to find him a better job, and then when Lisa was born they had both said she too would not be forgotten.

Sybil had three daughters and one son, Lucy had two sons. Now Lisa was receiving an education with the girls, although she had yet to meet the two boys.

Mary had no idea where they intended Lisa to go from there. Roger said they were trying to shape her life, but Mary recognised the independent streak in Lisa's nature and already it was surfacing.

She was well aware that Sybil would soon be relating the morning's events to Lucy and the two women would be wondering why they had ever decided to do anything with their ungrateful cousin and her family.

When Roger arrived for lunch he said caustically, 'What was your cousin's visit in aid of this morning? I saw her riding up to the house.'

'Nothing really, just a social visit.'

'Oh come on, Mary, when does the lady of the manor visit us socially? What did she want?'

'It was about Lisa—she's late arriving for lessons and the teacher has complained.'

'Well, she doesn't want to go there, does she? It's inevitable that she shows it in every way she can.'

'Roger, we've both got to talk to her. She's being given so many advantages—why can't she see it?'

'What advantages? She's never going to be asked to their balls. One day they'll convince themselves they've done the best for her and then she'll be on her own.'

'We don't know that, Roger.'

'Well, of course we do. Their charity extends so far and no further. We're never invited to the hall when they have guests, never for meals, never to social evenings. It's still there, the line your grandfather drew; the little they're doing for Lisa is merely a sop to their conscience, nothing more.'

Inwardly Mary knew Roger was right but some strange feeling of family loyalty wouldn't let her admit it. With a cynical smile he turned away and gave his full attention to the lunch she had set before him.

Roger had no illusions about his employers. He was good at his job, but he had already resolved that one day they would move on. It would be better for them all to get right away from old hurts and slights; better for Mary and obviously better for Lisa.

Later in the day he had no doubt that his wife would try to convince their daughter that she should be grateful for the lessons she was receiving, and that she should conform in every way, but Lisa had a mind of her own. He thought grimly to himself that the obstacles in store would be many; Lisa would be her own woman.

CHAPTER TWO

THE TWO WOMEN ENJOYED their lunchtimes together. There was a hint of rivalry between them but it was good natured on the whole.

Perhaps it was true to say that of the two, Lucy Hazelmere had exceeded her cousin in the matrimonial stakes, having married an earl whereas her younger cousin had married only the second son of an earl, but it was also true that the Jarvison-Noelles' lineage had existed for longer and produced more eminent sons.

On this particular morning, however, all their talk was of the third cousin whose daughter was giving problems.

'What is she like, then?' Lady Hazelmere asked curiously.

'Well, I've really seen very little of her. I never see her at the Hall and I only barely remember her playing in the gardens of their house. She's not really pretty, at least not like my girls. She's very dark, obviously like her grandmother.'

'Wasn't she Italian, or Spanish? I can never remember which.'

'Spanish, I think. Yes, she probably is like her grandmother. Can you begin to imagine how Grandfather would have hated foreign blood in the family.'

'He made that very clear. So what are you going to do now about Lisa?'

'Oh, Mary's promised to have words with her. Helena is twelve in August so I've promised she can have a party. I suppose I could invite Mary's girl—that at least might mend the situation, make the child feel more accepted.'

'You're being very patient, Sybil. Will you be inviting boys to the party?'

'Well, my son will be home from his school and there are your two. I'm sure they'd enjoy a party.'

Lucy didn't speak but stared reflectively through the window.

'How are the boys?' Sybil asked.

'Oh, we have good reports from their school. Dominic is obviously the clever one, Austin the sporty one. Will you be going to the garden party over at Dene Salton?'

'Oh, I expect so. You've said very little about your weekend in Bedfordshire.'

'There's a lot I have to tell you about that. The King was there with that Langtry woman. How does he get away with it?'

'We saw them together at the races. She is a very beautiful woman. I wonder how long it will last?'

'The Queen is a very beautiful woman too. Oh, he'll tire of her, I've no doubt, then he'll replace her with somebody else. Isn't that the way of things?'

'The old Queen would have been horrified.'

Lucy laughed. 'Yes, well, but it didn't stop a great many people kowtowing to both of them. Johnny and I kept ourselves to ourselves.'

'Well of course. Back to the party, Lucy. I do hope your boys will accept the invitation. It's August, so I rather thought a marquee in the garden—weather permitting, of course.'

'That sounds very nice; one hopes the weather will be good in August.'

'And the boys?'

'Oh, certainly if they have nothing else in mind.'

'Perhaps when you write to them you could mention it. That way they'll surely keep the date free.'

'Oh, I do hope so, dear, but they have friends at school and they get invited here, there and everywhere. I'm sure it's the same with Edwin.'

It would seem Sybil had to be content with that and as she rode home later in the afternoon she thought how diffident Lucy always was about her two sons.

Why for heaven's sake did she need to be like that? They were handsome and charming boys—Dominic was the quieter one, rather grave but friendly enough, while Austin was outgoing and likely to make a fuss of the girls. She wanted them at Helena's party and would insist that Johnny speak to Lucy about it; besides it would be nice for Edwin if his cousins were there.

As she rode her horse up the long drive to the Hall she was aware of a small plodding figure coming towards her, recognising her immediately from her long black hair and the school satchel thrown carelessly over her shoulder.

Halting her horse she said, 'Good afternoon, Lisa, have you enjoyed school?'

The child looked up at her out of unusual green eyes and in a small voice said, 'Yes thank you.'

'And you will try to be on time in the morning, I hope.'

No answer was forthcoming, and with a brief curtsy she took to her heels and ran across the grass towards her home.

For the first time that day Sybil began to have a fellow feeling for Anne Walton—teaching must be a terrible profession when faced with disruptive pupils; she only hoped her cousin would be able to instil some sense of propriety into her daughter.

From the front window of her house Mary had witnessed Lisa's brief meeting with her cousin and awaited her arrival home with some degree of trepidation.

For a few minutes she watched her swinging idly on the gate, then she rapped on the window with a frown, calling on her to come inside.

She met her in the hallway, where Lisa dumped her school bag on the floor and turned as if to go into the kitchen, but her mother said, 'Come in here, Lisa, I want to talk to you.'

She looked at her daughter with some degree of anxiety, at the sulky look on her face, at the long blue-black hair that shone indigo in the sunlight streaming through the window and the long black lashes hiding the green of her eyes as she looked down to avoid her mother's gaze.

'Lisa, you worry me,' Mary began. 'I've had Mrs Jarvison-Noelle here this morning complaining that you are always late for school. Your teacher has complained to her, and you left here in good time this morning. Where were you?'

'Walking to school,' Lisa murmured.

'Why didn't you walk quickly? Why dawdle on the road?'

'I didn't think of the time; it was lovely on the way there.'

'Never mind how lovely it was, Lisa, you must do better and appreciate all that is being done for you. Your friends in the village are not being given the chances you are being afforded, so try to be a little grateful.'

'Why do I have to go there, Mother? I was happy going to school with my friends; now they don't want to speak to me because I've left the school to go up to the Hall.'

'Well, they don't understand, do they?'

'No they don't, and I don't either.'

'Lisa, think about it. One day when you're grown up, education will matter—you could become a teacher like Miss Walton, or a governess in some aristocratic family. You could marry well, a vicar or a doctor, some man who is looking for the right sort of wife, a young woman who is educated and intelligent. We should be grateful to Mrs Jarvison-Noelle for her thoughtfulness, Lisa. The fact that you are being difficult is making me very unhappy.'

Lisa looked up into her mother's sad face and tears filled her eyes. Her mother was the most wonderful person in her life and she didn't wish to make her unhappy, but why was her mother's happiness so tied up with her own misery and an education she didn't want? What was wrong with the village school—that was education, wasn't it?

She rushed towards her mother and threw her arms around her, whispering, 'I'll try mother, I'll try.'

It was later when Lisa had gone to bed that Mary and her husband discussed the matter. She had known that Roger would be scathing.

'We don't need their charity, Mary,' he said angrily. 'It's a sop to their conscience that you were ignored as a child. If it's causing you so much distress we could move; I could get a job somewhere else.'

'No Roger, I won't have it. I'm happy here; you like your work; they're good employers. Instead of agreeing with Lisa why don't you make her see the advantages of an education?'

Later that evening he went into his daughter's bedroom and found her standing at the window staring miserably out into the night.

'What are you doing out of bed, child?' he said sharply. 'You'll catch your death; it's cold in here.' Indeed, as he took hold of her hand to lead her back to the bed he was aware of her pallor and the coldness of her fingers. He settled her into the bed and pulled the blankets round her, then said, 'Your mother's been telling me that you've been in trouble about school, Lisa. I promised I'd speak to you, but I hadn't thought to be doing it now. Why are you so unhappy there?

'I don't see why I have to go there.'

'Neither do I, love. You and me are of the same opinion; it's your mother who's being made unhappy about it, and really, I suppose she's right, love, it does matter that you grow up with an education behind you or you could end up marrying an old farmer like old Exton. You wouldn't want that, now would you?'

For the first time laughter filled her eyes and she smiled. Farmer Exton was obviously the most ridiculous example he could have made—a coarse, loud-mouthed boor of a man who all the village made fun of.

'I'll tell you what's a better idea, Lisa. Why don't you go up to the Hall and show them all that you can beat them, that you know more, absorb more, that none of them can hold a candle to you when it comes to learnin'?'

She stared at him uncertainly, as laughing he went on, 'Can't you see it, love? Instead of sulking and making life difficult for yourself, be the clever one, capture some handsome young man from right under their noses when the time's right—it'd make your mother so happy and proud of you.'

The doubts on her face turned into awareness, and she smiled, then her father said, 'Go to sleep now, Lisa, or you'll never be ready for school in the morning, and remember all we've talked about. Make tomorrow a whole new start.'

As he left her room he thought he'd done his best; it was up to Lisa now. As he entered their bedroom Mary looked at him anxiously and he smiled. 'I've talked to her, love, I think she's taken it in. I don't think either of us can do any more.'

When Anne Walton walked into her schoolroom the next morning she was amazed to find all her pupils assembled including Miss Lisa. Furthermore she was already sitting at her desk with her school books opened in front of her, her usual tumbling hair held back from her face by two tortoiseshell slides, her white blouse decorously buttoned.

She was even more surprised in the late afternoon when she perused the work they had each handed in at the close of their lessons.

She had never had a high opinion of her employer's children—they tried, they were adequate, but they would never be called upon to work for their living and they knew it; consequently it was sufficient if they could speak properly, read adequately and converse prettily. Lisa she had written off as entirely inappropriate.

Now she found herself staring down at her written essay which showed good grammar, a keen imagination and a questioning mind.

What had brought on this sudden transformation? she wondered.

Meeting Mrs Jarvison-Noelle several days later on her way to the schoolroom Anne Walton paused hesitantly, and her employer said sharply, 'I trust all is well, Miss Walton. Is Lisa behaving herself?'

'Oh yes, ma'am, she is always on time now and her

work is very good. Thank you so much for speaking to her mother about her.'

'Well, I'm very relieved to hear it, for your sake if nothing else.' Then to Anne Walton's surprise she went on, 'Join me in my study for a few moments; I'll ring for tea.'

Inside the study she was invited to sit, and in only a few minutes a maid arrived with tea and biscuits and after the maid had poured the tea, handed round the cups and departed Sybil said, 'I don't suppose you are aware of it, Miss Walton, but my daughter Helena is twelve at the beginning of August and we are proposing to give her a party here at the Hall. I take it you will be on holiday from the beginning of August.'

'Yes, ma'am, if that is convenient.'

'Of course.'

'That is good then, because we propose to be away for two weeks after the party so that school can commence at the beginning of September. Do you go anywhere nice for your school holiday?'

'Oh yes, ma'am, I go with my sister to Italy. We've gone there every year for the last five or six years.'

'Where exactly in Italy?'

'Tuscany, ma'am. Very close to Florence. We can't really afford to stay in the city as it's very expensive, but we stay in a small village not far from it and use the local train to take us there every day. Do you know Florence at all, ma'am?'

'I've been there, but I prefer Rome or Capri. You should go there when you have the opportunity.'

'Oh yes, I do want to do that. We both love Italy.'

'I think perhaps I should invite Lisa Foreshaw to Helena's birthday party. What do you think?'

'It would be very kind of you, ma'am, particularly if the improvement I find in her continues.'

'Yes, well, the girls are at school together, so I don't want her to think she is being excluded from something a little more exciting.'

On the way back to the classroom Anne Walton was considering it more than generous for her employer to be including Lisa Foreshaw in Miss Helena's birthday celebrations. She couldn't analyse what she really thought about the girl.

She was never disrespectful—those jade-green eyes merely looked straight ahead with cool detachment, and she wondered if underneath that stony indifference there might be a gentleness she had yet to discover.

When lessons were over and the girls came to hand in their papers Helena said, 'I'm having a birthday party in August, Miss Walton. Would you like to be there?'

'Oh, that is kind, Miss Helena, but I shall be on holiday in Italy. Your mother mentioned the party to me. I'm sure it will be quite wonderful.'

'I just hope the weather is good—Mother is hoping to have a marquee in the garden.'

'Of course. You will need good weather for that.'

'I am inviting a good many girls and boys.'

'Then I shall pray that the weather is lovely and that you will all have a wonderful time.'

Turning round to Lisa, Helena said, 'I think Mother

intends to invite you also, Lisa. I hope you will be able to come.'

Lisa stared at her without enthusiasm, and Miss Walton watched the quick intake of her breath coupled with the colour flooding her cheeks before she said, 'I'm not sure—perhaps we shall be away.'

Oh why couldn't she be enthusiastic, why so diffident? Anne thought angrily that if she'd been asked to such a party at Lisa's age she'd have died with gratification. Was there anything in the world that could shake that studied composure?

Walking home Lisa thought about the invitation to Helena's party. She would only know the Jarvison-Noelle girls, none of their friends and certainly none of the boys. What would they make of her? At the back of her mind were her mother's stories of her two cousins and their friends with whom she'd felt totally at a loss.

If she told her mother she didn't want to go she would be unhappy; in fact her mother already knew of the invitation and was thinking about the dress Lisa might wear. Something not too ostentatious—Lisa wasn't the frothy fairy-tale girl, but it had to be something right and affordable.

When she asked Lisa what colour she would like Lisa merely said, 'I don't really mind, Mother. Must I go?'

'Well, of course you must. Do show a little enthusiasm, darling. I think pale green would be so lovely with your eyes, or primrose perhaps. So many of the girls will be wearing white and your colouring is so vibrant.'

The material was chosen, pale green lawn, and a

darker green velvet cape for if the weather was cool. The material had been expensive and Lisa, staring at it, said, 'Are you going to make it, Mother?'

'No dear, I've asked Mrs Stedman if she'll make it up for you; she's really very good.'

'She's also very expensive,' her husband said drily.

'Darling, it's the first big party Lisa's been invited to, so she's got to look the part.'

She wished Lisa would show more interest both in the dress and the occasion. Sybil had already informed her that replies to the invitations were guaranteeing an enthusiastic response. There would be around twenty girls at the party and nearly as many young men. They had engaged a small orchestra and there would be dancing since most of the girls attended dancing classes and the boys obviously would be able to dance.

That last piece of information convinced Lisa she would not go to the party. She had never had dancing lessons—if a boy invited her to dance he would think she had two left feet, and she prayed silently that on the day of the party God would inflict her with chickenpox or something similar.

But God did not appear to be so obliging since the day of the party was to find her totally well.

CHAPTER THREE

FOR THE WHOLE OF AUGUST there would be no more school and Lisa was happy roaming the countryside, largely alone, since her friends from the village considered her too superior to be included in their pursuits, and the Jarvison-Noelle girls were invited here, there and everywhere.

The weather was gloriously warm, and every day the sun shone out of a clear blue sky, until the day before Helena's party when dark clouds loomed over the horizon threatening to bring thunderstorms and heavy rain. Unfortunately this was not a good omen for the party, so it was decided that the marquee was not a good idea. Consequently the party would be held in the Hall and the staff were busy moving furniture as well as expensive porcelain which the mistress said must not get broken.

The ballroom was a modest one but it was lined with small gilt chairs and at one end there was a fair-sized dais for the orchestra. Plants were brought in from the greenhouses and in the kitchen itself the staff were busily engaged in polishing cutlery, assembling crockery and Cook more than anybody was busy preparing her menu.

The girls were excited, their mother rather less so. She was annoyed with the weather, with the fact that the entire house was being disorganised and by her husband's lack of interest. She rode over to her cousin's house in a shower of rain and for most of the afternoon Lucy had to listen to a series of complaints about what she termed 'the whole wretched business.'

'I don't see what you can do about it,' Lucy said reasonably. 'You promised Helena the party; I'm sure it will be a great success.'

'I suppose so, but it was a mistake. We should have gone off to France instead; we could have spent the whole of August there instead of just two weeks.'

'Well, there's nothing you can do about it now, Sybil. The invitations have gone out and I'm sure everybody is looking forward to it.'

'Are the boys home?'

'Yes, out riding somewhere. I told them you were coming so I'm sure they'll be in to see you later.'

'Edwin tells me Dominic is going on to university. I hadn't realised he was old enough.'

'He's eighteen and he's clever. I'm sure he'll do well at university, while Austin is destined for the Army or the Navy, I think.'

'You mean he's not as intellectual?'

'No. He's the happy-go-lucky one. Dominic is very serious. Have you seen anything of Mary?'

Once again Sybil reflected that Lucy invariably changed the subject very quickly when they discussed the boys—if they were so wonderful, why did she do it?

'I really don't see much of her. She's busy in the house and now that school is over until September I don't see the daughter either.'

'But she'll be at the party?'

'I've invited her. Surely she'll jump at the chance.'

From outside the room they could hear voices and laughter, and Lucy said, 'Here are the boys. I'm glad they remembered.'

They were both handsome boys. Dominic was taller than his brother and was dark, whereas Austin was fair. They both greeted Sybil with charming smiles but it was Austin who had the most to say. He talked about horses and the sport he was playing at school, while Dominic merely answered questions that were put to him. There was a reserve about him, and occasionally she found Lucy looking at him questioningly.

After the boys had left them Sybil said, 'They're very different, Lucy.'

'Yes, I told you they were.'

'It seems to trouble you.'

'Not at all. People are different—just because they are brothers doesn't mean they should act alike.'

'But which one troubles you the most?'

'Really, Sybil, neither of them troubles me; they will both have very different roles in life.'

'You mean Dominic will have the title and Austin will be the adventurous one.'

'Something like that.'

'Oh well, fortunately I only have one son to worry about while the girls will make their own way in life, and hopefully marry well. Helena is only twelve, but she's always had a very soft spot for Dominic.'

'Really, I didn't know.'

'I know they're second cousins but it works in a great many families.'

Lucy didn't continue with the conversation but instead said irritably, 'Johnny is hankering after going over to Ireland before the end of the summer—some stud farm he's anxious to buy from. It simply means we'll miss so many things that are going on here.'

'Why does he need another horse?'

'Oh, Major's getting on a bit, and you know Johnny— he's always been horse mad.'

'And the boys?'

'Well, they're hardly ever at home, are they? So the party arrangements are going well?'

There it was again, that quick change of subject and the irritation behind her words.

Lucy had always been the restrained one, hiding her thoughts, keeping her doubts personal, while she had been the outgoing one, too ready with suggestions, too anxious to want to know everything; but it was only when her sons were mentioned that Lucy acted like that now.

Looking through the window at the lowering sky and rain that seemed to be coming straight down in unrelenting blasts, Sybil said angrily, 'This really is too awful, and it's August when we should at least be able to expect some sunshine. The entire house is disrupted because of this party; it will take days to make everything right again.'

'Perhaps on the day itself the weather will be kind.'

'Well, we've cancelled the marquee—I suppose the servants will cope. Arthur has washed his hands of the whole affair—on the day he'll be off to the races somewhere.'

Lucy laughed. 'He and Johnny have a lot in common.'

'Yes, but he could at least show a little enthusiasm and offer a little help. I'll get off now, Lucy. I'm glad I came in the trap but all the same I'll be drenched by the time I get home.'

'Shall I see you again before you go off to France?' Lucy asked with a smile.

'I'm not sure. There'll be so much to do and of course we'll see your two boys. Do encourage them to be charming with the girls, even when they are so much younger.'

'Well, of course. I'm sure they'll both be aware of what is expected of them.'

'Edwin thinks it's all a very big bore; he's anxious for it to be over so that we can get off to France.'

The two women embraced and then Lucy watched her cousin drive off into the rain. She wandered into the library where Dominic sat near the window, a book open on his knees; he looked up with his usual swift, sweet smile.

'Isn't Austin with you, then?' his mother asked him.

'He's in the billiard room, Mother.'

'Dominic, Aunt Sybil has asked if you and Austin will be nice to the girls at the party—ask them to dance, chat to them. I know they're a lot younger than you both but I don't want her complaining that you've been aloof and disinterested.'

'We have promised to be there, Mother.'

'I know, but neither of you are that enthusiastic.'

'Oh, I think Austin will enjoy it—lots of food, lots of pretty girls.'

'I'm not bothered about Austin, Dominic. I'm more concerned about you.'

'I don't see why.'

'Well, you've either got your head stuck in a book or you're out there riding in the park. You visit the homes of friends yet I never hear you speak of their sisters or any other girl you might have met.'

'Mother, I'm eighteen. Isn't there plenty of time for all that?'

'I was interested in boys when I was a lot younger than eighteen.'

'Don't girls mature earlier than boys?'

'You're so very mature in a great many ways, Dominic, and so very complicated in others.'

'I'll tell Austin of your concerns, Mother.'

'I'm not in the least concerned about Austin—you're the one I'm concerned about.'

He smiled, and at that moment she had to be content with that.

On the day of Helena's party Lisa stood at the window watching the girls arriving with their parents, in smart traps or expensive limousines; then there were the boys, smartly dressed, laughing and joking with girls they had obviously met before.

Most of the girls were in white, pretty frilly dresses, their hair tied back by ribbon bows the colour of their dresses; as they walked towards the Hall there was much laughter and high spirits.

She was wearing her pale-green dress and it was beautiful. It complimented her black hair which her mother had brushed with a silk pad until it shone and now it was tied back from her face with a huge satin bow the colour of her dress. As she regarded herself in the mirror, for the first time in her life she began to think that one day she could be pretty.

Her mother constantly reassured her that she was pretty; she talked about her grandmother who had been Spanish and beautiful, beautiful enough to capture the grandson of an English aristocrat, and disastrous enough to have robbed him of his inheritance.

Her mother had always told her that it hadn't mattered. She'd grown up surrounded by love and if they hadn't been rich, so many other things had made up for it. Lisa couldn't understand why she didn't mind, why she felt no envy for people like Mrs Jarvison-Noelle and Lady Hazelmere.

The resentment she felt in her own heart was deep and bitter. When she listened to her schoolmates talking about holidays they spent abroad, the splendour of Paris and Rome, the snows of Switzerland and Austria, she wanted to put her hands over her ears and tell them to stop.

She didn't want to go to the party, and when her father came in to tell her the pony and trap were waiting outside to drive her up to the Hall she said quickly, 'I can walk there, Father. It isn't far.'

'And suppose it rains and ruins your lovely dress,' he said quickly. 'Your mother won't be pleased about that, and you'll find that all the other girls are staring at you.'

There was no help for it and as he lifted her into the trap he said, smiling, 'You are going to have a wonderful time, dear. Do try to look a little happy about it for your mother's sake.'

So she smiled and waved her hand to her mother standing watching from the window.

'Goodness gracious,' her father said as they neared the Hall, 'we're going to have to wait until some of these move off. They don't look to be in any hurry.'

'I'll get off here, Father,' she said quickly. 'Look, it's only a little walk and it isn't raining now.'

'Are you sure, love?'

She put her arms round his neck and gave him a swift kiss, then jumped down onto the drive and the last he saw of her was her dark-green velvet cloak behind the row of vehicles, but he was unable to see if she had entered the Hall.

Lisa was aware of music coming from inside the Hall. As she looked through the window she could see boys and girls dancing in the ballroom and the chandeliers were lit, even though it was only early afternoon. It was a pretty sight: girls and boys beautifully dressed, each and every one of them accomplished in their dancing, the girls smiling up into the eyes of young men who looked down at them in the friendliest fashion, while others sat on the small gilt chairs chatting and laughing together.

They would look at her and wonder who she was; perhaps they would be kind and try to include her in their conversation, but what would be the point? She had been nowhere, done nothing; they would find her boring and inadequate, so instead of entering the Hall she set off towards the back of the house and the woodland that stretched towards the distant hills.

She knew it well, and loved it. The meandering stream that tumbled over the rocks, the glades filled with bluebells in the spring, the primroses that sheltered shyly in the hedgerows, the stepping stones that crossed the stream leading to the beech grove and the dark-green conifers beyond.

In only minutes she became aware that her satin slippers were damp and stained as the hem of her dress too swept among the grasses, and in some dismay she sat down on a stone bench to reflect on her stupidity.

Her mother would be hurt and angry—her stupidity would cause her parents to have words about her, and in the end apologies would have to be made. Perhaps they wouldn't miss her; perhaps she could go home saying that she had a headache, that she hadn't felt well all day, but would they believe her?

Although it was mid-summer a chill wind was blowing down the hillside and she began to feel cold. She couldn't go into the party now wearing her sodden slippers and the dress that had trailed in the mud; she would have to go home. So she made her way back to the front of the house, to the line of cars and carriages and the group of men standing together while they waited to take their young charges home.

As Lisa was keeping in the shadows they didn't see her, and indeed they were so engrossed in their conversation none of them bothered to look around. Standing on the terrace, however, she became aware of the solitary figure of a young man seemingly more interested in the gardens than the activities within the house. She paused, as she didn't want him to see her because it was obvious he was a guest at the Hall.

She waited in the shadows, her back against the stone wall, conscious all the time of her sodden slippers and damp skirt, but he seemed in no hurry to go inside. Then another boy called to him from the doorway, saying, 'What are you doing out there, Dominic? You're missing all the fun.'

Dominic seemed in no hurry to get back to the fun, and Lisa edged her way along the wall, willing him not to notice her, then he turned at last and moved towards the open door. Lisa was unaware that the silk of her dress fluttered in the breeze and caught the glow like a hovering dragonfly.

He was staring down at her and all she wanted to do was run for dear life along the drive, but he smiled, saying, 'You're a little late for the party. May I escort you inside?'

She shook her head almost angrily, then in a whisper she said, 'No, I'm going home. I have a headache.'

'Oh I'm sorry. May I take you to your carriage then?'

'No. I live on the estate. It isn't far.'

'Then I'll walk with you.'

'Please, there's no need, you will miss the party.'

'I'm happy to miss the party. Why do you suppose I was standing out here in the garden?'

She looked at him curiously and he smiled. He was good looking with a charming rather grave smile; without another word they set off together away from the house and towards Lisa's home.

'I'm sorry you have a headache,' he said gently. 'Were you looking forward to the party?'

'Not really, I won't know many people there.'

He looked at her curiously. 'You say you live on the estate?'

'Yes, my father's the Estate Manager.'

So this was Lisa, the distant relative his mother had mentioned on and off over the years. Some mystery in her background, but neither Dominic nor his brother had taken much notice when his mother had told them stories of old scandals that had affected the family.

As he looked down at her dark damp hair and the pretty dress spoiled by the soiled hem, and at the satin shoes with the colour unrecognisable, he felt a sudden surge of pity for a girl who hadn't wanted to go to a party where she would feel like an outsider.

When she stumbled over a stone on the drive he took her arm and smiled down at her, and in that brief moment something intangible was born in Lisa, a sudden sweet partiality—too soon for desire, too innocent for love.

Her mother had watched them walking along the path outside the house with something like dismay. Who was the boy walking with her? Why was he bringing her home so soon? The party would still be going on—what was Lisa doing coming home so soon? She went quickly to the door and crossed the garden to the gate, then Lisa saw her and her face crumpled into tears.

She saw instantly the state of her attire, and the concern in the young man's face, then Lisa was leaving him to run into the house, leaving her mother at the gate to ask for explanations.

He was handsome and troubled as he smiled down at her. 'I'm sorry, Mrs Foreshaw, but I saw Lisa in the grounds and she was obviously rather distressed, so I offered to walk home with her. I am Dominic Lexican.'

'Lucy's son?'

'Why yes.'

'I hope she hasn't been a nuisance. She didn't want to go to the party—I wish now I hadn't insisted. The only people she would know there are the Jarvison-Noelle girls.'

'I can see that would bother her.'

'I'm so sorry that she has kept you away from the party. Thank you so much for bringing her home.'

'Well, I wasn't particularly enjoying the party either. I was standing outside the Hall when I saw her walking towards me—please believe me, she hasn't spoilt my enjoyment of the event at all.'

'Well, thank you again. We will be making our excuses to the family tomorrow. It seems to me that I have to make so many excuses these days on behalf of Lisa.'

He smiled again before turning away, and she stood for a long moment watching his tall figure walking away along the drive.

Viscount Lexican, Lord Hazelmere's eldest son. Sybil would not be pleased that he had missed so much of the party in order to see Lisa home. There would be girls at that party earmarked already for his attentions—no, Sybil would be furious.

CHAPTER FOUR

As Mary helped Lisa out of her party dress and regarded the spoilt satin slippers with some dismay, Lisa cried, 'I'm sorry, Mother, I meant to go, honestly, but when I looked through the window and saw them all dancing I didn't know anybody and I couldn't do any of the dances. They've all had dancing lessons—nobody, just nobody would want to dance with me.'

'I'm sorry, dear, I never thought about it like that. I shouldn't have insisted that you go—it's as much my fault as yours.'

'No, Mother, it's all my fault. You bought me this beautiful dress and it cost a lot of money we can't afford. I'm mean and selfish; I didn't think of anybody but myself. They'll all be furious with me; I'll never be able to go back there, never.'

'Oh, I rather think you will, dear. It will all blow over. It was nice of Viscount Lexican to bring you home.'

Lisa's eyes opened with surprise. 'Is that who he was?'

'Yes, Lord Hazelmere's son. He was very nice, charming, polite and very handsome. Didn't you think so?'

'I suppose so.'

Her mother laughed. 'Oh Lisa, one of these days you are going to grow up. That young man who brought you home will be the aspiration of so many ambitious women looking for a blue-blooded suitor for one of their daughters. He was handsome, charming, and the fact that he left a party to spend time with you will not go unnoticed, I can assure you.'

Lisa looked at her mother uncertainly, then in a small voice she said, 'I've never heard Helena mention him.'

'I wasn't thinking of Helena, dear. They are second cousins. I was thinking of some other girl, one of Helena's friends perhaps.'

Lisa wasn't really interested. She would probably never see him again, but then in a whisper she said, 'What was he really called, his first name, I mean?'

'Dominic. It's nice, don't you think?'

'I suppose so.'

Later in the evening, when Mary related the afternoon's events to her husband, she was unprepared for his laughter.

'So while all those girls were wondering where their quarry was he was busily escorting Miss Lisa Foreshaw home to rather less salubrious surroundings.'

'Why are you so sarcastic, Roger?'

'Because it is a situation lending itself to sarcasm, don't you think? What did our Lisa think of him?'

'That he was nice, kind.'

'And she's far too young to offer any serious threat to any of them—it's my bet that your cousin Sybil will be here post-haste tomorrow morning to make sure there was nothing more in their meeting.'

'Well, of course there wasn't anything more. Lisa is eleven years old; Dominic is probably nineteen or so. What else could there be?'

'Even so, my dear, the lady of the manor will make haste to reassure herself—she could have him mapped out for one of her daughters.'

'I don't think so—more like one of their friends' daughters.'

'Well yes, from the sight of all those pristine carriages and motor cars they were a pretty well-heeled lot attending that party. They'll have somebody in line, and in a few years' time at some debutantes' ball they'll remember where they first met.'

'And Lisa will not be there, so we don't even have to think about it, Roger.'

'No, perhaps not. I'll be interested to know what tomorrow brings.'

Both Lisa and her father were out of the house when Sybil called the next morning. Mary watched her getting out of her trap with something like trepidation. Her face was stern, and there was a decided determination in her tread as she marched up to the house.

After she had been shown into the living room and before Mary could offer her any refreshment her first words were, 'Really Mary, what is your daughter about? She didn't come to the party and Dominic had to escort her home. What are we going to do with the girl?'

'I'm sorry, Sybil. She wasn't well and she was worried she wouldn't fit in. She hasn't had dancing lessons and she didn't know any of the girls apart from your daughters. I can understand how she felt and she didn't ask Dominic to escort her home.'

'Then why did he do it?'

'He saw her on the terrace—she was trying to hide but he saw her and he was kind enough to ask what she was doing there. Natural, I think, under the circumstances. I do hope he was able to explain the situation when he arrived back at the party.'

'His brother went out twice to look for him; there were girls at that party anxious to meet him and he spent hardly any time there. His mother won't be pleased.'

'Then perhaps I should explain matters to Lucy myself.'

'There's no need, I'm going over there now. Really, Mary, I only invited very nice girls to Helena's party; they would have been kind to Lisa—that she didn't dance wouldn't have been a problem.'

Mary didn't speak—surely Sybil must see that it would have been a very big problem to any eleven-year-old girl.

She watched Sybil staring impatiently through the window, her attitude one of frustration. She wanted to say more, but what good would it do? After a few minutes she rose to her feet saying, 'Well, I must go now, Lucy is expecting me. We are going off to France in the morning so while we're away do please try to instil some sense of purpose into Lisa. What did Dominic have to say to her?'

'I really don't know. She said he was kind; she told him there really was no need for him to bring her home, that she only lived on the estate, but he was insistent. I'm sure the young ladies who were looking forward to meeting him will have many more opportunities.'

Sybil looked at her quickly to assure herself that no sarcasm was intended. Mary's expression was bland even though her thoughts were not, then she was escorting her visitor to the gate and watching as Sybil drove her trap speedily away, taking her frustration out on the unfortunate pony.

Sitting opposite Lucy her frustration was immediately apparent as she told her that the party had been a great success even though the guests had seen very little of Viscount Lexican.

Lucy was staring at her with some surprise.

'Dominic has said nothing to me about taking Lisa home, so why does it bother you?'

'Because I'd promised Joyce Atherton that her daughter would be introduced to him.'

'You mean she's shown an interest in Dominic?'

'A very great interest. Melanie is fourteen and she's pretty. Her father's a marquis; think what a match that would be for him.'

'But he went back to the party, didn't he? At least Austin said they'd enjoyed the event.'

'Oh, he came back eventually, but he'd been missing most of the evening, either wandering along the terrace or taking that wretched child home. I introduced him to Melanie myself and he danced with her, then after one dance he wandered off again—where to I really don't know.'

'They're young, Sybil, there will be other opportunities.'

'You're probably right, but he's certainly let this one pass him by. You seem very complacent, Lucy,' Sybil snapped.

'I just don't see what I can do about it. Obviously Dominic was being kind to a girl hanging about outside the house; it was natural that he should take her home. Like I said, there will be other opportunities to meet Melanie, and opportunities for her to meet a great many young men.'

'Well, if it was my son I'd be worried.'

'Worried? Why should I be worried about Dominic?'

'Not Dominic, simply a wasted opportunity.'

Lucy was glad when her cousin decided to leave. She had evidently been extremely exasperated and didn't know how much or how little she had promised her friend Joyce Atherton.

Joyce Atherton too had three daughters like Sybil and they would both be looking out for suitable suitors for the girls—that Dominic was being considered for one of them, she had not been aware of until that morning.

Later in the day Lucy decided to question Austin about the affair.

'Wasn't Dominic enjoying Helena's party that he had to absent himself from it?' she asked him.

'Oh, you know what he's like, Mother. I told him he was missing all the fun but it didn't seem to worry him.'

'When? When did you tell him?'

'Well, he was standing outside gazing at the trees. He doesn't like parties—he likes riding and hunting; he likes reading and music; he's not interested in girls.'

'What do you mean by that?'

'Well he isn't. Don't worry, Mother. I more than make up for him.'

He left her, chuckling to himself, and she stared after him, her eyes filled with a strange doubt. She really would have to have a word with Johnny about Dominic—he was old enough to be taking an interest in girls. Then her face brightened. He had evidently been prepared to be gallant with young Lisa Foreshaw—maybe it was just the girls in his own walk of life that didn't interest him.

The opportunity to talk to her husband came later that afternoon. He was in a particularly good mood after one of his horses had done well in Doncaster. He had not been there to see the horse win as it had been totally unexpected, but now he brought out the champagne and was waxing enthusiastic about the horse's future.

After several minutes, however, he said, 'You're not very interested. What's on your mind, Lucy, aren't you pleased about Javelin?'

'Yes, of course I am, but I'm worried about Dominic.' Then she decided to tell him about Sybil's visit and the events of the previous evening.

'What's there to worry about?' her husband asked.

'Dominic walked a young girl home out of courtesy; maybe he didn't fancy young Melanie; maybe he doesn't want two pushy women ordering his future for him.'

'He doesn't know that they are. He never talks about girls; he never sees any.'

'How do you know? Besides, he's young—there's plenty of time to get interested in girls.'

'Austin is interested in them and he's considerably younger.'

'And he'd do better to attend to his studies and do something with his life before he gets too entangled with the opposite sex.'

'It's no use talking to you, Johnny, you're more interested in your horses than you are in your sons.'

'And you take more notice of that bossy cousin of yours than you do of me. It's my bet that she's earmarked fitting young blue bloods for all her girls and her husband won't have a word to say against her. I only met that other cousin of yours once, but I preferred her to Sybil.'

'You know the story, Johnny. You know why my grandfather objected to her being brought into the family.'

'Yes, well, it might be worth taking a look at that daughter of hers.'

'No, Johnny no, you can't be serious.'

'Why not? Your father couldn't say boo to a goose, and given the right preparation she's got the right genes, at least on her mother's side of the family.'

'And her husband works on my cousin's estate and her grandmother was unacceptable to the family.'

He was looking at her with eyes filled with malicious amusement, and she snapped, 'Stop it, Johnny, I'm very concerned about Dominic and you should be too. I think you should talk to him.'

'About what—an interest in girls or the lack of it?'

'The lack of it—have you thought about that?'

He stared at her in amazement, then sharply said, 'That's nonsense, of course he's perfectly normal. This is ridiculous, Lucy.'

'Well, it happens. Look at Claude Marshland—his family sent him abroad when they found out about it and nobody's seen him for years.'

'Well there was always something funny about Marshland. Nobody can say that about Dominic. He's a man's man and when the right girl comes along he'll be smitten.'

'Oh Johnny, I hope you're right. So you intend to do nothing and say nothing?'

'I intend to keep my eyes open and say nothing for the time being. We'll deal with anything necessary when the time's ripe.'

Lucy had to be content with that, but later in the afternoon when she saw Dominic walking back to the hall from the stables, the worried frown was back on her face. Johnny was right—Dominic was handsome and virile, the sort of young man a young girl could dream about, but what would be the use if he didn't care either one way or the other?

He came into her sitting room favouring her with his usual sweet smile and she said gently, 'You haven't said much about Helena's party, Dominic.'

'I think everybody enjoyed it, Mother.'

'Did you?'

'Well yes. They put on a very substantial buffet, the orchestra was fine and Helena was very happy with it all.'

'Sybil tells me you found Lisa on the terrace and escorted her home; that was kind of you, darling.'

'Well, she did look a little distressed. There was mud on her dress and her hair was wet with the rain; she hadn't been inside the Hall. She'd been walking in the woodland.'

'So I heard. Wasn't that a strange thing to do?'

'I don't think so. She felt out of her depth; I understood how she felt.'

'How very kind. Did you like her, Dominic?'

'She seemed a nice girl. Her mother did too. Lisa went in the house so I had a few words with her mother.'

'Is she pretty?'

'Well, I really didn't notice, Mother. She was troubled, and was also worried about her shoes and her dress.'

'Perhaps I should invite Mary and her daughter to tea one afternoon. I'm sure she'd like to thank you for your kindness properly.'

He looked at her steadily before saying, 'There's really no need, Mother, I only did what any man would have done and I'm sure she would prefer to forget the entire episode.'

With a swift smile he left her, but in Lucy's heart the doubts continued.

Lisa was happy. There were three whole weeks before she needed to go back to her lessons, three weeks to wander the countryside, walk the parkland with her father, visit the stables and the horses she loved but had never learned to ride. A situation which her father decided to remedy.

He found a docile mount for her, a gentle mare called Annie which normally would be riden by Sophie, the youngest of the daughters, and it was clear to Roger that his daughter was a natural. She improved every day and her confidence in the saddle grew; by the end of the holiday she was riding Barnaby, Helena's mount, and riding with considerably more panache than his habitual rider.

Soon the riding would have to come to an end when the family returned from France, and Lisa became unhappy with the situation. It was then Roger decided to have a word with his employer to see if she could continue to ride with his daughters during the months that followed.

'Sybil won't like it,' Mary argued. 'There's only so much and no more she will be prepared to do for Lisa.'

'I intend to ask nevertheless,' he answered her.

His employer saw no harm in it; it was only when he told his wife that the argument started.

'Really, Arthur, don't you think we do enough for Lisa? We're providing her with a good education so that she can earn her own living. I hardly think horse-riding will be an added accomplishment.'

'Well, I've promised now so I can hardly go back on my word,' he snapped.

'Let us just hope that there won't be much time for riding, then,' Sybil said. 'She'll be too busy with her studies.'

'I've promised she can ride with the girls, Sybil.'

'I'll speak to Mary, make her see that her education is more important.'

But before she could speak to Mary the opportunity came to visit Lucy—after she had told her cousin of her annoyance about Lisa's prowess as a rider she was unprepared for Lucy's views on the subject.

'That's really quite a good idea, Sybil. After all it will give her more confidence to mingle with girls at the next party you give for Cora.'

'What makes you think Cora will be having a party?' Sybil said sharply.

'Well, you can hardly treat her different to Helena, can you?'

'And why would I invite Lisa when she was so cavalier about her last invitation?'

'You can't be so petty minded as to remember that occasion—after all we did both promise to look after Mary and her daughter.'

'And I've done more than you, Lucy.'

'Simply because you had three girls and it was easy to involve her. I shall do what I can when the time is ripe.'

'Doesn't it enter your head that she might pose a threat to the other girls?'

'What sort of threat?'

'Well, she's growing up—some young man might like her, when he should be liking somebody more in keeping with his station in life.'

'That would be interesting, wouldn't it, Sybil, but nothing that couldn't be handled.'

'Supposing it was one of your boys, Lucy?'

'Like I said, we would handle it.'

'Have you forgotten that Dominic already knows her?'

'I haven't forgotten, but when I spoke to Dominic I had no reason to think that his interest in Lisa was anything more than good manners.'

'I'm glad to hear it.'

Sybil drove home with the knowledge that ranged against her were her husband and her cousin. Neither of them could see anything wrong in Lisa enjoying her time with the horses, and attending future parties—next thing Lucy would be suggesting she attend the dancing lessons, and where was that going to lead?

Lisa too was beginning to realise that she was happy with her lessons. She was beginning to get along with Miss Walton, she absorbed knowledge quicker than the other girls and she was a better horsewoman. None of this was lost on Sybil but always when she broached the matter to her husband he merely smiled, saying she was resentful and there was no need for it. 'Mary's had a hard deal,' he said. 'It was your idea to do something about things so you can hardly quarrel with the results.'

The same sort of sentiments were offered by Lucy, and in the end she realised nothing more could be done.

CHAPTER FIVE

MARY SAT IN THE LIVING room watching the dress-maker, making sure that Lisa's new dress was to her satisfaction.

Mrs Stedman was good at her job and her prices had gone up considerably over the years. She was well aware that she needed to make a good job of this dress because it would be in competition with many others that had cost considerably more, and some that had been bought from expensive and fashionable salons.

Not for Lisa the white silks and satins so many of the girls favoured. Her mother had realised over the years that her daughter favoured more exotic colours that went well with her blue-black hair and jade-green eyes. Consequently she had selected pale peach taffeta and Mary was well aware that she would stand out like a poppy in a field of daisies.

Over the years the parties had come and gone. Sophie's and Cora's birthday parties, Helena's eighteenth birthday and now Helena's engagement party. Lisa had never seen the need to be invited and she had never enjoyed herself, but it pleased her mother that she should be there and she had gritted her teeth and pretended an enjoyment she had never felt.

The girls had not been her friends—in the main they had resented her blossoming beauty, her mature intellect and her prowess in the saddle, and Lisa was well aware that she rode, danced and conversed with the best of them.

Helena had captured a young man eminently suitable—the second son of an earl and one likely to do well in his chosen army career. Her parents were well pleased, even though Sybil would have preferred it if she had shown more interest in his elder brother. Lisa's father had shown a degree of amusement in the match.

Mrs Stedman departed at last, well pleased with her work, and the dress was hung up in the spare bedroom, where mother and daughter looked at it with mixed feelings.

It was beautiful, but Mary thought of the economies she would have to make in order to afford it. Lisa feigned an enthusiasm in order to assure her mother that it had all been worthwhile.

She liked Helena the best of the three Jarvison-Noelle girls. Helena at eighteen was only a year older and they had the most in common. The two younger girls she regarded as immature—Sophie was frivolous and Cora was vain, so that though they had tolerated her in the classroom they had never considered her a suitable companion for their other pursuits.

As she sat down in the kitchen drinking tea with her

mother Mary said, 'This is going to be a wonderful evening, darling. There will be a lot of nice young men there and you will look very beautiful; try to enjoy yourself, Lisa.'

'Mother, none of those young men are going to be interested in me. They will all know one another, their families, their credentials. I get so bored listening to them talking about who is right for them, who has the right background, the most money, the best future; they never talk about love.'

'Perhaps it isn't really important, dear. Perhaps it's something that comes later.'

'Do you really mean that, Mother? Shouldn't it be all important?'

'Perhaps not in their station in life, Lisa.'

'How can you say that, Mother? It was important for Grandfather, important enough for him to choose somebody his father didn't agree with.'

'A great many people would think he wasn't very sensible, Lisa. To give everything up for love is not everybody's idea of the right thing to do.'

'Well, I think he was very brave. We don't need their patronage.'

'But we do, darling. Your father needs his job, I need this house and you need your education. Neither Sybil nor Lucy needed to take care of you; that they have done so is most admirable.'

She was aware of her daughter's disagreement, and to change the subject she said, 'I expect Lucy's two sons will be at this party; only Austin went to the younger girls' parties. You will be able to meet Dominic again.'

Lisa regarded her mother with some impatience.

'Oh Mother, surely you don't think he's going to remember me, some girl in a muddy dress, wearing muddy shoes, whom he was kind enough to walk home. If I see him there I'll hide. I don't want him to remember me.'

Mary looked at her sadly. With all the advantages she had what would Lisa's future be? She was rebellious, and would probably meet some young man who was destined to be a farmer, a vicar or a shopkeeper and settle down to a mundane future in the name of love.

All day Lisa had been aware of the activity going on at the big house—the arrival of caterers, florists, dressers, and then in the early evening the orchestra and the first guests. She stood looking at herself in the long mirror in her bedroom and for the first time she seemed almost surprised at the beautiful vision that confronted her. The dress was beautiful; its long sweeping skirt fell away from her slender waist and the low-cut bodice was edged with darker peach satin roses to match the roses in her dark hair. She had never considered herself a match for her schoolmates with their blonde tresses and blue eyes, but now she was looking at a different kind of beauty, a more exotic beauty she had inherited from her Spanish grandmother.

She turned to meet her father's eyes across the room and he smiled tenderly. 'You look lovely, dear. You'll be the belle of the ball tonight. Time to go.'

He draped the satin stole round her shoulders and after picking up a fan from the dressing table he took hold of her hand and led her from the room.

'Isn't she beautiful,' he said to her mother, standing at the bottom of the stairs, and Lisa was aware of the tears in her mother's eyes, as well as the doubts.

'Do enjoy yourself, darling,' she said. 'You can hold your head up high, Lisa. There will be nobody there more beautiful than you.'

Lisa smiled tremulously. Her mother would have thought so if she'd looked like a waif.

'Sorry we haven't a Rolls Royce,' her father was saying. 'There's only this old jalopy but I've given it a good clean and nobody's going to be interested with all these pristine models hanging around.'

She knew what to expect, but on this occasion there was more of it. More cars, more people, more music and yet as she entered the ballroom, for a brief moment there was silence—an exotic girl in a beautiful dress, a girl with raven hair and green eyes, a girl with a proud aloofness that hid a swiftly beating heart.

She was afraid; she didn't know where to sit, who to speak to. People were chatting in groups, then she became aware of Helena standing with her fiancé and her parents at the head of the room and instinct made her walk towards them.

She was being introduced to Helena's fiancé, who was smiling down at her, a nice-looking young man in army officer's uniform, and then Sybil and her husband were greeting her as Sybil said, 'You look very nice,

Lisa. Ah, here are Andrew's parents; do excuse me while I greet them.'

Somewhat bemused, Lisa realised that she was superfluous to the engagement party and turned away, her eyes hastily scanning the room for some means of escape. It was then that Lady Hazelmere descended on her with a nice smile and charming words of welcome.

'How nice to see you, Lisa. It's many years since we met—you won't remember, you were only a little girl at the time. I am your mother's cousin, Lady Hazelmere, and this is my husband Lord Hazelmere.'

A rather large handsome man smiled down at her, and then she was looking up into Dominic's eyes and he was smiling down at her gravely, as his mother went on, 'You remember Lisa, don't you, dear. That quite disastrous evening when she slipped in the mud and you kindly escorted her home.'

'I hope you're not going to slip in the mud this evening,' he said, 'particularly in that beautiful dress.'

'No, but then it isn't raining tonight,' she said, and everybody laughed even though her words were trite.

'This is Austin, my younger son,' Lady Hazelmere said, and a shorter young man was taking her hand, a young man with admiration in his eyes and a laughing confidence.

'Do you have a dance card?' he asked. 'I must put my name on it before too many beat me to it.'

With a smile she handed it over, and his mother said, 'Don't monopolise Lisa, darling, Dominic will want to dance with her I feel sure,' and with a smile Austin handed her dance card to Dominic as their mother said, 'Be nice, Dominic, dance with Lisa before supper so that at least she will know somebody here. I don't suppose you really know too many young men, do you, dear?'

Lisa was well aware that they were being watched by a great many haughty eyes, mostly from aspiring mothers with daughters, but Lady Hazelmere seemed determined to keep her in the party as they moved around the room. Austin chatted to her brightly until his mother said, 'There's Barbara Erskine, Austin. Didn't you rather like her the last time you met?'

He laughed. 'I like a good many of the girls here, Mother. Barbara no more than the rest.'

'Even so, it would be gallant if you asked her to dance, dear.'

'All in good time, Mother.'

'Now Austin, her mother is one of my closest friends. She was anxious to know if you would be here. I can't have you ignoring her daughter.'

Lisa felt uncomfortable, that in some way she was to blame for Austin's interest in her, but in the next moment Lucy said disarmingly, 'I'm afraid my younger son is a terrible flirt, Lisa, totally unlike his brother, who is far more reliable. Come, we will sit over there away from the orchestra; it becomes so noisy it's impossible to talk.'

Dutifully they followed her, but from across the room Sybil watched them with some degree of anger. What was Lucy about? Here were so many friends of hers who had made it a duty to ask if Dominic would be there, so many friends with eligible daughters dying to meet him—hadn't she reassured them that he was sure to be present? Now here he was being pressed by his mother into escorting Lisa to seats set well away from some of her other guests. Lucy had said that one day she too would do her best for Lisa; surely it didn't extend to earmarking her for her eldest son.

Turning to her husband, she snapped, 'Why is Lucy keeping Lisa with them? I didn't invite her for Dominic; we should do something.'

'What, break the party up, tell them who the lad has to mix with? I'll tell you something, the girl's a corker, best-looking girl in the room, and it's my bet Dominic thinks so too.'

'Really, Arthur, it's becoming increasingly obvious that you don't see further than your nose. We have obligations to our friends.'

'What sort of obligations?'

'The same sort of obligations that will ensure that our own daughters marry well when the time is right. Would you be happy to see a prospective suitor ignore either of your girls for a less than attractive girl?'

'Well, from what I can see young Lisa is as attractive or even more so than any young woman here. All the boys are looking at her.'

'She has no money, her parents are not of the right calibre, her ancestry is debatable.'

'It is tied up with yours, my dear.'

'But not in a way we wish to advertise, Arthur.'

'What do you propose we do about it then?'

'We break that little party up.'

'A little late, I think. She's dancing with Dominic—a host of young women and their mothers will be pea green with envy. I suggest we leave well alone, Sybil, and concentrate on why we are here.'

Oh but he was annoying! What was it about men that they couldn't see the wood for the trees? She'd get no help from him; she'd have to speak to Lucy herself.

Lucy proved to be charming and agreeable, but when it came to Dominic and Lisa she was uncooperative.

'Darling, they're all having a lovely time; your girls look lovely, particularly Helena and she's obviously very happy. Such a nice young man, Sybil.'

Thoroughly frustrated Sybil snapped, 'I wish I could feel the same way about Lisa, Lucy.'

'Whatever do you mean, dear? She looks enchanting and she's obviously enjoying every minute. You grumbled when she was difficult; tonight she's doing everything right.'

'With Dominic!'

'And with every young man who invites her to dance.'

'But particularly with Dominic. Really, Lucy, he should be circulating among the sort of girls he will one day marry, can't you see?'

'He seems perfectly happy to me, Sybil. I don't interfere with my boys; they're both enjoying themselves.'

'I'm not concerned about Austin. He'll flirt with anything in skirts, but Dominic is the serious one, the one destined to always do the right thing and never ever let the family down.'

'Is dancing with his second cousin letting the family down?'

'Not a lot of people know she's his second cousin; perhaps we should enlighten them so that they will not think he's dancing with one of your palourmaids.'

After conferring on her one of her haughtiest looks Sybil swept away. Gazing after her, Lucy's expression was rueful in the extreme.

Lisa had never been so happy in her entire life. Her dance card was full of young men who were gallant and charming, and she would be dancing the supper dance with Dominic, who was easily the most handsome man in the room.

She saw him chatting to a young man standing at the edge of the ballroom, a dark-haired, good-looking young man who had watched them dancing round the room with a half smile on his face, but now it would appear their conversation was particularly serious.

They both smiled as she danced an energetic polka with Austin and she asked, 'Who is the man talking to your brother? He smiles at me but he doesn't seem to want to dance.'

'His name is Oliver Cardew; he was at university with Dominic; they're old friends.'

Although many of the girls looked at them hopefully neither seemed disposed to want to dance, and it was only when the supper dance was announced that Dominic came to claim her.

A splendid feast had been laid on, and as she sat with Dominic in a corner of the room she saw that the young man he had been talking to was now standing alone helping himself from the table.

'Would you like your friend to join us?' she asked softly.

'I doubt if he will. Oliver is a bit of a loner; he either prefers to be by himself or with people he knows well.'

Lisa didn't answer, but it seemed to her a pity that there were so many beautiful girls sitting nearby looking at him hopefully.

Smiling down at her Dominic said, 'You didn't enjoy the other party, Lisa, but you're obviously enjoying this one.'

'Oh yes, I am. Now I can dance with the best of them; that night I would have been hopeless.'

'So you walked in the woods instead and spoiled your dress.'

'Yes, it was terrible of me, but you didn't seem anxious to join the festivities.'

'No.'

She looked at him sharply but he seemed not to want to elaborate on his answer, and after a few minutes he said, 'What are you going to do with your life when your education with your second cousins is finished?'

'My second cousins! Yes, I suppose they are; you too, Dominic.'

He smiled. 'You haven't answered my question, Lisa.'

'I don't really know, but I will have to think about it very soon. Miss Walton says I could teach young children. She says I could marry a young man who is looking for an intelligent wife who could help him in his profession.'

'And will you, do you think?'

'How can I say? I don't know any young men; the only ones I meet are at the functions Mrs Jarvison-Noelle has invited me to here, and they have their sights set on someone better than an Estate Manager's daughter.'

'You're sure about that?'

She laughed. 'Of course.'

She was unaware of the thoughts passing through Dominic's head. Why had they picked Lisa up out of obscurity merely to throw her back when the time was right?

That was the moment when Lucy Hazelmere descended on them and, taking her place next to her son, she said brightly, 'Are you both enjoying the evening? Your father wants to leave as soon as we've eaten, Dominic. As usual he's grumbling about his indigestion and you know how he hates dressing up in what he calls his monkey suit.'

Dominic laughed. 'I'll drive you home, Mother.'

'Oh no, darling, Jeffries will be waiting. You take Lisa home.'

She did not miss the sudden look of detachment in her son's eyes before he said quickly, 'I'm sure there are a host of young men anxious to escort Lisa home.'

Lisa was quick to say, 'I only live along the drive; I don't want to take anybody away from the party.'

'But you won't, my dear. You'll dance the night away until the stars pale and then Dominic will take you home. Heaven knows what Austin will do; he's surrounded by a gaggle of girls. Isn't that Oliver Cardew over there, Dominic?'

'Yes, Mother.'

'Do you see much of him?'

'Not a great deal; he's living over at Threpton.'

'Alone?'

'I think so.'

'Oh well, here's your father, darling, so I'd better go with him to say our farewells to Sybil and Arthur. Such a lovely party. You enjoy yourselves, make the most of the rest of it.'

They paused on their way out to speak to Oliver, and Lisa looked at Dominic doubtfully.

'Please don't think you have to look after me, Dominic. You've been very kind and I'm accustomed to looking after myself.'

Across the room she looked into Oliver Cardew's eyes and was taken aback by the cynicism in them.

CHAPTER SIX

LISA STOOD BEHIND THE CLOSED door listening to Dominic's footsteps walking towards the car, then the sound of its engine as he drove away.

She went to stand at the window from where she could see the lights around the Hall, the steady stream of car headlights, and she could guess the sort of conversations that would still be going on as the revellers made their way home.

At the door Dominic had unlocked it for her, then he had raised her hand to his lips and kissed it before favouring her with his cool, sweet smile, saying, 'It's been a lovely evening, Lisa, I've no doubt I shall see you again whenever there is another such function.'

She had wanted so much more. She had seen girls standing in the arms of young men in the conservatory, or in quiet corners on the moonlit terrace, and had hoped that Dominic would sweep her into his arms and kiss her on parting.

Of course, Dominic was a gentleman, and real gentlemen didn't do such things; they were circumspect—

passion was something reserved for women they intended to marry, but it had been a lovely evening. Whoever she danced with in the future, it could never be the same.

How handsome he was with his cool, sweet smile, his tall, slender figure, his grace on the dance floor and the low charm of his voice—how could she ever be expected to care about any other man when there had been Dominic? She loved him, and would love him for the rest of her life. Every dream she had had in her heart was realised in him; it would never be possible to replace him with some other inferior being.

In her heart she could still hear the sound of the music they had danced to, feel his hand warm in hers, feel her hair against his cheek whenever there had been too many people around them.

There had been that one moment when her eyes had met Oliver Cardew's as he watched them dancing nearby him, eyes that were filled with a cynical amusement, an amusement she couldn't understand.

From above she heard the opening of a door and then her mother's voice calling softly, 'Lisa, are you downstairs?' Hurrying to the bottom of the stairs, she said, 'I'm just coming to bed, Mother, it's after two in the morning.'

Her mother was running swiftly down the stairs, and taking hold of Lisa's hand she said, 'I'll make cocoa, darling. I want to hear about the party; who brought you home?'

Lisa laughed. 'We can talk about it tomorrow morning, Mother. We don't want to wake Father.'

'He's sleeping like a log, Lisa. Just a few minutes just to tell me if you enjoyed yourself. Who brought you home, Lisa?'

'Dominic brought me home, Mother. We danced the supper dance together and his mother was so nice to me.'

'But you didn't dance with Dominic all evening, Lisa. There were other young men?'

'Oh yes, Mother, a lot of young men, who were all so nice. I danced with Dominic's younger brother and he made me laugh. Dominic's so handsome, Mother. He made me feel that I was every bit as good as all the other girls, and some of them didn't seem very pleased that he paid me so much attention.'

It was all about Dominic, and in Mary's troubled heart she saw the danger in it. Her daughter had fallen in love with him.

Sybil thought she had sulked over her cousin long enough and so three weeks after the party she decided to visit her, telling herself that her horse needed the exercise and by this time surely Lucy must agree with her point of view.

Lucy greeted her as if they had met yesterday, with a calm smile, pointing out that the azaleas had been particularly beautiful and that she really should see the Japanese garden with its oriental shrubs.

Somewhat frustrated, Sybil said, 'I've been busy since the party, Lucy. That's why I haven't been over.'

'Well, we've been busy too. How long since we met? I've lost count.'

'At least three weeks.'

'So long! Oh well, time flies, I really hadn't noticed.'

'Are the boys away?'

'Austin's in Kent with the Lorevals and Dominic is out on the estate with his father. No doubt they'll be here before you have to leave.'

'I take it they all enjoyed the engagement party.'

'Yes, of course. I did write to you, Sybil, and I'm sure the two boys told you so.'

'I forget. People were very kind to Lisa; at least she made the effort this time.'

'And a very creditable effort, Sybil. I'm still hearing people say how beautiful she's become and how polished. You have to be congratulated on that score, Sybil.'

'I've done my best. We both said we would.'

'And you've done far more than I. I rather think it's my turn now.'

'What's that supposed to mean?'

'Oh, I'll think of something. I did promise.'

'I rather think we can now leave Lisa to sort out her own destiny. We've given her father a good job, the house and Lisa's education; from now on it's up to her. Surely you agree.'

'But I've done nothing.'

'You were kind to her at the party, and you allowed Dominic to escort her for most of the evening as well as escorting her home.'

'He didn't seem to object; as a matter of fact I think he rather enjoyed the experience.'

'But was it fair on Lisa? Might she not read more into his attentions than there actually was?'

'Oh come now, Sybil, a young man and a pretty girl having a wonderful time. Dominic likes her; I want him to like her.'

Sybil's eyes opened wide. 'Why, for heaven's sake? What future is there in him liking her? They're related to each other. If it's something deeper you're thinking about, he should look elsewhere.'

'Dominic doesn't exactly seem to be looking anywhere at the moment. He showed absolutely no interest in any of those girls at the ball. I'm sure their doting mothers must have been most exasperated, but like I said, Sybil, I am not going to push Dominic in their direction. If he wants it well and good, but I liked Lisa; she could be worth cultivating.'

'What has Johnny to say about it?'

'What does Johnny have to say about anything beyond his horses and his estates?'

'Well, doesn't that tell you something? His estates and their future.'

'All in good hands I can assure you. Now do let us go inside and have tea; I take it you have the time.'

'Not really, I have to get back; this was just a brief visit.'

'Oh, I am sorry. Well, don't leave it three weeks before you call to see me again.'

'It seems to me it is I who always does the visiting; you never take the trouble.'

'Oh, do forgive me, dear, but I have so many things on my mind at the moment and you were always the one with a penchant for horses. I believe Lisa has become a very competent horsewoman.'

'Who told you that?'

'Oh, it was something Dominic mentioned; they must have talked about it.'

Sybil decided it was time for her to leave and all the way home she thought about her cousin's attitude over the past few years—her changes of the subject whenever the boys were mentioned, her sudden secrecies and now her leanings towards Lisa Foreshaw.

As she left the stables she saw Mary in her garden gathering blackcurrants and somehow she didn't want to talk to her. She favoured her with a cool nod and Mary stared after her, aware that all was not right.

Lisa too was giving Mary cause to worry—the girl lived with her head in the clouds. Helena had given her photographs taken at the party when she had stood with Dominic under the lights on the staircase—two beautiful people in evening dress, with him looking down on her with a gentle expression and her looking up into his eyes with an adoring smile.

'Who took the photograph?' she had demanded.

'Oh, Mother, they were taking photographs everywhere,' was the only reply she received; at the same time the photograph took pride of place in her bedroom and she wished Lisa could forget him. Loving Dominic Lexican could only bring heartache; he was not for Lisa.

That sentiment was brought home to her very forcibly on the occasion of Helena's wedding when Lisa was not invited. Mary had to admit it was difficult, for how could they in all honesty invite Lisa when they showed no intention of inviting her parents?

Lisa went with her mother to the church to watch the wedding, a very sumptuous affair with the aristocracy well represented. Dominic acted as usher and Helena's bridesmaids had been chosen from girls whose mothers had him in mind as a prospective husband for one of them.

Lisa's eyes followed him outside the church as he went about his duties, escorting one pretty girl as they left the church, smiling down at her, every bit as gracious as he had been to her, and her heart ached.

Her mother was well aware of her distress and she whispered, 'We'll get right away, darling, before the photographs are taken; there will be an awful crush and I don't want Sybil thinking we want to be seen.'

As they moved away, however, Lady Hazelmere approached them with a warm smile on her face and annoyance in her heart.

'How are you, Mary?' she said brightly. 'It's ages since I saw you, and you too, Lisa. One day you must both come over to see us; I shall look forward to it.'

Mary blushed and smiled, and Lisa looked across the sea of faces to where Dominic and other young men stood with the bridesmaids in a laughing group.

Lucy did not miss any of it. Lisa was troubled. She had not been wrong when she'd thought the girl truly liked her son; now here he was with a bevy of hopeful young debutantes and nothing was going as she had planned it. Sybil had done it deliberately—she had never had any intention of inviting Lisa to the wedding.

She showed her displeasure by leaving the reception as soon as the banquet was over, so that Sybil hissed, 'You're surely not leaving so soon—why for heaven's sake?'

'I have things to do,' Lucy answered, and her husband looked at her in some amazement, whispering as they left the Hall, 'Why are we leaving now? What's got into you?'

'I'm bored by it all, bored by those women pushing their daughters onto every eligible young man in there.'

'Isn't that what they've always done? Didn't your mother do her share?'

'Yes, and it was a constant embarrassment.'

'It worked though, didn't it?'

'If you say so.'

There were times when Johnny Hazelmere didn't understand his wife, and he snapped shortly, 'I'm glad you didn't insist the boys left with us; that would hardly have been popular.'

'Perhaps not, but it's my guess Dominic will soon make his escape.'

'Why would he?'

'Because he isn't interested in anybody there.'

'How do you know?'

'I know Dominic.'

Lucy knew that Sybil would make it her business to make her annoyance plain when next they met and she was ready for her. Lucy had plans and she would not be thwarted. Austin would marry one of those aspiring young women; Dominic would play another role.

It was not yet time to take Sybil into her confidence; there was so much to think about, so much to tell Johnny and she could only feel some trepidation at his response.

Lisa and Mary walked back to their cottage, aware of the laughter behind them as the crowds gathered in their finery and Mary said gently, 'It was a lovely wedding, dear. Helena looked very pretty; I hope they'll be happy; he seems a very nice young man.'

Lisa didn't reply; her thoughts were on Dominic and the pretty bridesmaid he had escorted. She was no doubt the sort of girl he would be expected to marry, but the hurt refused to go away.

Her father's ancient car stood outside the gate and Mary said, 'Your father's home, Lisa. He said he might be late this afternoon.'

There was no sign of him in the downstairs rooms and she called to him. 'We're home, Roger, are you upstairs?'

When there was no reply she said, 'He's perhaps asleep. I'll see if he wants anything.'

She found Roger lying fully dressed on the bed, breathing heavily, his face pale and twisted with pain. She went immediately to his side, saying, 'What is it, Roger? You look awful.'

Clutching his heart he gasped, 'I can't get my breath, Mary. It came on so suddenly.'

'I'll get the doctor, Roger. Perhaps it's something you've eaten.'

He shook his head and groaned again. Running from the room she called to Lisa, 'Your father's ill, Lisa. Run quickly and get the doctor; tell him it's urgent.'

Unfortunately the doctor was out on his rounds and it was all of two hours before he could attend to Roger, by which time he had lost consciousness; his wife and daughter were frantic with worry.

The doctor diagnosed a heart attack, and shaking his head dismally he gave them little hope.

'But he's never been ill in all the time I've known him,' Mary cried. 'He's been out in all weathers and never even seemed to catch a cold.'

The doctor sympathised and ordered that an ambulance be sent out for him, saying that if he survived the night then he might have a chance.

They were with him three hours later when he died in hospital.

Mary and Lisa sat together in the living room in stupefied silence. Roger, who had always been so robust, with an undiminished sense of humour even when Mary had felt most vulnerable, now he was gone from them and the future loomed before them like a dark, impenetrable waste.

The men who had worked with him on the estate came clutching their cloth caps, standing with strained faces as they tried to find words to describe their sympathy.

'Will ye be able to stay on 'ere, Mrs Foreshaw?' one of them asked.

'Oh, I really don't think so, Garvey, this house is for the Estate Manager and Roger will have to be replaced,' she replied.

'But not right away, surely,' he insisted.

'Well, I don't know. Until I have spoken to Mr Jarvison-Noelle I really don't know what is going to happen.'

He shook his head sadly. 'Well, the lass will still be receiving 'er education, won't she?'

'Oh no, Garvey, that is finished now. Lisa will be looking for work, I'm sure. I really don't know what will happen.'

'Well, we shall all be at the funeral, ma'am, to pay our respects,' he ended, and Mary thanked him with a sad smile.

On the morning of the funeral the flowers began to arrive—flowers that had been grown in country gardens, small posies from children; then the Jarvison-Noelles' chauffeur arrived clutching several large and ostentatious wreaths from the family.

It was shortly before noon when Lisa answered another knock on the door to find Dominic standing there holding more flowers, his smile gentle and filled with sympathy.

'My mother and the rest of us have sent flowers, Lisa,' he said, 'May I carry them in for you?'

Without answering she stepped aside so that he could enter, then her mother was there and he was handing some of the flowers to her.

'Thank you so much, Dominic, your mother has been very kind,' she said.

'We are all very sorry; it seems sad that we were all enjoying the wedding party in the midst of so much tragedy here.'

'Yes, but you couldn't have known.'

He stared at her strangely. 'But you were to have been at the wedding?'

'Oh no, we came to the church to watch but Roger died in the evening.'

'I didn't know.'

His face was strangely puzzled, and Lisa said softly, 'We did not expect to be invited to the wedding.'

He offered no further comment but said instead, 'My mother would like you to visit her after all this is over. Will you be able to do that?'

'I would like to see her, but we may not be here much longer. The house will have to go to the new manager; everything is going to change for us but we don't really know how quickly.'

'I will tell my mother you will visit and I will drive over if that is agreeable.'

'Thank you, Viscount Lexican. You are very kind.'

He smiled at Lisa. 'Dominic, please. I remember you did call me Dominic when we ate supper together at Helena's engagement party.'

Lisa smiled tremulously, but it was Mary who escorted him to the door where Lisa joined her after he had driven away. Mary looked at her daughter sadly. Oh yes, he was kind and handsome, all the things a young girl dreamed of, but perhaps it might be as well if they did move away—far away to spare a broken heart.

CHAPTER SEVEN

MARY WAS SURPRISED AT the number of people who turned out for the funeral service at the small village church, villagers who had known Roger and liked him, and many of the men who had worked with him on the land as well as servants from the house.

His employer and his wife stood in the Jarvison-Noelle pew, distanced from the rest, and on leaving he had pressed Mary's hand, saying, 'We will talk soon, Mary, no doubt my wife will call to see you during the next few days.'

Three days later Sybil came riding her horse, clad in her pristine riding habit, her dark hair tied back under her hat, giving her a severity that was her hallmark.

Lisa made coffee and Sybil sat opposite mother and daughter for several minutes in uncomfortable silence before she said, 'This has been very tragic for you, Mary. Roger always appeared to me to be especially robust.'

'Yes, I thought so too.'

'My husband will be speaking to you about the house.'

When Mary didn't reply she said somewhat tetchily, 'It is all terribly inconvenient; obviously we have to employ somebody in his place and they will need the house whoever they are.'

Before her mother could form a suitable reply Lisa said, 'My father's death was a tragedy, Mrs Jarvison-Noelle, hardly an inconvenience.'

Mary gasped with mortification and Sybil snapped, 'I agree with you, young lady—the inconvenience was ours. The tragedy was for you and your mother.'

'Really, Lisa,' her mother murmured, 'that was very unkind.'

'Oh, young people are getting like that these days,' Sybil said sharply. 'Will you wish to stay in the area or would you prefer to move away?'

'I don't know. It's all come too soon but I've lived around these parts most of my life; even my father didn't want to move away in spite of his family problems.'

'And what of Lisa? You will need to find employment. I can't think there is much in the villages. You would do better in a town or city.'

Lisa didn't speak, and Mary said quickly, 'We will have to start thinking of the future very soon. Have you any idea how long we will be able to stay here before you will need the house for the new people?'

'I have no idea at all. Arthur thinks he might promote Peabody. He was Roger's right-hand man and he's capable enough, although personally I think he'd do well to bring somebody in from outside. The rest of the work-men would take more notice of a stranger than Peabody, who lives in the village.'

'Roger thought he was a good man.'

'On the land perhaps, but we're expecting a string of horses being brought over from Ireland. How good he is with that side of it I can't imagine.'

'His wife is a nice woman, and the two girls were very friendly with Lisa when she went to school with them.'

'Well yes, but they won't be involved with anything to do with the Hall. We have one or two small cottages in the village. One of them might be made available, we'll have to have thoughts on the matter. Would you be prepared to move into one of those?'

'I think we shall have to be very grateful for anything at the moment.'

'Yes well, I'm driving over to the Hazelmeres' now so perhaps they may have some suggestion to offer.'

Lucy listened to her cousin's problems, which were largely expected.

'Young Lisa was most rude,' Sybil exclaimed. 'Her father's death has been an inconvenience to us, but I meant nothing disparaging about it, but she picked me up very smartly. I've had the girl educated, it's given her ideas above her station obviously.'

'You surprise me, Sybil. From what I've seen of Lisa I'd have thought her sweet and malleable.'

'That's how I would describe her mother, not the daughter.'

'Perhaps under the circumstances your remarks were rather insensitive.'

'Surely I am allowed to express a comment on how Roger's death is going to affect us.'

'Perhaps, but obviously Lisa has taken her father's death very hard.'

'But what are we going to do with them? I've mentioned one of the cottages in the village—we can probably find one for them but isn't it time they moved away now? Arthur and I have done the best for them. Lisa should find employment.'

'Maybe it's my turn, after all I have done very little.'

Sybil looked at her sharply before saying, 'Your contribution has been to allow your son to look after her when I had particularly hoped he would give some attention to one of my other guests.'

Lucy smiled. 'I don't tell either of my sons what they must do.'

'Well, I didn't invite her to Helena's wedding. I didn't want a repetition of the incident.'

'And nothing whatsoever has come of your machinations on that occasion. Sybil, when the time is right Dominic will make his own decisions on how the rest of his life is going to go.'

'Then why do I often feel you are worried about him? Oh not Austin, always Dominic.'

Lucy had not bargained on Sybil's astuteness. She had been foolish, incautious and the time was not right. In some confusion she said, 'I'm not in the least worried about Dominic. There are times when I wish he was more like his brother, then there are other times when I wish Austin was more like Dominic. Do you never have problems, or worries about your children?'

'Perhaps it's different with sons, and one son in particular who must be seen to get it right.'

To change the subject Lucy said, 'I have asked Mary and her daughter to visit us here. Dominic will drive them here, and please, Sybil, no arched eyebrows, don't read more into this than I have intended. I've done very little for them, and I did say that one day it would be my turn. Perhaps Johnny can find them a house nearer here. It would solve matters for you.'

'Why? Don't you think it would be better if they moved away?'

'I think we should allow Mary to decide for herself what she wants to do.'

On the way home Sybil still felt unsure that Lucy wasn't playing some strange game of her own. She had been withdrawn about Dominic in spite of what she said to the contrary.

She pulled her horse up as two riders approached her and saw that it was Dominic and his friend Oliver Cardew. They greeted her courteously and Dominic said, 'Mother said you might be riding over.'

'Yes, I came to report on the Foreshaw situation. Your mother seems to think your father can find them something round here.'

'Really?' Dominic said. 'She hasn't discussed it with me.'

'Oh well, it's all in the air at the moment. Where are you living, Oliver? I thought it was over at Weaverham?'

'Yes, quite near to Martindale.'

'That's nice when Dominic elects to spend time there. You've been friends a long time.'

Both men smiled, and Sybil said, 'Well I must go, Arthur and I are expecting guests this evening. No doubt we'll meet again quite soon.'

She wasn't entirely sure that she liked Oliver Cardew. He always seemed cynical and in a world of his own. Helena had often said he seemed rather distant, and she couldn't recall that he had ever had a serious friendship with a girl.

At functions he always seemed a bit of a loner, never one of a group, always standing alone at the bar or occasionally chatting to Dominic. For the first time Sybil's thoughts turned onto something quite unacceptable. Oh no, surely Lucy couldn't have been concerned about Dominic's sexuality. Dominic was gallant and charming; the girls liked him. She pulled her horse up again and turned to look back to where the two men were galloping their horses down the hill in the direction of the mere, where they pulled them up, laughing, before dismounting and walking along the margin of the lake.

She'd talk to Arthur, ask him what he thought about Dominic and his friend. Arthur would think she was mad even to think there was anything wrong, but she was remembering Lucy's expression and her many withdrawals whenever her son was mentioned.

It was plain to Sybil that Lucy had misgivings. What sort of plot was Lucy forming in her mind and did it concern Lisa Foreshaw? Was Lisa to be the sacrificial lamb to save Dominic's reputation?

Of course it was ludicrous. Better not mention it to Arthur—he would think she was out of her senses.

Arthur was becoming a bore about the replacement of his Estate Manager. She'd had it all over dinner, and now he sat opposite her with a remote expression on his face, his thoughts miles away.

'I thought you were going to promote Peabody,' she said in some desperation.

'I'm not sure he's up to it. He's all right on the land, but he's hardly up to Roger's standard.'

'Then get somebody else.'

'It's not easy. He's expecting the job and I don't want any problems with the workforce.'

'What about that cottage for Mary? Will there be one?'

'I haven't got around to thinking about it yet. There has to be one, doesn't there?'

'I saw Lucy today. She said they might be able to find them something.'

'Then we should let them. It would be their problem and not ours.'

'I'm not sure.'

'Why, for heaven's sake?'

'Lucy's planning something. She's very devious and I'm sure it concerns Dominic and Lisa. If it does I can't think what she's thinking about.'

'Dominic and Lisa. Why, he's the catch of the season. Why would Lucy want Lisa for him?'

'I don't know, maybe I'm wrong, maybe I'm reading more into it than there is, but I have my suspicions about Dominic and Lucy's hardly been open about him.'

He was staring at her with some degree of bewilderment. 'What are you on about, Sybil? I like Dominic. I prefer him to the other one who is far too full of himself.'

'It's not that, Arthur, it's something else. She's worried. I've seen it for months even when she's never actually put anything into words.'

'Worried! Worried about what?'

'You'll think I'm being ridiculous like you usually do.'

'If I don't know what you're on about how can I think anything at all? I'm going into the study. I have letters to write.'

She watched him striding towards the door. She'd known it would be like this. Now he was impatient, and in reality what exactly could she tell him?

Left alone she decided to go outside onto the terrace where the summer evening was balmy. A soft breeze stirred the branches of the beech trees and perfume from the flower beds filled the air.

Why should she be worrying about Lucy and her son? She had enough problems of her own. Sophie was interested in a most unsuitable young man, a boy who had republican tendencies and an arrogant disposition, and Cora was too much like her father, interested in nothing beyond horses.

When she returned an hour later to the drawing room Arthur was sitting with his head in one of his field books, having helped himself to a large whisky and soda.

'Ah, there you are,' he said shortly. 'Now come along and explain yourself, woman, what's all this about Lucy and Dominic?'

'It's nothing. I don't want to talk about it.'

'And I won't listen to half a tale.'

'It's probably something and nothing.'

'Well, let's hear it. You've got some bee in your bonnet about Dominic and young Lisa, and it's probably rubbish anyway.'

'There you go, disparaging before I've even said anything.'

For a long moment he looked at her with some degree of impatience, then his expression softened and he said gently, 'I know, I'm an exasperating individual, but if you really are troubled, my dear, I'd like to hear about it. What is this about Dominic?'

'I think he's different, not interested in girls.' She paused and let the full meaning of her words sink in.

'What! That's ridiculous. Because he hasn't found some girl he wants to marry, and in any case what has that to do with Lisa?'

'Because it wouldn't do for it to get out—with Lisa we'd keep it in the family.'

'I never heard anything more ridiculous in my life.'

'I knew you'd say that, but you haven't been listening to Lucy all these months; you haven't been seeing the way she's changed the subject whenever Dominic and some girl was mentioned, the way she's decided to welcome Mary and her daughter.'

'Well, didn't you do the same? You educated the girl, against her will I might add, and you've no thoughts on marrying her off to our son.'

'Dominic's too close to that Cardew boy. They're always together. It's too close a friendship for comfort.'

'Nonsense. They were at school together, university together—it's natural they should remain friends.'

'I know it's no use talking to you, Arthur, but I know what I know. Lucy's worried.'

'And what about Johnny?'

'He's a lot like you, blinkered. He won't have noticed anything about Dominic; a mother's instincts are more profound.'

'Well, I've taken on board what we've talked about and I'll keep my eyes and ears open. I can't say more than that.'

'I hope I'm wrong, and please be discreet, Arthur, I don't want Lucy or Johnny thinking we're on to something.'

'Well, of course I'll be discreet. You surely don't think I'm going to tackle the lad. I've decided to give Peabody the job; give him twelve months to see if he's up to it. If not he'll have to be replaced, and we'll see about a cottage for Mary. That should keep Lisa firmly away from Dominic.'

Neither of them were aware that Lucy had already made arrangements for Dominic to drive Mary and

Lisa over to see her the next day. Lisa happily donned her prettiest dress and spent most of the morning in happy expectation.

He arrived immediately after lunch in the company of Oliver Cardew so that Lisa sat with her mother in the back seat of his car listening while the two men chatted together about all and sundry, leaving Mary and Lisa to gaze out of the window at the passing scenery.

Lucy received them with charming warmth, indicating that they should sit in the window where they could look out across the parkland, while inwardly she was annoyed that Dominic and his friend excused themselves on the grounds of exercising the horses.

'I want you back for tea, Dominic,' she said to him sharply in the hall. 'We do have guests and it would be polite, I think.'

'They're your guests, Mother,' he replied evenly. 'Surely they'll be happier chatting to you. Oliver hardly knows them at all.'

'Why is he always here? Isn't it time he spent some time away?'

'He's my friend, Mother. He likes it here.'

'And I like my son to be agreeable to my guests and to think a little less about his commitment to his friend. Oliver has little conversation anyway.'

'I find him entertaining.'

'Please Dominic, just do as I ask. Be nice to my guests and save Oliver for another day.'

* * *

Lisa was looking round her with great interest as Mary said, 'It is a beautiful house, isn't it, darling? I've been here just once many years ago.'

'Will it be Dominic's one day?'

'Of course, but he has his own house at Martindale. When he marries he and his wife will live there, then when he takes his father's title they will move in here.'

'You know so much about the way of things, Mother, and yet we've always been outsiders. Father was often scathing about it, Did you never resent it?'

'Oh yes, very often, but I tried never to show it. I was telling Lisa what a lovely house this is,' she said quickly when Lucy entered the room.

'Of course, Mary, when Dominic comes back I'll get him to show Lisa round. He's gone to exercise the horses but will be back for tea.'

'Does his friend live nearby?' Mary asked.

'He lives near Martindale but he visits here quite often. They've been friends many years. Now we must talk about where you are going to live. Has Sybil mentioned anything?'

'She thinks there may be a cottage in the village.'

'Well, I have a better idea. Do you remember the stone house near the crossroads that belonged to Aunt Jane? It's been empty since she died. It's a very beautiful old house and there have been a great many people interested. Johnny wouldn't part with it as he was very fond of Aunt Jane. I've often wondered what he would eventually do with it; now I've made one or two suggestions that it might suit you and Lisa.'

'But Lucy, it is very large and we don't have the furniture. It is also very grand. We're really not in that situation, Lucy.'

'Why ever not, Mary? We're cousins—my grandfather was a sad, unforgiving man and you've suffered long enough. I want you to have that house. I want Lisa to benefit from the education she's had and she'll only do it with the right address and the right atmosphere for advancement.'

'Oh Lucy, I don't know. What would Sybil have to say?'

'It has nothing to do with Sybil. It would be our decision—surely you can see the advantages.'

'But I'm not rich. I couldn't do justice to that house. Roger left very little money and Lisa wants to find employment.'

'There's no rush, Mary. We'll talk about financial matters later; in the meantime there is sufficient furniture left in the house to make it habitable and we have a great deal of stuff here tucked away in the attics. In the evening I'll get Dominic to come with us and we'll take a look at the place. You will both love it.

CHAPTER EIGHT

IT WAS LATER IN THE AFTERNOON when Dominic showed Lisa around the house. He took her to the long gallery with its portraits of Hazelmeres long gone—soldiers and admirals, bishops and politicians—and shyly she said, 'These are all your ancestors, Dominic?'

'Yes, some of them entirely pristine, others decidedly nefarious.'

'Surely not, they all look very proper.'

'In their immaculate uniforms or clerical garbs, yes, I suppose they do and yet here is the third Earl Hazelmere who was a notorious womaniser, and the sixth Earl who was a sadistic bully.'

'But there were some good ones, I'm sure.'

'Of course, but will we get any better do you think or will we simply decline in stature?'

'With you, Dominic, it can only get better.'

He smiled. 'You're something of a champion, Lisa. I hope I shall not disappoint you. I believe we are to look at Aunt Jane's house this evening. Mother obviously has plans for it.'

'She has said Mother and I could live in it.'

'Really? It's a beautiful old house—large for the two of you.'

Dominic looked down at her with some surprise. Aunt Jane's house had been empty since her death and his father had rejected all attempts to dispose of it, so he was surprised that his mother was suggesting it for Lisa and her mother, who would obviously not have the money to care for it. His mother must have a decidedly guilty conscience about the treatment Mary had been subjected to over the years.

Lisa fell in love with Aunt Jane's house against all her mother's misgivings.

'Darling, it's too big for us,' Mary exclaimed. 'We could never afford to live here—the rooms are large, the entire house is completely out of our reach. I can't think why Lucy has even suggested it. It will take a fortune to heat it. It's been a house with servants, parlour maids, butlers and gardeners; there are even stables for horses, which we can't afford.'

'But Lucy says I can ride horses from their stables, and we don't need servants. We can live comfortably in one or two rooms—we don't need all the house.'

'But Lisa, think of the waste. Lord Hazelmere could sell it for a great deal of money. All we need is a little cottage and for you to get some sort of job, teaching perhaps, or some other occupation your education will have equipped you for.'

While Lisa wandered through the house Mary complained bitterly to Dominic.

'She's so taken with the idea of living here, Dominic. I can't think why your mother has suggested it. Do you think you could explain matters to her?'

He smiled. 'Well, explaining things to Mother against something she's set her heart on will be very difficult, but I'll try.'

'Oh, I do wish you would make her see how silly it would be for us to come here.'

Dominic too was puzzled. If his mother wished to find them a home there must be suitable cottages on the estate, not this old manor house that his father could sell for a great deal of money.

The opportunity to talk to his mother came later after he had driven Lisa and her mother back to their home.

'I really don't see why they're so negative about it,' she argued. 'Sybil's done all she could for them, now it's my turn. You won't remember your great-grandfather, Dominic. He was distant and unforgiving. Sybil and I had everything, Mary had nothing; it's time matters were redressed.'

'Have you discussed it with Father?'

'No. Up to now he's refused to sell that house. Don't you think it would be better for somebody to live in it than standing idle and deteriorating?'

'Even when it's quite unsuitable for them?'

'Why is it unsuitable? Mary is still my cousin; she's

gentry, and Lisa is a very beautiful girl, or hadn't you noticed?'

'Her beauty has nothing to do with the house, Mother.'

'I asked you if you had noticed.'

He was looking at her steadily and Lucy was the first to look away. He was her son. She should be able to ask him if he had any interest in girls but the words wouldn't come out, so instead she said, 'I'll speak to your father and see what he has to say about the house. In the meantime I'll have words with Mary again simply to make her see that she has nothing to worry about. Did you say if you would call to see them again?'

'No, Mother, tomorrow I'm driving over to Martindale. I promised Oliver Cardew that we'd have a look at the old barn together.'

'What does Martindale and its barns have to do with Oliver Cardew? It's your house—one day when you marry you'll live in it. Any alterations to the house and its land can be decided then, not now between you and Cardew.'

'Two heads are better than one, Mother, and Oliver is my friend.'

'And it's a friendship I have difficulty in understanding. What is he doing with his life, does he have a job, does he earn any money? Where exactly is he living near Martindale?'

'He has an old house in the village, one his aunt left to him. He paints pictures and sells some of them. He has all sorts of irons in the fire—I never probe into his financial situation, Mother.'

'Well, he seems aimless to me. Oh, I know he gets invited to the same sort of functions you get invited to, but on what grounds? Because he's your friend or some other reason?'

'Probably because he's acceptable to the people who invite him—certainly not because of me.'

'Well, I hope when Mary and Lisa come to live in Aunt Jane's house you'll be nice to them. Take Lisa to one or two garden parties or other venues. Let people see that she's nice enough and good enough to be fully accepted, and it will be good for you too, Dominic, a pretty girl on your arm, a girl other men would probably envy you for.'

Without replying Dominic left her but his face wore a troubled frown as he walked up the stairs to his room. His mother was pushing him in some direction only she was contemplating. He liked Lisa, she was a nice girl and he wanted her to have a decent future, but this steady manoeuvring by his mother was disconcerting. What did she hope to achieve by it?

Lucy was every bit as purposeful as Sybil when she had made her mind up about anything, and Mary felt she was being swept along into a strange and alien future.

Sybil on the other hand thought Lucy was mad to even think that Aunt Jane's house was suitable as a future home for them.

'Aunt Jane had a houseful of servants to look after her and the house,' she argued. 'To offer it to Mary seems ludicrous to me. I'm sure Johnny would agree with me.'

'It's standing empty and deteriorating,' Lucy snapped.

'Well, I hope you're not expecting Mary to pay for the renovation, she hasn't the money.'

'It will all fall into place.'

'They need a small cottage and Lisa needs a job. I didn't have her educated to live like a debutante in that crumbling old house. I don't understand you at all, Lucy.'

'I'm doing my share for Mary and her daughter, that's all.'

'But to such lengths.'

'We have nothing else available at the moment and Arthur will want the house they're now living in for his new manager.'

'It isn't urgent. Peabody already has a house in the village.'

'But he'll want to move onto the estate,' Lucy said.

'We said we could find them a small cottage in the village.'

'And I said I'd do my share of looking after them. I never interfered in your plans for Lisa, Sybil. I don't expect you to interfere with mine.'

'I'm not interfering, I'm simply stating a point. The house needs work doing on it.'

'I'm aware of it. There are workmen in there now.'

'You mean Johnny approves?'

'I mean I've arranged for renovations to be made. Johnny and I are talking about it.'

She had to talk to Johnny soon as the bills were starting to roll in and he would soon want to know what it was all about.

* * *

Indeed it was over breakfast only a few days later that
he had the bills spread out in front of him, exclaiming
with horror at the size of them.

She was dreading the confrontation but the time had
now arrived to discuss her woes regarding Dominic with
her husband. Problems about the house would lead her
into them.

'Is something wrong?' she asked him gently.

'Something's decidedly wrong. These are bills for
work on Aunt Jane's house. I never authorised such work.'

'I know, dear, I did.'

'Without telling me! Aunt Jane was my father's sister. She wasn't your aunt and the house has nothing to
do with you. It was entirely my affair.'

'About which you've done absolutely nothing. People have been interested in buying it but you wouldn't
sell it. It's falling apart, the roof was leaking, the garden was a wilderness, the plumbing needed seeing to;
one of these days it's going to fall down and then what
are you going to say?'

'But why now? Why without saying anything to me?
What are you supposing will happen to it?'

'I want it for Mary and Lisa.'

There was silence for a long minute as Johnny's face
grew red with amazement before he said, 'Mary and
Lisa! They can't live there, they haven't the money to
maintain it and in any case they'd rattle in it.'

'They need a good address.'

'Why?'

'Because I want Dominic to be interested in Lisa. She's beautiful, intelligent and he likes her. It's the first time I've ever heard him say he liked a girl.'

'He will when the time is ripe, some girl in the right environment. He doesn't need to have a girl found for him, particularly the wrong girl.'

'Oh, Johnny, all these years you've been blinkered about Dominic. You really don't know what I'm talking about, do you?'

He stared at her with uncomprehending astonishment. 'No, I don't know what you're talking about. What's wrong with Dominic?'

'I think he's a homosexual.'

'What utter rubbish! Whatever gave you that idea?'

'Think about the difference between the two boys.'

'Yes, well, the young one's too frivolous by half, Dominic's the steady, safe one.'

'Safe, Johnny? Oh no, he isn't safe, he's simply more interested in men than women.'

Spluttering with rage, he said, 'What are you talking about? Where do you get such ideas?'

'All those young girls who like him, wish there could be more but there never is. Oh, I'll admit he's nice to them, he's charming and courteous, but there it ends. The only person he's really interested in is Oliver Cardew. They're at Martindale together now, supposedly talking about the barns, but that's not why they're there—they simply have to be together somewhere.'

'You've been on about this before. How do we go about changing him?'

'We have to change him, Johnny, and if we can't we have to stop anybody else knowing about it. He's got to marry, Johnny. If he's seen with a wife any likely gossip about him will stop. He needs an heir. After that nothing matters.'

'You're asking a lot from a man who has no interest in women, or has that escaped your attention?'

For several moments he remained staring into space. It was all too much—his son's sexuality and the long-term view of his life.

Lucy sat watching the expressions flit across his face—doubt, anger, anxiety—then he said, 'What a mess, Lucy, what are we going to do?'

'I hoped I was wrong. I wanted to ask him outright but the time was never right; now I'm sure and I have to protect Dominic and the family name. Nobody has to know. Think about the Marshland boy—he was shipped overseas and none of the family know where he is. Fortunately he was a younger son so people are not as quick to sit in judgement.'

'What about Lisa? Is this your idea of doing your best for the girl, tying her to a man who can never really love her, spoiling her chances with some man who would love her and give her children? Is that your idea of caring, Lucy?'

'She'll have money, a title, jewellery, travel wherever she wishes to go. The compensations are enormous and it is something she wants. I've seen the way she looks at him—there is no other man she's even remotely interested in.'

'So they move into the old house which gives her a decent address, he won't be seen to be marrying beneath him, and even if people do talk they'll soon forget about it once she's got a ring on her finger and a handle to her name.'

'Exactly.'

'Have you talked about this to anybody else?'

'No, but I'm sure Sybil guessed long ago that Dominic was different. She's never put it into words, but she would agree that the family has to be protected, and Lisa is family, however obscure.'

'So the suffering goes on. They were never acceptable with your grandfather, now they pay again; this time though it's the younger generation who pay.'

'Johnny, trust me. I know what I'm doing. Shouldn't you do something?'

'What exactly?'

'Talk to Dominic. You're his father, you can ask him outright. You can also make him see that he owes something to us, to his family name. Heaven knows, there's been enough scandal in the past, we don't want any more.'

'What scandal?'

'Well all right, it was a long time ago, but scandal lingers. When new scandal erupts the old ones come to light again.'

'Look, Lucy, can't we simply allow our son to do what he likes? If he doesn't want to get married that's his business, it's his life. He should be allowed to get on with it.'

'And have everybody saying he's different, he's not

getting married because he doesn't fancy women? And then there's that Cardew boy in the picture.'

'And what about the girl?'

'Oh Johnny, Lisa's an intelligent girl. She'll see all the advantages—she'll be the Viscountess Lexican and one day the Countess Hazelmere. She'll have status, money, all the prestige she's so far been denied. I don't think we need to worry about Lisa.'

'What about love and children?'

'Well, obviously we're not sure about children, but we needn't rule out love as long as she's discreet about it.'

'I always thought Sybil was the hard one; now I'm not so sure.'

'What do you mean by that?'

'I'm seeing a new you, Lucy, a manipulative woman who leaves me standing when it comes to plotting and planning the future.'

'What you are seeing is a mother and a wife concerned about her son and her family.'

'What exactly is your strategy, Lucy?'

'I want Mary and Lisa to move into the manor house. I want them to mingle in the right circles now that they will have the right address, and I want Dominic to be seen escorting her here, there and everywhere so that people will see that they are together. Then when they decide to marry nobody will be surprised.'

'And you really are expecting Dominic to rise to the occasion?'

'I'm expecting you to convince him that this is his duty.'

'Are you going to take your cousin Mary into your confidence?'

'No, Johnny, nothing and nobody has to interfere now that I've decided what we must do.'

'And Sybil?'

'What has Sybil got to do with anything?'

'She'll know what you're about. Hasn't she got friends who have been urging her to introduce their daughters to Dominic? She's hardly going to be pleased that he's looking elsewhere.'

'Sybil is family. She'll come to see the logic of it all.'

'Don't you think she might derive a certain malicious enjoyment out of it all?'

She stared at him coldly before saying, 'Sybil will agree with me that scandal and secrets must be kept within the family. She's fond of Dominic. If it was her son I'd be behind her all the way.'

'When is Dominic likely to return from Martindale?'

'He didn't say, and I didn't ask because the Cardew boy was hanging about anxious for them to be off. To-morrow or the next day perhaps.'

'You don't think you should telephone him?'

'No. At this stage I don't feel we should put any undue pressure on him. It will come soon enough.'

Johnny sighed. He would not relish talking to his son about such things. In his innermost heart he prayed that Dominic would deny adamantly everything his mother thought about him.

CHAPTER NINE

MARY EYED HER DAUGHTER over the breakfast table with the utmost consternation. All Lisa's thoughts were on their future in a house that was too large for them, too expensive to maintain and for which they did not have sufficient furniture.

Anything she said was discounted. All Lisa could think about was that she was leaving behind all the old feelings of being the poor relation, a girl sitting on the sidelines, with little hope that times would improve.

Then there was Dominic. She would be living nearer to him, perhaps seeing him every day, but although she said nothing to her mother, Mary was not deceived.

She knew that Lisa liked Dominic too well, but the situation was impossible. For one thing they were second cousins—when Dominic married it would be to a girl in a similar situation to his own, a girl with aristocratic associations and with money behind her, not a girl who his grandfather would have rejected as totally unsuitable.

* * *

Sybil too thought the entire situation preposterous and lost no time in telling Lucy what she thought of it.

'How can you even think of installing them in Aunt Jane's house?' she argued. 'They haven't the furniture, so do you expect them to live in a couple of rooms and ignore the rest of the house?'

'The house is furnished; it isn't a museum. They can make use of whatever facilities and furniture there is there.'

'Lucy, why?'

'Didn't we say we'd do our best for them? You've done your share now it's my turn.'

Dominic arrived home late that afternoon and Lucy was relieved that Oliver Cardew was not with him. She went out to meet him and in some surprise Dominic said, 'I thought you'd be over at the Carsdales', Mother. Isn't this the day of their garden party?'

'I had a headache and didn't feel like going. You too were invited.'

'I know, I made an excuse several days ago.'

'Anything to get out of a social engagement, Dominic. You'll be getting a reputation for being something of a wet blanket.'

He smiled. 'Yes, well, I'm sure Austin more than makes up for me.'

'Join me in the drawing room, Dominic. I have something to say to you.'

They sat opposite each other, Lucy's face adamant, Dominic's unsure.

'I'm glad you're home, Dominic,' she began. 'My cousin and Lisa hope to move into Aunt Jane's house in a few days' time and I'm hoping you'll be able to give them whatever assistance they require.'

'Assistance, Mother?'

'Well yes. Oh, they've arranged for removal men but there will be books to sort out and personal things. Mary's a bit of a dreamer and the onus will fall upon Lisa. You'd be such a help, darling.'

'Well, of course if Lisa asks for help I'll willingly give it, but she seems adequately capable to me.'

'Ah, but she's not. She's a young a girl in a strange environment who needs encouragement. She needs re-assurance that she's in the sort of world she should have been born into instead of all those years of rejection her mother and her grandparents had to endure.'

'I hadn't realised you felt so concerned about it, Mother. Why has it suddenly become so important?'

'It's always been important, Dominic, but it's only re-cently that I've been able to do something about it.'

'So what are you expecting the outcome to be, Mother?'

He was regarding her with a degree of cynicism she rarely saw in Dominic and in turn she was aware of her own embarrassment. She had to be careful—she should let Johnny handle Dominic, so in a lighter vein she said, 'I simply want Mary and Lisa to settle in happily and for Lisa to have a good future, meet the right sort of people and enjoy whatever is on offer.'

Rising to his feet, Dominic said, 'I'm sure it will all fall into place, Mother. At least it won't be your fault if it doesn't.'

She felt annoyed with him. He'd shown little enthusiasm for helping Lisa arrange their personal belongings and she was a beautiful girl. Most men, even if they hadn't wanted it to become serious, would not have been averse to spending their days in her company. She was right about Dominic, she had to be. If she'd suggested he spent time with the Cardew boy he'd have leapt at the suggestion.

She was not looking forward to dinner that evening. Johnny would be irritated and hardly looking forward to interrogating Dominic later in the evening, but she'd insist on it. She'd come this far; answers had to be found.

Conversation at the dining table hadn't been easy. Johnny's attendance without her at the Carsdales' garden party he'd considered something of a bore.

'I can't think why you didn't make an excuse for both of us,' he said grumpily. 'Lots of silly chatter from women in silly hats and bits and bats to eat that I didn't enjoy.'

'You had men to talk to surely. You'd know everybody there.'

'What do men talk about when they're surrounded by women?' he argued. 'They talk about Ascot and Goodwood, and they never get let off the leash.'

'Didn't Austin go with you?' she asked.

'He was off with some girl or other.' Then eyeing Dominic he said, 'What time did you get back then?'

'This afternoon.'

'Managed to tear yourself away from the Cardew boy then?'

Dominic looked at him enquiringly, and receiving Lucy's warning look he said, 'Well, he seems to spend most of his time here. I want a word with you in the study later—something I need to discuss with you.'

'It sounds very serious, Father.'

'It could well be.'

Dinner went on largely in silence and when they reached the coffee stage Johnny said, 'I don't want coffee. I prefer to get this over with now. I'll have a whisky; join me as soon as you can Dominic.'

'I'll join you now, Father. It all sounds very serious.'

Without another word Johnny got up from the table and walked out of the room and after a brief look at his mother Dominic followed him.

He found his father staring through the window onto a scene of indescribable beauty. Artists painted it, poets eulogised on it, now his father was looking at it with grim uncertainty as if he wasn't seeing the herd of deer strolling towards the lake, the setting sun lighting up the avenue of old trees, the banks of alpines nestling in the rockeries.

Dominic stood uncertainly, waiting for his father to turn round and take his seat behind the desk, but when he did so it seemed that the silence went on too long, too uncomfortably.

It wasn't fair, Johnny thought angrily. Lucy shouldn't have troubled him with this enormity. Of course Dominic was no different to any other man. There was plenty of time for him to think of matrimony. Lucy was wrong, and yet when he looked into his son's eyes he found them strangely wary; but it was Dominic who posed the first question.

'Is something wrong, Father?' he asked.

Blustering relief came to his assistance. Get it over with. Either let him admit to it or deny it. No use pussy-footing around something as serious as this.

'Yes,' he snapped. 'Something is very wrong, and it's you. Your mother's got some bee in her bonnet that you're different, that you've a thing against women, that you're not the son I want you to be.'

Dominic stared at him, but in his eyes he read only anguish, and in some exasperation Johnny went on, 'Well, are you denying it, or is it true?'

In a strangled voice Dominic answered, 'Does it matter, Father? Is it so important?'

Furiously his father replied, 'Yes it does matter. You're our eldest son. You carry the future of this family on your shoulders, and you owe it to the family to produce the next heir. Surely among all the girls who like you, there is one you might wish to settle down with—that's providing you don't prefer some man like Oliver Cardew, and that's what your mother's afraid of.'

'It seems that you've already made up your mind, Father.'

'I'm waiting for you to deny it,' Johnny snapped.

He watched his son sink weakly onto the nearest chair, his hands clenched on his knees, his face the picture of despair, before he said, 'I can't help it, Father. I've always known I was different, not because I wanted to be but because I couldn't envisage any other way.'

'And this lad Cardew, you're more than friends?'

Miserably Dominic looked down at his hands; he didn't need to answer.

The long silence was interminable and Johnny was wondering what he'd ever done to deserve this. Dominic was handsome, the sort of man any parents could be proud of, and yet families hid away sons of his calibre, sent them away to live separate lives, and if they were not forgotten, lies were told to friends and family about where they were and why. But dammit, Dominic was his eldest son, he couldn't be sent away, he had to stay here and do his duty.

Lucy should be here; she was the one who'd suspected it; she was the one who'd insisted it be brought out into the open; now she had to be the one to tell Dominic where she wanted it to go.

He got up from his chair and without another word he pulled the rope near to the fireplace. When a servant appeared he said briefly, 'Ask Lady Hazelmere to join us in here,' then he went back to his chair to sit in silent melancholy until his wife joined them.

One look at her son's aloof expression and her husband's despair confirmed the suspicions she had tortured herself with for so long. Taking the seat next to Dominic she waited for what was to come.

After what seemed an eternity her husband said, 'Well, you were right, he's admitted it. Where do we go from here?'

How still it was in that room lit by the setting sun, while three people remained strangely silent, each one of them plagued by uncertainties. Dominic was the first to break the silence by asking, 'What is it to be, Father, the French Foreign Legion or some far-eastern monastery nobody has even heard of.'

'Hardly a subject for flippancy,' his father snapped.

'I'm not being flippant, Father, I was merely wishing to bring a little normality into the proceedings,' Dominic answered.

'Normality! There's nothing normal about this situation. I've asked you to join us, Lucy, because you're the one who first agonised about something I had absolutely no conception of; now I'm relying on you to tell Dominic what you are expecting of him. We've done our part—see how well he repays us.'

Dominic was looking at his mother curiously and Lucy felt that she was wallowing in a quagmire of complexities completely alien to anything she had ever known. Dominic was her son and yet what did she really know about this new Dominic? He was a stranger living in a separate world, and yet she loved him just as much as she had always loved him. Nothing in his private life would ever change that, and yet behind it was tradition, the long tradition of wealth and privilege, of noble titles that were handed on from father to son through long interminable ages that was concerning her now. Nothing must be allowed to stop the destiny that fate had planned for them.

Both her husband and her son were looking at her

anxiously and with a voice filled with determination she said, 'Outside these walls nobody must know. Apart from we three no other person must be informed. Dominic, for the sake of the family you have to change your life. You have to make sure that you behave normally, that however you feel inside, this is how it has to be. Do you understand?'

'I can't help the way I am, Mother. How can I pretend to be something I'm not?'

'You can and you will. You will give up that friendship with Oliver Cardew to begin with.'

'I can't do that, Mother. We've been friends too long; it's more than friendship.'

'You mean you think you're in love with him,' she argued.

His father snorted disdainfully, but Dominic said, 'I do love him, Mother, we love each other. It's more than the friendship of two boys; it's something that's grown and intensified. Mother, you are asking the impossible. Oliver and I need each other.'

'Then I am asking you to be discreet, don't shout it from the house tops. Behave like every other young man with all his life in front of him and find yourself a wife.'

He stared at her with incredulous tortured eyes, and reaching out to cover his hand she said, 'Think, Dominic, some pretty girl who likes you, who thinks you're kind and wonderful, some girl who will want to be your wife. She'll have position, a title, money. You can spread your wings, take her abroad, let her see the world, shower her with gifts, jewellery, money. In the end she will accept what she cannot change.'

'Mother, it's dishonest,' Dominic cried. 'A girl who thinks she's in love with me will expect more than money and jewellery, more than some worthless title.'

'How can you say your title is worthless? It is what will encourage the right sort of girl to realise how fortunate she is.'

'Mother, all those aspiring girls with ambitious mothers are from blue-blooded families—they'll be looking for more than what I can offer them.'

'There's Lisa.'

'Lisa!'

'You like her, she more than likes you and she's by way of being family.'

'Are you suggesting that I tell Lisa about myself and then ask her to marry me?'

'Don't be silly, Dominic. I am asking you to get to know her. Invite her to race meetings, to balls, let the world see that you're like other men with a pretty girl on your arm; and now that Lisa and her mother are installed in Aunt Jane's house, she has the right address and can keep up with any one of them.'

'Why should that matter?'

'It does matter, darling. She's pretty, she rides as well as or better than any of them, she will have the right sort of clothes. I'll see to that, and in the end everybody will see that you're right for each other.'

'You're asking me to pretend, Mother. It isn't fair to me and it certainly isn't fair to Lisa.'

'Dominic, you're making me so angry. Because of your grandfather, Lisa and her mother have been deprived all their lives. Now she's being given advantages she never dreamed of. In the end she'll value what she has far more than love that can be transitory and often elusive. One day she'll be the Countess of Hazelmere and people will have stopped asking themselves questions years before.'

'And if she finds somebody else to love?'

'Then she will know how to be discreet. Look around you, darling, and you don't have to look much further than our respected king with his retinue of mistresses.'

Dominic's haughty expression told her nothing of his private thoughts but for the first time his father said shortly, 'What about your cousin, Sybil? She's not to be silenced about her thoughts on Dominic and don't tell me she hasn't expressed them.'

'You can leave Sybil to me, Johnny. She's as family orientated as I am. Sybil likes scandal, but not when it concerns members of her family.'

Turning to Dominic she said gently, 'Dominic, darling, you're the one we care about most. It's your future we're thinking about. Promise me you'll get to know Lisa—in the end you may realise you are a man after all, and, darling please no more Oliver Cardew in the immediate future.'

His expression was bleak as he excused himself from their presence, and when he had gone it was his father who expressed his doubts.

'It won't work, Lucy. It never worked with Brampton's

youngest boy. If they're born like that there's nothing anybody can do about it.'

'Johnny, we have to try. We have to encourage him, make much of Lisa, survive all this.'

'The girl will be a sacrificial lamb.'

'Sacrifices can be made to achieve something. If this sacrifice achieves what I hope it will achieve then it will all have been worthwhile.'

He looked at his wife long and thoughtfully before saying, 'You're a hard, wily woman, Lucy Hazelmere. I never had a chance after I met you, and now I can see why—you'd challenge Armageddon to achieve your ends and you'd win.'

She smiled. 'Oh do let us go back to the drawing room, darling, and have a drink. I feel quite exhausted by all this. We should forget it for the rest of the evening.'

CHAPTER TEN

SITTING OPPOSITE HIS WIFE in the drawing room Johnny couldn't think how she could possibly concentrate on her needlepoint when the events of the last few hours were causing him such feelings of trauma. He was not to know that Lucy's thoughts were a long way from her embroidery.

She was remembering Dominic's expression, or the lack of it. He had walked out of the room without looking at either of them, like a sleepwalker, with his mind refusing to see beyond the future they wanted for him.

'Now where is he off to?' came her husband's voice from where he had gone to stand looking out of the window.

Dominic was walking across the terrace and down the steps leading to the drive. He was walking slowly, his eyes on the ground, his hands thrust into the pockets of his hacking jacket, the disturbed figure of a man with many doubts and questions occupying his mind.

A solitary horseman riding in the opposite direction paused so that they could exchange words and Lucy said sharply, 'Is that Oliver Cardew, Johnny?'

'No, it's our younger son on his way back from the garden party. Perhaps it's time we had a few words with him. Heaven knows, until today he's been the one needing some sort of admonishment.'

'It was Austin's behaviour that made me view Dominic with suspicion,' Lucy retorted.

Austin was cantering up the drive, waving gaily when he saw his parents standing at the window. They returned to their seats. Several minutes later Austin joined them and sprawled out on one of the couches so that his father said sharply, 'Take your feet off the furniture, Austin. The mud in the stable yard will do nothing for it.'

Complying, Austin said, 'I've just seen Dominic on the drive looking as if he had the whole world on his shoulders. Had a row with Cardew, I suppose.'

'Why do you say that?' his mother retorted. 'What do you know about Dominic and Oliver Cardew?'

Austin stared at her with a smile on his face, to be removed instantly when he saw her haughty expression, and shrugging his shoulders he said, 'Well, they're old friends, aren't they? Did you never have a spat with one of your old pals? It was obvious he had things on his mind.'

'It's about time you had more on your mind than cavorting with every girl around. Who was that girl you disappeared with this afternoon? By the time I left nobody seemed to know where you were or who you were with,' his father said testily.

'She was perfectly legit, Father, a friend of Jemima Garnet. Her father's big in trade even though he hasn't a handle to his name. She was fun, a thoroughly nice girl.

A girl I could take to the May Ball and introduce into your kind of society.'

'There's no cause to be facetious—you wouldn't be the first man to latch onto the wrong sort of girl.'

'You should be talking to Dominic, Father, he's the one you should be expecting great things from, not me. He's the one with expectations. I'm the one who should be allowed to make my own life, just as long as I don't kick over the traces.'

Getting up from the settee he grinned at them, saying, 'Well, I'd better get out of these riding things. I've promised to meet a crowd of them over at the Bensons, later on.'

'What goes on at the Bensons'?'

'Oh, just a few young people enjoying an open-air buffet and a bit of fun. Nothing for you to worry about, Father.'

He left them with a broad smile on his face and his father said sharply, 'Before this afternoon I'd have been concerned about that one. Never in a million years did I think it was my elder son I needed to worry about.'

'Darling, you don't. We've sorted all that out and Dominic will conform.'

'And suppose he doesn't.'

'But he must. He's intelligent enough to know he can have no life with Oliver Cardew. His entire future must be seen to be normal, a nice wife, without any hint of scandal. Even Dominic must be aware of the alternative and what it would do to him and to us.'

Her husband was silent, staring morosely into space,

so in a gentler voice Lucy said, 'You're thinking about Lisa, Johnny, but I've told you before you don't need to. I'm quite sure Lisa is a materialistic girl capable of weighing up the advantages against the disadvantages.'

'I can see all that, but suppose she's in love with him, suppose she's more interested in love's young dream than position and money. Will she forgive him? Will she forgive us, do you think?'

The sound of footsteps crossing the hall brought their conversation to an abrupt end and Lucy said quickly, 'No more tonight, Johnny, we've said our piece. Let Dominic see that after today it's up to him. We must act as if that is how we've left it. We trust in his intelligence, in the pride he has in his family, Johnny, we've done all we can.'

Dominic's eyes met theirs across the room and Lucy said gently, 'Austin is going out for the evening, darling. Do come and sit with us a while in the drawing room.'

The atmosphere was dreadful though. For the main part Dominic was deep in thought, responding to his mother's attempts at conversation while his father made absolutely no effort to lift the gloom.

Lucy suggested they all have another drink but Dominic said immediately, 'If you don't mind, Mother, I have letters to write. I don't want a drink and must ask you to excuse me.'

'I hope you're not sulking, darling,' she said reproachfully.

His gaze met hers calmly but without another word he left the room.

His father said gruffly, 'We've set the cat among the pigeons. We don't know which way he's going to jump.'

She smiled complacently. 'You worry too much, Johnny, it will all come right, I'm sure.'

'When? When will it all come right?'

'Be patient, darling. You'll see that I'm right.'

They saw little of Dominic during the next few days—he was often out riding his horse across the fields and lanes—indeed it was several days before he joined his mother for lunch and said in a restrained voice, 'I thought I should tell you, Mother, that I have invited Lisa to the garden party the Holdsworths are giving at the end of September.'

Her eyes lit up with delight. 'Darling, that's marvellous. All the county will be there.'

'That's what I thought, and it's what you wanted, isn't it? That we should be seen together, that people would be able to say, "We must have been wrong about him after all, he seems pretty normal to me."'

'Oh Dominic, darling, don't be like that, please. You know that your father and I have your welfare at heart, we only want what is best for you, and for Lisa.'

It was an entirely different story in the manor house that Lisa and her mother had moved into. Mary was watching her daughter arrange flowers in one of Aunt Jane's most prized pieces of Spode.

'I don't think you should be using that, dear,' she said thoughtfully. 'They are being kind enough to let us live here, but we really have no right to treat Aunt Jane's belongings as if they are ours.'

'Mother, Aunt Jane is dead. We're not living in a museum. Surely it is better for them to be used than keep them simply as ornaments and use our inferior things.'

'Perhaps we should ask Lucy first.'

'Oh Mother, how long are you going to keep up all that second-class citizenship nonsense? You're every bit as good as either of your cousins. It wasn't your fault that grandfather disowned your parents and you.'

'I know, dear, but old memories die hard. I'm not really ready for all this, although I must say you've taken to it very well. You've seemed particularly happy today. Why is that?'

She was aware of Lisa's blushes before she said, 'Dominic has invited me to a garden party at the end of September, Mother. I know you've told me not to read too much into his kindnesses but he really didn't need to ask me anywhere if he didn't want to.'

'Where is the garden party?'

'Somewhere near Lichfield; the Holdsworths', he called it.'

'Sir Ronald Holdsworth's place?'

'Do you know them, mother?'

'No, I only know of them. Landowners, rich people.'

Lisa looked at her mother doubtfully. 'You think I shouldn't have accepted his invitation, Mother?'

'Oh darling, I don't know. Perhaps I should speak to Lucy to see if it has her approval. They've been more

than kind to us. I don't want them to think we're looking for more.'

'Perhaps you would prefer me to tell Dominic I can't
accept his invitation, that I have nothing suitable to wear,
that I am not sufficiently versed in the right sort of conversation, or that I don't exactly have the right sort of
background for such an occasion.'

Mary looked at her daughter's expression helplessly.
Lisa's face was filled with resentment, an expression she
was familiar with but which had not been quite so much
in evidence of late.

'Darling, I'm so very proud of you,' she said gently.
You're very beautiful. I always knew that one day you
would be, but I don't want you to get hurt.'

'Why would I be hurt?'

'Because I know how much you like Dominic. I've
seen you looking at him, worshipping with him your
eyes, hanging on his words, wanting more. But suppose
there isn't any more, Lisa, suppose that one day you'll
be told that he is to marry some other girl from his own
station. What will that do to you?'

'From his own station, Mother? What does that
make me?'

'You know what I mean, darling.'

'No, Mother, I don't. You tell me I'm beautiful, and
somewhere in me is some of the blood that is in him. The
fact that you don't think I'm good enough for him is
hurtful.'

'Lisa, I think you're good enough for the most noble
family in the land. It's not me you have to think about,

I'm your mother. It's what the rest of the world thinks that matters.'

She watched as Lisa put the remaining flowers in the vase before she stood back to look at them, then in one quick movement Lisa removed them and, gathering them together in her hands, she said angrily, 'I'll look for another vase, Mother. They're evidently not good enough for the Spode, like I'm not good enough for Dominic.'

With a sob in her throat she ran out of the room and Mary followed her with a sad and aching heart.

In the next few days she would speak to Lucy. It was better for Lisa to be hurt now than mortified at a function at which she would be made to feel inferior.

The opportunity came several days later when she saw Lucy exercising her horse in the park. Lucy pulled up her horse with a warm smile on her face and almost timidly Mary said, 'I'm so glad to have seen you, Lucy. I intended to call upon you as I'm rather worried about something.'

'I hope it's nothing at the house, Mary. Haven't the builders finished putting everything to rights?'

'Oh yes indeed, everything is perfect, we're very happy there. It's something quite different.'

Lucy waited, but there was no denying the worried look on her cousin's face so she said gently, 'You look worried, Mary. Nothing wrong with Lisa, I hope?'

'No, not at all, but it is something to do with Lisa that is worrying me.'

'Really? What can that be?'

'Did you know that Dominic had invited her to attend the Holdsworths' garden party with him in September?'

'Yes, he did mention it to me.'

'And you don't mind?'

'Mind! Why should I?'

'Shouldn't there be some other girl he should be taking? Sybil said she knew a dozen girls who had aspirations about him, girls from his own walk of life, girls whose mothers had designs on him.'

Lucy laughed. 'I know about those girls. Dominic knew about them also. Quite evidently Dominic preferred to invite Lisa instead of any one of them.'

'And you don't mind?'

'Of course not.'

'Will Dominic's father mind?'

'Of course not. You should know by now that Johnny leaves the boys to make their own arrangements, particularly Dominic who he attributes with a great deal of common sense. Surely Lisa wants to attend the garden party with him?'

'Yes indeed, she's very happy and wants to go with him.'

'Then there's nothing more to be said, is there.'

With a bright smile she galloped off into the woods leaving Mary staring after her but with more relief than she had expected to feel.

Over their evening meal she told her daughter about the conversation she had had with her cousin but she was unprepared for Lisa's response.

'Mother, am I supposed to be grateful that I now have his mother's permission to attend? It's demeaning.'

'It isn't meant to be, dear. I felt you would be pleased that she likes you so much.'

'I don't care whether she likes me or not, only that he likes me. I had intended to decline the invitation.'

'Oh Lisa, no. Why hurt Dominic?'

'I'm not so sure that he would be hurt; relieved maybe.'

Mary looked at her daughter sadly. 'Oh Lisa,' she murmured, 'it's always been there in you, that feeling of hurt pride, that desire to repay slights with anger and revenge. Go with Dominic with the knowledge that he has invited you because he wanted to, and that his parents have no objection.'

'You know, Mother, I was so looking forward to it. That's what I had thought, that I'd been invited because he liked me; now I can only wonder.'

Mary accepted the fact that her daughter would never be like herself. Within Lisa was some of the high-handed pride that her grandfather had been capable of. Perhaps Lisa would always be her own worst enemy, but then Dominic was nice—perhaps he would be capable of changing her proud, insecure daughter into another sort of woman, less prickly, more gentle. She offered a silent prayer that Dominic would never hurt her.

If they could have heard Lucy and Sybil talking together later that day they would both have been more troubled.

'You mean Dominic has actually invited Lisa to the

Holdsworths' in September?' Sybil asked in some amazement.

'Of course, why shouldn't he?'

'Because it's ridiculous. What about Marcia Shepple-ton, what about Pheobe Bart, girls with money, position, all of them waiting for him to approach them?'

'I don't put pressure on my sons to seek out girls they don't particularly aspire to. It's evident Dominic likes Lisa. I like her, she's beautiful and intelligent; he could do worse.'

'But people will talk. They know our history; they'll never understand why he would invite a girl his family would never have stood for.'

'You're biased Sybil. You're talking about our grand-father who's been dead these many years. We're her family, we've accepted her. Let them all see that we both deplored our grandfather's treatment of Mary and her fa-ther, that we've atoned for it.'

Sybil stared at her in amazement. 'You mean there's likely to be more to it?' she asked.

'How can I tell, but if there is Johnny and I will not object.'

'Is any of this your doing, Lucy?'

'What is that supposed to mean?'

'You had suspicions about Dominic—are you push-ing him into this?'

Lucy stared at her cousin with the utmost exaspera-tion. 'I would not attempt to push my son into anything. I had doubts because he showed absolutely no interest in those girls you've just spoken about. The reason is obvious—he didn't care for them. He quite obviously cares for Lisa, and neither his father nor I have any intention of interfering.'

Sybil realised she would have to be content with that, but it did not stop her from railing her husband about the unsuitability of it all.

'I don't know why you're going on and on about it,' he snapped. 'It's evident nothing you say is of any importance. They like the girl, so does Dominic; he should be allowed to please himself.'

'Oh, he will and it could be a disaster.'

'But not your disaster, and possibly not a disaster at all. She's an intelligent girl. What did that governess have to say, that she'd worked hard and come along marvellously. She's a good looker, at par or even better than some of the other girls that have been trotted out. You should stay out of it, Sybil.'

So in the weeks before the garden party Lisa saw more of Dominic. They rode together across the parkland, they went boating on the river and walked together through the village so that family and villagers alike smiled on them as a pair.

Lisa was head over heels in love; Dominic enjoyed talking to her—she had a lively mind and she was fun.

One day when Lisa was entering the house she saw a solitary horseman riding towards her. At first she thought it was Dominic until he drew nearer and she recognised his friend Oliver Cardew.

She smiled at him but was completely unprepared for

his haughty stare and the cold expression in his dark eyes. He passed without a smile or a word and for a long time she stood staring after him. She could not understand why Oliver Cardew should have looked at her with quite that degree of cold anger, but she let herself into the house with a feeling of deep hurt.

CHAPTER ELEVEN

MARY WATCHED HER DAUGHTER setting off with Dominic to the garden party she'd been looking forward to for weeks. It was a perfect Indian summer day when the countryside basked under an azure blue sky and Lisa had never seemed more beautiful in her pale peach gown and large straw hat decorated with gardenias.

She and Dominic were a handsome couple in any-body's estimation, both of them tall and slender, both dark, both elegant. Dominic had been gracious and charming while there was no disguising Lisa's expression of deep and tender love.

Mary couldn't see why she should feel in the least disquietened but beneath it all she couldn't rid herself of a strange feeling that none of it could last. Dominic was invariably kind, but was there more? She remembered what it was like to be in love, to look into a man's eyes and want his arms around her, but somehow or other there had to be a sense of distance where Dominic was concerned.

Perhaps he did not feel the same affection for Lisa that

she felt for him, or perhaps it was something that would emerge later, a passion that would grow, a strengthening of desire that was latent in a young man brought up to respect the niceties of life.

Lisa had no such qualms. People were wandering around the gardens in smiling groups, greeting them courteously, seemingly seeing nothing amiss that Dominic had chosen to escort a girl who had until lately been outside their circle of friends.

Lord and Lady Hazelmere had greeted them charmingly, Lucy telling her that she was looking very beautiful and Dominic standing beside her with a half smile on his handsome face.

Watching them stroll away his father said gruffly, 'What do you make of it, Lucy?'

'They seem very happy and relaxed together, but then I always knew they would be.'

He looked at her wondering how she could be so blind and decided to say nothing more. From further down the path Sybil was sharing his disquiet. She had seen Lisa's expression as she looked up at Dominic's face, seen the way she leaned against him, a girl asking to be loved, asking to be held close, and she had seen Dominic's restraint. It was all going to end in tears, she felt sure.

They were chatting to a group of other young people when one of the girls asked innocently, 'I haven't seen Oliver Cardew here, Dominic. Come to think of it I haven't seen him for some time. Is he away?'

Dominic smiled. 'I'm not sure, it's some time since I've seen him.'

'But you were always so close. Has he got some girl he's interested in?'

'You would have to ask him that,' Dominic replied cagily, and with a little smile the girl said, 'Oh, I will when I see him. Actually I didn't think he was much interested in girls.'

When they were on their own Lisa said, 'I don't think Oliver likes me very much, Dominic.'

He stared at her for a few moments without speaking, then he said, 'Why do you say that, Lisa?'

'I saw him one evening on the road and smiled at him, but he just rode on without speaking or even smiling. Perhaps he resents me.'

'Why would he?'

'Well, like that girl said, you were nearly always together; now you don't see very much of him, if hardly at all.'

'Oh well, times change, people move on.'

'You don't strike me as the sort of man who would forget old friendships, Dominic, you're too kind, perhaps Oliver's the one who has moved on.'

'Perhaps. Oh one of these days we'll meet up again, but I'm sure he has nothing against you Lisa, please don't think that.'

That evening her mother was waiting to hear all about the events of the day and Lisa, nothing loath, described the dresses the women had worn, the refreshments on offer, the glory of the gardens and the day's perfection.

* * *

Now she was accepted as Dominic's girl and when their engagement was announced near Christmas the bluest blood in the county arrived at Hazelmere to celebrate with them. Dancing in Dominic's arms until the stars paled had been Lisa's idea of complete and utter bliss and when it was over and she went to collect her wrap she noticed that Dominic was chatting to Oliver Cardew in the hall.

The hall was decorated with tinsel and holly branches while a huge Norwegian spruce occupied pride of place in one corner. Log fires burned in the huge stone fireplace and people were laughing and exchanging Christmas wishes before they went out into the frost-laden night.

Lisa approached them shyly, concerned that Oliver would display the unfriendly attitude he had shown before, but this time he raised her hand to his lips and bowed his head over it. When he looked into her eyes, however, she still felt a vague misquiet at the veiled amusement in his dark eyes.

'Allow me to congratulate you on your engagement,' he said evenly. 'When is the wedding to take place?'

'We thought in the spring or early summer,' Lisa murmured.

'And I take it you will be moving into Martindale immediately.'

She looked up at Dominic wishing he would contribute something and he smiled, saying, 'Yes, it will be our home after we return from Italy.'

'So you are spending your honeymoon in Italy?' Oliver asked.

'Yes, Italy and Spain. Lisa is anxious to see something of the country her grandmother came from.'

'Of course, I'd forgotten your grandmother was Spanish.'

'I never knew her,' Lisa said. 'She died before I was born, I only know that she came from a small village near Seville.'

'A little country girl who made her presence felt quite potently when she arrived in England,' Oliver said with a half smile on his face and Lisa looked at him uncertainly. What did he know about her grandmother? And yet obviously he knew something of the trauma of her arrival into the family. But then Dominic was saying calmly, 'We all have skeletons in our families, Oliver. There have been some in your family or I have been misinformed.'

Oliver laughed, a sly, amused laugh, before saying, 'I can see that Aunt Dolly didn't waste any time in telling you about them. Oh yes, we had our disasters. I'm sure more were on their way; perhaps now they have been averted.'

Dominic was quick to change the subject by saying, 'Have you plans for Christmas?'

'I'm going home to see the parents. I shall miss you, Dominic, we've spent so many Christmases together.'

Dominic merely smiled and, bidding him goodnight, they left him gazing after them with a strange smile on his face. Lisa said anxiously, 'He really doesn't like me, Dominic. It's in his eyes, in his voice. He really does resent me and I can't think why unless he thinks I've come between you.'

Dominic made no effort this time to assure her that that was not the case; instead he exchanged words with his parents' guests as they climbed into their cars and prepared to drive away.

Over the weeks and months that followed her mother was in constant consultation with her two cousins. The expense of the wedding was troubling her, but immediately Lucy said, 'Dear Mary, of course we understand, you can't possibly be expected to take care of it all on your own. See to Lisa's dress and the flowers; we'll take care of the guest list, the food, the location, and of course the wedding will be at the Cathedral and the guests will dine here.'

'And Arthur will give her away. After all he is by way of being an uncle and I've already asked him and he has agreed,' Sybil assured her.

Mary felt that in the end she was having very little say in the proceedings, but as she surveyed her daughter on the morning before her wedding when she tried on her wedding gown complete with one of Lucy's exquisite tiaras, she thought that Lisa must be the most beautiful bride any of their guests had ever seen. The cream satin gown with its long train showed off her slender figure to perfection and her blue-black hair gleamed under the delicate veil finding its echo in the glittering diamonds in the jewelled diadem.

Her four bridesmaids laughed around her, admiring her gown, and Helena said, 'Did Mummy and Aunt Lucy interfere a lot in your choice of gown, Lisa? They had a lot to say about what I should wear.'

'They've been very kind. The dresses are beautiful, don't you think so?'

'Well, I really would have liked a darker blue. I'm so fair, and I don't want to look insipid.'

'But you're so pretty, Helena, of course you won't look insipid,' Lisa told her.

'I always wished I was dark like you. There's nobody else I know with that beautiful blue-black hair and jade green eyes. Isn't Dominic the most wonderful lover? He always seemed so remote, but we think underneath it all he's probably the most passionate lover.'

The girls giggled expectantly but Lisa was not to be drawn. Over the last few years she and Helena had become good friends and Helena had confided in her something of the passion she shared with her fiancé. It was one she did not share with Dominic. Dominic was invariably gentle, kind, thoughtful, but passion was never there and she longed to confide in Helena. Of course all men were not alike—passion would be worth waiting for. On their wedding night Dominic would be the perfect lover; she had nothing to fear.

She was surprised that he had not invited Oliver Cardew to be his best man—instead he had asked his brother and that of course seemed entirely fitting, but when he said Oliver was not even invited she had stared at him in some surprise.

Quickly he said, 'Oliver was very apologetic but he

has unfortunately another engagement on the day of our wedding, something he is unable to get out of. He said he would call upon us at Martindale before we leave for the continent.'

She asked no questions, nor was she to know that his mother had been rather more curious.

'You mean there has been no difficulty with Oliver?' Lucy had asked.

'No, Mother, did you expect there to be?'

'Frankly yes, Oliver has never been an easy boy, and he can't have accepted the situation with any degree of comfort.'

'He knows your feelings, Mother, he knows the position. you and Father have given me little choice.'

'But you are fond of Lisa, surely, Dominic. She is very fond of you.'

'I am aware of it, Mother. I am fond of her and I shall be a good and kind husband to her; that much I can promise but no more.'

'Oh Dominic, time alters many things. You will have a beautiful wife who loves you and she will give you all the joys you could never have got from Oliver Cardew. He belongs to the past; Lisa is your future.'

For a long moment he looked at his mother in pitying silence before he turned away. Oh, she thought, surely everything would turn out well. They'd been two young men who were friends, unaware that they could change. Now Dominic was being given every chance to change and in time Oliver too would accept it and move on.

That her husband shared no such feelings she was well aware. Johnny was wishing the wedding was well and truly over, his son and his bride out of their house and in their own place. Dominic and Lisa would rub along—they had to—but he didn't want to be a witness to the trauma that was sure to come. His future daughter-in-law was no pushover. She had a mind of her own and if Dominic was not prepared to love her the way she needed to be loved who knows what her answer would be.

Lucy firmly believed he would be able to change, but Johnny had known too many men like him, men who were known to be homosexual and who could never change.

It was undoubtedly the wedding of the year in spite of the fact that some mothers couldn't understand why Dominic Lexican had preferred a girl from nowhere instead of one of their more acceptable daughters. It was true that the girl was oustandingly beautiful and would shine like a star in her new exalted surroundings.

Later, after all the speeches had been made and the toasts drunk, Lisa and Dominic departed for Martindale surrounded by well-wishers, and with the laughter of their guests ringing in their ears.

During the two-hour ride to Martindale Lisa felt utterly contented; everything had gone so smoothly, her mother had embraced her with tear-filled eyes saying how enchanting she had looked, and similarly her mother-in-law too had assured her that only happiness lay ahead of them.

Aunt Sybil had said little beyond the usual expression

of congratulations, and Dominic's father had been reticent, merely kissing her cheek briefly and assuring her that she would enjoy both Spain and Italy.

'Never seen much of Seville,' he told her, 'but I've always had a soft spot for Italy, particularly Tuscany.'

'I simply wanted to see where my grandmother came from,' she answered shyly.

'Quite right too. Never knew the lady, but if she was anything like you I'm not surprised her husband cut loose and ran off with her.'

Lisa laughed. She liked Lord Hazelmere—he was brusque but she liked his humour. He was never condescending, never distant; indeed there was times when she wished Dominic was more like him, times when she looked at his handsome remote face and wished she understood the thoughts behind the calm impersonal mask he showed to the world.

It was early evening when they arrived at Martindale and outside the door the staff were lined up to greet them. As they walked from their car the butler came forward to present the rest of the servants while the men bowed correctly and the maid servants bobbed quaint country curtsies.

It was smaller than Hazelmere but there was a distinct charm about it with its tall mullioned windows and occasional pointed towers and turrets. The gardens stretched onwards into woodlands and later Dominic showed her round the house and into the gardens. She thought it was charming.

'Do you want to look at the stables,' he asked her, 'or would you prefer to wait until the morning?'

'I'd like to see them now, Dominic,' she answered. 'Have you many horses?'

'Three or four. You must find a mount you like, or I could get you another.'

'I'm sure I shall find one of yours most suitable.'

How stilted it was. They walked together like two polite strangers. He did not even take her hand and she longed for him to put his arm around her and behave like any other man on the first day of his marriage.

One horse in particular stood with his head over his stable door, watching her gently from eyes edged with long lashes, his satiny coat shining like burnished copper. Stroking his long neck she said, 'Oh I like this one. What is he called?'

'His name is Maxton. He's gentle and predictable; he's yours if you want him.'

She thanked him warmly, putting her arms around his neck and kissing him gently. She felt his rigidity when she had expected him to respond with an ardour to match her own.

They dined in the ornate dining room at the long table, where Dominic sat at one end and Lisa at the other, served by soft-footed servants, and because of the distance between them the conversation was minimal.

The meal was excellent, and later when they moved into the drawing room a fire had been lit and coffee was served to them. It was a ritual she had experienced at Hazelmere and at that moment she thought about her mother in that too large house on her own. Seeing her expression Dominic said gently, 'Your mother will be missing you, Lisa. I told my mother that house is really too large, particularly now that she is alone.'

She had to agree, even when she knew she had been the one wanting it.

'I hope we can have Mother to stay with us for a few weeks, Dominic. She would love this house—I do so want her to see it.'

'Of course. I spend a lot of time on the estate, so she would be company for you.'

She looked at him doubtfully. She wanted his company—would there ever be what she wanted there to be?

They talked about the day they had just spent, the guests, the good wishes, the presents. They discussed the gowns the women had worn and the music that had surrounded them, but now and again she looked questioningly at the clock on the mantelpiece thinking how slowly the fingers moved. When could she suggest that they should go up to their room? In the end it was Dominic who said, 'I'm sure you're tired, Lisa. It's been a long day for both of us—would you like to retire now?'

She smiled, and getting to her feet said, 'I am tired, Dominic. I'll go up first, please join me soon.'

He escorted her to the bottom of the stairs and stood waiting until she reached the head of the first flight where the stairs divided. Looking up she saw that in front of her stood a large painting of a man and woman standing with two young children in a garden surrounded by several dogs; turning, she looked down at him questioningly.

'My great-grandparents,' he said softly. 'One day perhaps your portrait will take its place.'

She smiled. 'Oh yes please, Dominic, our portrait. Just like this one with our children around us.'

CHAPTER TWELVE

LISA STOOD UNCERTAINLY BESIDE her bed in her pale cream satin nightgown, watching her maid put away the things she had recently discarded. Then the girl turned and with a bright smile said, 'Is there anything else you require, Milady?'

'No thank you, Hannah,' Lisa answered.

The girl said softly, 'Goodnight, Milady,' and after bobbing a gentle curtsy left the room.

How soon before Dominic came to her? How soon before he held her in his arms and whispered the words of love she longed to hear from him? How sweet would be the enchantment she had been waiting for, how potent the ecstacy in the long hours before the dawn.

She climbed into the large bed with its silken sheets and the vague perfume of lavender around her, and then the events of the day began to take their toll and incredibly she fell asleep. She had no idea what woke her, whether it was the sighing of the night wind outside the window, but as she struggled to sit up against her pillows she was strangely aware of a deep sense of foreboding.

It was so still within the house, and fearfully she reached out to clasp the ivory clock on the cabinet nearest to her. It was after two o'clock and Dominic had not come to her.

She got out of bed and struggled into her robe, then she went to open the door, walking cautiously to the head of the stairs and looking down into the deep darkness of the hall below. There were no lights anywhere, only a sense of deep penetrating emptiness.

Where was Dominic? Why hadn't he come to her? Then quickly she thought that perhaps he had found her asleep and had been reluctant to wake her, but as quickly as it had come she discarded the idea. Of course he would have wakened her—surely his ardour would have been as great as her own, his needs as demanding.

She should look for him—perhaps like herself he had fallen asleep somewhere downstairs. Suppose the servants found her wandering around the rooms downstairs, but the servants would be in their rooms—all the same she had to do something.

She was trembling with some unknown emotion—was it fear, anger or despair? But she made herself go back into the bedroom where she lit a three-pronged candelabra.

She was unfamiliar with the house, with the light switches—the heavy silver candelabra cast its light eerily along the corridor and down the stairs. For what seemed eternity she wandered round the house, into rooms she had never been into before, into the vast library and the billiard room, into reception rooms she had yet to discover and along corridors that seemed to go on forever; then at last she let herself into the large conservatory from where she could look out into the gardens.

Wearily she sank down onto one of the chairs from where she could see the silver moonlight shining through the beech leaves and hear the gentle rustling of their leaves. The light scudding clouds cast purple shadows against the glass and she felt suddenly cold.

This was her wedding night but she had never felt so alone. She had anticipated warmth and tenderness, passion and emotional joy, and here she was alone in a strange house looking down the long drive in a world devoid of human happiness and companionship. She had no idea how long she stayed there—inside she felt like a dead thing with no past or hopes of a future; only the feeling that there was something terribly wrong.

She felt no need to sleep, only to go on staring out of the window, feeling nothing, thinking nothing, as the sky grew lighter heralding the approaching dawn.

Mechanically she extinguished the lights on the candelabra, and rose wearily to her feet. Dominic had not come looking for her. Wherever he was it was evident he had not missed her and she turned to walk away from the window. She had almost reached the door leading into the house when something made her turn round again, and dimly along the drive she saw the solitary figure of someone riding towards the house.

She stood quite still within the shadows. Who was this lone rider coming slowly towards her? She felt herself trembling, as she waited to recognise him, but even before he came closer she knew for a certainty that it was Dominic. She watched him take the path towards the stables, riding unhurriedly, looking straight ahead, unknowing that from the conservatory his young bride watched him with mounting anger in her heart.

She fled through the house, leaving the candelabra on a side table somewhere in the hall, rushed into her room and stood breathless with her back to the door, her ears straining for any sound from below. It seemed like an eternity before she heard the first faint closing of a door, then footsteps, unhurried and barely audible crossing the hall.

With the first hint of panic she went to her bed, waiting with a fluttering heart for the husband who should have appeared hours before; then she heard the soft closing of another door further along the corridor. She waited until the first pale glow of the sun illuminated the room, knowing with chilling certainty that Dominic would not come to her now. With that certainty was the knowledge that he must not love her, had never loved her. So why had he married her? It was then that she realised that she not only hated Dominic but his entire family as well.

They had been pushed into it—she had been made welcome, bought like a piece of jewellery for the price of a house, clothes to wear, and an education she had never asked for or wanted.

How many times had she heard it? What must be done for Lisa, how much they had to make up for slights and hurts—like a fool she had thanked them for it, even when her mother had seemed uncertain.

And Dominic. He must have agreed to it all, but why? He could have had any aristocratic girl from his circle of friends and acquaintances. Why did it have to be her?

She slept no more that night; instead she got dressed in her riding apparel and went down to the stables, where a sleepy groom eyed her in amazement. He had only just come on duty and had certainly not expected to find the lady of the house waiting to have her horse saddled so soon after dawn.

She waited while he saddled Maxton, then climbing into the saddle she rode off along the drive in the direction she had seen Dominic coming from only an hour before. The road outside the tall iron gates led to the village, a village that had not as yet come to life.

A square-towered stone church occupied pride of place at the top of the village street along which a brook gurgled and bubbled into a small tarn where the lanes divided. Wooden seats stood round a large oak tree, but it was too early for the residents to sit on them. Window boxes filled with summer flowers adorned the walls of the Trantom Arms Inn and flowers bloomed profusely in cottage gardens. It was a village she could have loved, but now even its normality made her angry. It seemed to Lisa that morning that there would never in her life be love for anything ever again—she felt only resentment and bitterness. As she rode onwards along the lane she passed a square stone house with gardens leading onto a piece of meadowland and from the stables at the back of the house a man was leading a horse; then another man left the house to join him. There was something in his walk that she recognised, a kind of arrogance, and she waited with a compulsion that she could hardly understand.

Taking the horse's reins from the groom he climbed into the saddle, then pulling the horse round he rode down the path towards the gate. As their eyes met Lisa saw once more the hostility in his gaze, the cynical amusement that she now understood but had never understood before.

He hated her because she had become Dominic's wife, and Dominic had married her loving Oliver Cardew. This was where he had spent the night, in Oliver's house, in Oliver's bed, and no doubt he had poured out all his anguish to a listening lover who had offered him sympathy and promises that between them nothing had changed.

Pulling her horse around she galloped back along the way she had come and leaving Maxton with the groom she strode back into the house and up to her room. Her maid was already in attendance but impatiently Lisa dismissed her—she didn't want the girl to pamper her and report later to whoever was prepared to listen that her mistress had been riding alone on the morning after her wedding, and that her mistress's husband appeared to have spent the night in his dressing room.

In the breakfast room servants waited to serve her, smiling their good mornings, anxious to pander to her every need and she made herself accept their courtesies, making herself eat when the last thing she wanted was food, wondering how long before Dominic found the courage to face her.

She heard his voice outside the room and willed herself to sit quietly finishing her breakfast while a servant came forward to pour coffee. Across the room she looked into his eyes and was instantly aware of his pallor and the shame that was flooding his whole being.

Impatiently he waved the servants hovering around him away, and Lisa waited—the first words had to come from him, whatever they were.

She sat quietly, at first unable to look into his face, heard his sudden intake of breath, realising his nervousness, wanting him to be nervous, wanting him to suffer, praying that he would never know peace again; then he said quietly, 'Lisa, I'm sorry.'

She stared at him in amazement. He was sorry, what sort of a word was that? There were no words that could ease the pain of what he had done to her, and looking at her cold, angry face he was aware of it.

For a long moment there was silence, then he said quietly, 'I can't blame you for hating me, Lisa. It is what I deserve but perhaps I should be allowed to explain some of it.'

'Don't you think it's too late for explanations, Dominic?' she answered coldly. 'You should never have married me—you didn't love me. What made you think that I was so insecure and desperate that any sort of marriage was better than none, that whatever you were able to offer me would make up for the only thing that mattered and that I would be missing?'

'I tried very hard to make them see that. I'd hoped that you would realise that I couldn't love you the way you wanted to be loved and that you would see it wasn't going to work. You didn't, Lisa, you wanted me, and I can't understand why.'

For a moment she stared at him helplessly, then the tears started to roll down her cheeks, and without hesitation he came to take her in his arms. It was the embrace of a man for a child, for another human being for whom he had compassion, and she recognised it as such. Easing herself away from him she said quietly, 'I don't want your pity, Dominic, there will be enough of that in the years to come.'

'Lisa, I have promised to honour you and keep you and I will do all the things I promised. I will keep you in sickness and health for as long as you live and you will be my wife, the one being I have sworn to protect.'

'But your love, Dominic, who will you give that to?'

Holding her hands in his he stared down at her solemnly then he said calmly, 'I can't help the way I am, Lisa—I was born this way. I have loved Oliver Cardew for a long long time; it may not last, like the love between a man and a woman does not always last, but the regard I feel for you is very different. I shall always be there for you, Lisa, because you are my wife. If you can live with me like that, as friends—is it possible do you think?'

'And one day I might love somebody else—have you thought about that?'

'It is possible; I'm aware of it. I shall not stand in your way, Lisa.'

'But that is not how it was meant to be, is it, Dominic?

No hint of scandal, no scurrilous tongues saying things about you, no hint that I would seek lovers to compensate for your inadequacies. Oh Dominic, there are at this moment so many people I shall never forgive for what they have done to me. You will have Oliver Cardew, I shall not have a husband in the accepted sense of the word, but I'm glad the pretence has stopped here. You could have pretended to love me, simulated a passion you didn't really feel, but in the end I think I would have known it wasn't real and the bitterness would have been twice as bad. I think I could have killed you for that, Dominic.'

Dominic didn't answer, but remained holding her hands gazing sadly into her eyes.

For the rest of her life she would be acting a part: devoted wife, loved wife, and Dominic too would be playing a role he had never wanted. And what of Oliver? Would he be content to stay in the background, or would his dislike of her make him careless so that in the end the world would see them all for what they were?

All those guests at their wedding, thinking of their joy, some of them with envy, all those other girls who had wanted Dominic and who would marry other men and live happily with them, while Dominic's envied bride envied them and wished she had what they had.

'What do we do now?' she asked him miserably. 'Do we go on as if we were two normal people, or do we stay on here living our separate lives like two lost, lonely souls who are afraid to face reality?'

'It needn't be like that, Lisa. We will go to Spain and

Italy as we had promised ourselves. There is more to life than passion, more than love perhaps. Can't we search for it?'

What else was there? They had both made promises—to deny them solved nothing, but that night in the emptiness of her room Lisa made a vow that the people who had conspired to salvage their pride at her expense would be made to pay. She did not at that moment know how she would achieve it, but she would find the way. One day the proud family who had put themselves before her happiness would wish they had never set eyes on Lisa Foreshaw.

She had been so looking forward to their time in Spain and Italy—now she couldn't work up any enthusiasm for it. She spent the last few days before their departure riding her horse around the countryside surrounding the house and in the evenings she listened to music and read books. She didn't know where Dominic spent his time but she suspected it was with Oliver Cardew. She would have been surprised if she had seen him riding alone across the hills as he wanted to be with Oliver, but in his innermost heart he felt he needed to punish them both by keeping his distance.

The night before they left for the continent Oliver rode up to the house. Lisa saw him arriving from the drawing-room window and the hatred she felt for him surfaced anew. How dare he appear on their doorstep as if he was simply a normal guest, but the next minute a servant was showing him into the room and they were staring into each other's eyes—Lisa's haughty, uncompromising; his, filled with a strange anxiety.

'My husband is out,' she said coldly. 'I have no idea when he will be back.'

'I know he is out, I came to see you,' he replied softly.

She raised her eyebrows but offered no comment, and she saw for the first time that he was nervous when he had always seemed so confident, so self-assured.

'I came to ask if we could be friends. I know I really have no right to ask this of you but I had to try. Dominic is very unhappy with the situation. I see it in him every time we meet and I don't know what to do.'

'Did you expect him to be happy?' she cried. 'Or did you really think things would go on as normal, you and Dominic, and me his wife. Did either of you think of my happiness or the rest of our lives?'

He sat down weakly on the nearest chair, his face grey.

'Lisa, we can't help the way we are. Dominic tried to explain matters to his parents over and over again but they didn't understand. His mother particularly thought he could change, that he could come to love you in the way a man loves a woman, but it was impossible. They talked to him about duty, about family, about pride. They thought that for you the material things he could give you would be enough. Now it seems to me that everybody was wrong except you—those things are not enough, are they?'

'No. I'm twenty years old and for the rest of my life they seem to be all I shall ever have.'

'Some man will love you, Lisa. A great many men could love you.'

She smiled cynically. 'Love me, perhaps,' she murmured. 'Marry me, no.'

He looked down at the floor without answering, and in a strained voice she said, 'I shall keep Dominic's secret, Oliver, for his sake and mine, but there will be no forgiveness in my heart for what they have done to me.

'You and Dominic will have each other, his family will have their brave, perfect son and there will be those who envy me for having the best of husbands—faithful, generous, extraordinarily kind. I shall never reveal that I have a husband who does not love me, has never loved me, and only married me to hide the fact that he is in love with somebody else, another man.'

He looked at her helplessly, his face grey with pain, and with all its usual cynicism gone from it. He bowed his head in farewell and after a few moments she heard the closing of a door and stood at the window to watch him walking slowly towards the fence where his horse was tethered.

She felt shaken by his visit. At first she had thought the mere sight of him would make her wildly angry, but instead she felt consumed by a desperate pity.

Pity for herself in a world gone mad, and pity for two young men who society judged as different.

CHAPTER THIRTEEN

THEY TRAVELLED IN ROMANTIC style through Europe—
the luxury of the best hotel in Paris, the glamour of the
Blue Train, and everywhere they went and from every
person they met they were treated like the English aris-
tocrats they were, made welcome and venerated.

Lisa looked beautiful in her furs and jewels, while
Dominic was the perfect example of a nobleman, tall and
aristocratic, gracious and charming with a beautiful
woman on his arm, equally charming, undoubtedly gracious. But as Dominic began to unwind Lisa inwardly
seethed.

She wondered if the men and women who served
them in the hotels and on the train asked questions as to
why they occupied separate rooms. Maybe they came
across other people like them and they were not so
unusual after all. These people would be accustomed to
guests with their idiosyncrasies, after all their faces
were bland, their expressions unconcerned. What did it
matter anyway? Yet underneath it all the fact that they
were living a lie persisted.

It was late afternoon when they arrived at their hotel in Seville and from across the reception counter several pairs of eyes watched her closely. As they made their way to the lift Dominic said with a smile, 'They will be speculating as to whether you might be Spanish, Lisa. It is your colouring I think.'

'I saw them staring at me. Do you think it is that?'

'Undoubtedly. I once saw a photograph of your grandmother. You are very like her, you know.'

'I've never seen her photograph. Who did it belong to?'

'My grandfather had it—perhaps the only one that escaped the family's censure.'

Later when they took their places in the dining room they were the pivot of all eyes, and again Lisa felt it was she the other guests were most interested in. She was wearing a cerise silk gown with the sheen of diamonds round her throat and in her ears, and against the sheen of her gown her hair shone blue under the lights and never had her jade green eyes appeared more unusual or more provocative.

Looking at her Dominic thought her the most beautiful woman he had ever seen, and this woman was his wife. She was dear to him, so why wasn't he able to love her? Other men had watched her progress across the room with admiration, even envy, so what bitter fate had excluded him?

In the days that followed they absorbed Seville's history, the beauty of the cathedral and other churches, the fascination of the squares and streets, the religious processions and the clamour of a people thirsting for life in the greeting of famous matadors or the playing of gypsy music for the dancing that enlivened the city's squares under dark, starry skies.

Lisa bought colourful swirling skirts in the markets, delighting in her new gypsy earrings and high-heeled Spanish shoes, and when Dominic was happy to sit in the hotel gardens reading his English newspaper she ventured out onto the street where she was no longer the English lady but a Spanish señorita with a beautiful smiling face under her dark flowing hair.

It was on one of those days when she sat at one of the cafés watching the crowds sauntering across the square that she became aware that a young man was watching her closely out of dark sombre eyes, so she looked away quickly, afraid to give any indication that she was looking for company.

He paused beside her table with a half smile on his face, causing her to look away haughtily before getting hurriedly to her feet. He was quick to say, 'Pardon me, my lady, but I am Paulo from the hotel. I recognised you. I am very sorry.'

Her gaze faltered when she saw his embarrassment, and she smiled. She recognised him now, the handsome young man who handed her her key, wished her good morning, and had handed her only that morning her mother's letter.

'I'm sorry, Paulo,' she said gently, 'I didn't recognise you out of your uniform.'

He smiled. 'It is my holiday today. I go to see my mother.'

'Your mother lives in the city?'

'No, in the hills over there. To live in the city is expensive.'

'I see. May I buy you a drink, a glass of wine perhaps?'

'Thank you, my lady, but no. We are not allowed to drink with the hotel guests.'

She could not have explained what prompted her to insist that he sit with her at the table. They were some way from the hotel—she had chosen the café for that very reason since it was in a square where there was little interest for visitors to enthuse over; but still he hesitated until again she insisted, pushing the chair forward for him to sit on.

He fancied her and was nervous. She had seen his eyes following her across the hotel reception area, seen the delicate colour illuminating his cheeks, the caution in his dark eyes. 'Are you happy working at the hotel?' she asked him gently, for something to say.

'Oh yes, my lady. I need to work, and the money is good.'

'And in time you will receive promotion?'

'Promotion?'

'Why yes, perhaps you will be the manager one day.'

His smile was rueful and depreciating, and after a moment she said, 'You say your family live in the hills above the city. In one of the villages?'

'Why yes, my lady, my family are farmers; we are not rich.'

'My father too understood farming, and we too were not rich.'

He stared at her in something approaching disbelief. 'But you are a titled English lady, so why do you say you were not rich?'

'My father was not rich. I married into the aristocracy very recently.'

'English ladies are fair-haired and fair-skinned—you could be Spanish, an aristocratic lady from my country.'

'My grandmother was Spanish, from a small village outside Seville, perhaps even from one near your village.'

His face lit up with a warm smile. 'You are going to see your family? They know you are coming?'

'No. I don't even know if any of my relatives are still living here, or if they are alive. It is a long time ago since she left Spain. I just wanted to see the city and the country where she was born.'

'You know her name?'

'She was called Carmelita de Sanchez.'

He shook his head doubtfully. 'I do not know the name. We are part of a large farming community. There are many villages around the big house. I have a grandmother who might know. She is very old.'

'Old enough to have known my grandmother?'

'Why yes. She does not see well, and she never goes far from the door but she still has a good memory for things in her youth.'

'When are you going to see your family again?'

'On my next free day—one day next week perhaps.'

'Have you a large family?'

'Oh yes—mother, father, aunts, uncles. My eldest brother Juan is in charge now. He is very handsome. I am his little brother. He laughs at me because I am not strong enough to be a farmer. I had illness as a child, but his laughter does not mean he does not care for me.'

'Well, of course not. I'm sure he cares for you very much. And then there is your grandmother?'

'Yes, Suanita. She is frail now, over ninety years old, but her mind is good, very good.'

He tapped his forehead with a broad smile on his face and Lisa said, 'Perhaps you could ask her if she remembers Carmelita de Sanchez.'

'Oh yes, my lady, I will ask her next time I go home, now I should go, I am seeing my mother today.'

He rose to his feet with a smile and a little bow, then he walked away from her quickly, followed by a great many pairs of eyes—such a very fortunate young man to have been in the company of such a beautiful young woman, and they had seemed to have had much to say to each other.

Lisa was aware of their interest and was quick to pay for her glass of wine before making her way back to the hotel.

It was some time before dinner but she had made several purchases in the city so decided to go straight to her room to leave them there.

As she placed them in a drawer of the dressing table she looked in the mirror thinking how different she appeared to the English Lisa in the formal glamour of her wedding finery—the Lisa who had looked forward to a future as serene and unchangeable as a summer's day.

There was a light tap on her door and before she could open it Dominic entered her room. She stared at him in surprise—it was the first time he had ever entered her bedroom, but she realised instantly that his expression was worried and not a little anxious.

'Is something wrong?' she asked quickly.

'Yes, I'm sorry, Lisa, but my father has had an accident, a fall from his horse and my mother seemed very concerned. She didn't seem to know how bad the fall was or how badly he was injured but she thinks I should return home as soon as possible.'

'I'm sorry,' was all she could find to say.

'There is no need for you to return with me, Lisa. I'm sure they won't expect you to. I'll be in touch as soon as I know just what is happening and I'll return here as soon as possible. I dare say Mother is making mountains out of molehills.'

'They will think it odd if I don't return with you.'

'I'll explain that I didn't think it was necessary— after all, what can you do, what can either of us do for that matter? My father rides unsuitable horses. I've often told him so, but he never listens.'

She didn't want to return to England and Dominic would prefer to go there alone—after all England meant Oliver Cardew who he had undoubtedly been missing. Some of her thoughts conveyed themselves to Dominic who said gently, 'I am not going back there because I want to see Oliver, Lisa. I'm going at the request of my mother and I hope to return here at the earliest opportunity.'

'It doesn't matter, Dominic, I hope you will find your father is not badly injured.'

Her tone was petulant and she knew it. As he left

Dominic pressed her hand and kissed her gently on her cheek—gestures she might have expected from a brother or a good friend, whereas she would have preferred a brief smile and casual goodbye.

She dined alone in the vast dining room that evening aware of the curiosity of those sitting around her, and as she crossed the hall to return to her room Paulo smiled at her from his place behind the desk. She knew that he would be aware that her husband had left the hotel.

Two days later Dominic telephoned her to say his father had suffered a broken shoulder and two fractured ribs; otherwise he would make a full recovery. He hoped to be back in Spain within two weeks as he had several business engagements to attend to.

She had two weeks of freedom before he returned, freedom to search for her grandmother's family in the hills above the city, but she would have to ask Paulo to help her.

In the meantime Dominic faced his mother across her sitting room and it was evident she was angry.

'I can't understand why Lisa didn't return with you, Dominic. Surely you both should have known it would be expected of you to return here together—she is your wife.'

'I told her it wasn't necessary, Mother. What could she have done? And Father is recovering very nicely.'

'But to leave her in Spain on her own.'

'She is happy there. She wanted to find some remnants of her grandmother's family, so it will give her something to do.'

'Gracious me! Her grandmother's been dead many years. All the people she knew there will have long since died or left the area. What can she hope to achieve by raking over old scandals?'

'I understand that the scandals started here, Mother, not in Seville. I'm sure the lady came from a respected family who would have been horrified at the treatment of their daughter in this country.'

'Yes well, I still think it's very silly to go looking for things and people that have no place in the present. I shall make my displeasure known when I see Lisa again.'

'I wouldn't if I were you, Mother, Lisa is no longer the little girl who tramped up to Aunt Sybil's to receive her education, or the girl you were kind enough to install in Aunt Jane's house.'

'She should be grateful all the same.'

'We should be grateful, Mother. Think about it.'

Her eyes were hostile as they followed him out of the room. What was he talking about? There was cousin Mary installed in Aunt Jane's house, living the life of a gentlewoman born and bred, and there in Spain was Lisa in her Parisienne gowns and jewels that had been in the family for centuries—Viscountess Lexican, no doubt being fawned upon by all and sundry and loving every minute of it. Besides, Dominic had probably long since forgotten his dalliance with Oliver Cardew and become the husband Lisa had wanted. She obviously adored him—it was probably the sort of adoration that would make him forget Cardew.

Dominic's father thought his son had been right in allowing his wife to remain in Spain. It was enough that his wife and his servants were fussing round him—there'd been no need to bring Dominic back, let alone both of them.

When he voiced his thoughts to his wife she merely said, 'Hasn't it occurred to you that he came back alone to see the Cardew boy—with Lisa with him there would have been no problem.'

He'd looked at her in pitying silence for several minutes before saying, 'If he'd wanted to see Cardew neither Lisa nor either of us could have stopped him.'

'You're so wrong, Johnny. Dominic is different, he's changed.'

'How do you make that out?'

'He just has, I know it. He seems happier, contented. I think he's come to terms with his marriage; he takes her side, even against me.'

'Well, that's something at any rate. We should stay out of their lives and let them get on with things.'

'We are his parents, Johnny.'

'I know, but we've done enough damage. I don't want there to be more.'

'Oh, I know I'll never convince you that we were right. You'll see it for yourself one day. One day they'll have children, then you'll know I was right.'

He looked at her with pitying scorn. Let her go on living in cloud cuckoo land if that was what she wanted. Changing the subject he said, 'When is he going back?'

'I'm not sure. She's out there looking for remnants of

her grandmother's family. Did you ever hear of anything more stupid?'

'Why is it stupid?'

'Well, they've probably all died out by this time, so who will know them?'

'There could be descendants, just as you are a descendant of your grandparents.'

'Well, we're a notable family—I expect those people were peasants.'

He decided not to argue with her further. His shoulder was paining him and he needed to rest. He should never have gone riding on a horse he was unused to however pristine its pedigree, and he was well aware that his two sons endorsed that view.

Lisa's mother received Dominic in her sitting room and he watched while she poured tea from Aunt Jane's priceless china. Lisa was not in the least like her mother. Mary had fair fine hair that framed a pretty pink and white complexion and candid blue eyes. It seemed strange that Lisa had inherited all the fire and glamour of her Spanish ancestors.

'Will she be safe on her own in Spain?' she asked him anxiously.

'Of course. She did not wish to return to England with me, and I am returning there myself very soon. I will tell her I have seen you and that you are well.'

'Thank you, Dominic. I am so glad that you are happy together.'

He had not mentioned their happiness, but she was

looking at him gently, waiting for confirmation, and he smiled. He liked her—she was sweet and caring, and although she just wanted her only daughter to be happy, he could only give her the material things in life, never the reality she craved for.

'She will have a great deal to tell you when she returns,' he said, ignoring her remark. 'Seville is a very beautiful, vibrant city. Lisa seems very much at home there with her vitality and her colouring.'

'Yes indeed. She's not at all like me, or her father. When she was a little girl I felt I had constantly to explain to people that her grandmother was Spanish and that Lisa took after her. You know how village people gossip.'

'Yes, usually about things they know nothing about.'

'I see very little of your mother, Dominic. Is she well?'

'Very well. Father is the one who is suffering.'

'I hope he will soon recover. Lisa and I are both very grateful for so many things—this house, the furniture and the gardens; and then there is you, Dominic. We owe them so very much.'

CHAPTER FOURTEEN

LISA WAS EXPERIENCING A sense of freedom that had been lacking in the weeks since her marriage. Although Dominic had shown her friendship and undivided attention, they were like two elderly people who had been married for many years, caring and considerate—a husband who showed her nothing but gallantry and charm; a wife who had accepted such feelings after a lifetime together. But they were not old and had not been married for years—they were young and demanding, but alas, not of each other.

As she left her door key at the desk the day after Dominic's return to England she found Paulo alone, smiling at her with his usual shyness. She said quickly, 'Have you spoken to your grandmother about me, Paulo? Does she know anything about my family?'

Paulo had spoken to his grandmother only the day before, taking his place on the bench beside her where she invariably sat day after day, looking down on the sprawling city below. Her thin hands, gnarled and splashed with liver spots, clung steadfastly to the walking stick she was never without. Although she smiled, wrinkling up her face in that grotesque smile that never quite reached her eyes, it was doubtful she could see him.

'Is it Paulo?' she'd asked in little above a whisper.

'Yes, grandmother. I met a lady at the hotel, an English lady, who would like to meet you.'

She frowned. 'I know little English,' she replied at last.

'I can interpret for you, grandmother.'

'Why should an English lady wish to meet me? I have never met an Englishwoman. What is she like?'

'Young, beautiful. She is of Spanish descent; she looks more Spanish than English as she is dark like our people, and she is very nice.'

Her mouth twisted into a smile and she gave a little chuckle. 'And you like this English lady eh, but not too well I hope. The hotel would not like it, Paulo.'

'She speaks to me, grandmother. She is interested in finding out more of her family. I told her you were old, but she's hoping you might remember.'

'Ay well, there is much to ponder over when one is old—my eyesight is going, I am forgetful of many things—but the past is always with me, even though yesterday eludes me. Who were her family?'

'De Sanchez, from one of the villages above the city. Did you ever know a de Sanchez?'

She stared across the field and was silent so long he thought she had wandered off into one of her dozes. He was about to walk away when she suddenly said, 'Oh yes, I knew the de Sanchez. Farmers they were, like my family.'

'Then you must have known her grandmother, Carmelita.'

'Carmelita de Sanchez. Oh yes, I knew her, but not that well—she went away to a convent school to be educated. She never came back to the village—some said she had gone to England to work.'

'Why would they educate her, grandmother?'

She chuckled. 'You might well ask, Paulo. She was the youngest of seven children and she was not like any of the others. It was said that the lord of the manor had educated her because she was his daughter. I do not know.'

He looked at her, puzzled, and after a few minutes she chuckled again saying, 'Inez de Sanchez was free with her favours, or she was sadly belied. She was beautiful, wild, married too young to a lout of a man who was a drunkard and had other women. If she found other men, who could blame her?'

'But the owner of these lands, grandmother, would he look at a peasant woman?'

She chuckled throatily before saying dryly, 'He would look at Inez de Sanchez with her black hair and green eyes. I can see her now dancing round the fire in the evening, with the men ogling her and the women giving her looks that could have killed her.'

'Was her daughter like her?'

'Like I said, Paulo, she was young when she went away to England. And so she married an Englishman, so much better than coming back here to face only the scorn of a bunch of envious women.'

'Will you meet this lady if I bring her to see you, grandmother?'

'It will be more interesting than looking down on the

city which I see through a cloud. Is it always cloudy over the city, Paulo?'

He smiled gently. There was no cloud over the city, only the old woman's fading eyesight. At that moment Juan, Paulo's eldest brother, joined them saying, 'I have to go down to the city, Paulo. Are you ready to return there?'

'Yes, Juan. Goodbye, Grandmother. Next time I come I will bring the lady with me.'

'What is this?' Juan cried. 'Found some young city girl already?'

Paulo merely smiled and as they walked together down the hill to where Juan's ancient car waited for them their grandmother's head fell forward—she had missed her midday siesta.

'So,' Juan said teasingly, 'who is this lady you bring to meet our grandmother?'

'A great lady from the hotel. She is English but her grandmother was Spanish. She thinks our grandmother may have known her.'

'And is she beautiful, this English lady?'

'Yes.'

'And she has a husband?'

'He has had to return to England for some reason, but he will be back.'

'And my little brother admires her, although not too much, I hope.'

'Oh Juan, it is not like that. She is a very high born lady with a title.'

Juan threw back his head and laughed. 'Then it would

seem the Spanish señorita who was her grandmother did very well for herself.'

Paulo remained silent. He was accustomed to his brother's teasing, mostly about the type of girls he was likely to meet in the city.

'So, when will you bring her to the village then?' Juan asked.

'The next time I have time from my duties.'

'Why don't I come to the city to bring you to the village? That way I can keep an eye on you.'

'There is no need. The lady will obtain transport for us, she has said so.'

'Oh well, I shall still wish to meet this lady, just to see that my little brother is in no danger from an English lady whose husband has had to return home.'

He laughed with obvious enjoyment at Paulo's expression, while Paulo jumped down from the car and walked quickly away.

It was several days later that Lisa met Paulo close to the cathedral in the car she had travelled in from the hotel. He was waiting for her at the place they had agreed upon, and if the driver was surprised when he was asked to pick up another passenger he did not show it.

As they drove up through the hills Lisa thought how beautiful it was with the sun shining on the slopes covered with vineyards and where tall, graceful cypress trees stood out starkly against the blue sky. This was the Spain her grandmother would have known: the men and women working in the fields, the huge oxen pulling the carts, the children screaming with laughter, running into the fields.

They left the car and Paulo said, 'My brother will take us back to the city, my lady, if you wish to dismiss the driver.'

'Are you sure, Paulo?'

'Oh yes, Juan always drives me back when I come to the village.'

The village church stood at the head of the long straggling street and they were greeted with long stares from a group of women standing gossiping at the well. One or two called out to Paulo, and from his blushing face Lisa could only assume that they were teasing him about his companion. She was aware of a very old woman sitting outside one of the small stone houses, an old woman who leaned back in her chair with her eyes closed, her hands resting idly on her lap, oblivious to the bright morning and the laughter around the well.

Paulo touched her gently on the shoulder saying, 'Grandmother, we are here. This is the lady I told you about.'

She opened her eyes and peered upwards, raising her hands to shield them from the glare of the sun, and then after a few minutes she nodded her head, speaking in a throaty whisper to Paulo, who said apologetically, 'My grandmother does not know any English, my lady. I am sorry.'

'What did she say?' Lisa asked.

'She says that now she remembers.'

'She remembers my grandmother. Oh, please ask her

to tell me all she remembers—what she was like, where she lived, how well she remembers her.'

Paulo spoke rapidly to the old woman. After a few minutes she shook her head, and reaching out a thin bony hand she took hold of Lisa's, pulling her down to sit beside her on the low stool at the side of her chair. She placed her head close to Lisa's so that Lisa could see the brown wrinkled face and clouded dark eyes, the wrinkled mouth with broken and missing teeth, the grey wispy hair that hung loosely onto her shoulders, and smell the decaying aroma of wine and food on the old woman's shawl. Then turning to Paulo the words came thick and fast in low, gutteral Spanish and Lisa waited expectantly for Paulo to tell her what she said. At last he raised his hand to halt his grandmother's flow of words and turning to Lisa he said, 'My grandmother says you are very like Inez de Sanchez. She was beautiful; she danced out there in the village square in the evenings when the work was done.'

'But my grandmother was Carmelita—can she not remember her?'

'Inez was her mother. She did not know your grandmother well. She went away when she was very young and did not come back to the village.'

Lisa's face was filled with disappointment—it was going back too far. She knew nothing of Inez de Sanchez and suddenly she felt herself wishing that she hadn't come. What good did it do to search for something here in this alien place, amongst people far removed from those she had grown up with? Her grandmother had moved away, so why had she felt this urgent need to discover her history? What did it matter now that she and her mother had endured so much pain which had all been laid at Carmelita's door?

But of course it mattered. She was married to Dominic, and because of the past she had been specifically selected by the family who had rejected them for so many years.

The old woman released her hold on her hand and Lisa looked down to where her long fingernails had cut into the skin, then opening her purse she took out a handful of silver and placed it in the old woman's hand, before rising to her feet and saying, 'There is nothing more she can tell me. Paulo. I did not know Inez and she does not remember Carmelita.'

When he told his grandmother what she had said she merely chuckled, speaking quickly, and Paulo did not tell Lisa that she had merely repeated the rumour that Carmelita had been the daughter of the great lord from the big house. After all, it was village gossip, and he knew what those women were like who hung around the well talking about all and sundry. He would tell her later when the time was right.

He looked up the village street, saying, 'Juan is here. It is early—perhaps he will not be ready to go to the city so soon.'

'Then I will look in the church,' Lisa said. 'See a little of the village where Carmelita lived.'

Juan greeted her with a smile and she thought him handsome and bold. As he smiled into her eyes he thought she was the most beautiful woman he had ever seen and Paulo read the signs well. Juan was a flirt who loved women as every pretty girl in the village could testify, but this Englishwoman was not for him.

Words were exchanged between the two brothers but it was Juan who accompanied Lisa to the church while Paulo stayed with his grandmother.

The church was very old but it had character, and as Lisa sauntered along the aisle she thought that perhaps her grandmother had worshipped there in the company of other young girls.

Carmelita had been a Roman Catholic, another reason why her husband's family had disowned her, but as time passed her descendants had reverted to their Anglican religion. Now Lisa felt intrigued by the ornate statues of the Virgin Mary and other religious figures.

Juan walked behind her, explaining the things she paused to look at, and it was only when they had left the church that he said, 'My grandmother is a very old lady who forgets many things. You are not happy with what she has been able to remember about your family.'

'I didn't expect too much. Your English is very good.'

He smiled. 'I learn it at school. I did not want to be a farmer but Paulo was not strong and my sisters could do nothing. I was asked to forget any ambitions I had and follow in my father's footsteps.'

'Do you mind very much?'

'Oh yes, I mind, but it is what I must do.'

'Do you own the land your father and you farm?'

'We own the farm. The land belongs to the Fernandos

Capriates family, who have lived here for centuries at the great house.'

'And where is that?'

'I would like to show it to you if you will come again. It is some little distance. We could walk, or we could ride there. I take it you ride?'

'Yes. Would Paulo come with us?'

'He is no horseman.' His bold eyes smiled down into hers. 'Would you be afraid to ride with me alone?'

'No, why should I be? I would expect you to behave like a gentleman.'

He laughed, and looking up into his face, at the gleaming teeth behind the wide smile and the dark eyes staring boldly into her own, she felt the first faint stirrings of alarm. Seeing the sudden doubt in her expression he said swiftly, 'My lady, you will be very safe with me. I will promise my little brother that I will take care of the young lady he so admires.'

Paulo was waiting for them beside the ancient car and regretfully Juan said, 'The vehicle is disreputable, my lady, at the moment I cannot afford to exchange it, but it is in good repair, so we shall arrive at the city without mishap.'

Paulo allowed her to sit with Juan while he perched in the back among the crates of oranges and vegetables. It was only when they were in the city and on their way back to the hotel that Paulo said, 'My brother admires you. There is a girl in the village my father would like for him; her name is Maria.'

Lisa smiled. 'Your brother has said he would like to

show me the great house. I promise you, Paulo, that I shall not tempt him away from Maria. If you are afraid for him why don't you come with us?'

'I do not ride well, and he likes a fast horse. All the money he has goes on horses he can ill afford.'

Lisa thought it was time to change the subject so she said softly, 'Your grandmother intimated that Carmelita was the daughter of the lord from the great house. Do you believe her?'

'How can I tell? My grandmother must know something to make her say that. Is that why you wish to see the house?'

'It might help in some way to bring the pieces together.'

'How long before your husband comes back to Seville, my lady?'

'I don't know. Soon perhaps.'

He looked at her long and hard before bowing his head and leaving her to walk back to the hotel alone.

It was ridiculous of him to be so concerned for his brother. She had come to Spain to look into her grandmother's history not to embark upon a love affair with a Spanish farmer she hardly knew, although as she walked through the gardens of the hotel she found some amusement in the idea of it.

What a way of paying them back for what they had done to her—retribution for what they had done to Carmelita and the greater evil of what they had done to her.

She pictured her mother-in-law's welcoming face

and the treachery behind it, and all those years when she had trudged angrily up to Sybil's house to achieve an education meant to prepare her for it; then she thought about Dominic.

She had loved Dominic, and even now she couldn't hate him. Wasn't he as much a sacrificial lamb as she was herself? Suddenly anger took its place when she thought about that dark night when she had roamed through the house needing him, wondering where he was, why he hadn't come to her.

She remembered Oliver Cardew's cynical smile, his pitying expression at her naivety and then his all-conquering disdain.

She should hate Dominic as much as the rest of them.

There was a letter from Dominic waiting for her at the hotel when she arrived there and it was Paulo who handed it to her, his expression strangely thoughtful. The letter told her very little except that his father was recovering slowly, needing much attention and there was a great deal to do on the estate. The English weather was becoming more wintry and he hoped she was enjoying Spain's sunshine. He would return to Seville at the earliest opportunity; in the meantime his parents sent her their love, and he signed himself 'Yours as Always, Dominic.'

She smiled bitterly. Dominic would never be hers. The 'Always' was farcical—how could Dominic expect her to believe it?

CHAPTER FIFTEEN

SYBIL AND LUCY WERE ENJOYING their weekly get-to-gether sitting in Lucy's pristine sitting room overlooking the gardens. It had been a convivial meeting with Sybil anxious to discuss the forthcoming marriage of her middle daughter, and Lucy seemingly at ease with her husband's health and her younger son's attachment to Lady Heather Stretton.

Sybil was more interested in watching Dominic walking from the stables to the house as she asked, 'How long does Dominic intend to stay here now that Johnny is recovering?'

'I intend to ask him this evening. He's had a lot to do. You know as well as I do that Johnny's affairs never took first place with him—as long as there were horses and racing he was content to let things slide.'

'It can't be much fun for Lisa on her own in Spain—after all she doesn't know anybody there. What has her mother had to say about it?'

'Not very much. After all, Mary can hardly be described as worldly. All she knows about Spain is talk about her mother and that was hardly salubrious.'

'All the same this is supposed to be their honeymoon. They were married in August and it's now November. You can hardly call it a honeymoon when she's out there and he's here.'

'I agree with you, and like I said I intend to talk about it to Johnny and Dominic this evening.'

Sybil had to be content with that, but later when Lucy broached the subject to Johnny he said testily, 'If he wants to get back there I shan't prevent it, but before he goes I don't want any loose ends left for me to sort out.'

'Oh Johnny, you've got a perfectly good Estate Manager, but you've got used to Dominic being here. The doctors say you're almost well again, and in no time at all you'll be back on the race course or in the saddle.'

'The fun's gone out of racing. When the old king was alive it was interesting—his horses, his women—now it's all circumspect and dull. When did we last have a nice juicy scandal to look forward to?'

'When he gave us a scandal you called it deplorable.'

'Well of course, but we did make the most of it, old girl. After Victoria we really couldn't have enough of Edward. He was like a breath of fresh air, but now we've gone back to boring respectability. It strikes me there's not a lot to get better for.'

'Oh well, if you want to talk like that I'll leave you to it. We'll talk at dinner, and do back me up, Johnny. You leave everything to me.'

'Is the younger lad here or is he galivanting as usual?'

'He's staying at Heather's for the next few days—her sister's eighteenth birthday I think.'

'Something going on there?'

'I hope so. She's a delightful girl, pretty, intelligent and with all the right connections.'

'In keeping with our daughter-in-law who didn't wish to return here with her husband.'

'Stop it, Johnny. Dominic told her there was no need. You're the one who's kept him here longer than was necessary.'

She did not miss the cynical expression in his eyes as she marched towards the door, slamming it shut behind her.

Over the dinner table she gave her husband an encouraging glance which prompted him to say, 'Had thoughts on when you're going back to Lisa, Dominic?'

'I've been waiting for you, Father,' he said steadily. 'Are you able to manage now?'

'Just prime Hesketh with all that's necessary, then you can get back. What do you suppose she's been doing all these weeks? I was never over the moon about Spain, unless she's found a Don Juan to chauffeur her around. Those Spanish Lotharios have an eye for the girls.'

'Really,' his wife snapped, 'must you be so vulgar?' while Dominic went on with his meal in inscrutable silence.

It was fortunate that none of them had any conception of the problems occupying Lisa's mind at that moment.

* * *

It had all started so innocently. The walk to the church, the drives through the hills and that one golden afternoon when they had sat on the hillside looking up at the towers and turrets adorning the grey stone castle set high on the hillside.

There were so many castles, so many hills, but this one castle spoke to her of depravity and innocence, the cold seduction of a poor young woman by a man who had everything—this castle and riches. But in the end he had reckoned without Inez de Sanchez's demand that the child he had fathered should be educated. How could her Spanish mother have foreseen that she would end her days married to an Englishman whose family were as ruthless and cold-hearted as her father had been?

Juan had extracted her story from his grandmother in every detail she could remember, and Lisa had sat listening to it while his dark eyes absorbed her beauty and his hands caressed her body, evoking the response he longed for.

She did not love him, but she was a warm, young and passionate woman crying out for love. She had wanted this sort of passion from her husband so that when he couldn't give it to her she had felt unloved and worthless. She had once told herself that she would find love out of revenge—now it was the last thing she thought of; now she was simply a woman responding to a man's desires with every fibre of her being, and regardless of the consequences.

When her eyes met the eyes of his grandmother she

was well aware of their cynical amusement and she knew what the old woman was thinking. She was no better than Inez, fashioned in the same mould as the woman the rest of the village had looked upon as a harlot.

She was more concerned when Paulo looked at her. He did not look at her with scorn but with a strange disenchantment. He had liked her, looked upon her as a good English lady; now his grandmother was telling him she was worthless.

One afternoon when they walked together, largely in silence, through the streets of Seville, she asked, 'Paulo, I'm sorry that you dislike me so much—you really don't understand any of it.'

He looked at her sorrowfully before saying, 'I understand, my lady. You make my brother love you, but you do not love him. When your husband returns you will go with him to England and forget Juan.'

There was no answer because he was right. She would go back with Dominic because she did not love Juan, had never loved him—he was simply fulfilling a need her husband had been unable to provide.

Every day she told herself that she would not see him again, but it had now reached the stage where she could not venture out of the hotel without finding him waiting for her in the street outside. She became afraid, afraid that the guests at the hotel would see her with him. She imagined that they were looking at her with suspicion and a certain disdain.

She took her place in the dining room looking neither to right or left, wearing her jewels and beautiful gowns, but inwardly burning with a terrible fear. It was on one of those nights when she looked across the room to see Dominic walking towards her and she was aware of the silence around her and the expectation on people's faces, then he was kissing her cheek, favouring her with his slow, sweet smile, saying, 'Lisa I'm sorry it's been so long, it was impossible to come back sooner. I hope you haven't been too lonely.'

She smiled. 'No. I've got to know Seville and the countryside. I've learned nothing about my grandmother.'

'No, I didn't think you would, it's all too long ago.'

'How is your father?'

'Much better. Walking around with two sticks and hating every moment of it.'

'And your mother?'

'Very well. I have been several times to see your mother; she's very well, missing you and hoping you'll return very soon. We did promise ourselves Italy, Lisa, what do you think?'

'It's not the same, Dominic. Then it was summer, now it's autumn and even here the weather is changing.'

'I know. Perhaps another time we can take in Italy—in the spring perhaps.'

'Yes, that would be nice.'

What else could they talk about? She could not ask him about Oliver Cardew and he would not mention him. In some desperation she said, 'How is your brother, still making his mind up about some girl or other?'

'I'm afraid so. He's decided to join the Army, so girls are hardly at the top of his list at the moment.'

She stared at him in surprise. 'Why would he join the Army, Dominic? Isn't that a strange thing to do?'

'I don't think so, Lisa. Something's going on in Europe and we're heading for a scrap, I think.'

'You mean war?'

'Perhaps. I hope not, but we have to think about it.'

'But war with whom? Nothing's been said around here, but then I've only known one or two English people to talk to.'

'I know, dear, it's been difficult for you.'

'But war, Dominic, war with whom?'

'Well, Germany's a problem, the Kaiser has ideas of grandeur and there's trouble in the Balkans, Austria, Hungary, even Russia. It may come to nothing.'

'But your brother must think something serious is brewing, Dominic. What would you do in the event of war?'

For a long moment he stared at her without speaking, then he said, 'I would do what Austin has done, Lisa, and join my father's old regiment. What do you expect?'

When she continued to stare at him he said somewhat irritably, 'I may not care too much for women, Lisa, but I am a man, and would do what every other man would do, I hope.'

'Oh Dominic,' she cried. 'I didn't mean anything, it was a stupid thing to say. Of course I didn't imply that you were less than a man; please forgive me.'

After a few moments he said, 'If we are not to go to Italy perhaps we should think of leaving in a few days, you will need to pack and I will make arrangements regarding travelling.'

'Oh yes, I can soon pack. In fact, I'd like to get away quickly now that we've decided to go.'

'So Seville has lost its enchantment?'

'I'll never forget it, the city I mean and its history, but if there's going to be trouble I'd prefer to be in England.'

He was looking at her earnestly, and under his gaze she felt strangely disturbed until he said, 'You're different, Lisa, I'm trying to think how.'

'I want to know, Dominic, how am I different?'

'A new maturity perhaps. The wide-eyed little girl look has gone. What is left is a very beautiful woman, a woman I should be very proud of.'

'No Dominic, no. Just a woman who has been manufactured out of loneliness and bitterness. I hope to rise above it.'

'And you will, my dear, we both will.'

'Didn't your mother think I should have returned to England with you?'

'My mother's always been a great one for setting rules and regulations and my father allowed her to take charge. She's been a good mother and I have the greatest regard for her, even when I have often wished she would take more of a back seat. But she obviously has no intention of doing so. I hope in time you and she will be friends.'

She decided to say nothing more about his mother. Only time would resolve their differences and at that moment she was staring into an unknown future.

They crossed the reception hall together to ask for their room keys and as Paulo handed over her key she said gently, 'My husband and I are leaving in a few days; we need to get home to England.'

He bowed his head courteously but she had not missed the consternation in his dark eyes. He was thinking about his brother, what he must tell him, hating her for the anguish she would bring into his life; then she turned away, waiting for Dominic at the bottom of the stairs so that they could ascend them together.

She was going home to what? Wealth and respectability, family pride and a husband who would treat her kindly but would never love her, and in her mind she thought grimly, 'Fear no more the heat of the sun, all passion is spent.'

Two days later they were travelling north on the Blue Train through the peaceful fields and vineyards of France, past the ancient villages which surely could never be touched by the cruelty of war, unaware of the ignorance of a people who toiled to extract a living from the soil with never a thought that one day it could end in brutality and pitiless uncertainty.

They arrived at Dover in the early hours of a cold November day with the sea a churning mass of grey against the bows of the ship and sleet falling from leaden skies.

'Do you wish to stay overnight in London?' Dominic asked but she shook her head quickly saying, 'No, please Dominic, I'd rather go straight home.'

'Then I'll telephone Mother to have a car meet us at the station. We'll go straight to the Hall.'

'Not to Martindale then?'

'No. They are not expecting me and I rather think my parents and your mother will wish to see us.'

'When shall we be returning to Martindale?'

'You're anxious to go there?' he asked looking down at her gravely.

'Well, I thought you would be—it is your home after all.'

'We'll talk about it in a day or two,' he replied.

She wanted to ask him if he didn't wish to see Oliver, or had he already spent those recent weeks in Oliver Cardew's company, but somehow or other she was unable to mention his name, and if Dominic knew what was in her mind he ignored it.

Lisa was not to know that in all those long weeks he had not seen Oliver, although he had known that Oliver was in the vicinity. Once he had seen him in the distance when he rode his horse across the park but deliberately had turned away to ride in the opposite direction. He had been able to imagine Oliver's frustration, his anger that Dominic had cast him aside as though he had never existed, as he refused to acknowledge the difficulties Dominic was facing with his parents and his new wife.

For years he had been accepted as a guest in Dominic's home, but that was before his mother became suspicious about their feelings for each other; now he was anathema to Lady Hazelmere and probably to the rest of the family.

Dominic learned that Oliver had returned to his house near Mapleton and it had been Lisa's mother who had said innocently, 'Your friend Oliver has been in the village, Dominic. I suppose you have seen him.'

'Very briefly,' Dominic had replied, but Mary had never been overly curious about their relationship beyond that of friendship.

He wanted to tell Lisa that he would never see Oliver again but it wasn't possible. How could he tell what passions would draw them back together? How could he explain to his wife feelings she would never understand?

Later that evening Lady Hazelmere embraced her daughter-in-law, thinking that she looked pale and strained, but when she remarked on it Lisa merely said, 'The sea crossing was terrible and we've been travelling for days. I do feel rather tired.'

'Then you must have something to eat and go to bed immediately, or would you rather I had something sent up to you, dear?'

'No really, Lady Hazelmere, I just want to sleep. I'll feel better in the morning.'

Dominic realised the problem immediately when Lisa retired. His mother would expect them to occupy the same room but he said quickly, 'I shall sleep in my old room tonight, Mother, so that Lisa can rest.'

'Oh well, darling, of course if you're sure. I'm sure she'll be feeling much better tomorrow.'

'Tomorrow we should go home, Mother,' he replied evenly.

'But why? Surely there's no rush to do that. Lisa will want to see her mother and your father has all sorts of things he wishes to discuss with you.'

'We're not a million miles away, Mother. I intend to spend some time here but there will be things to do at Martindale and it is our home after all.'

Lucy had to be content with that. This was a Dominic she didn't altogether understand—firmer, obdurate and more distant. The charming, gentle side of him was still there, but behind it was the steely side of him she hadn't bargained for.

Perhaps Lisa could persuade him to stay. She'd talk to Lisa in the morning, tell her her mother was aching to see her, that Johnny needed Dominic here. Surely Lisa would see that there were so many things to keep them at Hazelmere.

Her words to Lisa over breakfast the next morning had little effect. Lisa looked tired and strained. She had not slept well in the huge bedroom with her mind obsessed by the need to keep their private lives private.

Why was Dominic's mother pretending that all was well? Why keep up a pretence that was meaningless? They should go to Martindale and pretend in private.

She felt lethargic but it was Mary who said anxiously, 'You're so pale, darling, it must have been dreadful spending all that time on your own in Seville, and the long journey home. Would you like me to come to stay with you for a while, at least until you're feeling better?'

'No, Mother, there's no need. Like you said, the journey home was not something I'm anxious to do again. Although the train was luxurious, the channel crossing took longer than we'd anticipated because it was so rough, but we're home now. I'll soon be feeling better.'

Mary had to be content with that, but Dominic too was concerned about her pallor and unresponsive reticence.

CHAPTER SIXTEEN

LIFE AT MARTINDALE CONTINUED its pattern. They dined together in the evening with Dominic sitting at the other end of the long dining table while they were waited upon by deferential servants.

Lisa did not see Dominic during the day. He was busy on the estate so she invariably breakfasted in her room and went riding in the afternoons. Whenever she passed Oliver Cardew's house she looked for some signs of life but he was never around. Riding home at dusk she saw lights in one of the downstairs rooms, but if he came up to the Hall she never saw him.

She knew that Dominic was concerned about her. He thought she was unwell and suggested that she should see the doctor, but he was not aware that it was fear that was making her ill.

She knew the reasons for her illness, the sickness that left her weak and fractious every morning. She knew that she was pregnant.

Lisa had promised revenge, but revenge had been far from her thoughts when she had revelled in Juan's ardent lovemaking. She had simply been young and alive, a girl needing to be loved, delighting in the warmth in his dark eyes, the feeling that this was something she had a right to, when the real world she would soon be returning to could only be bleak and barren.

How could she have been so stupid to think that she would escape unscathed, and now she was afraid of the consequences. She told herself that the family deserved it, that she was making them pay for what they had done to her, but she knew that in the end she would be the loser. She could not force another man's child onto her husband—Dominic would divorce her and the world would know the reasons for it.

What would she do? What would her mother say? How could she ever stand a chance against an all-powerful family who would fight her all the way—yet there was one ray of hope. Would they really want the world to know that she had turned to another man because her husband was homosexual?

She would never name the child's father and supposition would be rife, but Dominic would know that it had been some man she had met while he had been absent from Spain. She thought about the men at the hotel, most of them with their wives, the only men on their own hardly worthy of a second glance because they had been either too old or too mindful of her station.

It was over dinner that Dominic said, 'I've invited the doctor to call in to see you tomorrow, Lisa. He's an old family friend, Doctor Meredith, and will simply give you something to make you feel better. I'm worried about you, Lisa.'

'Really, Dominic, there's no need. You shouldn't have called the doctor without telling me first.'

He raised his eyebrows maddeningly before saying, 'I rather think I should, my dear. You have no appetite, you're very pale and I don't think you should go riding looking as you do.'

'I have to do something, my horse is my one pleasure,' she retorted.

'Then I suggest we invite your mother to stay with us. She would like that.'

'And have her question all those things we are desperate to keep private.'

'My dear girl, my parents have occupied separate rooms for years. It is not uncommon in our exalted society.'

'But not in the early years of their marriage, I feel sure.'

'Perhaps not—I couldn't be expected to know anything about that.'

Oh, but he was so annoying when he was being superior, and once again the fear consumed her, so jumping to her feet she ran weeping from the room.

Dominic stared after her with real concern, but with every intention of inviting the doctor to reassure him about the state of her health.

He appeared the next morning while Dominic was eating breakfast alone, and after a few minutes' conversation when Dominic explained something of his wife's problems, he escorted Doctor Meredith personally up to Lisa's bedroom.

He introduced them and then left them together, and Lisa looked up into a kind face which had taken in immediately her ashen face and the dark circles under her green eyes.

'Perhaps you will allow me to examine you,' he said gently. 'Dominic is very concerned about you.'

'There's really nothing wrong with me, Doctor Meredith, nothing that I haven't diagnosed for myself,' she said shortly.

He raised his eyebrows, surprised by the brusque nature of her reply. 'And what diagnosis have you reached, Lady Lexican?'

'That I'm pregnant,' she answered shortly.

After a brief moment he said gently, 'And not entirely happy about it.'

She looked away quickly, but he was aware of her eyes filled with tears and the sudden tightening of her hand on the arm of her chair.

'Most women would be delighted to give their husbands news of that nature. Why is it causing you so much unhappiness?'

She didn't answer, so he took a chair and drew it in front of hers so that he could look at her face. 'You can talk to me,' he encouraged her, 'tell me what is wrong. It is obvious all is not as it should be.'

'It's too soon,' she said, already realising that she had not wanted a third person to be concerned with her dilemma. She was the one who had to tell Dominic, not some doctor who thought it would please him. It shouldn't have to be like this.

'I understand,' he said gently. 'You had thought there would be months, years perhaps to enjoy life together, but a child need not destroy that, Lisa. May I call you Lisa?' he added. 'I've known Dominic since he was a child.'

She nodded without speaking.

'My dear lady, be happy with your condition, have your baby and enjoy your life. Do you want me to tell Dominic?'

She looked up quickly. 'No please, I will do that.'

'Then when he asks me what is wrong I'll simply tell him nothing at all, and that he must ask you.'

She nodded again, and rising to his feet he gently patted her shoulder. 'Dominic will be delighted, my dear, indeed all the family will be delighted. A new heir for Hazelmere, or if your first child is a girl let her be as beautiful as her mother—we can ask for nothing more.'

He felt strangely sad that his words had done little to reassure her, but after a few moments she held out her hand saying, 'Thank you for coming, Doctor Meredith. I'm sorry if I've appeared ungracious.'

'No, no, my dear, the next time we meet I'm sure I shall find you serenely smiling.'

He was thoughtful as he walked down the stairs, hesitating a little before he knocked at the study door where Dominic had said he would wait for him. Dominic sat in front of the fire but immediately he rose to his feet indicating that the doctor should sit opposite him. 'What can I get you to drink?' he asked. 'Your usual whisky?'

'Yes, thank you, just a small one. I am calling to see Mrs Langstone when I leave here. She's not at all well. I suppose Oliver has told you something about it.'

'No, I haven't seen Oliver for some time.'

'I didn't know. His aunt is suffering from arthritis and is becoming increasingly forgetful. Not unusual, I'm afraid. She is well into her eighties.'

'I'm sorry. Isn't she Oliver's great aunt?'

'Yes. She was always very fond of him, doted on him. I'd rather like him to be there when I call.'

'Of course. Please give them my regards, Doctor Meredith.'

'You and Oliver have always been great friends, but marriage alters many things—perhaps he's feeling a little left out.'

Dominic looked at him sharply, but ignoring his words said, 'How did you find my wife?'

'She's perfectly all right, a little out of sorts perhaps, but absolutely nothing for you to worry about. I would go up to see her when I've gone so that she can put you in the picture.'

'Better than you can, do you mean?'

'Well of course. Women have a way with words that we poor men have difficulty in understanding. She'll want to talk to you, Dominic, and now I must leave you. Thank you for inviting me to dine with you one evening, I shall look forward to it.'

The two men shook hands and Dominic escorted him across the hall to the front door, then thoughtfully made his way up the staircase to his wife's bedroom.

He paused in the doorway, staring at Lisa where she sat before her dressing table. She was still wearing her negligee, her blue-black hair falling onto her shoulders, but she did not immediately turn round. Dominic went to stand behind her so that their eyes met through the mirror. He felt the tightness in his throat, aware that his heart was hammering against his ribs, and then she turned and in a low halting voice she said, 'Dominic, I'm pregnant and I don't know what you are going to think about it. That it was revenge, that it was the worst thing I could do to you and your family. I could never blame you for thinking these things of me and expect to be punished in any way you think fit.'

She was dismally aware of the expressions chasing themselves across his face—dismay, incredulity, and a sudden cold anger—then he said stiffly, 'Am I to be allowed to ask who you chose to be the father of your child?'

'Somebody you don't know, will never know. I shall never see him again, but that is beside the point. I am not expecting clemency.'

'I want to know who he is, Lisa.'

So the entire wretched story came out: the village above the city and the old woman sleeping in the sunshine, her wizened old face and claw-like hands, the cynical amusement in her faded eyes as she described Inez de Sanchez, and the two young men who had listened to the story, two brothers.

She told him about Paulo who had liked her, and Juan who had loved her, and she told him about the animal passion that had consumed them both.

'Did you love him?' he asked coldly.

'No. I liked him. We were young, I needed him, I needed somebody to adore me, look at me with eyes filled with love instead of resentment, and I had no thoughts beyond that. Once I had thought it a way of taking revenge on you and your parents, a child, possibly from the gutter, a child from nowhere that would inherit your name and because your family would not wish to divulge your failings they would have to accept him. Dominic, it wasn't like that. I forgot revenge, I forgot everything except the need to be loved; now you can denounce me for the wretch that I am and let me get out of your life.'

For a long time they stared at each other, then he turned away and walked out of the door.

All afternoon she rode her horse across the countryside, meeting nobody, her thoughts bitter and agonising. Where would she go? She could not allow her mother to stay in her house, as they would not allow it. They would have to go away, and she would have to find work after the child was born. Tomorrow she would leave Dominic's house, leave her jewels and her clothes, return to being Lisa Foreshaw—with the tears streaming down her face she thought of her mother's sorrow. That her treasured, beloved daughter had brought them both to this.

Then she thought of Dominic. He too would be bitter, betrayed and anguished. He had given up his lover for what he had considered to be his future, and then suddenly she was angry again. Both she and Dominic had been pawns in a larger game, one that went back centuries when the lords of this realm had everything and the peasants little. She had been the peasant, marrying a lord who must be seen to be unsullied, a fitting person to take his father's place one day—they would not allow this child of hers to usurp the ancient name of Hazelmere.

How could she ever have thought herself capable of revenge when now she must pay the price of treachery?

She ate alone in the vast dining room and if the servants who waited on her thought it strange, their obsequious behaviour gave no sign of it.

How slowly the time passed. The chiming of innumerable clocks only emphasised the empty hours as she wandered from room to room expecting the memory of them to tantilise her for the rest of her life.

All those shelves filled with books bound in leather and embossed with gold in the library, had they ever been opened, and the grand piano, how long since it was played? There were great urns filled with flowers, some of which she had arranged, others by the servants—she would be gone from here before their petals fell, and she looked across the hall to where an empty space waited for the portrait of herself and Dominic, and then at other portraits of long dead Hazelmeres around the rooms.

She felt sure that Dominic would be with Oliver. He would need to talk to him, tell him about her perfidy, reassure him that he had never loved her, married her only for expediency; and throughout those long weary hours one minute she was ashamed, then she was angry, one minute afraid, the next filled with bitterness.

It was almost midnight when she went to her room. A fire had been lit with the flames from it lighting up the damask curtains at the long windows and around the huge ornate bed, with tints of rose that gave the huge room a gentle warmth. She knelt on the rug in front of the fire and held out her hands to the blaze. She realised for the first time that she was cold after wandering into rooms that were unheated, and she shivered at the sound of rain lashing against the windows.

Surely Dominic hadn't gone to Hazelmere—the butler would have said something, but then why should he? Dominic did not need to tell anybody where he intended to spend the night—he was answerable to neither his servants nor his wife; but then even as she thought it she heard the sound of a car from outside in the courtyard.

She stood near the door listening for any sounds in the house and then she heard the closing of doors and voices. She recognised the low murmur of Dominic's voice but could not tell if he had brought guests home with him or if they were the voices of servants.

She needed to see him, and yet she was afraid of the coldness in his eyes, the resentment in his voice. The old Dominic who had always been courteous and intrinsically kind would surely have gone forever.

She stood with her back to the door waiting, exactly as she had waited months before, but this time she was not waiting for a man who she would expect to be her lover, rather a man she had betrayed; then suddenly she heard the sharp closing of a door further across the corridor and realised that Dominic had gone to his room.

What would he be thinking as he retired alone in that lonely room? Would he blame her for everything without a hint of pity that like him she had been a victim?

She couldn't sleep; the hours seemed endless on that cold autumnal night when the only sounds came from outside: the sighing of the night wind and the shrill barking of foxes. The sound of the rain was continuous, and flashes of lightning lit up the walls so that she got out of her bed to draw the curtains at the windows. As Dominic drove up to the house he must have seen the lights shining from her windows but he hadn't thought it necessary to see her; now she waited miserably for the dawn and the answers that had to be found.

It was barely light when she heard the opening of his door so apparently he too had been unable to sleep. For one moment she thought he was coming to her room, and she listened, hardly daring to breathe; thick carpets in the corridors and down the stairs deadened the sound of his footsteps; cautiously she opened the door only to be met with darkness, and yet from somewhere below a lamp had been lit and as she stood at the top of the long shallow staircase she heard the opening of a door, then from the library saw the faint glow of another lamp.

She went back to her room and picked up her robe, then went to switch on the lights that would illuminate the stairs. She had to know what he intended to do—after all, however guilty she felt he could not in all honesty expect her to take the blame for everything. She was a woman first, his wife second, and however much he blamed her, surely the blame deserved to be apportioned.

She opened the library door quietly to find him sitting at the huge mahogany desk staring in front of him, unseeing, at that moment unaware that she stood staring at him. He was wearing his dressing gown, and like herself had evidently been unable to sleep.

She turned to close the door, then when she looked round he was watching her, his face expressionless. Full of anguish she cried out, 'Dominic, I have to know, I don't care what you do to me, how things are resolved, but I have to know. Isn't it enough that you leave me alone for hours, waiting, thinking all sorts of things, sick with worry even when I know I have really no right to expect anything else? Just tell me what we must do, when you need me to leave. I need to see my mother. I need to be with her.'

He stared at her in silence, at a woman distraught with fear, trembling with guilt, unprepared for the calmness of his voice as he said, 'Go back to bed, Lisa. This is no time to talk about anything, I'm in no mood to think beyond the here and now, and you are obviously too distraught to listen to me.'

'But you're upset or you wouldn't be here in the dead of night alone, and I can't sleep with all this hanging over us. We need to talk now, surely you must see that.'

He rose to his feet and walked towards her. At the door

he switched off the light and looking down at her in a calm, quiet voice said, 'Tomorrow, Lisa, we'll talk tomorrow when we're calmer. Please go back to your room.'

She had to go as there was no alternative, and at the bottom of the stairs he waited for her so that they could walk up to their rooms together.

CHAPTER SEVENTEEN

A NEW DAY—A DAY OF DANK dismal mist and rain, a day when the last remaining leaves on the trees hung dejectedly from the branches, reluctant to fall on the wet grass, and when even the birds had fled to more hospitable lands.

The mood reflected her own and as Lisa looked into the mirror all she was aware of were the dark circles underneath her eyes and the pallor that had erased the beauty from her face. Dominic too would be as heavy hearted as herself. Today answers had to be found, and she had little hope that at the end of the day she would be the survivor.

She heard the closing of Dominic's door but still she waited afraid and tearful until she realised she could wait no longer—today either one way or another their future had to be resolved.

As she entered the breakfast room Dominic stood at the side table pouring coffee and she watched while he carried it to his place at the table. There was an array of food laid out for them but he'd not taken any, and looking up he merely said, 'Good morning, Lisa,' and following his example she went to pour her coffee. They sat facing each other like two polite strangers, until at last it was Dominic who spoke, saying mechanically, 'Don't you want breakfast, Lisa?'

'Don't you?' she answered dully.

His brief smile was merely a polite response.

'Nevertheless,' he said, 'the staff have prepared breakfast for us so perhaps we should make an effort. May I help you to something?'

'Fruit juice and scrambled eggs, if you insist, Dominic. I'm really not hungry.'

'Nor I, but I think we should make an effort.'

She went with him to the table but the mere sight of food nauseated her. Nevertheless she made herself take scrambled eggs and toast, and seemingly Dominic too was entirely uninterested in the food laid out before them.

Breakfast was a silent meal where two people had so much to say but neither of them could find the words to begin. It was Lisa at last who rose to her feet saying, 'We can't talk in here, Dominic, the servants will be here to clear away. Where do you suggest we go?'

'In the study, I think,' he answered. 'I'll join you there. I have a telephone call to make first.'

Was the telephone call to do with her? she wondered. Wasn't it something that could have waited? But she waited nonetheless in the study, appreciative of the blazing fire that vied with the rain lashing against the window panes.

At last they faced each other and she waited anxiously for him to collect his thoughts before he said,

'Our lives are going to change radically. You do realise that, Lisa?'

'Well of course. I just want you to tell me when I must leave and what we are going to say to your family and my mother. Obviously I can't simply disappear—how much does the world need to know?'

'I have just spoken to my mother on the telephone. They are expecting me later today.'

She stared at him in disbelief. Oh, surely not so soon; she needed to tell her mother first, she thought wildly. Seeing her immediate distress Dominic said, 'Perhaps you should come with me and stay with your mother, Lisa. She will need to know; my parents also.'

'And then what, a divorce? We shall have to move away.'

'Lisa, if we stay together you are always going to think it is a cover-up for my inadequacies; if you go the world will judge you harshly unless you are prepared to tell them the truth which you have every right to do. Whatever the outcome only you and I can really know how we want this problem to be resolved.'

'I've been an unfaithful wife, Dominic. You have every reason to reject me.'

'And I have been a cold and unloving husband, Lisa. Isn't that the true reason for your taking a lover?'

'Yes, Dominic, it is. I loved you, I wanted you to love me but it wasn't possible. You have no idea how I needed a man's love, partly because I felt worthless and un-wanted, but I never loved him, never.'

'So you used him?'

'If you like. We used each other. He will forget me,

find some other woman to love and he will never know about the child. I shall never go back to Seville. I can go to live with my mother and we can move away. I will promise never to tell the truth to another living soul, never to divulge the name of my baby's father, never to say why I had felt it necessary to seek love away from you.'

'And I shall be the aggrieved husband, the English gentleman cuckolded by a selfish wife and deserving of something better. Oh no, Lisa, I don't think I could live with that.'

'That is how your family would like to see it.'

'I am sure that you are right, my mother in particular.'

'Then tell me what we must do.'

For what seemed like an age he was silent, standing at the window and gazing out into the wet misery of the morning before he returned to take the chair opposite her. His voice was grave and measured, his expression sincere. 'Lisa, I am not sure at this moment if I will ever be able to love your child but I will be kind to him, I will educate him and try very hard to be a good father to him—that is the most I can promise at the moment. As time passes I may feel resentment that one day he will inherit Hazelmere and all that goes with it. I shall surely feel he has no right to it, but it will not be the child's fault—he will have been educated into it and I must try to put the rest behind me.'

'You say he—suppose it is a daughter?'

'Then there will be no problem. She will no doubt grow up to be as beautiful as her mother and possibly as spirited. She will probably marry into the nobility and there will be no questions asked.'

'And Oliver Cardew?'

'I beg your pardon?'

'Will you tell Oliver, and what is he going to think? That you have fathered a child or that I have chosen some other to fill your place?'

'I have not seen Oliver Cardew since our wedding. Oh, I know that you must have thought we were together when I was here and you were in Spain but it wasn't so. I did not see him; I have no thoughts on seeing him.'

'But you love him, Dominic.'

'And I don't want to discuss him with you or anybody else, Lisa. You haven't told me what you think about my suggestion.'

'Are you going to tell your parents?'

'That you are pregnant, yes. Nothing more.'

'That the child is yours?'

'They will assume that it is mine. I shall not enlighten them otherwise.'

'I don't want to meet them just yet.'

'Of course not. I will take you to stay with your mother, but I have to say that my mother will not be able to contain her enthusiasm and you may expect to see her soon. Will you be able to play your part?'

'Oh yes, Dominic. We will both be playing our parts for a great many years. Will it be easy do you think?'

'No, Lisa. You will still long for the love I cannot give

you and I have no doubt there will be other men in your life. How discreet will you be?'

'And you too, Dominic. Oliver Cardew will be there for you, and you will tell him the truth if you never tell anybody else.'

'I shall not tell him anything.'

'But Dominic, that isn't fair. You love him, he loves you, if you keep everything else to yourself he has a right to know.'

'No, Lisa, he does not. He is still seething with bitterness over our marriage—another delusion will not come as too much of a surprise.'

He stared at her long and hard for several minutes then in a lighter vein he said, 'I will tell Harding that we intend to go away for a while. I'm not sure how long I intend to stay at Hazelmere but your mother will be delighted to have you with her, so stay as long as you like, Lisa.'

'What time are we leaving?'

'Late afternoon. Telephone your mother; let her know when to expect you.'

She sat on in the study after he had left her thinking about the pattern of their future together. She had a husband who could never be the husband she needed— would he ever be able to look at her child without condemning her for her immorality?

The romantic young love she had felt for Dominic had long gone, but the fondness remained. More than anything else she truly liked Dominic for his intrinsic dignity and consideration, whether she deserved it or not.

The journey to Hazelmere was taken largely in silence—not an oppressive silence, but rather the silence of two people who were facing irredeemable changes. Lisa was the first one to speak by asking, 'What are you going to tell your parents?'

'I can only tell them the truth.'

'That I have betrayed you and that I am expecting another man's child?'

'That you are pregnant and have decided to stay with your mother for a while.'

'And you expect them to believe that you are the father?'

'My mother will believe that the old Dominic was a myth and that I have come to my senses; whatever doubts my father might have she will repudiate. And your mother?'

'My mother will be happy for me, for us.'

'My mother too. Be patient with her, Lisa. She will make a fuss of you, let everybody know how delighted she is. Try to keep the sarcasm out of your eyes for all our sakes.'

'I will try, Dominic.'

'I expect you would prefer to go immediately to your mother rather than go with me first to Hazelmere?'

'Yes please, Dominic, I need a little time before I can face your mother.'

He nodded, and once more lapsed into silence. Dominic was not relishing his meeting with his parents—his mother's joy based on a lie, his father's amazement, and another thought had come to trouble him.

One day his brother would marry and have children,

who would be denied their birthright in favour of a child who had no right to the title handed down to him; yet the pledges he had made to his wife must come first.

When all the arguments had been said, Lisa was still the innocent pawn who had been sacrificed on the altar of family pride.

Mary received her daughter with motherly affection, and if she was surprised that Lisa decided to stay with her and allow her husband to travel on without her she merely said, 'Are you sure, darling, that you want to stay here instead of going on to Hazelmere?'

'Yes, Mother, we've seen so little of each other and Dominic really doesn't mind. I have a lot to tell you.'

Dominic merely smiled, then they both stood in the doorway to watch him drive away.

'You're very pale, Lisa,' were her mother's next words. 'Have you been ill?'

'No, Mother, I'm quite well. You always fussed too much.'

'I don't like to see you looking so wan; you were always so vibrant.'

'I'm pregnant, Mother. That may be why I've lost my colour.'

Her mother's eyes lit up with immediate joy, and drawing Lisa into her embrace she cried, 'Oh darling, how wonderful. Lucy will be ecstatic, and Dominic too. Isn't he delighted?'

'Yes, Mother, we both are.'

'Lucy will be here in the morning, I'm sure. As soon as she's able to get out of the house. I've seen very little of either Lucy or Sybil, you know what they're like, they both have so many commitments. Sometimes I do wish I could do more to keep me occupied.'

'Such as what, Mother?'

'Well, you know. They do all sorts of things for local charities, and then of course there's racing and hunting, and the functions associated with both pursuits.'

Lisa smiled. 'Don't tell me you're thinking of taking up hunting, Mother.'

'Well of course not, dear, but there are other things. Anyway with a grandchild in the offing I hope you'll keep me busy. When exactly is the baby expected, Lisa?'

'May or early June. The doctor says one can never be very sure with a first baby.'

'No. Oh I do hope you can stay with me a few days before you need to go up to the Hall. Perhaps Dominic could stay here for a short while.'

'Well, you know what it's like, Mother. Dominic's father relies on him so very much.'

How long would they be able to make excuses to their friends and families? Separate rooms—what possible excuses for such an arrangement and yet neither of them would want it any other way? She could not visualise sharing a bedroom with Dominic—it would be like sleeping with a brother—and yet here they both were talking about the advent of a baby. Sooner or later doubts would begin to creep in and there would be no answers from either of them.

As she unpacked in the bedroom she had once occupied she thought how wrong both she and her mother had been to accept the house. It was far too large, with so many of the rooms permanently shut off—her mother must hate the vastness of it.

Her mother's questions were intrusive. 'How long does Dominic intend to stay at Hazelmere? How long do you intend to stay here? Really, darling, it isn't necessary for you to be with me. You should be with your husband.'

'Mother, please don't go on. Dominic and I talked about it before we left home; we are both happy with the arrangement and I really did want to spent time with you.'

'Do you ever see anything of that young man Dominic knew from school?' her mother asked innocently.

'Which young man is that?' Lisa replied, knowing full well who she was referring to.

'Oliver, his name was. A rather dour young man, I seem to remember, although he was always at ease with Dominic.'

'No, Mother, we haven't seen Oliver Cardew for some time.'

'But they were very good friends and spent an awful lot of time together.'

'Yes I know, but like I said we haven't seen him. Perhaps he's abroad somewhere or he's left the area.'

'Oh no, Lisa, I saw him in the village several days ago. I met him in the post office. I smiled at him and said good morning but that was all.'

'Was he alone?'

'Oh yes. You know, Lisa, I don't really think I need a

servant. There's precious little for her to do and I like to do my own cooking. It's what I've been used to.'

'It's a very big house, Mother.'

'Too big, Lisa, haven't I always said so?'

'Doesn't a servant give it some sort of ambience?'

'An ambience I don't really need, dear. I'm sure Lucy will be round in the morning. She only ever has a cup of coffee but perhaps on this occasion I should offer her lunch or something. What do you think?'

'I really don't know, Mother. She probably won't stay for lunch, after all she has so many commitments.'

'That's true, but I feel I should offer—'

'Don't worry, Mother, we have to eat lunch—if she wishes to join us she will be very welcome.'

Her mother's expression was doubtful. As always she was still in awe of her aristocratic cousins, but in the next moment she said, 'I'm sure Lucy will insist on your going back with her to Hazelmere. If she does what will you say?'

'The same thing I said to you, Mother, that Dominic and I had discussed it and the present arrangement suits us both.'

'But all that long time when you were alone in Spain, Lisa, and he was here seeing to his father's affairs. Even Lucy thought it was asking too much of both of you. Didn't you think to come back with him?'

'We talked about it, Mother. It went on longer than we had expected. Do you see anything of Lord Hazelmere?'

'No, but I believe he has recovered quite well, although he isn't riding yet.'

'I'm glad.'

'Dominic rode his father's horse every day; he often called to see me.'

'Did he ride alone or did Oliver ride with him?'

'Oh no, he was always alone. If he rode with Oliver I didn't see them.'

What had prompted her to ask that question? She hadn't believed Dominic when he'd said he hadn't seen Oliver, and later when she lay sleepless in a room gently lit by moonlight she felt an overriding pity for Dominic.

Hurt and angry, she had thought only of herself, but Dominic was suffering too. He had loved Oliver Cardew and it appeared he had put him firmly out of his life, while she had been having a passionate affair with a man she had not loved.

It seemed to Lisa that she had grown up too quickly— one minute she had been a young girl in love with life and with a man she had believed had loved her, then she had been thrown into a nightmare.

She had no doubt that her mother-in-law would appear in the morning and she was doubtful if she could disguise her antipathy towards her.

Lucy would appear all smiles and congratulations. She would embrace her warmly, go on and on about the baby, say her piece that they should be together, and unwittingly her mother too would agree with her.

What was Oliver Cardew doing near Hazelmere and where was he staying? Of course he knew people in the area quite apart from Dominic and his parents, but if they were seen together eyebrows would be raised.

She had been naive and foolish, but older, more so-phisticated people might have found something unnat-ural in their friendship.

It was almost daylight before she slept and as a conse-quence she overslept and it was the sound of dogs bark-ing and women's voices that roused her.

She leapt out of bed and went to the window and saw that Lucy's horse stood tethered near the path. Her moth-er-in-law had arrived, and then her mother was in her room saying urgently, 'Lisa, darling, do get dressed. Lucy is here and dying to see you.'

'I'm sorry, Mother, I overslept. I didn't sleep very well.'

'No, you do look a little wan, dear. I'm sure Lucy will notice. Do get dressed quickly and put on a little make-up, a little rouge perhaps. You know how Lucy fusses.'

CHAPTER EIGHTEEN

DOMINIC HAD WATCHED HIS mother cantering off along the drive and surmised that she was on her way to see his wife.

He had waited the evening before until they sat down to dinner to tell his parents his news, and watched with cynical amusement the delight on his mother's face and the amazement on his father's.

His mother had been triumphant. Of course she'd always known that her elder son was no different to any other man. Given a wife he would quickly realise that a woman was what he really wanted—after all hadn't she always said that schools given over exclusively to boys were asking for trouble?

Later in the evening he had heard his parents' voices in his father's study and surmised they were discussing the events of the evening.

From where he sat in the library, going over his father's correspondence which had been left out for him to sort out, their voices carried—his father's mainly sceptical, his mother's entirely jubilant.

'Didn't I tell you, Johnny, that everything would turn out right? Of course Dominic was interested in girls. It was simply he'd never met the right one until Lisa came along, and wasn't I absolutely sure that he'd quickly forget the Cardew boy? Why are you so unconvinced?'

'Because I've known men like him.'

'How can you say that? He's your son. Anyway this proves you wrong. He's fathered a child and I for one am delighted, so should you be. Why are you so sceptical?'

'She was in Spain long enough on her own. Who knows who she was cavorting with. Like as not we could have some Spanish Lothario carrying on the family name.'

'Really, Johnny, that is despicable. I wouldn't like Dominic to hear the things you are saying, and tomorrow we should go to see Lisa together to express our joy at the news.'

'You're the one who is happy about the forthcoming event; I'm not so sure.'

Dominic had heard the opening and slamming of the study door and his mother's rapid footsteps across the wooden floor.

In the next few weeks the rest of the family would descend on Hazelmere to offer their congratulations and he would have to receive them with smiling pride and a less than jubilant heart.

Lisa had suffered her mother-in-law's warm embrace and expressions of heartfelt delight; now she watched while the two older women chatted easily about christening robes, invitations to Christmas festivities and later to the christening itself.

'Lisa says the baby is expected in May or early June,' her mother said, 'so he'll be a summer baby which is nice.'

'Oh I do agree, Mary,' Lucy said warmly. 'Those rooms at Martindale, and here at Hazelmere too can be decidedly chilly in winter. Of course, you know his first name has to be John, don't you, Lisa? Dominic's first name is John.'

'Suppose my baby is a girl, Lady Hazelmere,' Lisa said evenly.

Lucy's eyes opened wide. 'Oh gracious, I haven't even thought of that contingency. We'll just have to think of names for a girl. But there's lots of time and you'll have other children—one of them's sure to be a boy.'

'I hope you'll stay and eat lunch with us,' Mary said quietly.

'Well, I'd love to, darling, but I have to get over to see Sybil. I don't want to tell her the news by telephone. She'll be absolutely thrilled. I'm going to suggest to Johnny that at Christmas this year we should have a huge family party. I do hope Austin will get home for Christmas. Why he had to go off to join the Army I'll never know.'

'Dominic said Austin seemed to think there was some sort of scrap in the offing,' Lisa said, only to be met by Lucy's silvery laughter before she said, 'Oh that's so silly, all those young men dreaming up some sort of war in which they can all become heroes.'

'We must get together soon, Lisa, to think about

Christmas, family and close friends, I think. And of course you'll be with us at Hazelmere. Your mother can come to stay or come up for the festivities; she's quite close anyway.'

She has it all planned, Lisa thought, just as she's had my life and Dominic's planned, and we'll all comply, but as she watched Lucy riding away a small secret smile curved her lips—her baby would never be Lucy's grand-child and she would never know it.

When they returned to the house Mary said doubtfully, 'I'm not sure that I want to be a part of the Christmas celebrations, Lisa. There'll be people there I don't know, all sorts of things will resurface.'

'Oh Mother, why should you care any more? I don't and you mustn't either.'

All the same Christmas at Hazelmere posed a prob-lem. She and Dominic would be expected to share a bedroom and she would need Dominic to find a way out.

Dominic on the other hand was troubled by a far more worrying episode. His father was insistent that Dominic exercised his horse. 'Manners doesn't ride him like I would,' he insisted. 'That horse cost me a bomb and I don't want any apprentice practising his horsemanship on him. You must ride him; you'll know how to look after him.'

So on a grey blustery day in early December Dominic rode his father's horse across the vast parkland surround-ing the house and it was only on returning to the stables that he saw a solitary horseman riding towards him, his head bent against the wind; but he knew immediately who the horseman was.

He rode slowly towards him and then their eyes met and in Oliver Cardew's eyes he saw a sudden joy, immediately replaced by anxiety.

'I heard you were here, Dominic,' he said. 'I hoped you'd come here before I returned home.'

'I thought you'd be staying with your aunt, Oliver. I heard she wasn't well.'

'No, that's true. She has a friend staying with her, but in any case I'm not much use at looking after an old lady. I'm going back there next week. I thought I might see you around Martindale. I couldn't very well come up to the house when Lisa was there.'

Dominic didn't answer but remained sitting on his horse, his expression inscrutable, as Oliver said gently, 'Dominic, I've missed you. I thought when you came home to see your father you'd make an effort to see me; after all Lisa was in Spain.'

'I told you it was over, Oliver,' Dominic said evenly.

'I know what you told me, but how can it be over? You don't love Lisa, you didn't love her when you married her, you still love me.'

'People fall out of love,' he answered gently.

'Of course, but not people like us, not over a woman.'

'Lisa is expecting a baby in the summer, Oliver, so perhaps that should convince you. Lisa is my wife, Oliver. She needs me to take care of both of them.'

He was aware that Oliver was looking at him with such an expression of pain on his face that he felt an urgent need to go to him, then with a strange heartbroken cry Oliver wheeled his horse round and galloped as fast as his horse could carry him towards the gates.

Dominic stared after him with pain-filled eyes—he had bitterly hurt the person he cared for most in the world and there had been no other way. Oliver would never forgive him for what he would regard as betrayal; it might be that they would never meet again, unless Oliver wished to taunt him by his presence.

He rode back to the house with his thoughts in chaos. He should have defied his parents, let the world see him for what he was regardless of the contempt he would be subjected to. But the world was not ready for the likes of Oliver Cardew and himself. This way only three people were hurt—Lisa, Oliver and himself—the other way they would all have been hurt.

The groom took charge of the horse and Dominic made his way to the house, walking with his eyes on the ground, unseeing, unaware of the wind tearing at his jacket as from the window of the study his father watched him. He had witnessed his encounter with Oliver, and seen that neither of them had dismounted from their horses, and that Oliver had ridden away as though all the hounds of hell pursued him. He knew instinctively that Dominic had informed him of his wife's pregnancy and that the news had filled Oliver's heart with pain and bitter rage.

He felt a sudden surge of pity for his son. He had always been proud of Dominic, the serious, handsome boy who had done well at school, always been studiously polite, gentle and courteous and had a charm that drew people to him.

He had never suspected there was anything different about him—after all a boy didn't shout his affairs from the housetops, and it had only been maturity that had raised so many problems.

Why had Lucy seen it when he hadn't? Why not Lisa?

But surely along the line they must have been wrong. He had fathered a child, come to realise that he could love a woman. It was no wonder boys were confused, herded together in boys' schools from the age of six until they were young men. Obviously Lucy had been right.

He called to Dominic from the study door. 'Come and have a hot toddy with me; it's freezing cold out there. Horse perform all right?'

Dominic joined him reluctantly. He would have preferred to have gone straight to his room, but his father was ringing the bell above the fireplace and instructing the servant to bring their drinks.

'Horse behaved well?' his father asked again.

'Yes, Father, very well. You'll soon be riding him yourself again.'

'I'm not sure. He's a bit of a handful; I expect I've lost a bit of confidence.'

'Oh I don't think so, after all you've had tumbles before. Your confidence will come back the next time you ride him.'

'I'm not sure. It's my belief that you should get on his back immediately after you've had a fall. I was unable to and now it might be too late. After all, I'm not getting any younger.'

'Couldn't Mother ride him?'

'He's not a mount for a woman.'

'You mean you don't want him to be.'

His father chuckled at the logic of Dominic's words.

'You know, your mother's intent on having a huge family party at Christmas. I suppose even more so now she's heard your news.'

'Yes, she did say something about it.'

'I take it you and your wife will be together?'

'Well obviously, but not I hope in the room I occupied when I lived here.'

'Oh, do you want a change?'

'Well, I have a beautiful house of my own and we don't exactly live a thousand miles away. We could drive over for the party.'

'Your mother wouldn't like that. She will want you both here and we're hoping your brother'll get leave. What he wanted to join the Army for I can't imagine.'

'The news from Europe is not good, Father. Austin made up his mind that there was going to be some sort of scrap. He wanted to be in on it.'

'Did he indeed? And what will you do if there's some sort of scrap as you call it?'

'What most young men in the country will be expected to do, Father—I shall go into the Army.'

'You've thought about it, have you?'

'Of course. Your old regiment, I think. Weren't you very proud of it?'

'Very proud. But of course there won't be a war, just lots of silly warmongering. We went off to South Africa praying the war wouldn't be over before we got there, but of course it was, or at least we saw nothing of it.'

'This might be very different, Father, and certainly more widespread.'

'Well, don't talk about it to your mother. Let her have her Christmas party, and don't think too much about joining the Army—your wife and child will be needing you at home.'

'If there is a war, Father, there will be a great many women and children needing their fathers at home. I don't intend to be an exception.'

'No, I suppose not. You know your mother's gone to see Lisa?'

'Yes, Father.'

'She'll be planning all sorts of things. She's quite thrilled with your news you know, then I expect she'll ride over to see Sybil and her husband. They'll all have to be in on the act; she'll not be able to contain herself.'

Dominic smiled.

There were so many questions Lord Hazelmere needed to ask but as always he was conscious of that strange reserve that existed between him and his elder son. He could say anything to Austin—deplore his late nights and his choice of female companions, his ability to lose money on indifferent horses and at the card table—but always Austin just grinned at him, before offering the usual abject apologies.

Dominic had never needed his censure. He was the

serious, proper, elder son, and his wife's anxieties had shocked him; now perhaps they had both worried needlessly.

He couldn't stop himself asking, 'Ever see the Cardew boy, Dominic?'

'I saw him for a few moments this morning. He's returning to his aunt's house near Martindale, I believe.'

'Does he visit you and Lisa there?'

'No. I doubt if Oliver would enjoy taking afternoon tea with a married couple.'

'You were never apart. He seemed to enjoy the social events here then, the tea parties, the garden parties and the dances the young people laid on.'

'Would you mind if I left you now, Father, to take Hassan out? It'll be dark around four and the wind seems to have got up.'

'No, of course not. It's time your mother got home. I don't like her riding across the Downs in a storm, and I think there's one blowing up.'

After Dominic had left him he reflected that the need to ride Hassan had merely been an excuse to avoid any more questioning. He'd had the horse out in the morning—taking him out again had merely been an excuse to get away.

Dominic had been aware of the constraint as soon as Oliver Cardew's name had been mentioned, but of course why wouldn't there be? He was well aware of his parents' opinion regarding his friend and himself; now it was time they forgot about it.

Dominic walked to the stables with his head bent against the wind. There really was no need to take the horse out again but he had wanted to get away from his father's questions. As he entered the stable yard he was aware that his mother had arrived back and the groom was leading her horse away while his mother said, 'You're surely not intending riding again today, dear?'

'Well, I'd thought of it, but it's looking like a storm, so I'll return with you to the house. Aunt Sybil and family are well, I hope.'

'Oh yes, dear, and so thrilled with your news. I called to see Lisa and her mother. I thought she was looking a little pale, dear. I really do think she should come up here to be with you.'

'Well, Lisa hasn't been too well, Mother, and she's happy with her mother. I doubt if she'd be too happy in that boy's bedroom you insist on putting me in.'

Lucy stopped to stare at him. 'Oh Dominic, of course not. Why on earth didn't you say something about it? You and Lisa must occupy the Rose Room. It's always been a guest room but you shall have it now; it's huge and there's a bathroom and dressing room. There will be no reason for her to stay on with her mother, and Mary can visit whenever she likes.'

Dominic thought with relief that at least one problem would be solved. He would sleep in the dressing room so that neither of them would feel embarrassed, and at least it might put an end to his father's lingering doubts.

'I'll go down to see Lisa in the morning and tell her what I've arranged,' his mother said.

'I shall see Lisa in the morning, Mother. I will tell her.'

'And do tell her she should return with you, Dominic.'

'Leave it to me, Mother.'

Lucy smiled complacently. It was all going so well; there was so much to look forward to.

'I told Mary and Lisa about the Christmas party I shall be planning. Family and favourite guests, and hopefully Austin will be home. Your father's not happy about the situation in Europe; your uncle was on about it too. Why are men always so intent on looking for trouble somewhere or other?'

'The news isn't good, Mother.'

'Why did your brother have to join the Army? He had several very nice girlfriends from good families; surely one of them could have pursuaded him against it.'

'Obviously not, Mother.'

As they made their way to the house Lucy's thoughts were on her younger son.

They had hoped Austin would marry well and produce the heir Dominic would never have; now it was all going to be so different. Austin would be in no hurry to marry. Hadn't he always played the field? Now there was no need for them to urge him on.

Hadn't she always said it would all come right in the end?

CHAPTER NINETEEN

THE LARGE BLUE SPRUCE THAT had been brought in that morning from the estate stood resplendent in the hall while an army of servants brushed away the branches that had fallen and formed a path from the door. Now they were assembled to decorate the tree and Lady Hazelmere was in her element directing operations.

'Lisa darling, we'll let the men clamber to the upper regions while we concentrate on the lower branches,' she said gaily. 'We mustn't have you falling, must we.'

Lisa had been in residence at Hazelmere for two weeks and the many problems that she thought would materialise had not happened. They were installed in the Rose Room overlooking the rose garden—Dominic slept every night in the dressing room while Lisa slept in the huge bed under its draped silken canopy.

That first morning she had heard the closing of the dressing-room door very early, and consulting the clock on the table beside the bed she found that it was only just seven o'clock. Dominic had already left the room so with a fast-beating heart she hurried across the room to look inside the dressing room where she found the bed already made and the entire room appeared to have been unoccupied.

Dominic apparently was not taking any chances that the servants would be able to comment on their sleeping arrangements, and if she felt an acute gratitude, she also deplored the necessary subterfuge.

Between her and Dominic was the friendship that had always been there. Once she had thought that friendship would never survive but strangely enough it seemed to be the one true value left. She had nobody to confide in— neither her mother who was looking forward with great anticipation to being a grandmother, nor the girls who had been her bridesmaids and who she thought of as friends who envied her aristocratic, handsome husband and had high hopes of finding similar eligible suitors.

Every day they rode together, visited friends together and took part in helping Lucy with her party arrangements.

Lord Hazelmere's worries slowly subsided. All he saw was his daughter-in-law's contentment, his son's concern for her—his wife was right, they could both have been wrong.

Two days before Christmas Austin came home on a week's leave, filling the house with a mixture of girl-friends, entertaining them with talk of his army training and the fact that there was going to be a war. Europe was seething with problems, Austria and Hungary were at loggerheads and Russia was interfering. The German emperor was a loose canon likely to go off at any moment and there was no way the British would be able to stay out of it.

It was during the second evening over the dinner table that Austin said easily, 'I forgot to mention it sooner, Dominic, but I ran into Oliver Cardew in London on my way to the station. I suppose you already know he's joined the Royal Artillery. If there is a war they'll be one of the first to go out there.'

He was not aware of the strained silence around the dining table until Dominic said quietly, 'I didn't know. I haven't seen much of Oliver recently.'

'No, he said you'd lost touch. I was a bit surprised about that as at one time you were inseparable.'

'Well, Dominic is married,' Lady Hazelmere said sharply, 'so obviously things have changed. Oliver is a free agent; no doubt he has many other friends.'

'I wasn't sure if he'd heard about your becoming a father but he didn't show much interest. He seemed more concerned with the state of the troubles abroad.'

'What made him join the artillery?' Lord Hazelmere asked shortly.

'He said he wanted to be in at the outset, said he got bored in the country with an aunt who was more or less senile and wanted some excitement in his life.'

'His aunt's been a very good friend to him,' Lucy said sharply. 'To my knowledge he's never found a job to suit him; spent most of his life partying and riding round the countryside on one of his aunt's horses.'

'At his aunt's request,' Dominic interrupted quietly. 'It

was impossible for the old lady to ride her horses—she relied on Oliver for their well-being.'

'I'm sure you're right, darling, but I think the Army might be the making of him. I hope so anyway.'

Lisa felt the tension round the table, and it seemed only Austin was unaware of it as he said brightly, 'I asked him if there was a girl in the offing but he laughed and said no. Come to think of it I've never actually seen him with a girl, except to dance with of course.'

'Has your mother decided to spend Christmas here with us?' Dominic asked Lisa in an effort to change the subject.

'She hasn't decided. She lives so near, she'll probably decide to go home after the party is over.'

'Quite unnecessary,' Lucy said sharply. 'Most people will be staying. I'll speak to Mary and get her to change her mind.'

Lisa was aware for the rest of the evening that Dominic appeared to be listening to the conversation going on around him but she was convinced his thoughts were miles away.

Later in the evening they sat listening to Dominic playing Chopin, sensitively and artistically. He played well as he did everything else, but from the room across the hall Lisa could plainly hear the sound of billiard balls which Austin found preferable to listening to music.

After a while she got up quietly and went to join him. On her arrival he looked up with a grin. 'I'm no performer on the piano,' he said. 'Dominic was always better than me when we were both having lessons. I was better at snooker.'

'Do you really think there's going to be a war?' she asked him quietly.

'Sure to be. The government wouldn't be going to all this expense if they didn't think so.'

'Expense?'

'Well yes—recruitment, training—they're even setting up nursing homes here and there. Don't be surprised if they approach you about that stately pile of yours.'

'Martindale!'

'Why yes. You'll not want to soldier on there on your own with a young baby—Dominic will go into the Army. Nobody's going to get out of it, Lisa, unless he conscientiously objects, that is, and even then someone will take his place.'

'Dominic would never object.'

'No of course not. So you see what I mean about Martindale?'

'Where will that leave me?'

'Here, dear girl, or with your mother. Your mother is literally rattling round in that old house of Aunt Jane's.'

She laughed. 'My mother would agree with you; I was the one who wanted it.'

'You know, Lisa, I'm jolly glad you married Dominic. It certainly took the heat off me. I'm not ready for marriage. Although actually I'm quite fond of several of the girls I play around with, marriage to any one of them would be something else.'

'One day you'll fall in love, Austin.'

'Don't bank on it, old girl. I think the family were a bit tetchy about Oliver Cardew—after all, they invited him constantly so why are they so scathing about him now?'

'Did you like him, Austin?'

'He was all right, I suppose. He and Dominic were friends; some of the lads used to think there was more to it than met the eye but Dominic's proved them wrong by getting married. When I mentioned you to Oliver he seemed uninterested, too uninterested.'

'What do you mean by that?'

'Well, either it's because he resents your intrusion into their friendship or the fact that his free holidays here, there and everywhere have come to an end.'

'You're too materialistic for me, Austin.'

He grinned. 'I am, aren't I? Have you chosen any names for the new baby? One will have to be John, of course.'

'Yes, I've already been told that.'

'Any others?'

'He could be a she.'

'Then she'll have to be Jane something or other.'

'If it's a girl then the heat will be back on you, Austin.'

'Why? You'll have other children.'

The sound of the piano had ceased from the music room; after a few minutes the door opened and Dominic joined them.

'Join me in a game,' Austin invited.

And looking at Lisa, Dominic said, 'Would you mind, Lisa?'

'Not at all; I'll join the others.'

'You'll find them in Father's study,' he replied. 'He prefers to sit in there with his rum toddy and Mother'll be glad of your company.'

It was strange how Lisa remembered that Christmas when so many others faded into insignificance.

She remembered the walk to church along frost-laden paths when the mist hung low over white-encrusted fields, the soft pealing of bells and the bright red berries on the holly bushes in the ancient churchyard.

The Christmas carols were the same, the Christmas story centuries old, but over it all was the warmth of a people whose lives had suddenly become unsure. They had been so confidently sure of an unchanging world, the stability of a proud empire, a calm uncluttered way of life that had seemed indestructible, and now even among this rural congregation there were young men in uniform, and the threat of war from countries they had hardly read about.

They sang their carols, exchanged their greetings and after the last strains of the final carol ended the congregation moved out into the chill morning air. In mansion and cottage alike there would be Christmas meals, roasting chestnuts and decorated trees. Children would run around in excited delight showing off their new toys, and at the end of the day they would all agree that there surely couldn't be anything to worry about; nothing would change. Next year, another year, it would all be the same.

At Hazelmere the servants served hot toddies and hot mince pies, and then they all congregated round the giant tree to open their presents.

There seemed so many of them, and Lisa looked down somewhat doubtfully at the gaily wrapped parcels around her feet before Dominic placed a small package in her hand saying, 'It wasn't with the others, Lisa. This is from me.'

She smiled at him uncertainly before giving her full attention to the opening of the parcel. Inside it was a long velvet box and on opening it she found a long gold chain adorned with a large, beautiful emerald and long emerald earrings.

She looked up at him with startled surprise. 'It's beautiful,' she said. 'I love emeralds.'

'Of course,' he replied, 'they are the colour of your eyes.'

It was beautiful and romantic, and as the other guests enthused over his gift they must have thought so also.

That evening she wore his gift and there were those present who thought she had never seemed more beautiful with the exquisite stones gleaming under the lamplight, and her green eyes in which they found their reflection had never seemed more wonderful.

Throughout the evening other guests enthused over the perfection of the gleaming jewels and the deep love that had prompted the gift; through it all Lisa could only think that it was a lie.

She sensed the undercurrents around the table as they sat down to dinner—the gratification of Dominic's parents, the nervousness of her mother and the cynicism of the Jarvison-Noelles. Through it all her husband's charm never wavered, and it seemed that only his brother brought an air of normality to the proceedings.

Austin chattered on about the state of the country and the outcome of hostilities until his father said sharply, 'We'll have no more talk of war this evening, Austin, this is Christmas Day. Can't we forget it for one night?'

'You can forget it, Father—I'm going back to it.'

'You're going back to talk and more talk. It will all come to nothing and you'll be back here before we're ready for you.'

'I was talking to Anthony Pierce outside church this morning. He's in the same lot as Oliver Cardew; their preparations are well ahead of ours, he tells me.'

His father fixed him with a stern look but it was Dominic who said, 'What sort of preparations?'

'Well, they're talking of moving them out to France very soon.'

'A precaution,' snapped his father.

'I don't think so, Father. The Army are already commandeering horses from whatever sources they can find them—don't expect to keep yours for much longer.'

'That's rubbish. What good will our sort of horses be to the forces?'

'A horse is a horse, Father. It can pull things men cannot pull; it can carry men into battle. You mark my words—you can say goodbye to your horses in the immediate future.'

Furiously his father said, 'We'll have no more of this.

Can't you see you're spoiling our evening, the evening your mother's looked forward to and made such plans for? If the war comes it comes, but for tonight at least we'll have no more of it.'

People were laughing and chatting, but their laughter was largely to cover up the trauma underneath, and looking at Dominic's face Lisa saw only a grave and deep anxiety.

That night when the house was quiet and Lisa lay unsleeping she listened fearfully to the sounds from the dressing room next door. Drawers opening and closing, the drawing back of curtains, and finally the opening and closing of the dressing-room door. Dominic was unable to sleep and had gone downstairs.

After several minutes she got out of bed and shrugging her arms into her dressing gown she opened her door quietly and crept downstairs. Dimly from across the hall she could see a light in the library and went cautiously to stare through the door.

Dominic was sitting looking into the dying embers of the fire, his expression desolate, his entire appearance one of acute despair.

She wanted to go to him, to comfort him, just as she might have comforted any other human being in the depths of such utter misery, but she could not go to Dominic. He was her husband, but wasn't she largely responsible for so much of his misery, mainly the fact that she was his wife.

Slowly she crept back to her room, but it was several hours before she heard the closing of the dressing-room door.

Both Lisa and Dominic arrived at the breakfast table heavy-eyed and lethargic, so much so that her father-in-law said sharply, 'You both look as though you're sickening for something. There's influenza about, so don't say one of you has it.'

Dominic looked at her curiously, but she gave her full attention to the act of pouring orange juice and coffee at the breakfast bar.

Her mother relieved the situation by saying, 'I shall walk home after breakfast, dear, as I have to see to the animals—poor darlings, they'll wonder if they've been deserted.'

'I'll run you home, Mary,' Dominic said. He had always called her mother Mary, and somehow it had always seemed right.

'Oh you don't need to do that, dear, I like to walk,' she replied.

'It's icy on the paths outside,' Dominic said adamantly, 'and we don't want you falling.'

'I have the right sort of footwear for the walk,' she insisted, and with that Dominic decided to let her have her way.

'I hope you'll return later in the afternoon,' Lady Hazelmere said quickly. 'The holiday isn't over until tomorrow.'

Before Mary could answer, however, Sybil said,

'Well, we're also thinking we might drive home this afternoon, Lucy. The weather is deteriorating; I think it's going to snow. What do you all say?'

Before any of them could reply Austin said, 'Well, isn't this what we all hoped for, a white Christmas, something we can remember when we're saving the world? Let the older members sit in the drawing room before a glowing fire while the younger element get the sledges out. It'll be glorious up there on the Downs. Who is in agreement?'

It appeared that most of them were in agreement and the older people had little chance of changing their minds. Consequently after lunch, under a threatening sky and falling snow, they set out to enjoy what was left of the day.

'You shouldn't go,' Lucy admonished Lisa. 'Think about the baby; we don't want you catching cold and you looked decidedly peaky over breakfast this morning.'

Anything was preferable to sitting with the older element, Lisa thought, so she said with a smile, 'I don't intend to be too adventurous but I think I would benefit from some fresh air.'

'Oh well, Dominic will be there. He'll look after you.'

It was exhilarating on the Downs with the falling snow and the keen wind that blew the dry snow into drifts of shimmering white. There was laughter and foolishness, the fading illusion of joy that for one brief afternoon brought forgetfulness.

Looking back over that Christmas it was the thing

Lisa remembered most, not the tinsel-decorated tree and stately rooms, not the silken dresses or the sparkle of jewels, but the snow falling from leaden skies and laughter.

For that one brief afternoon she had seen Dominic laughing with his brother as they swept down the hillside to land in a boisterous heap in a mound of snow, and then they were all laughing again as they forgot their hurts and heartaches, and even the approaching threat of war.

Book Two

CHAPTER TWENTY

LISA STOOD IN HER MOTHER'S garden looking anxiously down the road towards the church. She seldom found her mother at home these days, and Antony, her small son, was tugging at her skirt, anxious to be away.

'Darling, we have to wait for Grandma,' she said softly, 'she won't be long.'

Antony was almost three years old; christened John Roger Antony he was a beautiful happy child, and although Dominic's parents saw little resemblance to his father in the child, they cared very deeply for him.

They thought he was too Spanish, too much like Lisa and the grandmother they had tried to ignore. Lisa never thought of the boy's Spanish father—he had been unimportant in her life and his memory had long since faded.

For almost three years the war had raged in Europe and there seemed no end to it. Young men were being slaughtered in the trenches and Dominic had been away for all of two years. The last time Lisa had seen him was soon after he joined the Yeomanry, handsome in his officer's uniform, and somehow distant. He had looked at her son with kind affection but little else; if he was spared she knew he would be a good, kind father to the boy but she could not tell if he would ever be able to love him.

Occasionally letters would arrive from him, but they told her little and she felt she was living in a quagmire she could never escape from.

Martindale was now a nursing home for wounded soldiers; Dominic had allowed the government to commandeer it as such and she never went there. The horses had all gone, both from Martindale and Hazelmere, and only the pony that pulled the small trap was left.

Hazelmere too was different. Soon after Martindale had been taken over Lady Hazelmere had decided that the East Wing would make an admirable nursing home. It was her contribution to the war effort, and confiding in Lisa she said, 'God will take care of my sons; after all, I am doing all I can to repay Him.'

Lucy invited the villagers up to the Hall, where they sat in a group knitting sweaters, gloves and scarves. They made biscuits and cakes for the Red Cross and at dusk they returned to their homes across the frozen fields to spend their evenings talking to each other about the day's events.

Lisa had to go back soon, as later that afternoon a new influx of young officers was arriving and Lucy had stipulated that they should both be there to receive them.

Lord Hazelmere had said somewhat tetchily, 'I don't see why you find it necessary to welcome them, Lucy, there is a perfectly good matron and a bevy of nurses.'

'It is necessary, Johnny,' she'd replied. 'This is our home they are coming to, and I do try to walk around the wards and chat to as many of them as I can. I write letters for them and I take them books. I know I don't do any nursing but I can cheer them up with other things, just as Lisa does.'

Johnny had known it was no use trying to argue with his wife—the East Wing was her resolve. War had taken her two sons and this was her promise to God in exchange for their safety.

Sybil came several days to help with whatever was being done but in retrospect she really came to gossip and Lisa was wary of her questions.

Antony tugged again at her skirt and pointed down the road to where she could see her mother in the company of the new vicar. Antony ran down the road to his grandmother and immediately the vicar picked him up and hoisted him onto his shoulder. Lisa hardly knew him. The younger vicar of St Mary's had joined the Army as a padre soon after the war started and the Reverend Blanchard had taken his place.

He was a tall, well-made man with silver hair and a nice face. He had made himself very popular with his congregation and, it would seem, particularly with Lisa's mother.

'Oh darling, I'm sorry I'm so late,' Mary said embracing her. We've been gathering holly and doing a little to decorate the church. Have you been waiting long? Do come along in and we'll have tea.'

'No, Mother, there isn't time, but I'll come again later

in the week. We have a new influx of wounded soldiers in today. I promised I'd be back to receive them.'

'Mr Blanchard kindly offered to walk to the house with me. Do be careful on the way back, dear, the roads are a little icy.'

'I'll be careful, Mother, but Jenny is very sure-footed.'

'If there's anything I can do up at the Hall, Lisa, you will tell me,' her mother said anxiously.

Lisa smiled, and the vicar said, 'Your son is very like you, Lady Lexican. I haven't met your husband.'

'He's not like Dominic at all,' Mary said. 'He's going to grow up into a real Spanish grandee.'

'I'd prefer an English gentleman, Mother,' Lisa said evenly.

'I know, dear. Mr Blanchard doesn't know anything about our family history. You'll come in for tea, vicar?'

'Thank you Mrs Foreshaw, that is very kind.'

They stood together to watch Lisa drive away and on the way back to Hazelmere Lisa began to ask herself how involved her mother had become with the vicar.

Mary was a pretty woman, young enough to want more from life than a lonely existence in a house that was far too large for her; and she believed the vicar was a widower.

As she drove up the long drive to the front of the Hall she was already aware that several trucks and ambulances were standing outside the entrance to the East Wing. Urging the pony on she pulled her up outside the main door and lifting Antony down she hurried inside.

Lucy met her in the Hall, faintly agitated as she always was when new arrivals were expected, and saying sharply, 'You're late, Lisa, I thought you'd forgotten.'

'No, I'm sorry, my mother was out; we waited for her to come back.'

'Oh well, leave the boy with his nanny and we'll go in there together. Leave your coat on that chair; one of the servants will move it; and do straighten your hair, dear, it's become windblown.'

Lucy marched on ahead and Lisa followed wishing with all her heart that the ceremony would be over soon. She was cold, and it really was completely unnecessary that both she and her mother-in-law should be part of a welcoming committee.

The nurses stood in a long row near the door, and the matron came forward to meet them. She was a large woman in a voluminous white uniform and a large headdress covering her white hair. They took their place next to her in front of the nurses and then the butler opened the door and the men trooped in.

They were the usual contingent of men in dusty khaki, most of them carrying walking sticks, their limbs either plastered or bandaged; a few of them had head wounds.

Some of them came in with hardly a glance at their opulent surroundings, whilst others stood in some degree of awe. Lucy enjoyed the ceremony but Lisa was convinced most of the men would have preferred to go immediately to their rooms. They had travelled some way and many of them were either in acute pain or very weary.

The welcoming ceremony over at last the men were

shown upstairs to their dormitories and Lisa went in search of Antony. He was in her bedroom watching the ambulances leaving and she went to stand beside him in time to see a large staff car coming towards the house.

Staff cars usually conveyed senior officers, either to inspect the East Wing or to bring an officer who had sustained injuries, and she watched curiously as the driver went to open the door so that a man carrying two walking sticks could climb out.

For several minutes he stood looking up at the house before he limped painfully towards the steps and the driver followed in order to reassure himself that the officer was capable of climbing the steps unaided. Underneath her window he paused, leaning heavily on his sticks, then he looked up as if he knew he was being observed.

Their eyes met, and in that one breathless moment she felt that his was a face she had known always and yet she knew they had never met before. He was tall, and under his peaked officer's cap his face was bronzed, his chiselled features wracked with pain, and yet she was strangely aware that underneath the pain there was serenity. He smiled before walking on towards the East Wing.

It was later that she learned from her mother-in-law that his name was Lieutenant-Colonel Adrian Lawson.

'We've put Lieutenant-Colonel Lawson in the Green Room which was always such a favourite with many of our guests,' Lucy said. 'He was quite adamant that he wanted no special treatment but he is a very senior officer so that has to be respected.

'We must prevent Antony running wild in the men's

quarters, Lisa. I know they make an awful fuss of him but they are here to recuperate and children can be so disruptive.'

'I rather think they enjoyed his company when they were feeling much better,' Lisa said evenly. 'He's very proud of the boat that young corporal made for him.'

'I know, dear, but we must keep our distance. We are family; they are merely our guests until it's time for them to leave.'

Lisa was accustomed to her mother-in-law's strictures on how the family should behave towards the wounded soldiers. One day they were part of a welcoming committee, the next they kept their distance, and then on another day when Lucy felt she should be more involved with their progress she suggested visiting them and offering to write letters for them.

Antony looked plaintively at the closed doors leading to the East Wing. Behind those doors were young men who would be kind to him, laugh with him and make toys for him; now Grandma was being difficult, telling his nanny to make sure he stayed away from that part of the house where he had found such friendship.

It was over dinner that Lucy raised the question of her mother's friendship with the new vicar.

'It would be a very good thing for her, Lisa. He's very well thought of according to the villagers, and she has been a widow for some time now. How do you feel about it?'

'My mother hasn't discussed him with me,' she replied tersely.

'Well, perhaps you should discuss it with her, dear. She's probably a little diffident about saying too much in case you feel she isn't being fair to the memory of your father. She was always a very good and loyal wife to Roger; now she has to move on. You surely wouldn't offer any objections?'

'No. I wouldn't interfere in my mother's life.'

'You like him, don't you?'

'I really don't know him; it would be enough for my mother to like him.'

'Of course. I must have a word with Matron to make sure Lieutenant-Colonel Lawson is comfortable in the Green Room. He's Indian Army, I believe. How strange to be serving in France in those rain-soaked trenches so far away from India's sunshine.'

'Do you know anything else about him?' Lisa asked.

'No. I don't know if he's married or if he has family in this country. No doubt we'll find out more during the next few days.'

Her husband took very little part in his wife's preoccupation with her military guests. He hadn't been keen to turn half his house into a nursing home as he didn't think it was necessary—after all they had Martindale, what more did they want?

Lisa was aware that he viewed her son with cynical detachment. The boy was nothing like his father, he was too Spanish, and he couldn't resist the sneaking feeling that Dominic was not the boy's father—after all Lisa had been left to her own devices in Seville and could have taken up with anybody.

He remained unconvinced that they were a normal couple, and if he was right he couldn't really blame her for seeking consolation elsewhere. At the same time family pride made him look at Antony with some degree of distrust.

One afternoon the villagers were sitting at the table in the vast drawing room with their knitting and sewing, while others worked with the kitchen staff preparing food to fill the large baskets waiting on the tables. Lisa sat with them in the drawing room listening to their views on life in general. Most of them were middle aged or considerably older since the younger members had left to work on munitions or on the land.

She was cold. The meagre fire in the grate hardly reached the outer limits of the room, and invariably they sat with shawls round their necks, many of them with fingers red and swollen from chilblains.

Halfway through the afternoon a servant came in with tea and with her came Antony's very agitated nursemaid.

'Master Antony has gone into the East Wing, Milady,' she said anxiously, 'I called to him but he wouldn't listen, and I didn't think I should go in there after him.'

The villagers smiled, and Lucy said sharply, 'Really, I did warn you about this. Why weren't you looking after him, Hannah?'

'Well, I was, Milady, but he's been determined to get in there. The young men who were here before made such a fuss of him. Have I your permission to go in there and get him?'

'No, his mother will go; you will apologise to the matron, and assure her that he will not go there again, Lisa, and make sure that you are displeased with him.'

Lisa was glad to have something else to do. How was it possible to put such strictures on the shoulders of a young child?

The matron was not in her office, but meeting a young nurse outside she asked if she had seen Antony. Smiling, the nurse said, 'I've only just come on duty, Milady, sure and the boy isn't doin' any harm though.'

'No, I'm sure he isn't but Lady Hazelmere doesn't want him here, I'll look around for him.'

'Well, if I see him, Milady, I'll tell him his mother's looking for him. Sure and ye can't blame the young lad for displayin' some curiosity; after all it can't be much fun for him sitting in there with the villagers.'

Lisa smiled. 'No, but he doesn't sit with the villagers, and his nurse is finding him more than a handful.'

The nurse smiled and hurried away when she heard the matron's voice in one of the rooms.

After opening one or two doors and being met with wide-eyed stares from the men in there and some of the nurses, she found no trace of her son, and it was only when she walked up the wide shallow staircase to the rooms above that she heard his voice, his laughter and the deeper tones of a man's voice.

He had found his way to the larger rooms on the first floor, rooms that overlooked the vast parkland and which were given over to the doctors and senior officers and as she crossed the hall she called to him, but received no response.

Again she heard his laughter so she knew immediately that it came from the Green Room and she saw that the door was open; as she pushed it open wider she saw that her son knelt by the chair in the window which was occupied by the lieutenant-colonel who looked across the room and smiled.

'Antony, what are you doing here?' she scolded him. 'I told you you must not come into this part of the house.'

Uncontrite, the boy looked at her with a bright smile and she saw that in his hands was the wooden boat he was so proud of. The lieutenant-colonel said, 'He tells me one of the men made this for him, and very good it is too. Please don't scold him, he's been keeping me company.'

'Oh but really, you need to rest, I'll take him back with me. I don't want Matron thinking I'm upsetting her regime.'

'Please don't worry; I'll tell Matron that he's done me a power of good. Is he your son?'

'Yes, his name is Antony.'

'He's very like you. I am Adrian Lawson, and you are?'

'Lisa, Lady Lexican.'

'Lady Hazelmere's daughter-in-law.'

'Yes, my husband is in France.'

'You live here?'

'Temporarily. Our house is a nursing home like this one, but we have given it over to the War Office in its entirety until the war is over.'

'Very generous, Lady Lexican.'

'I hope you're very comfortable here. Is there anything else you need? If so please don't hesitate to ask.'

'Thank you. I'm hoping to get back into harness after a few weeks so that I can return to the front. Perhaps you'll allow this young man to visit me from time to time. The loneliness is the worst, you know—perhaps you would condescend to call to chat to me.'

Lisa smiled.

'If Matron doesn't object, Lieutenant-Colonel,' she said gently.

'Oh, bother Matron. I doubt if she has the time to chat and you'd probably be doing us both a favour.'

'I'll consult with my mother-in-law,' Lisa said, and he laughed.

'She's that sort of mother-in-law is she?'

'I'm afraid so.'

'Oh well, we can leave the door open to reassure her that everything is most circumspect. While I'm bandaged and plastered it could hardly be anything other.'

His smile was engaging in his bronzed, handsome face and for the second time she was strangely aware of the attraction she felt for this man who was nothing more than a stranger.

She had loved Dominic with a young girl's first intensity but it had been something that had grown and blossomed, not this blinding sudden attraction that seemed both blissful and senseless.

She took Antony by the hand and led him towards the door, then once more their eyes met and he smiled, a smile that she would not forget.

At that moment she felt she was looking at him for

the last time, but as she made her way back to the West
Wing she was acutely aware of an impulsive urge to see
him again. What harm would it do? The men were
lonely; it wasn't enough to see to their wounds. They
wanted sympathy, tenderness, and she could see no hint
of danger in that.

CHAPTER TWENTY-ONE

LUCY SCOLDED HER GRANDSON and told him that he must not go into the East Wing again; the child sulked a little before he ran off to his nursery holding his wooden boat aloft.

'Really,' Lucy grumbled. 'I doubt if Hannah is able to control him—he should have somebody older.'

'He's a child,' Lisa said. 'If he did everything he was told I'd think there was something wrong with him.'

'Well, his father was always most obedient, but Austin wasn't. Perhaps he's more like Austin. Where did you find him?'

'He was in the lieutenant-colonel's room. We chatted for a while. He said the worst thing about all this is the loneliness. They need companionship, and the lieutenant-colonel is on his own up there. I think he enjoyed talking to Antony.'

'Oh well, perhaps I'll chat to him occasionally; perhaps he would like you to write letters for him; that would help.'

'He didn't mention letters, simply conversation.'

'I'm not sure, Lisa. These man are lonely, many of them are married; why put temptation in their way?'

She walked away and Lisa's eyes followed her. Temptation! Men who were absent from their wives and sweethearts, but who were sick and wounded and under the stern eyes of a matron and numerous nurses. Oh yes, there could be temptation, but in just a short time they would move on to be replaced by others similarly handicapped.

A few days, a few weeks perhaps, not long enough for temptation to take the place of sympathy and consideration. What harm was there in writing letters for men who couldn't see, or talking to men whose wives were far away? Then she remembered his smile, the appeal in his dark eyes, the blinding attraction that had set her heart racing uncontrollably.

On the days when Lucy and her cousin Sybil sat cossetted in the warmth of the morning room Lisa invariably went to see her mother. She still had the urge to address Mrs Jarvison-Noelle as Ma'am, and she believed Sybil still looked upon her as the difficult, rebellious child who had tramped up the long drive to receive an education.

What did they talk about during those mornings? Like her mother-in-law, Sybil was none too happy with Antony's resemblance to his mother rather than Dominic, and she knew that his appearance would be discussed from time to time. Now there was her mother's friendship with the vicar.

Fewer of the rooms were used these days because of the heating situation, and one morning she had overheard them discussing her mother while she sat in the study writing letters.

'Suppose Mary decides to marry the vicar,' Sybil said. 'People are talking about their friendship—do you think it would be a wise thing to do?'

'I'm not sure. I suppose if she does marry him she'll move into the vicarage, which is a large draughty old house. They couldn't really stay in Aunt Jane's house as it's some distance from the church and the parishioners would have something to say about it.'

'What does Lisa say about it?'

'Very little. I always thought we would be such good friends after all I've done for her and her mother, but I never seem to get through to her.'

'I suppose she's missing Dominic—women all over the country are missing their husbands.'

'She rarely mentions him. I think she's bored. The horses have gone, she helps when the villagers come here, but most of the time she's in a world of her own. I've suggested that she tries to get involved with some of the wounded, listen to their problems, write letters for the men who are unable to write and generally be a little sympathetic—after all she has a husband in the Army. It would be nice to think he was able to rely on similar generosity should he ever be in the same position as these men. Don't you agree?'

'I'm not sure. Men in these circumstances are very vulnerable and she is after all a very attractive woman.'

'They are also ill and in pain, Sybil. I think they are more interested in their recovery than the pursuit of a flirtation.'

'What had Lisa to say about it?'

'Very little really, but I'm sure she'll agree.'

'What sort of men are they?'

'War weary, young, apart from one or two older men, regular army types; then of course we have a lieutenant-colonel. He was wounded on the Somme and is desperate to get back into action.'

'And will he, do you think?'

'Oh yes, I'm sure he will. I haven't spoken to him for several days but I really must. He's quite charming, very good looking.'

'Is he married?'

'I don't know, and I really don't think I should ask personal questions unless he volunteers to tell me.'

'And is this one of the men you are suggesting Lisa chats to?'

'Well of course. She's a married woman with a child, married to my son. Lieutenant-Colonel Lawson will have every respect for her position, I feel sure.'

Lisa had heard enough. The more she got to know Lucy the more she began to realise that Lucy's world was one she had created. The perfect world of wealth and privilege where she could manipulate the people around her in the way she wanted them to go.

She had a husband who was content to allow her to do this just as long as she didn't involve him; when for one reason or another she did involve him he became taciturn and uncooperative and would invariably retreat into his study to sulk.

Lucy believed her world was inviolate, that she was

always right and in the case of her eldest son, hadn't she proved it? Lisa had the power to shatter that confidence but she could not be the one to do it; only Dominic had that power.

It was too cold to take Antony to see her mother and as she drove the pony and trap across the parkland flurries of snow swirled around her so that she was glad to drive into the sheltered stable yard and leave the pony in the capable hands of the young boy who looked after the garden.

Her mother came to greet her with a warm smile saying, 'Oh Lisa, I'm so glad you've come today; I thought perhaps that you wouldn't want to when it began to snow. Is everything well at Hazelmere?'

'Yes, Mother, Sybil is visiting.'

Her mother's face registered some confusion and Lisa said with a smile, 'You will be discussed, Mother—they talk about all and sundry but don't let it worry you.'

'It does worry me, darling. Do you know what they say?'

'They are naturally curious; I'm curious, Mother. Don't worry about them—is there anything you need to tell me?'

'Come into the sitting room, Lisa, and I'll ask Alice to make tea; we'll talk in there.'

She watched her mother's preoccupation with serving afternoon tea while inside she screamed at her to talk. That her mother was embarrassed she was well aware, but Mary was not to be hurried as she asked about Antony and the wounded soldiers who had arrived days before.

'The Reverend Blanchard visits them,' Mary informed her. 'They have morning service and he comforts them. He tells me the matron and nurses are excellent and so is the accommodation. Knowing Lucy, how could it be otherwise?'

'Tell me about the Reverend Blanchard, Mother. I know that he visits you; I believe you like him very much but that is all I know. Is there more?'

She looked at her mother's blushing face, heard her quick intake of breath, saw the trembling of her hands, and then her mother said quickly, 'Oh Lisa, I really don't know. I'm lonely here. I've always said the house was too big for me and I really don't feel I've any right here. I haven't enough to do. I sometimes go with the villagers to Hazelmere and do things at the church, but there's so much more I could do.'

'At the church do you mean?'

She nodded wordlessly.

'Things that you couldn't do here?' Lisa prompted her.

'Well yes. Richard is a nice man, a very good man, and he has so much to do for the church, the parishioners, the district, and he too is lonely in that vicarage on his own, just as I am lonely here.'

'What are you telling me, Mother?'

'He has asked me to marry him, Lisa.'

'And?'

'I haven't said I will. There's the family, this house, you. I'm forty-seven years old, Lisa. I was a good wife to your father and we were happy together, even though we never had much money. We tried to bring you up as well as we could, but then Sybil interfered and then Lucy.

'Oh, I knew they meant to be kind but I'd have been quite happy for just you and I to make our own niche in life until I realised that you had fallen in love with Dominic, then I knew what I wanted for us wasn't enough.

'I didn't think Dominic would marry you. I thought he would marry one of the girls from his own station in life but then Lucy made so much of you. She really liked you, Lisa, and wanted you for Dominic. Now, by marrying the vicar, I feel I shall hardly be in the right position as mother to the future Countess of Hazelmere.'

'Oh Mother, you haven't got to think like that. Marry the vicar if you love him, be happy and I shall be happy for you. It has nothing to do with your cousins and if they disapprove I shall tell them so.'

'I don't want there to be trouble between you and Lucy, Lisa.'

'There won't be, I promise.'

'What about this house?'

'Mother, you can't build your life around bricks and mortar. Like you said, you never wanted this house and now you have the opportunity to leave it. Go with Mr Blanchard to his vicarage and be happy. You'll be a splendid vicar's wife.'

'What will Dominic think?'

'Dominic is away at the war, Mother, and I don't know when I shall see him again. Dominic won't interfere in any case. Leave it to me to tell Lady Hazelmere.'

'Very well, dear, but do say what a good man he

is, how well respected he is, how popular he is with the bishop.'

'Mother, why should you care so much? It really doesn't matter what Dominic's parents think, it matters what you think.'

'I know, dear, but you know what they're like.'

Conversation usually flagged at the dining table. Lucy was concerned with her innumerable charities for the war effort, and Johnny was invariably glum thinking about his missing horses, the state of his investments and the disasters on the Western Front that seemed to be never-ending.

Lisa deemed it a good moment to tell them about her mother's decision to marry the vicar, a statement that was received with mixed reactions.

'Oh I really don't think that this is a good idea, Lisa, at this particular time,' Lucy said. 'Marriage is a big step to take at any time, but when one is settled into one's life why change things? I see nothing wrong in their friendship, it is nice for both of them, but marriage is something else.'

'Where will they live?' Johnny asked.

'I'm sure they will wish to live at the vicarage,' Lisa replied.

'So back we'll be with Aunt Jane's house standing empty. I told you, Lucy, that it wasn't a good idea to offer it to Mary. It was always too large for her, even when Lisa was still with her, and now it's going to be back on our hands.'

'Well, you never made an effort to dispose of it. Aunt

Jane was a spinster who lived there with a horde of servants; she never complained.'

'Mary couldn't afford a horde of servants.'

'Well, I really don't think marrying the local vicar is the answer. One day you'll be installed here, Lisa, and it's hardly a good idea to have your mother installed in the vicarage.'

'I don't see the problem,' Lisa said.

'You'll be Lady Hazelmere—don't you think your mother should aspire to something better than the vicarage, or the vicar?'

'She's not aiming to marry the local dustman,' Johnny said acidly. 'Besides it's none of our business who she marries.'

Lucy favoured him with an exasperated look that spoke volumes and Lisa felt the utmost urge to burst into laughter. It was all so ridiculous and their comments brought back to her very vividly the sort of conversation she'd heard over the years.

Silence descended on the dinner table for some time until Lucy said sharply, 'I think it might be a good idea to invite Lieutenant-Colonel Lawson to dine with us one evening. I intend to ask him in the morning.'

'Why, for heaven's sake?' her husband asked.

'I find him charming. I was talking to him this morning in the park where he was walking to exercise his legs. I'm sure he's very lonely. The other men have companionship, but because of his rank he's alone. I simply think it would be a very nice gesture on our behalf. What do you think, Lisa?'

'I have only spoken to him for a short while.'

'I know, dear, but he's very cultured and I'm sure he would be a very interesting man. He's lived in India for many years and none of us have been there. His conversation at least will make a nice change from the long silences I've been subjected to.'

'Please yourself,' Johnny said sharply.

'Oh I shall. Perhaps in the morning, Lisa, you would call to see him and issue my invitation; find out what sort of food he likes, although perhaps that isn't such a good idea since we're very much at the mercy of what the butcher sends round to the kitchens. I'm sure he won't mind what we have, but I do think he might enjoy a chance of scenery and a little company.'

'I thought you'd decided not to get involved with any of the wounded heroes. Why this sudden change of heart?'

'I simply want to invite the lieutenant-colonel. Besides, we have two sons in the Army—I would like to think some kind person would do the same thing for either or both of them.'

Johnny realised he had lost the argument, and as soon as dinner was over he said tersely, 'I don't want coffee. I'm expecting the Estate Agent round; we'll have drinks in the study. What did Sybil want? She was here most of the afternoon.'

'We simply chatted about this and that.'

'And I suppose you discussed Lisa's mother and Aunt Jane's house.'

'I might have mentioned it. We didn't labour on it.'

'Well, if she marries him it'll be a nine-day wonder; there's more important matters occupying the country these days than the marriage of Lisa's mother to the local vicar.'

They watched him stomping across the room and after he had closed the door behind him Lucy said dolefully, 'Really, Lisa, he really is a most exasperating man. I hope he takes the trouble to be gracious to our dinner guest tomorrow evening. I know he can be when he sets his mind to it but he can be difficult. Perhaps we should invite Sybil and her husband; what do you think?'

'And my mother and the vicar perhaps,' Lisa said with a wry smile, a comment that Lucy received with her most disdainful smile.

Lisa was more concerned as to whether the lieutenant-colonel would accept the invitation. She wanted to meet him again; he was attractive—there had been that one blinding moment when their eyes had met and she had felt a sudden rush of feeling which of course must be ridiculous. They knew nothing of each other; he was simply a man like so many others who had arrived at Hazelmere to be cared for, and yet she had not felt this sudden heart-stopping warmth for any of the others.

She distrusted her feelings. She was a woman alone with a husband at the war, but a husband who was different, a man who could never be what she wanted him to be. Wasn't she wide open to danger? Weren't her needs greater because the love she craved could never be hers?

She would take Antony with her and they would talk about banalities. She would show him that she was a proud wife and mother bringing him a dinner invitation from her mother-in-law, entirely innocent, while in her heart she longed for him to accept so that she would see him again.

There was danger for her in their meeting, but perhaps not for him; after all, what did she know of him? Somewhere there could be a wife, a fiancée, some woman he was in love with; tomorrow he might talk about his life, his family. If he had a family she would have to listen to him talking about them, and when their eyes met she knew her foolish heart would race and perhaps even he would be aware of the attraction she felt for him.

For the first time in months she thought about Antony's Spanish father and that wild, foolish, madcap affair that had produced a son, although she had looked upon it as nothing more than revenge. She had not been looking for love, and all it had ever been was passion, lust—now her need was for love.

As she lay sleepless she was wishing with all her heart that she was like other women whose husbands were serving their country but were longing for their homecoming, hoping that the war would soon be over.

Those women would be looking forward to real love between them, not polite friendship which was all she could expect from Dominic.

Was that really what the rest of her life would be like? Was that all there would ever be?

CHAPTER TWENTY-TWO

ADRIAN STOOD AT THE WINDOW of his room watching Lisa and her son walking across the terrace towards the gardens. She had delivered Lady Hazelmere's invitation to dine with the family and of course he had accepted with grateful thanks. He had listened to the child's chattering with a tender smile and Lisa had said, 'I hope Antony hasn't been bothering you, but he does like to talk to the men and some of them who have children of their own enjoy his company.'

'Yes I'm sure they do,' he'd replied.

'Do you have a family?' she asked.

'Parents. My father's a general as was my grandfather. We are army motivated you might say. My parents are in India now.'

She had smiled politely and left him taking the boy with her.

Why hadn't he told her about Catherine? Catherine who he had known since childhood; Catherine whose father was a general and who had been earmarked for far too many years as suitable material for an ambitious young officer. Promotion had been rapid for Adrian and always Catherine had been there—regimental balls and polo matches, holidays in Kashmir and mule rides through the mountain passes of Nepal. She was beautiful, gracious, loved by both his parents and very dear to him.

They had all hoped he and Catherine would marry before he left for England but some strange whim had told him they must wait—he could be killed in action and would worry about her if she was his wife far more than if she was simply his fiancée, so they had agreed to get engaged after the war and he had seen her eyes fill with tears as they had said their farewells on that last evening together. Catherine loved him, he had believed he loved her but so many things had convinced him of the littleness of love.

He had seen men he had known for years slaughtered in rat-filled trenches, or suffer the excruciating pain of wounds. He wondered in his heart if there would ever be an end to it. Now he had no doubt that during the evening ahead polite questions would be asked about his life in India.

They had reached the gardens now and he watched Antony running ahead wrapped up warmly against the wind, while Lisa chased after him, laughing as she swept him up into her arms.

He was so like his mother with her raven hair and strangely exotic beauty. The child's eyes were brown, however, but he was remembering the green of his mother's eyes, like pieces of chipped jade.

It was stupid and illogical, that first blinding attraction he had felt for her. He didn't know her, only what she looked like. He didn't know if she was kind and intelligent, if she truly loved the child's father or if it had been a marriage of convenience as so many aristocratic marriages were; somehow behind her smile there was sadness and a hint of regret, and there was something else, the same sort of awareness he felt for her.

A servant escorted him to the drawing room in the West Wing where the family were assembled, Lord and Lady Hazelmere, Mr and Mrs Jarvison-Noelle and Lady Lexican. They drank sherry and discussed the latest war news. They were sympathetic about his injuries and hoped he was recovering well; Lord Hazelmere anxiously made enquiries about the welfare of the horses on the Western Front.

'You are missing your horses?' Adrian said thoughtfully.

'I am. I had a nasty fall so I don't suppose I'm much up to riding these days, but all we've got is the pony that pulls the trap and I'm surprised they haven't asked for him too.'

Adrian smiled. 'Your son is in the Yeomanry, I believe.'

'Dominic is in the Yeomanry; Austin is in the Artillery. God knows where they are at this moment.'

Across the room his eyes met Lisa's and seeing the look that passed between them Lady Hazelmere said quickly, 'Lisa is missing Dominic terribly. It is so hard for their child to grow up without his father, but this is happening in all too many families. Do you have a family, lieutenant-colonel?'

'Parents. I'm not married.'

'Sensible precaution, eh,' Lord Hazelmere said. 'Plenty of time for the other stuff when this rumpus is over.'

'Any more news about your mother, Lisa?' Mrs Jarvison-Noelle asked pointedly.

With a small smile Lisa said, 'I've no doubt my mother will keep everybody informed.' Then turning to Adrian she said, 'My mother is a widow but she is friendly with the local vicar. I'm sure she will keep everybody informed on whatever they decide.'

'Does she live locally?' Adrian asked.

'In the large manor house at the other side of the village,' Lord Hazelmere said. 'It was my Aunt Jane's house and if she decides to marry Blanchard it will be back in our hands.'

'It's never been really off your hands,' Mrs Jarvison-Noelle said sweetly. 'I've always considered it far too big for Mary; no doubt she'll be far happier in the church vicarage.'

'Lisa's mother is our cousin,' Lady Hazelmere explained. 'We've always looked after her; isn't that so, Lisa?'

Lisa merely favoured her with a small smile and at that moment the butler announced that dinner would be served in the dining room.

They dined well as Adrian knew they would, the madeira flowed freely and the brandy, but what did they talk about for most of the evening? When he later returned to his room he had difficulty in remembering since all he could remember was Lisa sitting opposite him dressed in midnight-blue chiffon, with the gleam of diamonds round her throat and in her ears. The ladies had dressed for the occasion, and Lord Hazelmere said, well mellowed after the wine, 'Well, lieutenant-colonel, the ladies thought they should dress up for you and I was instructed to wear my monkey suit. I don't think any of them realised your dress uniform would be put aside in mothballs until after the war.'

'Put away in mothballs in distant Delhi,' Adrian said with a smile, 'but I admire the ladies for dressing up; it is a reminder of more gracious days which I hope will one day return.'

It was almost midnight when he asked to be excused on the grounds of still needing to rest, and quickly Lord Hazelmere said, 'Well of course, it's late and these ladies would chat forever. I'll get one of the servants to take you back to your room.'

'Really, Lord Hazelmere, there's no need. I'm quite capable of finding my own way there. Thank you so much for a delightful evening; it was most kind of you to invite me.'

'Oh we must do it again, and soon,' his wife said graciously. 'Lisa darling, why don't you take our guest to the door leading into the East Wing; the lighting isn't so good as we have to cut down on it like everybody else.'

Before Lisa could comply, however, Mr Jarvison-

Noelle said, 'I'll escort the lieutenant-colonel, Johnny, I know the layout.'

After they had left the room Lord Hazelmere said dryly, 'That was a better idea, my dear, perhaps you hadn't noticed that the officer is a very attractive man. We don't want our daughter-in-law falling for his charms, do we. It's the sort of thing that happens to women when their husbands are away.'

Lucy favoured him with a frown of disapproval while Sybil smiled cynically—not even Lisa's son had convinced her of Dominic's sexuality. Lisa merely smiled politely, said she was tired and would retire for the night.

As she bade them goodnight Sybil said pointedly, 'Do try to find out exactly what your mother intends to do in the near future, Lisa. People are beginning to talk. It is understandable, I think, a man on his own and a parishioner who is available.'

'Available?' Lisa asked coldly.

'Well, you know what I mean, dear. A widow in too large a house, particularly a widow connected to the family; it's bound to give rise to talk.'

Lisa once more murmured her goodnight before closing the door behind her.

Back in his room the lieutenant-colonel reflected on the evening he had spent with his hosts but it was Lisa who was the enigma.

In spite of her position within the family she seemed strangely ranged against them, whether it was because of her mother's involvement with the local vicar or some other reason he couldn't fathom.

Surely her mother was old enough and wise enough to plan her own future. Lisa was beautiful with a delightful child, and from what little he had heard about her husband he was both charming and well liked. So what was that indefinable something that made him see undercurrents in the life of a family that should be untroubled?

He admitted to himself he was attracted by her beauty, her singular reserve, and when their eyes met he saw the reciprocation of that attraction too. It was ridiculous, of course. As soon as he was well enough to leave Hazelmere he would be returning to the front and would never see Lisa Lexican again. If he was spared her husband would return to a life of wealth and privilege, his beautiful wife and son, and a close and well-knit family, while he would return to India, but for how long?

India was resolved in her fight for freedom from British rule and if she got it there would be no place for the Army in India, in which case he would have to rethink his life; and then there was Catherine.

The letters he received from her had been few, but they had been filled with love and sentimental imaginings of their future together; he resolved that his thoughts must not dwell on the desirability of Lisa but rather on the sterner aspects of the life to be.

His resolutions came to nothing when he met her the next morning in the gardens where he exercised when the weather was fine, and when she told him she had decided to visit her mother.

'Perhaps I'll walk with you a little way,' he said gently. 'Normally I just wander around here; it will do me good to walk a little further.'

'It isn't really very far,' she said with a smile. 'Just at the other side of the village, but if you grow tired you must come back.'

The route they took was further than he had previously walked, but as they chatted amicably together it didn't seem so. At last she pointed out her mother's house and he said in some surprise, 'It is a large house for a lady living alone.'

'Yes it is, and I do feel very responsible for that. I wanted to live there; mother always said it was too large.'

'Where did you live before?'

'When my father was alive we lived on the Jarvison-Noelle's estate; my father was the Estate Manager, but when he died Lady Hazelmere offered us Aunt Jane's house.'

'I see.'

He didn't see, but next moment Lisa said quickly, 'My mother and the two ladies you met last evening are cousins.'

'So they feel they should have a say in who she should marry?'

She laughed. 'I suppose they do. I hope my mother will please herself.'

Her mother greeted them with smiles of welcome, inviting them to eat lunch with her. Adrian, seeing them together, could only think how very different they were—Mary with her English colouring and Lisa, vibrant and strangely exotic.

He found her mother charming and gentle, asking questions on his recovery and if he found Hazelmere beautiful, and Lisa said, 'The lieutenant-colonel joined us for dinner last evening, Mother. The Jarvison-Noelles were also invited.'

Mary smiled. 'And I suppose they said something about the vicar and myself.' Then, smiling ruefully at Adrian, she went on to say, 'I am not sure I have their approval.'

'As a mature woman shouldn't you be asking yourself if you need it?' he replied.

She turned to Lisa to say, 'I hope you told them that, dear.'

'Yes, Mother, and perhaps a little more.'

'Are you sure you will be able to walk all the way back?' she asked gently. 'I can quite easily return for the trap and drive you back.'

'Oh no, I wouldn't hear of it. I've had a good rest here; I'm sure the walk will do me good. The sooner I get over these disabilities the sooner I can get back to our efforts to finish off this wretched war.'

Their eyes met and in hers for a split second he saw real pain, and something else, something he felt for her, that raw, incredible attraction that he had felt the first moment he saw her face.

As they walked back through the parkland the wintry sun was setting like a great red ball leaving the sky tinted rose against the dark conifers. They could see the deer sheltering under the distant trees, while the lake shone silver under its coating of ice. Shivering a little, Lisa said, 'Are you warm enough in your room up there, Adrian? If not do ask for more logs for your fire—fortunately we still have plenty of those.'

'I couldn't ask for anything better than I am receiving here, Lisa. I'm sure all the men are also most grateful for such kindness.'

'And I'm sure Lord Hazelmere invited you to read anything from the library; there are scores of sporting and field magazines, more serious reading too if you want it.'

'Thank you. I hope to take advantage of his offer.'

For several minutes there was silence then she said unexpectedly, 'More than anything I miss the horses. You ride, of course?'

'Yes. When the war is over you'll soon get back into the life you're missing.'

They parted on the terrace and taking her hand in his he said, 'I've enjoyed today, Lisa. I enjoyed meeting your mother, and having somebody to talk to; perhaps we can do it again soon.'

She nodded without speaking, and then she was walking away from him towards the door.

Somehow there was an inevitability about it—in her case a desperate need, in his a sort of dismay that he had become a part of this wild sweeping passion that consumed them both.

It had started that same evening after dinner when Lisa sat at the piano playing the Chopin she loved and Lucy had sat in front of the fire with her needlework. Over dinner they had discussed the usual news about the war, and Lisa had told them she had introduced the officer to her mother. Lucy had been quick to ask, 'And did your mother mention the vicar, Lisa?'

'Only in passing.'

'It was a fair way for him to walk,' her husband commented.

'He did very well; he said it was good exercise and he's anxious to get back to the front.'

'I think it's quite ridiculous to expect wounded men to get back into action before they're ready for it,' Lucy snapped. 'I'm so worried about the boys; why don't the letters get through?'

After dinner Lord Hazelmere said, 'I'm going to the study to write some letters. I'm fed up with the war, the weather and the winter.'

His wife had watched him go with a sigh. 'Really,' she complained, 'you'd think he was the only one affected; after all he's still waited on hand and foot—all he's missing are his horses and the race meetings. Oh, I know the house doesn't feel like his own any more but we're no different to many other families.'

Two hours later when he joined them again he seemed in a happier frame of mind when he said, 'I've been chatting to the lieutenant-colonel; he's in the library. We've been talking about India and home rule; they don't know when they're well off, but it's certainly on the cards. His life'll change; can't think he's looking forward to it.'

It was an evening like all the others—Lucy with her needlework, Johnny with his hot toddy and Lisa amusing herself in any way she pleased. Invariably they retired early but up in her room Lisa could look across towards the East Wing and Adrian's window in darkness. Making up her mind suddenly she went downstairs through the silent house in the direction of the library and found him there sitting in front of a blazing log fire. He rose to his feet but immediately she sensed his diffidence, the anxious uncertainty of a man who was afraid of his own feelings.

She didn't know what to say. She needed an excuse as to why she had gone into the library but his expression did nothing to help her, so after a swift smile she moved quickly to the table and started to sift through the magazines lying on top of it. She knew he was watching her, and in desperation she picked up one of the magazines and moved towards the door while he moved forward to open it for her. Their eyes met, and she said quickly, 'I'm sorry to have intruded, I have found what I was looking for.'

He turned to switch off the lights saying, 'I was about to retire. I'm afraid books are no substitute for reality.'

'You did not find what you were looking for?'

'Nothing in particular; simply a means to pass the time.'

'I know. I feel like that sometimes, that I am simply waiting but I'm not sure what I'm waiting for. You're anxious to get back to your men.'

'I seem to be recovering far too slowly.'

'But surely they will not send you back until you are well enough.'

He shrugged his shoulders, and after a few moments said, 'I see some of the men going back every day; none of them seem ready for it. One day sooner rather than later I hope it will be my turn.'

She smiled and wished him goodnight, but she was aware as she walked away from him that his eyes followed her although she willed herself not to look back.

In the days that followed, Lucy's insistence on inviting him to dinner meant that they were constantly in each other's company, but they were occasions that filled Adrian with unease. More and more the fascination for Lisa grew, but it was more than the normal attraction a man could expect to find for a young beautiful woman. It was the fact that she was something of an enigma and he sensed behind her politeness, her position within the family, a barrier that set her apart from the Hazelmeres, their relatives and even from her own mother; that somehow behind the gracious smiles and quiet serenity there were undercurrents only she was aware of.

He began to avoid her in the park, waiting until she was out of sight before he ventured out for his daily exercise. His feelings for her troubled him and added to his reasons for a swift return to the front, but it was one day more than any other that made it inevitable that they should meet.

He had walked behind the house through the narrow

paths that edged the river, knowing that she had driven across the park to see her mother and that their paths that morning were unlikely to cross; it was when he returned to the terrace that he saw her walking quickly towards him from the stables. She seemed agitated and against all his better judgement he went to meet her. Aware of the anxiety in her eyes he said quickly, 'Is something wrong, Lisa?'

She nodded. 'I'm afraid so. I saw the messenger walking away from the house.'

'The messenger?'

'Yes, the telegraph boy. Oh, please will you come with me; I'm so afraid that he has brought us bad news.'

The telegraph boy was not an uncommon sight in towns and villages alike, at the doors of cottages and mansions, with news that loved ones had either been killed, wounded or were prisoners of war. The Hazelmeres had two sons at the front, and one of them was Lisa's husband.

They hurried towards the house and the two gardeners they met on the way stared at them anxiously, they too having seen the messenger boy.

As they entered the hall a group of servants stood together, immediately going their separate ways with downcast eyes so that only the butler came to meet them, his eyes filled with sympathy as Lisa gasped, 'We saw the messenger, Brownson. Are they in the drawing room?'

'Yes, Milady,' and another servant came forward to take her outdoor clothing while Adrian said quickly, 'I'll leave you now, Lisa. I don't want to intrude in what is such a private matter.'

Their eyes met, he took her hand and squeezed it; as the tears came into her eyes she turned away quickly and hurried across the hall.

'You may go into the East Wing from here, sir,' the butler said, but Adrian said quickly, 'No, I would prefer to go in from the terrace; you have had some bad news, I think.'

'Yes, sir. I am not aware yet of its precise nature.'

Adrian shook his head sadly and left.

CHAPTER TWENTY-THREE

THE SCENE THAT MET LISA'S eyes when she opened the drawing room door was not unexpected.

They sat apart staring into the fire, but it was Antony scrambling down from his grandmother's knee who rushed across the room to fling himself into her arms that troubled her most. His face was pale and afraid and as she took hold of his hand to lead him towards them Lucy said shrilly, 'Come here, Antony, I want you here with me. You are our future—they are not going to take you away from me.'

She looked at her father-in-law believing at once that it was Dominic the messenger had brought news of, but he shook his head and held out the telegram for her to read. It was Austin who had been killed in France.

They stared at each other in anguished disbelief and the sound of Lucy's choking sobs filled the room. She took her seat beside Lucy on the sofa and immediately Lucy reached out to hold Antony, smothering him with her embraces, the child's face was a mask of bewilderment.

Words were not enough. Nothing she could have said

would diminish the misery of the moment; only the long empty silence made it possible for them to reach out into a past when Austin had been vibrantly alive and joyful. They were remembering his laughter, the frivolous humour that had made him the butt of his father's severity, the handsome smiling face that so many girls had fallen in love with, and their despair when none of them had meant anything to him. Now they would see him no more, and Lisa realised that she had known Austin more than she would ever know Dominic.

'Leave the child be,' Johnny admonished Lucy. 'He's frightened by all this and you're in danger of suffocating him.'

'He's all we've got,' Lucy cried, while the child strained away from her towards his mother.

Lisa said gently, 'You have Dominic; you have another son.'

'How do we know that the war won't take him too?' Lucy cried, and there was no answer, only the patter of rain against the window and the rumble of thunder like the sound of distant gunfire.

A servant came in to stoke up the fire and light the lamps, avoiding their eyes, his attitude one of deferential melancholy while Johnny went to stare out of the window before pulling the drapes.

'They've brought another contingent of soldiers in; the trucks are just leaving,' he said before taking his seat near the fire.

Lucy looked up. 'I should be there,' she said sharply. 'I'm always there; why didn't somebody inform me?'

'Because nobody would expect you to be there,' he replied. 'They don't need you, Lucy, there are enough nurses there to see to their needs. Let the child go up to the nursery; he's had enough of the atmosphere down here.'

She drew him tighter into her embrace, but it was Lisa reaching out for him that finally allowed him to escape.

As she walked with Antony towards the door Lucy said, 'I invited the lieutenant-colonel to dinner; nothing has changed.'

Johnny said tartly, 'Everything has changed, for today at any rate. Perhaps you would inform the lieutenant-colonel, Lisa, of what has happened. Like other families we shall get over it; we are not cancelling the dinner engagement, merely postponing it.'

Later that afternoon as she made her way to Adrian's room she was aware of the glances of compassion from those she met on her way and realised that already the bad news they had received had reached its way into the rest of the house. Adrian looked at her across the room, his eyes searching; shaking her head she said, 'It's Austin, Dominic's brother, killed on the Somme.'

He took both her hands in his and breathlessly she said, 'My mother-in-law has asked me to tell you she is sorry about dinner this evening.'

'Lisa, of course I understand. Austin was the younger one, wasn't he?'

'Yes. He was nice, friendly, always smiling, so much fun. We could have become good friends, I know; now I am left wondering just how many friends I have.'

'You will have your husband, Lisa, and your son. Surely the family care for you; you are after all Dominic's wife and there is your mother. Aren't you forgetting all the blessings you have and thinking only of the sad things in your life?'

She stared at him long and hard for several seconds before leaving his room.

He cared too much for her without understanding her—the bitterness in her smile, the sadness in her beautiful eyes. It was time to leave and get back to his men, time to forget Lisa Lexican, and yet in the days that followed he was aware of her walking through the parkland, always alone, her head bent against the wind, her mind obsessed by too many problems.

The dinner evenings were resumed much against his better judgement, but always he was aware of Lisa's preoccupation with her own thoughts and the Hazelmeres' increasing differences.

It was at the end of one such evening when Lady Hazelmere said, 'I'm driving over to see Sybil in the morning. I shall take Antony with me. Tell his nanny to wrap him up warmly and bring him to my room at ten o'clock.'

Lisa looked up sharply, saying, 'I hoped to take him myself to see my mother in the morning; she hasn't seen him for some days now.'

'I need him more than your mother does,' Lucy said adamantly. 'I have suffered a tragic loss; your mother is looking forward to a serene and peaceful life with Mr Blanchard; Antony is all I have.'

'You have a son,' her husband snapped sharply.

'My son is far away and may never return; like I said Antony is all I have.'

'The boy has a mother, Lucy.'

'Well of course he has a mother, who is young with all her life in front of her. Lisa understands, don't you, dear?'

Adrian was glad the meal was over and declined to join them in the drawing room with the excuse that he had letters to write and would return to his room.

'Why not write them in the library?' Lord Hazelmere said. 'I'm sure you'll find it more comfortable than that room in the East Wing. I always hated that part of the house; when we were children we always said it was haunted.'

'And was it?' Adrian asked with a smile.

'Well, you know what it's like. All these old houses are said to have their ghosts. I never saw anything but some of the servants were convinced they were here. We had a nanny who frightened the life out of us with her stories.'

'Then I'll take up your suggestion, Lord Hazelmere, and retire to the library. I'm not very anxious to encounter your ghosts this evening.'

Lucy retired early leaving her husband sitting moodily in front of the fire, while Lisa leafed through a magazine. She rarely played the piano since Lucy deemed music inappropriate for a house in mourning.

After a long silence her father-in-law roused himself to say, 'I'm rotten company, my dear. There's not much of anything for you with us at the moment.'

Lisa smiled. 'I understand,' she murmured.

'It'll be different when Dominic comes home—you'll get back to your own place and make a new life for yourselves. It's all this uncertainty that's the worst thing to take. I wonder if our guest needs some company; letters to write were an excuse to get away. What do you think?'

'He has parents and friends he must write to,' Lisa murmured.

'I suppose so. I'll turn in and leave the chap alone to get on with whatever he's doing. You don't mind do you, Lisa?'

'No of course not. I'll read a little more then I'll go up to bed.'

As she crossed the hall she was aware of the light from under the library door and hesitated—perhaps he would resent her intrusion. But even while she hesitated the library door opened and Adrian stood silhouetted against the the light.

Like a magnet she was drawn to him until they stood facing each other, then he turned and pushed open the door so that she could enter in front of him.

The room was cosy with firelight and Lisa walked towards it, his eyes following her, aware of the danger. All through the meal they had recently sat through he had been aware of her sitting next to him, adding only briefly to the conversation, a woman strangely at variance with the people she called family.

'Did you write your letters?' she asked him.

He shook his head. 'No, it was an excuse. They were

kind enough to invite me for dinner, but I don't think any of us were in the mood for conversation.'

She smiled. 'No. I'm sure you're right.'

'You've all suffered a grievous loss; only time will erase it.'

'And sometimes time isn't enough.'

He looked at her curiously. 'For them do you mean or for you, Lisa?'

'Perhaps for all of us. I puzzle you, don't I? You can't understand a woman who you think has so many of life's blessings—wealth, a title, a child and a husband, everything most women would die for and yet you find me difficult to understand. Is it that you find me mercenary, acquisitive or merely sulky? Sometimes when you look at me I see the doubt in your expression; you don't know whether to dislike me, distrust me or condemn me.'

'Lisa, whatever tragedy lies behind your demeanour I am sure there is a reason for it. I don't condemn you and I could never dislike you. How could you think that?'

'By the way you avoid me. Adrian, you do avoid me, admit it.'

'Not because I dislike you, Lisa, because I don't want to feel something for you that is wrong. I am here as a patient being cared for in Lord Hazelmere's home. They have been very good to me in a great many ways, so I owe them a lot, we all do. Whatever feelings I have for you must not be allowed to surface. They would be futile.'

'And the feelings I have for you, Adrian—you think I am a disloyal wife, unworthy of this family and my husband?'

When he didn't immediately answer her he has aware of the cynicism in her expression as, turning away, she said, 'Think what you must, Adrian. You know nothing of the circumstances that have made me what I am.'

'And if you are not prepared to tell me of those circumstances, Lisa, what else am I to think? Was your husband unfaithful to you? Was he cruel, unkind, do you not love him?'

'I did love him, Adrian. I loved him when I was young and foolish, before I knew that he could never love me, before I knew that there were such men as Dominic.'

He stared at her long and searchingly and after a few moments she said, 'My husband is not a bad man, he is not unkind, he is not unfaithful, at least not where another woman is concerned. My husband should never have married me—he is homosexual; he cares for men not women.'

'You knew this before you married him?' he gasped.

'No. I discovered it on our wedding night when he left me to spend it elsewhere, with the man he was in love with or alone, I still don't know.'

'But you had his son.'

'No, Adrian, Antony is not his son,' and when he continued to stare at her incredulously she told him the long sordid story behind Antony's birth.

'I was angry; it was childish and stupid, at first prompted by revenge on a family that had used me to cover up their son's inadequacies, then the desperate longings of a young girl needing to be loved, to feel desirable in a man's eyes. I didn't love Antony's father; I cannot even remember what he looked like, but for one brief time he gave me back some sort of belief that I was capable of inspiring passion or even love.'

'But your husband, he knows that he is not Antony's father. Has he willingly accepted him?'

'Homosexuality is a criminal offence in this country, Adrian. I have covered up for Dominic; he has covered up for me. That is what our marriage has come to; that is all there will ever be.'

She turned away with a sob in her throat, then he was holding her, comforting her, kissing her, as passion swept away every other thought and memory. If there had been no war they would never have met, they would have been worlds apart; and yet war had brought them together and now for both of them there could be no going back.

It was almost dawn when he left her room to return to the long empty corridors of the East Wing; his room felt cold and dismal even while his body still burned with memories of the passion they had shared. None of it would be easy—there was this old and powerful family to face, there was Dominic, and what he had so readily been able to forget, there were his parents and Catherine.

Perhaps he would not survive the war, perhaps Dominic would not escape alive, but if he did not, would come the breaking of Catherine's heart and all the hurt he would bring to his parents and hers. In Lisa's case there would be the ending of a marriage that had never been a marriage, and a future they would have to face separately.

He couldn't think clearly about the future. Soon now he would be well enough to return to the front and he felt a fierce sense of betrayal against the family who had nurtured him and helped him to recover. The pain he would bring to his family and Catherine was considerably more straightforward than that Lisa would have to face, and they would not be able to face it together.

In the first early light of dawn he stood at the window of his room staring out across a parkland silvered with frost, but his thoughts were far away from the present. He thought about a future when he would have Lisa beside him in India. Bridges would have to be crossed, mountains would have to be climbed but in the end they must love her as he loved her. They must be made to see the inevitability of things, face things as this family would be forced to face them.

To Lisa, lying awake watching the first faint gleam of the wintry sun imprinted across the ceiling of her room, there were far too many uncertainties. Adrian had been so sure that in the end they would be together, able to surmount whatever difficulties there were in their path, but Adrian did not really know this formidable family with its pride and its intransigence.

She remembered the young Lisa tramping up to her lessons, resentful and rebellious, her mother's persuasions that it was all for her own good, her father's cynicism; then she remembered Dominic as she had first known and loved him, handsome, caring, very kind, pushed and persuaded into a marriage he had never wanted; always it had been the family that had had to come first, while human emotions and needs had been disregarded.

Even now she could face Dominic; they had both been pawns in a greater game. But how could they face the rest of them? Austin had gone, and with his death Dominic was all important. Suddenly her thoughts turned to her son. Already in Lucy's eyes he was all important, he was the future, the grandson who would one day be Lord Hazelmere—how could they ever tell them otherwise?

Moaning with anguish she buried her head in the pillows. There had been so many times she had thought about the future with Dominic. That they would go on living together in their separate worlds, with Antony growing up to the sort of luxury that had been expected of the sons of Hazelmere. Dominic would find men to love, and she too would have love affairs, none of them meaningful. She would be the beautiful Countess of Hazelmere with her clothes and jewels and the countless men who admired her, but none of them would count—she and Dominic would stay together until their lives were done.

In the days that followed she listened to Adrian's thoughts on their future together in a country she did not know, and the more he talked the more she disbelieved that they had a future together.

It was a fairy tale born out of love and passion, the trauma of a war-torn world and too many uncertainties. Adrian believed the one certainty was their love, but even that became insignificant when several days later he told her he was being recalled to Headquarters.

She stared at him in disbelief. 'But Adrian, you're not well enough. How can you go back to war when you're still limping on two sticks, when you're still in so much pain? What will they expect you to do?'

'Well, obviously I won't be returning to the front immediately but there are other things I can do. I can't argue against it, Lisa. I do what I'm told and I'm not the only one to be going back to war.'

Lord Hazelmere received the news in silence although privately he believed Lisa was seeing too much of the officer. True, they had encouraged him to spend time with them, use the library, dine with them, and he'd found him charming and intelligent, but it was time he left; he'd been at Hazelmere long enough.

Lucy had no thoughts on the matter. In fact, she had few thoughts about anything beyond working with the villagers, taking her grandson on her visits to the East Wing, the people she knew in the area and to see Mary and Sybil.

When Lisa told Mary that the Lt. Col. was leaving Mary too heaved a sigh of relief. She had seen them together, absorbed in each other's company and it wasn't fair to Dominic. There were too many temptations put in the way of young Englishwomen with husbands overseas, by wounded heroes and young Americans, too, now that they had entered the war. When she said as much to the vicar he merely smiled, reassuring her that her daughter was merely a good, kind, young woman doing her best to comfort a man so far from home.

Adrian tried to reassure Lisa that what they had together would last. The war would be over, they would sort out their future and he would be with her to face the Hazelmeres together. Dominic would be reasonable—hadn't she always maintained that even though they didn't love each other, they were friends?

On the morning he left she stood at her window looking down to where the staff car and driver waited to take him away. Lord and Lady Hazelmere stood with the nurses to shake his hand and wish him well and later she knew that they would be annoyed that she was not there with them.

For one brief moment he looked up and their eyes met. Adrian would understand why she couldn't be there, and Antony standing beside her waved his hand saying, 'Mummy, why can't I go to be with Granny and Grandpa? Why is he going away?'

'He's going back to the war, darling.'

'Will he come back?'

'Perhaps one day, Antony, I don't know.'

'Granny says Father will be coming home after the war. What is he like?'

'He's nice, darling. You'll have to get to know him all over again.'

'Uncle Austin isn't coming back, is he?'

'No dear. Would you like to visit Grandma Mary this afternoon? She hasn't seen you recently.'

'I know. Granny is taking me to somebody she knows at Brampton. We're going in the trap; one day I shall be able to drive it.'

This was the usual pattern when Lucy insisted on taking Antony everywhere—he had become her crusade, the one being she was building her life round and their togetherness both humiliated her and shamed her.

Would Dominic feel nothing but cynicism for his mother's feelings for the boy, a cynicism that would accuse Lisa of duplicity, or would he care? Didn't they all deserve one another?

A week later Adrian wrote to Lisa at her mother's address informing her that he was to remain in London for some time, at least until he was fighting fit. The letter ended:

Darling Lisa, please believe me that we shall be together when all this is over; it is the one certainty in my life. Write to me, darling, we so badly need each other.

CHAPTER TWENTY-FOUR

THEY WERE OVER, THE LONG, desperate, violent years, the victory marches and the rhetoric, but it seemed to Lisa standing with the family and surrounded by a throng of villagers, that there really were no winners in what was left.

Wreaths had been laid around the war memorial on the village green, a white cross consecrated after the Boer War and now once more honoured by the names of twelve villagers who had lost their lives in this one.

They shivered in the damp mist that swirled across the green on a grey November day and Lisa watched as Dominic stepped forward to lay the family's wreath of bright red poppies followed by members of the families who had lost sons.

The villagers had welcomed Dominic warmly. They had known him since childhood, he was their young lord of the manor, and as they walked towards the church the men and women clustered around smiled their greetings, particularly at Antony who clung closely to his grandmother's hand.

Lisa stood beside Dominic in the family pew, aware of his tall figure in his major's uniform, gravely handsome, acknowledging the good wishes of all and sundry with his remote charming smile, the smile she had fallen in love with and lived to regret.

Antony had loved the military band and the marching: now his child's face looked bemused. He did not remember the man standing next to his mother, a man who favoured him with a kind smile, a man who had greeted him the day before with a handshake and few words.

The hymns were traditional as well as patriotic and Dominic read one of the lessons while the daughter of a dead hero read the other. The Reverend Blanchard gave an appropriate sermon and Lisa's mother sat in the front pew opposite with a gentle smile on her lips. They had been married two weeks and as she joined the rest of the family outside the church Lord Hazelmere said, 'Good sermon, Mary, very appropriate.'

Dominic took her hand and gently kissed her cheek. 'I believe congratulations are in order,' he said with a smile.

'Thank you, Dominic,'

'I hope you'll be very happy, Mary. I understand you've moved out of Aunt Jane's house?'

'Yes, into the vicarage; it seemed more appropriate.'

'I suppose so.'

'And you'll soon be wanting to get back to Martindale?'

'I need to take a look at it. I believe the nursing contingent and the rest of them have finally gone.'

'I hope they've left it in good order.'

'Yes well, that is why I need to see it as soon as possible.'

'Taken everything you need from Aunt Jane's, Mary?' Lord Hazelmere asked.

'Everything that was mine,' Mary answered him.

'Well of course, my dear, that's what I meant. I'll have to have thoughts about what to do with it; it could be a problem.'

'It's a very beautiful house, Johnny.'

'Well of course, but perhaps a white elephant. It needs servants and gardener; perhaps some city gent who's loaded and needs a good address might be interested.'

His remarks were cynical, and in some exasperation his wife said, 'If we hang onto it long enough it could be the right sort of place for Antony one day. Not too far away from his parents and close to us. Young people are wanting their own establishments these days.'

Antony rode back to Hazelmere with his grandparents leaving Dominic and Lisa to ride back together and when they were settled in the car Dominic said, 'My mother seems very close to the boy; has it always been so?'

'Very much so after Austin was killed. Somehow or other she replaced Austin with Antony, and she has very fixed ideas about his future.'

'You don't agree with her ideas?'

'Not all of them.'

'I'm not sure I agree with her thoughts on a private tutor for him. He should go to school.'

'Oh yes, Dominic, I do agree with you. He knows no other children, and although Mr Pickering is a very able learned man I can't think it's good for Antony to feel so isolated at his age. He should go to school.'

'Well, we went to school. My mother was glad to get us off her hands in those days; she had so many social engagements, so many commitments, but now she seems completely wrapped up in the boy.'

'She became like that after Austin was killed.'

'I'll talk to her, Lisa. I'm surprised Father hasn't said something. He was very concerned that Austin and I should go away to school.'

Lisa remembered those mornings when she had tramped along the drive to take private lessons around the nursery table as a girl, but even then she had had the company of three other girls.

'I must drive over to Martindale in the morning,' Dominic was saying. 'I need to see what needs doing there.'

'Perhaps I could come with you, Dominic.'

'I doubt if that's a good idea, Lisa. The house could be a shambles, there are probably no fires laid and I'm not sure about the servants—how many have stayed or returned. I know the government retained a few of them but I am rather anxious to learn how the house has been left.'

Lisa's immediate thoughts were that he needed to see Oliver far more than he needed to see the house, but adamantly she persisted. 'Dominic, I need to get out of the house. I feel stifled by family, by the same environment day after day, even if it's only Martindale it will be a change of scenery. I could be of help.'

'Very well, if you insist, Lisa, but I would rather you'd

have waited until the house could have been made to feel more like home.'

Home! When had Martindale ever felt like home, and yet she could see the logic of his argument.

Dominic raised the question of Antony's education over lunch, and immediately his mother said, 'I have found the best tutor it was possible to find and he assures me Antony is a very intelligent child who is learning well; five seems to me far too young to send him away from home.'

'I recollect that you sent both Austin and me away when we were seven,' Dominic replied dryly.

'Oh, things were different then, the world was a calmer, safer place; soon he'll have riding lessons and the horses will be coming back. This talk of school isn't a good idea at the moment, Dominic. I'm sure Lisa agrees with me, don't you, dear?'

'Actually, no, Mother-in-law, I think Antony should go to school and be with other children.'

'I'm surprised to hear you say so. A private education did a great deal for you.'

'In what way?'

'It enabled you to marry well, mix with the cream of society.'

'Antony isn't remotely thinking of such things at his age, Mother, and in any case Mr Pickering may not wish to travel to Martindale which is where Antony will be living,' Dominic said.

His mother looked at him with astonishment. 'Well of course Mr Pickering won't be able to travel to Martindale.

Antony will stay here during the week and spend his weekends with you.'

'Entirely impractical,' his father snapped, entering into the conversation for the first time. 'The boy's place is with his parents, either that or in school. Ever meet with Lieutenant-Colonel Lawson, Dominic? Nice chap, Indian Army, sent here to recover from wounds he had received in France.'

'No, I never came into contact with any Indian regiment.'

'Lancers, I believe, upholding the white man's burden then sent over here to sort the Germans out. We invited him for dinner several times and gave him full use of the library. The ladies got along with him very well; change of face, quite a handsome one too.'

Dominic merely smiled, but Lisa found her heart fluttering stupidly and hoped her father-in-law would drop the subject. With Adrian's departure love and tenderness had gone from her life. Soon he would be returning to India, to the life he knew and the people he knew there, while she would be at Martindale living the life of the lady of the manor in a house she barely remembered.

Indeed she hardly recognised it from the brief time she had spent there. The servants had gathered to restore much of it that had suffered at the hands of patients and nursing staff, but it still retained a clinical austerity that she knew Dominic was finding hard to live with.

The servants knew better than she where pictures should be hung and ornaments should be placed and she was wishing she hadn't come, particularly when Dominic spent time at the stables leaving everything at the house to the servants.

When he returned to the house in the late afternoon she sensed a strange restlessness in him and she asked, 'Have you been into the village at all?'

He looked at her in surprise saying, 'No, I spent time at the stables and with the workmen there. There's been nothing done there for four long years and soon I shall be bringing horses back.'

'When do you expect to see Oliver?'

She had to ask, but she realised as soon as she'd done so it was a question she should never have asked from the hauteur of his expression and the coldness of his reply.

'Oliver was killed on the Somme at the same time my brother was killed. I would have thought you would have known.'

'Oh Dominic, how could I have known? Not from your parents, and nobody has ever mentioned Oliver to me. I'm sorry, my question was insensitive; I should never have asked it.'

His expression softened. 'It doesn't matter, Lisa, a great many men lost their lives in the war. I never saw Oliver in France; the last time I did see him was before the war.'

It was all so hopeless. Once there had been comradeship, affection even, now there seemed to be nothing and as if he too seemed to recognise it he said, 'Perhaps we should think of getting back to Hazelmere; it's a typical grey November day and the mist is coming down.'

'We need to come again tomorrow.'

'It's not a good idea for you to come, Lisa, the rooms are cold and the servants know exactly where everything should go. I'm sure you'll be far happier sitting beside a warm fire than shivering in these empty rooms.'

He was right of course. There was nothing for her at Martindale in rooms devoid of furniture and where even the mist seemed to creep into rooms where curtains had yet to be hung.

Dominic smiled. 'In a few days it may look altogether different, then you can come back here and see if everything meets with your approval.'

The next day she remained at Hazelmere and Lucy said after breakfast, 'Antony went to meet Mr Pickering at the door. He looks forward to his lessons; I do think school is a ridiculous idea until he's older.'

Again her husband prevaricated. 'I went to school at his age and so did the boys. What is a ridiculous idea, Lucy, is for you to tie him to your apron strings. He should be with other boys, play games, be allowed to grow up; the child is being stifled with affection.'

'I want to spend time with him now while he's young and vulnerable. When my two boys went away I only saw them when they came on holiday and then they'd made friends with other boys and were rarely in the house.'

'And now you're expecting the boy to compensate you for what you consider you lost then. He won't thank you for it, Lucy.'

'I'm driving over to Sybil's,' she answered with a frosty stare. 'I can't talk to you when you're in this mood. Go and spend some time with the horses; it's what you do best anyway.'

Lisa felt superfluous in that great house. She was never asked to visit Sybil with Lucy because between Sybil and herself was always the old animosity and she felt sure her father-in-law would prefer to visit his stables without her. She went to answer the telephone that was ringing stridently soon after they had left the house, surprised to hear her mother's voice strangely agitated asking, 'Lisa, are you alone?'

'Yes, Mother, quite alone. Are you all right? You sound a bit edgy.'

'Lisa, I want you to come to the vicarage, and please come alone, without Antony or Dominic.'

'Antony is at his lessons, Mother, and Dominic has gone to Martindale. What is wrong?'

'Nothing is wrong, I just want to talk to you alone. Can you come now, Lisa? It's very important.'

'I'll come immediately, but I do wish you'd tell me if there's anything wrong.'

There was nothing more, only the replacing of the receiver, and in some trepidation she debated with herself whether to take the trap or walk to the village through the parkland. Her mother had said to go alone so if she went for the pony and trap she would have to tell Johnny where she was going, so instead she set off to walk quickly through the gardens where she only encountered the gardeners.

It was a pretty vicarage, she thought, as she opened the gate and walked up the path, even on a cold autumnal morning when late summer roses dropped their weary heads and leaves crunched under her feet; then before she reached the door it opened and her mother was there smiling nervously, saying, 'I'm making coffee, dear, go into the parlour; there's a warm fire in there.'

'Mother, we can have coffee later, after we've had time to talk.'

'No dear, we'll have coffee and then we'll talk, please.'

Lisa frowned. Why all the urgency and agitation if coffee was more important? she wondered. She could hear the sounds from the kitchen but as her mother had insisted she opened the parlour door and stared into the sober eyes of Adrian Lawson.

For several minutes she stared at him in anguished surprise before he stepped forward to take her in his arms and she said, 'Adrian, why are you here?'

'I told you I'd see you again, Lisa. Surely you didn't think I wouldn't.'

'You're still in uniform.'

'Of course. Your mother tells me Dominic is back.'

'What have you told my mother, Adrian?'

'Very little until we can tell her together.'

'Adrian, it's hopeless, just as I knew it would be. Dominic is back and there is peace between us and very little else. He's at Martindale as the house needs putting to rights and he preferred to go there on his own. It was sensible really; there was little for me to do.'

'Not even when it meant you would be together.'

'Oh Adrian, that is how it will always be. He doesn't need me, we don't need each other, but it's how it's got to be. I told you that anything between us was hopeless.'

'You mean you're not going to fight to make it different, that you're simply going to drift like a torpid river into eternity.'

'Don't think I haven't thought about it, but there's no other way, Adrian.'

'Yes perhaps, but I don't intend to, not without a fight anyway. I'm here to talk to Dominic. I'm returning to India next week sometime, so there's very little time; if he's as decent and honest as you say he is then he'll understand. Did you say he was at Martindale?'

'Adrian, you can't see him there.'

'Then I shall see him at Hazelmere. I do intend to see him, Lisa.'

'For what purpose? You're going to tell him that we love each other, that while he was in France we were sleeping together, that I've betrayed him not once but twice?'

'And how many times has he betrayed you?'

'Not with Oliver; Oliver is dead.'

'By being as he is, Lisa, by being unable to love you. Do you really want that for the rest of your life or do you intend to soldier on? Oh there'll be other men—I'm not flattering myself that I'll be the solitary passion of a lifetime, but one day there'll be other men, for him too. The world will smile and chatter amusingly about the beautiful countess with her string of suitors, but you and

Dominic will stay together, protecting each other, and in the end people will wonder at the waste.'

'What have you told my mother?'

'Very little as yet, but she's probably guessed there's more by my being here and wanting to see you.'

'Can you imagine what it will do to her? The vicar's wife, with a daughter who has betrayed her husband, a daughter who is married to Lord Hazelmere's son. They love Dominic and they're so proud of him. What will they think of me?'

'The worst, Lisa, I'm sure. We didn't promise ourselves that it would be easy.'

'It won't affect you, Adrian. Your family and your life are a long way from here. I shall be here to suffer the scandal divorce would bring, and I shall be the one they will blame because I am the one who has stepped out of line.'

'You could tell the world why you stepped out of line, Lisa, but I know you won't.'

'No, and I know that Dominic will keep his word about Antony. He will never tell a soul that Antony is not his son.'

'But not simply to protect you, darling, to protect himself.'

'What a mess it is. Think how easy it will be to walk away from it, to go back to your world and leave me to make the best of what I have.'

The door opened; they both turned to face Lisa's mother and Adrian went forward to take the tray out of her hands. She looked at them nervously, and Lisa said quickly, 'Sit here, Mother. I'll pour the coffee. Is the vicar out?'

'Yes dear, visiting some people over at Carling; he'll be home for lunch. Will you both be able to join us?'

Lisa looked at Adrian helplessly as he said evenly, 'I have to get back to London in the morning and I have things to do, Mrs Blanchard, but I don't know about Lisa.'

'Antony will have finished morning lessons, Mother. Perhaps I too should get back,' she said quietly.

Her mother looked at them before asking, 'I wish you'd tell me what is wrong; evidently something is.'

Lisa left it to Adrian to explain why he had suddenly arrived on her doorstep and her mother listened without interrupting, her hands clasped tightly together, her expression anguished. When the tale was told all she found to say was, 'I knew there was something. I watched you together, walking in the gardens, then those weeks when you tried to avoid each other, and then before you went away, Adrian, the way your eyes followed her, the feeling that you had come closer together.

'I didn't want to believe it, telling myself that you were just two young people who had been brought together in an unnatural world, that soon you would be going your separate ways and that would be the end of it. When you came here this morning, Adrian, I knew it was more than that. What are you going to do now?'

'I intend to speak to Dominic.'

The ready tears filled her eyes and she cried, 'Oh surely not. Dominic is nice; he's always been so kind and generous. Lisa, how could you have done this to him?'

'You don't know it all, Mrs Blanchard,' Adrian said gently.

'What are you saying?'

'Don't be too ready to blame your daughter; there are circumstances you are not aware of.'

'Circumstances, what circumstances? Oh, I know Lisa's not been entirely happy with his mother or his aunt; her young life was difficult, but since she married Dominic things changed. What are you expecting him to say?'

'I don't know. If you say he's kind and generous I'm expecting him to understand.'

'How can he understand that his wife is in love with somebody else? Would you understand it?'

He didn't answer her. There was no answer nor did Mary understand or know anything about the traumas and undercurrents in her daughter's marriage. All Mary remembered was that Lisa had wanted Dominic and been ecstatic when he married her. What terrible thing had there been to kill that love? None of them would be left unscathed by the scandal.

She thought about her husband preaching morality from his pulpit. He was a good man but how would he feel about her daughter's divorce and infidelity? They would be subjected to all the whisperings around the village, the condemnation levelled against Lisa, even against the mother who had raised her.

CHAPTER TWENTY-FIVE

LISA PUT ANTONY TO BE BED and read him a favourite story, then she joined Johnny and Lucy in the drawing room. Dominic had not returned and Lucy said querulously, 'I suppose we might as well have dinner since he hasn't informed us when he hopes to be back.'

'There's probably a lot to do,' Johnny said.

'Well of course, but at the moment none of us seem to know where we are from day to day. You should have gone with him, Lisa.'

'He wanted to go alone; he said there was nothing for me to do there.'

'Well, you could have kept him company; the servants don't know everything. What time did Mr Pickering leave?'

'I'm not sure; I went to see Mother.'

'Well, at least the stables are getting back to normal,' Johnny said. 'I might ride round the estate tomorrow—come with me if you like, Lisa, there are three horses down there.'

But Lisa didn't take him up on the suggestion. By the

time tomorrow came her entire world could be torn apart, and as she made a pretence of eating she thought of Adrian and Dominic, where they were, what they were talking about and what would be the outcome.

'I've invited Sybil and her husband to dine with us tomorrow,' Lucy was saying. 'Sybil said they've seen nothing of Dominic and it's time we got back to dinner parties and family get-togethers.'

'Dominic may not be here,' Johnny said.

'Then we'll have to make sure that he is. If you and Lisa can't get through to him, I will.'

Let them all come, Lisa thought wildly. Better to meet their righteous indignation as an entirety than many times over.

Dominic did not come home that night but in the early morning light Lisa heard the sound of a car's engine below her bedroom, and hurrying over to the window she saw him letting himself into the house.

Quickly she donned her dressing gown and slippers then ran down the stairs knowing immediately where she would find him—in the library where Adrian had first made love to her, the room where long-dead Hazelmeres stared down in lofty disdain at the foibles of a new generation. He was there standing at the window looking out on a cold grey day with an expression of acute melancholy on his face.

He turned at the opening of the door and for a long moment they stared into each other's eyes until Lisa said shakily, 'Dominic, I'm sorry, I'm so dreadfully sorry.'

He did not immediately answer her, then he said, 'Don't you think we should forget these expressions of sorrow, Lisa? They are unnecessary and superfluous. We should all be sorry. It's time to move on.'

'Move on,' she echoed stupidly.

'Why yes, isn't that what you want?'

'How can we move on?'

'Sit down, Lisa,' he said patiently. 'Isn't that why your lieutenant-colonel came to see me yesterday? Isn't that what you're both hoping in your hearts? He tells me he's in love with you, that he wants to marry you. Do I take it that that is what you want also?'

'Dominic, I didn't think I'd ever see him again. I thought it was over, that he'd return to India and we'd be together; I didn't plan it any other way.'

'I'm aware of that. He explained everything to me very succinctly. Actually, I liked him. I found him honest and straightforward, something new in our less than honourable relationship.'

'What are we going to do?'

'Divorce obviously. You could have the marriage annulled on the grounds of non-consummation, but where does that leave the boy? You can divorce me—quite the done thing these days, I believe. Some woman I've never even seen can be found who will agree to share a room in some hotel with me and leave in the morning considerably richer than she'd ever hoped to be.'

'Oh no, that's a terrible thing, besides I'm the one who's betrayed you, I'm the one who has broken my marriage vows, not once but twice.'

'And I am the one who should never have made them.'

'Oh Dominic, why did he have to come back into my life?'

'Do you really mean that, Lisa?'

She shook her head and the tears rolled slowly down her cheeks. 'No. From the first moment I saw him, even before we'd even said one word to each other, I felt something for him. I didn't expect him to feel the same and I can't believe now that he did.'

'He's coming here to see you today, well not here, your mother's house, and perhaps I should meet you both later. We have to talk it through, Lisa; there isn't much time; he's returning to India at the end of the week.'

'It all sounds so cold and businesslike. Not like the ending of a marriage at all; not about love or friendship—so incredibly cold.'

'And civilised, Lisa. It's better this way, coldly, logically, not burdened by passion or anger, and when we've talked you and I will face the rest of them. Why don't you go back to bed for a while? It's very early.'

'Dominic, I couldn't sleep; I have to find something to do.'

'Then why not take one of the horses out? Father said they were coming back; he won't mind, I'm sure.'

'Then why don't you come with me? We used to ride together when we were friends, but we don't seem to have been friends for such a long time; please come with me.'

For what seemed an age he stared at her, then his face relaxed into a smile and he said, 'I'll meet you down at the stables, Lisa. Choose the horse you want; I'll be with you presently.'

She had been dreading this meeting and there was still a long long way to go, but for the first time in years the Dominic who had been her friend was coming back to her. Whatever the rest of them thought of her, whatever the world might think, Dominic at least would play his part.

It was like the old days riding with Dominic in the chill wind with a sudden squall of rain against their faces and she thought about those early days when life had promised so much and none of it had come true.

Her face was rosy with colour as they brought their horses to rest at the edge of the forest and she cried, 'How wonderful to be able to ride a good horse again; I've missed them so much,' then her face sobered as she added, 'but they're not my horses; I shall be going away and may never ride them again.'

As if he knew her thoughts Dominic said, 'There'll be other horses, Lisa. You'll ride with Adrian in India, in the foothills and the sunshine, then you might remember this morning.'

'Oh I shall, Dominic, I promise you, but before that there is so much heartache to be got through—your parents, my mother, Antony.'

'We'll talk later, Lisa, nothing can be resolved right now. Come on, let's get back to the stables.'

* * *

Lord Hazelmere watched them cantering along the drive in some surprise. He had not expected his son and his wife to be riding so early in the morning, and in such evident enjoyment. Perhaps Lucy was right after all, perhaps they could be happy together; perhaps she'd been right all along.

He met them in the hall, smiling and affable. 'Well, it's plain to see you've been enjoying yourselves,' he said. 'What do you think of them then? I was hoping we'd get Caliph back but I've heard nothing about him; perhaps it's too early.'

'I'll make enquiries, Father,' Dominic said. 'There's nothing wrong with those two.'

'I thought I might ride round the park myself this morning. Think I'm up to it, eh?'

'How do you feel about it? Take it easy and I'm sure you'll be fine.'

'Your mother's not keen, but we should be getting a pony for the boy. What do you think, Lisa?'

Lisa smiled. Plans were something they couldn't make; when the family heard their story a pony for Antony would be the last thing they would think about. She left them together as she went upstairs to change out of her riding clothes.

She dressed for Adrian that afternoon in his favourite jade green that he had said reflected her eyes, and over luncheon Lucy regarded her gown with some surprise.

'I've never seen you in that before,' she commented. 'You hardly ever dress up these days. How long has that been lying in your wardrobe?'

'I did wear it for one evening, Mother-in-law, don't you remember?'

'I remember,' Johnny said with a mischievous smile, 'and so, I think, did our guest. It relieved the boredom of war-torn Britain and made us all think that perhaps there might be light at the end of the tunnel.'

Dominic smiled, and his mother said, 'Oh well, perhaps my mind was on other things.'

'You're going down to see your mother, Lisa,' Dominic said and she smiled.

Lucy immediately said, 'I may come with you; it's weeks since I've seen her and I need to see the vicar about the design of the plaque in memory of Austin, and where he intends to put it.'

'Another day perhaps, Mother,' Dominic prevaricated. 'I need to talk to you about some of the things at Martindale, your things, I think.'

'You've never mentioned them before. What sort of things?'

'Pictures, china, family things.'

'Well, we shan't be wanting them, we've enough things here; they'll still be in the family so what does it matter?'

'Nevertheless, Mother, I would rather discuss them with you. You can see Mary another day surely.'

'Well, of course, I simply thought I'd be company for Lisa. That gown hardly seems suitable for sitting in the trap.'

'I'll drive her there, Mother, and come straight back,' Dominic said evenly and with that Lucy had to be content.

Dominic deposited her at the vicarage gate, saying he would drive back for her in a couple of hours, then he helped her down onto the path.

'You need to see Adrian,' she murmured.

'No, Lisa, actually I don't, not today at any rate, and he did say he could only spend a very short time here. He is going back to London this evening.'

Adrian's car was already parked in the lane and Lisa hurried up the path expecting to encounter her mother, but only Adrian came into the hall to greet her.

'Your mother and the vicar are both out,' he said. 'I think they both decided it was better so.'

They stood for a moment with their arms around each other, then he said with a wry smile, 'I take it Dominic has told you a little of what we talked about.'

'Yes he has, but it all seems so unbelievable. Adrian, do you realise how little I really know about you, your family, your friends. You know considerably more about me, but in the end we're just two people thrown together in a world neither of us had expected to find ourselves in.'

'What do you want to know about me, Lisa?'

'I know you're not married, that you have parents, brothers, sisters, some girl that you liked—loved even?'

They sat together in front of the fire, her hand held

gently in his, and he talked about his parents and something of his life.

'My father is General Sir Robert Lawson; he was decorated in honour of his various contributions to uprisings, old largely forgotten battles, and I am never destined to inherit his title. My mother is Lady Lawson, a title that will not be passed on to my wife, I'm afraid.'

'Oh Adrian, as if I care. It was never Dominic's title that seemed important.'

'No, I suppose not. I'm an only child. My mother doted on me and spoiled me; my father less so. He was a very demanding parent.'

'And the girl?'

He didn't answer immediately so that she looked at him with some apprehension, then after lifting her hand to his lips he said gently, 'There was a girl, Lisa; her name is Catherine and I've known her since I was a child. We grew up together, same environment, same sort of life. Her father too was army; she came to cheer me on at the polo matches; we went together to the same balls, the same soirées, applauded the triumphs and wept at the disasters, and I cared very deeply for her.'

'You said cared; don't you mean love?'

'I thought I did. My parents and hers thought we would become engaged before I came to the war, but something told me it wasn't the right time. I told myself I might not survive the war, made excuses if you like, but I told Catherine that after the war it would be different, we'd have a life together. I believed in it, Lisa, then I met you and realised I had never been in love until that moment. I'd been a normal, contented sort of chap living the life I knew with the people I knew and nothing was going to change it; now I have to go home to India and confess that I'm not the same man I was then. I've been to hell and back, and the old values I believed were inviolate have flown out of the window as if they never existed.'

'But when you see her again, Adrian, it could be there still, the old feeling you had for her; if not you'll break her heart.'

'And if I go back there loving you but determined to forget you, do you really think I can go back to caring for Catherine—as a friend, like a sister—will that make either of us happy? I shall know it isn't enough and in time she will know it too.'

'And your parents? They'll be disappointed—they think you're going home to marry the girl they want for you. What is it going to do to them?'

'Hurt them, antagonise them, but it is my life, Lisa. Nobody can live it for me; and you too will have to be strong, Lisa. You'll be aware of their resentment— can you face it do you think?'

She didn't immediately answer him. Her mind was troubled by old resentments, a child who had been made to feel inferior to other children, a child who had been told she should be grateful for an education and other crumbs that had fallen from the table of richer, more aristocratic relatives; and then that other more sinister resentment that she had been encouraged to love Dominic when Dominic would never be able to love her. Now Adrian was asking her to face the obvious hostility of his family. They would not want their only son to marry a divorced woman when divorce was an anathema to decent-minded people.

'You're not sure,' Adrian said quietly.

'I was thinking of other things.'

'What other things, darling? Things more important than our future?'

'No, but things that mattered so much to me at the time. You met Dominic—did you like him?'

'Yes. I understood how you could have loved him; I saw him as a decent man who was prepared to listen to me. If you hadn't told me anything about him I would never have assumed that he was not like most men. I can understand why the world assumed it too.'

'If it ever became known, Adrian, society would castigate him.'

'So you're prepared for them to castigate you?'

'I will be living in a different country; here in England there are too many people to hurt. Dominic and his family, my mother and my son.'

'And what about Antony, Lisa, will they allow you to take him away?'

'He is nothing to do with them; he's my son.'

'But by taking him away you'll rob him of his future, you'll hurt the Hazelmeres and questions will be asked as to why a divorced mother has a right to take her child away from a father who has done no wrong.

Then Dominic's right to the child will be questioned again.'

'Oh Adrian, there's so much we have to talk about—not just me and you but Dominic and me. You're going away, so far away. How is it all going to end?'

'By us being together, Lisa. Nothing is going to alter that.'

How could he be so sure, and yet she believed him. It seemed to Lisa that the one certainty in her life was a future with Adrian, and softly she asked, 'When do you have to leave?'

'Soon, darling. I have to get back this evening and it's a long drive. I'll write and telephone. We'll talk some more very soon.'

'But you'll be in India?'

'Lisa, I'll make sure that India or no India, I'm never very far away, and in the meantime you too have a great deal to think about. You'll need to talk to your mother; I've already told her as much as I was able, so it will come better from you.'

'What did she say? Oh Adrian, she'll be so unhappy about us.'

'Yes, I was aware of that.'

'And her husband?'

'I met him only briefly, but I can imagine he won't be happy either.'

'Dominic's parents will be outraged, and the rest of them will be unable to come to terms with it.'

'You'll have Dominic, Lisa. I don't think he'll let

you take all the blame. I shall have to face my parents alone; you at least have Dominic to take some of the weight off your shoulders.'

'And will he, do you think?'

'What do you think?'

Lisa thought back to all those other times when Dominic had understood her problems as well as his own. There had been so many faults on so many fronts but in the end they had been able to talk, he had never once closed the door in her face and strangely enough she didn't believe he would do so now.

Adrian smiled. 'Believe me, darling, in the end it will all come right, our future together; you'll have to be brave, and in being brave remember that I love you; that whatever your mother might think she will never stop loving you; and in Dominic I think you will have a friend.'

'When I saw you leave Hazelmere I believed you were going out of my life forever; now you will be going back to India and it is so far away. I feel once again that you will be going out of my life forever.'

'Not this time, darling. We will be together soon, I promise.'

In spite of so many reassurances the future seemed too uncertain, she watched him leave from her mother's front gate, gazing down the lane until his car turned the bend into the main road; then, utterly desolate, she turned back into the house.

She left before her mother and the vicar returned to the house for the simple reason that she was well aware of the sadness she was about to bring into their lives. Soon she and Dominic would have to confront his parents and she was desperately afraid of their reactions.

To her knowledge there had never been divorce in the Hazelmeres' history; divorce was a sin, particularly where adultery was concerned, and in the England of 1919, homosexuality was another. It seemed to Lisa as she walked back to Hazelmere that both she and Dominic would be damned, but she also began to realise that it was she who would have to take most of the blame if she was to protect her son.

As she neared the house she saw Dominic walking towards her and she realised that something must have prevented him from seeing Adrian before he left. His expression was troubled, but then how could it have been otherwise.

He smiled. 'I'm sorry, Lisa, it wasn't possible to leave the house before Lawson had to leave. My mother is intent on holding her family party and neither you nor I can face it. I have told my parents that our marriage is in trouble and that we intend to divorce; you can well imagine the trauma going on there.'

'I should have been there, Dominic.'

'I've told them what they need to know; neither of them was in the sort of mood to listen to more. I have told them that we are going over to Martindale for a few days and that we'll talk some more on our return, by which time she'll have spoken to Aunt Sybil and we can come back here and try to talk calmly about the rest of our lives.'

'What exactly did you tell them?'

'That there was no future for either of us in a marriage that should never have been. That you and I will be friends as long as we live, but that isn't enough for either of us. I have told them that you love somebody else, and that when we come back we'll discuss the implications, how it is going to affect the boy, his future and ours.'

'Why did you have to tell them today, Dominic, and what about my mother?'

'We'll discuss matters with your mother on the way to Martindale, Lisa, it's better this way; better to take the bull by the horns, don't you think, than having it hanging over us for days, weeks even. Could you have faced a family dinner knowing about all this? I couldn't.'

She had to agree that it would have been an ordeal, as Dominic said urgently, 'Pack a few things, Lisa, enough for a few days away from here and be ready to leave soon. I don't want another confrontation before we leave; we'll face that when we return.'

CHAPTER TWENTY-SIX

THE JARVISON-NOELLES WERE entertaining their eldest daughter and her husband when the telephone rang and Sybil went to answer it, her expression one of amazement at the inarticulate noises coming from her cousin, interspersed with sobs and anguished moans of distress.

'Lucy, I can't understand what you're saying,' she said eventually. 'Is it Johnny? We're meeting this evening, can't it wait until then?'

The line went dead, and Sybil said, 'I've got to get over there. Something is evidently wrong; she's so distressed I couldn't understand what she was saying.'

'Well, surely it can wait until we've finished lunch,' her husband said testily. 'This is the first time we've seen Helena and her husband for months.'

Helena said practically, 'We'll finish lunch, Mummy, then I'll drive you over to Aunt Lucy's. It's probably something and nothing; you know how she goes on about things.'

'Something is very wrong. I don't want any more lunch; I want to leave now.'

Resignedly Helena looked at her father who shook his head dismally while her husband said, 'Do you want me to drive you?'

'No, dear, Mummy and I will go. You stay here with Daddy. He'll tell you what he intends to do with the outbuildings; you can tell him what you think about his ideas.'

'He won't change his mind about anything,' Sybil snapped. 'I've been trying; I don't think you're likely to have any more luck, John.'

So Helena and her mother left them to finish their lunch and on the way there Sybil said anxiously, 'Something's very wrong, Helena. When we were young Lucy was always the calm one, the humorous one, while I saw difficulties that weren't really there; she's changed so much, now she's too possessive with her grandson, too remote from Lisa, even from Johnny. I thought she'd be different when Dominic came home, but she isn't.'

'Well, Mummy, it was terrible when Austin was killed and it must have had an effect on Aunt Lucy; perhaps that's why she's so engrossed with Antony.'

'Perhaps. Isn't that Johnny stomping across the parkland towards the stables?'

There was no mistaking his tall portly figure, hands thrust deep inside his pockets, eyes staring morosely at the ground, and Sybil said, 'Well, there's evidently nothing wrong with Johnny; it must be something else, probably the child, measles or something.'

Instead of driving on to the house Helena turned the

car round and drove in the direction of the stables so that they met Johnny on his way there. He stared at them uncertainly before walking over to the car, and through the open window Sybil cried, 'What's wrong, Johnny? Lucy was very upset.'

'She is, we both are. She'll be glad you've driven over. I'm saying nothing; let her tell you what she knows.'

They had to be content with that so they drove on to the house, where they were shown into the drawing room by the butler, whose expressionless face told them nothing.

Lucy sat facing the fire, and their only greeting came from her Yorkshire terrier, who rushed over from his place beside her chair, wagging his tail and evidently unconcerned with his mistress's ravaged face and the sobs that started afresh.

It took several minutes for her to compose herself, while Sybil and Helena merely sat there waiting for the sobs to subside, then Sybil said gently, 'What is it Lucy? We've just seen Johnny, so evidently the problems are not of his making.'

Almost savagely Lucy cried, 'As though we haven't had enough tragedy to contend with. I've lost Austin, now it's Dominic.' The sobs started afresh.

'Dominic?' Sybil prompted. 'Surely Dominic isn't ill; he looked extremely well when I saw him in church the other Sunday.'

'He's not ill; he's unhappy with his marriage, with a wife who is in love with somebody else, and he is saying they both intend to separate, divorce. Have you ever heard of anything more dreadful? Where does that leave their son, the family?'

For a long moment there was silence, then Sybil said, 'You say Lisa is in love with somebody else. Who? Where did she meet this person? We've never seen her with another man; she's always been on her own all through the war. I don't believe it.'

'She's in love with Lt. Col. Lawson. It's probably been an affair that's been going on here right under our noses, and to think we made him so welcome in our house. He had the run of the place and was kind to the boy. I can't believe that none of us knew what was happening.'

'But isn't he Indian Army? He'll be going back there; he's probably got some girl there; it'll all blow over, I'm sure of it.'

'You mean Dominic should forget the adultery, behave as though nothing has happened?'

'Well no, not really, but divorce!'

'They've driven over to Martindale where they intend to stay for several days, talk about things, discuss their future, then I suppose when they've decided what to do they'll have the courage to come back and tell us.'

For the first time Helena spoke, saying, 'Lisa was always so much in love with Dominic, I can't believe she fell out of love with him.'

'Well, evidently she did,' Lucy snapped. 'He was away serving his country, Lieutenant-Colonel Lawson was convalescing here and making overtures to his wife.'

'He didn't seem that sort of man to me,' Sybil said slowly.

Lucy rounded on her by saying, 'You can be very wrong about people, Sybil. He was handsome, obviously an officer and a gentleman, but also not averse to forgetting all that when confronted with a young woman whose husband was not here to take care of her.'

'Dominic must be either devastated or terribly angry with his wife. What are they going to talk about? Surely there can only be divorce and for her to get out of his life as quickly as possible,' Sybil volunteered.

'Isn't there my grandson to talk about? Isn't he the most important thing to talk about?'

'He is her son, Lucy.'

'He is Dominic's son too, and my grandson. She is not going to take my grandson away from me; he is the future Lord Hazelmere after his father and should be brought up either here or Martindale, not with a mother who could end up living at the other side of the world with some man who is not even related to him.'

'Don't the courts decide this sort of thing?' Sybil murmured.

'Perhaps they do in the case of just anybody, but Antony is not just anybody—he is the heir to a long and noble name, the son of a father who has done no wrong. We will fight her all the way to keep Antony, Dominic will fight her; I shall make that very clear to both of them.'

For some time there was silence, the only sounds Lucy's sobs, the crackling of logs in the grate and outside the staccato sounds of rain on the window pane; it was Helena who finally said, 'So many of my friends were in love with Dominic. He was always so reserved, so remote if you like, and that only made them more keen. When Lisa captured him they couldn't believe it. She wasn't exactly in our circle although she was so beautiful. Even so, she didn't have money or position and that counted so much.'

'What do you mean, Helena?' Lucy asked. 'She did have some sort of status; she was related to us, to Dominic; surely they saw that.'

'Not really. I only know that most of the girls were pretty stunned when they didn't get a look in and he went for Lisa instead.'

'You did rather push it, Lucy,' Sybil said.

Immediately Lucy said sharply, 'I could see the way things were gong. Dominic was not in the least attracted to the girls who were trotted out for most of the boys. It was probably the mere fact that Lisa was not one of them that attracted him to her in the first place. Anyway, none of that matters now; Antony matters. I want Lisa out of here—she can go to her mother, so there won't be any problem with that.'

'Don't you think there could be a very large problem there?' Sybil answered.

'Oh, you mean the vicar, I suppose. Well, I'll admit he's not going to be very happy with divorce, the Church does not accept it, and divorce involving the son of Lord Hazelmere will be even more difficult for him to swallow. But that has to be their problem, Sybil. We didn't ask for this trouble, neither did they, but that is surely something for them to surmount.'

It was not the time to discuss the Church's prejudices or the effect Lisa's divorce was likely to have on the vicar's career or his relationship with his wife's daughter, and when Sybil and Helena left Hazelmere to drive home no amount of talking had resolved whatever the future had in store.

As they drove past the vicarage Sybil said, 'I can't think that is a very happy household at the moment.' She was right.

Mary faced her husband only too aware of his morose expression. He had spent much of his life counselling some of his young parishioners against the evils of divorce and the greater evils of adultery. He had met their tears of despair with stern righteousness, admonishing them to forget love, forget misery within their marriage, and think only of their children, that love outside marriage was transient and meaningless, that only their marriage vows meant anything and were inviolate. Those who disregarded his advice were cast out, no longer welcome, pariahs within society, even when in his innermost heart he knew that some of them were being returned to a life of cruelty and fear. It didn't matter—they were the teachings of his Church, and it was his duty to see that they were honoured. Now here was his wife's daughter involved in a scandal he had preached against.

At last he said, 'You heard them, Mary, they are not

going to listen to anything anybody says; they are intent on divorce at any cost.'

Mary nodded, and he went on, 'It's early days, perhaps when they've had time to think about it, but no, as I said, they've made their minds up; it's divorce, and what then?'

'I spoke to Adrian; he loves Lisa and intends to marry her; Dominic will not oppose it.'

'That is what I cannot understand. No mention of his son, no thoughts about his family; he is willing to let Lisa go without even trying to make her change her mind. It seemed to me that divorce was something they both want—I can understand Lisa, she's found somebody else, but Dominic will be alone.'

'I know.'

'Can you understand that, Mary?'

'There have been many times when I have not understood Dominic. I have always liked him, but there were also many times when I thought he should never have married my daughter. Oh, she wanted him, heaven knows how much she wanted him, but I was never sure if he cared for her to the same extent.'

'What do you mean?'

'He was always kind, approachable, generous, but I was never sure that he loved her. She assured me that everything was perfect, but she wanted it to be.'

'And the boy?'

'I don't know. Oh, surely Antony will go with Lisa, but what sort of life will it be for him in India? He should be in England at school.'

'Well, it's out of our hands, Mary; we can only advise. I'm sure Dominic will concern himself about the future of his son.'

'I'm worried about you, dear. How will it affect your work here? What is happening is against everything you believe in; I feel responsible that all this will affect you, make it impossible for you to carry on here as vicar, and that it is I and Lisa who have done this to you. How will you be able to face those people who need your advice when in your own family there is going to be this awful scandal?'

'I don't know, my dear. The bishop will be made aware of what is going on; he will no doubt advise me how to handle it.'

'Suppose he suggests your resignation? You love it here; where would you go, and would the scandal follow us wherever we go?'

'I don't know, Mary. For today at any rate there is nothing we can do; for the immediate future we can simply live one day at a time, and remember we are not the only ones who will be suffering. There is Dominic's family, and Adrian's family. We don't know anything about them, do we?'

'He has parents in India.'

'There you are, you see. Two families who are going to be hurt by this. Do you think we should visit Lord Hazelmere and his wife? Will it help, do you think?'

Startled, Mary looked at him. 'Oh no, not yet at any price. I think we should wait until Dominic and Lisa can tell us what has been decided. I couldn't face Lucy at this moment; she will be distraught and Sybil too. They will be so angry with Lisa, I can't think they will want to see me.'

'None of it is your fault, Mary.'

'Perhaps not, but I think for the time being we should keep our distance.'

Back at the Jarvison-Noelles' house Helena and her husband sat listening to her parents voicing their opinions on the scandal waiting to erupt, and as they said their goodbyes a little later to walk back to their car Helena said, 'I wonder where Lisa will go. I suppose I could invite her to stay with us until things get sorted.'

'I never heard such nonsense,' her husband said. 'Your mother would be furious.'

'She needn't know. How often do we see them? And Lisa'll need somebody before she goes off to marry her Indian army officer.'

'She must have other friends.'

'Not really. Privately educated, and not exactly one of us. I liked her. She hated coming up to the house to be educated; she was made to come very much against her will and she could be rebellious. When I really got to know her she was lovely; she had a wonderful sense of humour and she was so clever. Mother didn't like her being brighter than us, but she was.'

'I don't think it's a good idea, Helena, I would hate your mother and Lady Hazelmere to think you were taking sides.'

'I'll talk to Dominic; he'll not object, and he's the person most concerned.'

'I never really got to know him.'

'Getting to know him wasn't easy. Austin was the easy one; he was fun, a terrible flirt and totally undependable, whereas Dominic was always nice; you always knew you could rely on him to keep a secret or be kind to your friends. The only thing you couldn't rely on him for was to return their affection.'

'I say, you don't think he was suspect do you?'

'Suspect! What do you mean by that?'

'You know, fonder of chaps than he was of girls?'

She looked at him in amazement before saying, 'What a ridiculous thing to say, of course he wasn't. He married Lisa and they had a child, he's reserved, predictable, but he's not homosexual. That's what you meant, isn't it?'

'I suppose so.'

'Honestly, darling, you should get to know Dominic better. He's a brilliant horseman, got mentioned in despatches during the war and he's totally all male; I won't have you thinking anything else.'

'Well you started it, darling, with your talk about having Lisa to stay with us. It's not a good idea so forget it, will you.'

For the days Lisa and Dominic were together at Martindale they discovered a friendship that had been denied them in their manufactured marriage. They rode their horses together around the village, and the villagers smiled at them, unaware that soon they were to separate.

They dined together and talked over the meal like old friends, then in the evening they listened to music before retiring to their separate rooms.

Lisa was no longer plagued by the old punishing desire to have him make love to her, that he should be a lover never a friend; now that he was a friend she was content because his friendship was stalwart and enduring. The Dominic who had seemed so remote was now like she'd always imagined he would be—humorous and companionable—and they could talk about their separate futures in the knowledge that however far apart they might be they would both care about each other.

They talked about Antony and Lisa asked, 'Could you ever love him, Dominic? Remember that he is still only a child.'

'I will be a good father to him, Lisa, and one day when we have truly got to know each other I will care very deeply for him. I think we are being wise to send him to school in this country—my old prep school and then college. My mother loves him very dearly and she will be kind to him during the school holidays when he is at Hazelmere or here for only a couple of weeks. In the summer he can be with you wherever you are.'

'But he is only a child. How could he come to India?'

'He won't always be a child. When I was at school we had a great many children whose parents lived overseas. They saw nothing unusual in being asked to journey home to be with them, and their parents came to England to see them. Lisa, our lives are going to change, Antony's too.'

'Will there ever be anybody for you, Dominic?'

He shrugged his shoulders. 'I don't know—perhaps. You can be sure that people will speculate on my lifestyle, my solitary state which is perhaps unnatural.'

Lisa was dreading their return to confront his parents and perhaps even more so her mother and her husband. She received a long letter from Adrian written on his voyage to Bombay. The ship, the *Empress of India*, was filled with returning Indian Army officers and men and he was looking forward to seeing his parents again, but he did not tell her that he was also dreading that meeting. Nobody more than Adrian was aware of his father's intransigence or his mother's long-held desire that one day he would marry Catherine.

Lisa only read about the superficial things that were happening to him—the light-hearted camaraderie on the ship between men who had lived through the horrors of war and were now going to the country they called home to live out their days of service. Adrian told her that she would love India—the pageantry and the magnificence, the sunshine and the proud patriotism, the regimental balls and the soirées—and he never told her of the underlying resentment of a people who felt their country was not their own.

Those same people realised that although the British had given them a great deal, it was not enough; those same people would have been willing to face starvation, poverty, disease even, if they could call their country their own, and Adrian knew that these were cravings Lisa would find out for herself. Closer to his heart were the feelings of family and friends; India would sort out her own salvation.

She was leaving Martindale for the last time, the beautiful house that she had thought would one day be her home. She stood on the terrace looking up at the stone facade, the large mullioned windows and the exquisite symmetry of the chimneys and roof, and at the gardens leading down to the slow meandering river. One day Antony would live in this house; one day when he was Viscount Lexican he might bring his young bride here; one day he might tell her about his mother. That she had never really lived here, that she had merely always been a passenger in the life of this house and the family who owned it.

Dominic came down the steps to join her, and seeing the look in her eyes he said gently, 'Forget Martindale, Lisa, forget the last few years; relegate them to something neither of us had a right to. Your future is somewhere else, with somebody else who will love you as you need to be loved.'

CHAPTER TWENTY-SEVEN

IN INDIA ADRIAN FACED HIS mother's anguished disbelief and his father's anticipated truculence.

'You're telling us you've fallen in love with a woman you hardly know, another man's wife, the mother of his son, and while you were convalescing in his parents' house. What sort of honour is there in that?'

'I know that's how it seems to you, Father, but there's more that you would never understand, more that I can't tell you.'

'Why? Why can't you tell me?'

'Because in these times we live in it would be considered too scandalous, too shameful.'

'And so it is. An affair with a married woman, and now you say you're going to marry her, that she's coming here as your wife. What is she expecting from you that she's willing to give up her title for?'

'I can assure you, Father, that she is not concerned about her title; she is giving it up gladly and all the things that go with it.'

'What about Catherine?' his mother asked plaintively.

'They'll be coming here on Saturday to dinner. I've already invited them and they'll be expecting you and Catherine to announce your engagement. Her mother said as much only yesterday.'

'I shall endeavour to speak to Catherine in the morning, Mother. I hope she'll understand.'

'How can she understand?' his father snapped. 'You've known her since you were little more than children and you're giving her up for a woman you hardly know. What is there to understand in that?'

'Father, it's happened. Perhaps I knew Catherine too well, as a friend, even like a sister; I know now that I had never been in love until I met Lisa.'

'You'll say that to Catherine, will you?'

'I'll try to be as kind and considerate to Catherine as you would want me to be, Father, but I can't help the way I feel. I hope you will accept Lisa and make her feel welcome here.'

'You're asking a lot, Adrian. You're asking us to accept a woman you've had an affair with, a woman who will leave her husband and son to come here to be with you, and we were expecting a very different kind of daughter-in-law. No, Adrian, I doubt if we can ever accept Viscountess Lexican.'

Adrian winced at the sound of Lisa's name on his father's lips then he said evenly, 'In which case, Father, it will have to be the parting of the ways. Lisa will be my wife, and if you can't accept her then you will have to lose me.'

'You know what society here is like; it will be on everybody's lips.'

'I shall get a transfer; that shouldn't be too difficult—Burma, the Sudan, perhaps the Punjab. I had a good record in the war, my promotion's been excellent, some of it thanks to you I've no doubt, but I do want you and Mother to understand that Lisa will be my wife; she will have to come first.'

'So it doesn't matter, then, all the years you've meant everything to us. Is this how you're going to repay us?'

'Father, it doesn't have to be like this. Meet Lisa before you judge her; try to see in her the woman I fell in love with, the woman my life with you conditioned me to fall in love with.'

'Isn't that why we thought it should be Catherine?' his mother asked plaintively.

Adrian looked at her sorrowfully. 'Like I said, Mother, I'll speak to Catherine in the morning. Perhaps one day there'll be somebody for her, somebody new in her life, not a man she's been conditioned for without the enticement of somebody new.'

Adrian had no means of knowing how it would go. He knew his father's intractability, his belief that he was always right and other people's opinions could usually be discounted, but he knew too that his mother would often agree with him when everything in her wanted her to clash with his opinions.

Adrian knew that life in his parents' house would be insupportable in the time leading up to Lisa's arrival in

India. His mother's tears, the long silences, his father's condemnation and he realised he would need a transfer so that Lisa would not be subjected to any of it.

For a while the following morning he watched a polo match between two friendly sides, and he was asked why he'd decided not to play. Instead he simply smiled and said he was waiting for someone, and their returning smiles told him that they knew exactly who he was waiting for.

Catherine arrived promptly and he watched her walking towards him, occasionally pausing to speak to people she met on the way; his heart ached at the thought that he was very soon about to break her heart. She smiled, and he thought instantly that she was so very different to Lisa, with a cool English beauty of dark blond hair and blue eyes, wearing a cream shantung dress and a large cream hat to shade her from the sun.

He went forward to embrace her, kissing her cheek gently, while her eyes showed a surprise that his greeting was not more loving.

'You decided not to play?' she asked him.

He nodded. 'Yes. Shall we walk over to the pavilion? It will be cooler there and we have so much to talk about, Catherine.'

They walked slowly and discussed banalities. Catherine was aware that he was troubled, that this was far from the greeting she had expected after four long years.

They found seats on the verandah away from the others, and after ordering drinks Catherine waited for Adrian to be the first to break the silence.

'I believe my parents have invited you over for dinner this evening,' he said.

'Yes. I wasn't expecting to see you until then. I thought you would have things to do.'

'Nothing that couldn't wait. I had to see you alone, Catherine. I haven't been looking forward to it—nothing I can say will come easily.'

He saw the sudden anxiety in her eyes, and he hated himself for what he was about to do to her. As gently as he could he told her about Lisa, the sudden blinding attraction, the realisation that whatever he had felt about being in love in the past had been an illusion, an illusion that had perished as if in a dream.

After he had told her there was a long silence, but he was unprepared for her question, 'Is she very beautiful, Adrian?'

'Yes she is, but it has nothing to do with that.'

'What then?'

'At first she was an enigma. I wanted to know her better, but she seemed incredibly lonely; she lived surrounded by a rich and powerful family and yet she never seemed to be one of them. Her husband was serving in France but she never spoke of him; her son was like her, and yet it was his grandmother who demanded all his attention. As I said, she was an enigma and I became afraid of the feelings she was arousing in me. I had never experienced them before. We tried to avoid each other, but whenever we did meet I knew that she too felt as I did. In the end it was something neither of us could fight.'

'And her husband will divorce her?'

'Yes. I have met him and I liked him, but that is as much as I can say about him.'

'And the boy?'

'He is old enough to go to school. You know how it is with us, Catherine, an English education no matter where our parents live.'

'But he will come here surely?'

'I have left all that for Lisa to resolve. In the summer holidays I have no doubt either he will come here or Lisa will go to England to see him. She will arrange all this with his father.'

'It all sounds very civilized, somehow cold.'

'I know. This is how I found them, cold and detached, yet capable of arrogance.'

'And yet they were capable of turning over half their home for wounded servicemen.'

'I admit it sounds incongruous, but it is what a great many stately homes were expected to do during the war. They were patriotic. One son was killed in France. I did not say that they were bad people, Catherine, only that where Lisa was concerned there was this strange barrier I couldn't understand.'

'You've told your parents, of course?'

'Yes, last evening. It was difficult as you can imagine.'

'I expect your father was the difficult one.'

'I knew what to expect: Mother was tearful, Father intransigent.'

'They will accept her when they realise there is nothing they can do about it.'

'I don't think so, Catherine. You know my father. I'm a grown man with four years of war behind me, but in something like this he still thinks he has a right to expect obedience, just as he did when I was a boy on holiday from school. Your own father is no different.'

'No. He too will be furious about all this. I really don't think it's a good idea to dine with your parents this evening. I couldn't sit through all the recriminations. What are you going to do, Adrian?'

'I'm going to request a transfer. Lisa will have had enough trauma in England—I can't expect her to face it here and we can't start our married life together in an atmosphere of anger and disappointment. I may opt for the Punjab or Burma, there are endless possibilities and I have a good rank and reputation, I think.'

'Oh yes, Adrian, the best, even your father would have to admit that; there doesn't seem to be anything else to say, does there?'

'Only that I'm so terribly sorry and I know how trite and meaningless that sentiment sounds. I hope we're still friends, Catherine. You know I think a great deal about you; nothing of this can alter that. But will you still want to be my friend, I wonder?'

'Yes, Adrian. Perhaps we did know each other too well; perhaps we might have drifted into marriage without ever knowing there had to be more. One day I might find some man I hardly know, but someone who is capable of filling all the empty places in my heart.'

'You will, Catherine. When we were together we never

looked at anybody else; we thought we had it all—without me as your shadow who knows who you might meet.'

For a long moment they looked into each other's eyes, then she turned away and he stood staring after her until she passed through the gates.

There were so many regrets in his mind at that moment, memories of other years, dances and soirées when they were happy in each other's company—a handsome young officer and a beautiful girl basking in the approval of their respective families, and now almost in a dream it had all gone. He thought about Lisa, a girl he hardly knew, a woman he had yet to discover. What would his parents make of her exotic beauty and how much reproach would there be from the men he had served with, their wives and families who had believed he and Catherine were inviolate?

His parents had believed that the evening ahead of them would be one of celebration, two families toasting the coming together of a son and daughter who meant so much to them; now the evening would be nothing to celebrate—only his father's dour expression and his mother's misery.

Tomorrow he would have to put in motion his early departure; he certainly couldn't be expected to stand weeks and months of sulks and tears. One day perhaps when his parents realised their marriage had worked, that their love had lasted, perhaps when they realised they were grandparents to his children, then there could be peace between them. But all that was in the future; the present had to be got through first.

Catherine too would be suffering the astonishment and displeasure of her parents, and they would hate him for the sadness he had subjected her to and a disloyalty they would never have thought him capable of showing. He would have to visit them, to make them understand, even when he knew he would be setting himself an impossible task.

His father had made good use of his time by informing his friends about his son's transgression, and his general was aware of matters when Adrian put in his request for service elsewhere.

'Are you sure this is what you want, Adrian?' he asked shortly. 'All this for a woman, a woman you've known for such a short time. Your father's furious and your mother's inconsolable, and the Kelshaw family too—they're all convinced you're making a mistake you'll come to regret.'

'I'm sure they are, sir. If it is a mistake then I shall have to bear the consequences. At the moment I don't think it is a mistake. I'm a grown man; I think I can be expected to know my own mind.'

'You've suggested Burma or the Punjab; any preference?'

'The Punjab perhaps; Lahore or one of the stations.'

'Lahore, I think. It is a little more civilized and your wife will hardly be looking forward to life on the frontier.'

Adrian looked at him pointedly but offered no answer, and after a few minutes the other officer said in a more conciliatory tone, 'I shouldn't have said that, after all I don't know the lady, but I can't help thinking you're making a very big mistake.'

'You've already spoken to my father?'

'Yes, this morning, and if I were you I'd give him a wide berth this evening. He told me you'd be moving out and I was to discourage you.'

'I don't see why when he doesn't exactly want me and my wife living in the vicinity.'

'He's hoping you'll change your mind.'

'I've told him there's no chance of that.'

'Isn't she some countess or something, used to high living, English aristocracy? Does she know what she's letting herself in for?'

'My father is surmising what she will be like without even having met her. Lisa has survived worse than anything India can do to her, I can assure you. I shall be quite happy to settle for Lahore, sir.'

'In that case I'll recall Peterson. He'll be highly gratified to be back in Delhi and he doesn't have a wife to contend with.'

'When shall I be expected to arrive there?'

'The sooner the better, I'm sure, from your point of view. Give it a couple of weeks. You'll take over Peterson's living accommodation. It's quite reasonable, I believe, and since he went there he's made few complaints. When are you expecting the lady to arrive?'

'I'm not sure; there are several matters to resolve.'

'She'll sail into Bombay, I suppose?'

'Yes.'

'Then you'll be wanting leave to meet her?'

'Yes sir, and to get married by special licence.'

'Hmmm. So you're not expecting a bevy of guests at the ceremony?'

'No. sir. Unimportant, I think. Guests who don't wish to be there would only be an encumbrance.'

'Oh well then, that's all arranged. Lahore within the next two weeks, and one day I hope we'll see you here again. You're a good officer, one of my best; I deplore all this both for you and your parents.'

Adrian saluted and made his escape. It had worked out quicker than he had thought but still ahead of him lay the evening with his parents, and later his visit to Catherine's house. On arriving home, however, he was informed by the houseboy that his parents were out, dining with Sahib Kelshaw and his family. The houseboy favoured him with a sympathetic smile which told Adrian that he was well aware of the tension within the family.

Catherine too was unhappy with the events of the evening, listening to Adrian's father's condemnation and his mother's quiet sobs in which her mother joined.

His father said tetchily, 'Couldn't you persuade him, Catherine? After all, he hasn't seen you for four years; I thought when he saw you again he'd quickly realise where his true loyalties lay.'

'I didn't attempt to change his mind, General Lawson. It was already made up.'

'All the same—' his father murmured.

Then her father snapped, 'You can't expect my daughter to beg, Lawson. After all most of the chaps in the regiment have envied him because of Catherine; now that he's out of her life there'll be somebody more worthy of her.'

'Well, I hope so. I'll be the first to wish him well and wish it was my son, that's all.'

Catherine was weary of it. When at last they made their farewells she escorted them to the door and Lady Lawson embraced her with tear-filled eyes, saying, 'I am sorry, my dear. You won't forget that we love you very dearly and that our regrets are very real. You will come to see us, Catherine; never forget that you are the daughter-in-law we wanted.'

It was in the end a nine-day wonder. Other matters arose to hold people's attention—uprisings in Madras and Calcutta, skirmishes with the Afghans on the frontier, and in Delhi the usual regimental balls, soirées and polo matches.

The bungalow on the outskirts of Lahore was pleasant enough, but looking round the small rooms with their wicker furniture and shuttered windows, Adrian thought about all that Lisa was exchanging it for. Would she forget the splendour of Hazelmere and Martindale, the rolling hills and vast parkland when she viewed the small bungalow with the one houseboy as servant?

It was true the garden was charming with its lotus pond and fragrant bushes, but this was a serving officer's domain, hardly a stately home. Would his love for her make up for other things she would be missing, her mother and her son, friends she had locally and the familiar pleasures of music and books in the vast library where they had once made love?

There would be days when she would be alone when he was off to quell some trouble spot, and how would she regard the absence of his parents and the fact that they had not wanted to meet her?

He had known most of the other officers and their wives for a great many years and they had known Catherine. They asked no questions of their commanding officer and he volunteered no answers, but he knew in the mess they conjectured about why so much in his life had changed.

To put an end to their suppositions he made it his business to inform the Adjutant and his wife that he intended to marry a woman he had met in England during the war and that she would be coming over to join him in the not-too-distant future.

They were too polite to ask questions, but he imagined the story would be circulated amongst the others. They would be aware that his parents were not in favour of the marriage since they never visited nor did he go to see them, and because they had known Catherine too they would no doubt extend all their sympathy to her.

He was glad of the treks to distant outposts, the pageantry that they kept so palpably alive, from the parade of elephants to the ceremonies each day at sundown, but he deplored the loneliness of the nights he spent on his own in the bungalow composing letters to Lisa in which he told her how much he wanted her to join him and prayed it would be soon.

His parents' behaviour was a constant source of grief to him—his father's inflexibility, his mother's compliance—but Catherine wrote to him occasionally, telling him the news from Delhi and very little about herself. She dined with his parents frequently and said they were both well, but she never said if his name was ever mentioned or if there was any hint of forgiveness.

She had met Major Peterson, who had told her something of his bungalow and the life he would be experiencing in Lahore. Her letters always ended with expressions of love and friendship and the hope that all would go well with him when Lisa eventually joined him.

Her sentiments upset him. He felt he did not deserve them, but if he'd married her as planned would the living of a lie have been right for either of them?

What would Lisa think of the bungalow? He'd give her a free hand to make any alterations she thought fit, but what pleasure would she derive from it when she remembered Hazelmere?

Then he realised he was being foolish. Lisa would not compare it with Hazelmere. Hazelmere had never given her love or the real feeling of belonging; surely a tent in the desert was incomparably better than a palace without love.

CHAPTER TWENTY-EIGHT

LISA WAS INVITED TO JOIN a group of women as she sauntered across the garden path to where she could watch the polo match. They were the wives of other officers, and they made way for her in their midst with smiles and greetings.

The divorce on the grounds of her adultery had seemed almost a formality and, as she sailed out to Bombay, she found it hard to believe that behind her she had left a legacy of bitterness and that only Dominic was able to show any sort of understanding.

At first she had been lonely in Lahore, particularly when Adrian was away in some remote part of the Punjab. She was treated with politeness, but always she had the feeling that she was being assessed, realising that they knew something of her background and they were waiting for her to make the first move.

She had been surprised to find Adrian serving in Lahore when he had spoken only of Delhi and quickly became aware that she was to receive no welcome from his parents. It seemed to Lisa that she had brought problems into so many lives, not least her son and her mother, and now it would appear into Adrian's family also.

She asked for explanations and although he told her that nothing mattered now that they were together, she understood their resentment and their hurt. When he told her about Catherine's reaction it only seemed to add to the list of those they had injured.

'Did you ever love her?' she asked him plaintively. His reply was that he had believed he had until he met Lisa, but then he knew that he had never really known what it was like to fall in love.

'How she must hate me,' she murmured, but he was quick to say that Catherine would come to terms with her life and find another man to love her; perhaps she would discover as he had done that what they had had never been love at all.

She understood then why the other women were wary of her, and that only time would alter things. She went to polo matches and regimental dinners, and Adrian gave her full rein to change whatever she felt was necessary to the furnishing of the bungalow.

That was the start of new friendships. When she asked one of the women where she could buy silk for curtains and cushion covers they were kind enough to take her to the bazaars and show her where she could find exquisite silks and shantungs.

It was in one of the bazaars one morning that a woman stood beside her as she fingered the material; their eyes met and Lisa said, 'They are exquisite but I'm not sure

I'm capable of making drapes and cushions. I've never been a great sewer.'

The woman smiled, and in a voice that was pure West Country she said, 'Eh ma'am, I can make 'em up for ye. I does most o' the sewing for the officers' wives, even their frocks. I'm Mrs Emerson, mi 'usband's a sergeant in't forty-ninth.'

'Oh Mrs Emerson, I would be so grateful. I'm Mrs Lawson, the lieutenant-colonel's wife.'

'I knows who you are, ma'am, I've seen you at the polo and I asked who you were. It was your colour-in', ye know. Ye looked Spanish, if ye'll forgive mi sayin' so.'

'My grandmother was Spanish.'

'Is that right? Well, I'll do whatever ye wants with these silks. Just tell me the measurements, and ask any o' the other ladies—they'll vouch for me, I'm sure.'

'Thank you, I don't need to ask them; I'm sure you will do an excellent job. Perhaps you would care to come round to the bungalow so that you can see for yourself what is needed.'

'Well yes, Mrs Lawson, if that's all right. I'll call round this evenin' or in the morning if that's what you prefer.'

'Perhaps in the morning, Mrs Emerson. My husband is coming back this evening and I'm not sure of the time.'

When she told Adrian he laughed. 'Mrs Emerson's well known, Lisa. She's a good sort—when the others know she's doing work for you they'll ask questions about you, and no doubt she'll put them right.'

* * *

Mrs Emerson was indeed a good ambassador for Lisa, since she informed anybody who cared to listen that the lieutenant-colonel's wife was a lovely lady and whether she was English aristocracy or not she was very kind and approachable.

When his parents and Catherine were mentioned Mrs Emerson said that indeed Miss Catherine had been a very nice girl but they'd been more like brother and sister than two young lovers. It didn't do to tell children who they should fall in love with and evidently the lieutenant-colonel had gone to England and found somebody else.

Lisa found friends, at first to chat to and then to visit, and in time they endorsed Mrs Emerson's views of her. They found her charming and friendly but none of them were able to discover anything about her life before she had joined Adrian in the Punjab.

Lily Jessop, who was always the most forthcoming of the wives, did have the temerity to ask, 'Will your son be joining you here, Lisa? Isn't he at school in England?'

'Yes, I do hope so, perhaps for holidays,' Lisa answered and changing the subject said, 'The next time Adrian gets leave we hope to visit Kashmir; I believe it's very beautiful.'

Embarrassed by Lily's question, they were quick to reassure her that indeed Kashmir was beautiful and a houseboat on the lake would be wonderful.

In the early days Lisa waited eagerly for the post from England but it often disappointed her. Her mother told her they were thinking of moving, somewhere into

the Cotswolds, that the vicar was thinking of retiring
and Lisa read between the lines that she had been the
cause of such thinking. He wasn't old enough to retire, and they both loved the church and the vicarage,
but now it was probably impossible for him to remain
in the vicinity of Hazelmere and the bitterness she
had left behind.

The brief stilted letters she received from Antony
were no better.

His housemaster had the view that boys with parents
abroad should write to them often, and he supervised the
letters they wrote. Antony told her about his lessons,
cricket and swimming lessons. He never mentioned
Dominic but constantly told her that Granny Hazelmere
sent him tuck boxes while making no mention of the presents Lisa sent him from India.

The most lively correspondence came from Helena,
who wrote about the garden parties they were attending
and the race meetings. She said that her mother was interfering too much in the way they spent their money or
their leisure time, and that Aunt Lucy agreed with her
when it was really none of her business.

She told her that Dominic was living at Martindale
permanently now so was seeing little of his parents,
but Antony spent more time with his grandmother
than his father during short school holidays. Her last
letter ended with the suggestion that perhaps one day
they would be able to spend some time in India, that
she'd always thought she'd like to go there, and it might

be an idea for them to bring Antony over for a month in the summer.

When Lisa showed Adrian her letter he merely smiled and said, 'Do you want Helena and her husband to come here?'

'Not really, but it would be nice for Antony to travel with them.'

'And suppose he doesn't want to come.'

'Oh Adrian, surely he will. He can't have forgotten me.'

Even when she said it she had to admit that Antony could quite easily have forgotten her. Lucy would have wanted him to forget her and she would have exerted all her power to see that he did so.

In the early spring all thoughts of the past were swept momentarily from her mind when she realised she was pregnant and although she wrote to tell her mother she decided against telling Helena. Helena had a mischievous mind and would take great delight in informing her mother who would then inform Lucy and no doubt Dominic too.

They belonged to the past and this new child would be the future.

Her baby was expected to be born in early January so she decided to return to London in August to see Antony and consult doctors in London regarding her condition. Adrian was unable to get leave but he insisted that she should go, and she waited in some trepidation for Antony to join her in his housemaster's study at the beginning of the summer holiday.

Her first thoughts were that he had grown. He was tall and incredibly handsome with his dark blue-black hair and dark eyes, and even his housemaster remarked how much like his mother he was.

'We'll go wherever you want to go,' she promised him. 'I haven't made any plans as I wanted you to tell me what you want to do.'

'How long am I to stay with you, Mother?' he asked shortly.

'Well, I was rather hoping you would stay with me until you have to go back to school.'

She saw the doubts casting shadows across his expression. 'I'm having a new pony at Hazelmere, Mother. Grandma Hazelmere said it would be arriving in just two weeks and I do so want to be there when it arrives.'

'You know that when I return to India you may not see me again for a long time, darling. You can see your pony every holiday that you get.'

'I know, Mother, but he's being got specially for me and has cost an awful lot of money. Grandpa said I needn't hurry home but Grandma said I should think about it.'

'I'm sure she did, darling. What did your father say?'

He shuffled his feet in embarrassment before saying sulkily, 'He said like you that I'll see the pony often.'

'Do you stay with him at Martindale, Antony?'

'Sometimes. He takes me fishing for trout and he's teaching me to play chess. He has a friend who goes fishing with us, Mr Jeffries, who spends a lot of time at Martindale. They go riding together and they play chess and snooker.'

'Is he nice, this Mr Jeffries?'

'I suppose so. He's nice with me and gets along with Father.'

Had Mr Jeffries taken the place of Oliver Cardew in Dominic's affections? she wondered. After all there surely had to be someone—she had Adrian, so why shouldn't Dominic have found somebody to care for?

She did her best to make the days she spent with Antony a success but realised he had been conditioned to think of her as somebody who had gone away—that she had come back if only briefly did not make the feelings he had once felt for her resurface; she was his mother, but there was Lucy and all that she offered.

When Lisa asked him if he ever saw his other grandmother he looked at her solemnly, saying, 'Well, they went away, didn't they, just like you went away. She wants me to go to stay with them but they don't have horses or anything, and I couldn't take Charley, could I?'

'Is that what you've called him?'

'Yes. He's got another name, some pedigree name, but I like Charley better.'

As she said goodbye to him on the station platform before she put him on the train for Hazelmere she was aware that there was a certain relief in his attitude. He was going home to people who had been there for him for all too long, his mother was going back to India, and when she asked him if he would visit them there when he was a little older, his reply was that he was learning about India at school and wasn't there always trouble there, some man called Ghandi and soldiers being killed on the North-west Frontier when they went to buy horses from the tribesmen.

'I haven't seen any trouble, Antony, but I know that it exists sometimes. If you visit us I am sure you won't see any either.'

Her reassurances didn't seem to fill him with enthusiasm to visit them and as the train pulled out of the station and he stood waving to her from the open window she was left with the feeling that the last two weeks had somehow been a waste of time from her son's point of view.

She would go back to India and over the years his letters would arrive, each one more impersonal than the last until he ran out of things to write to her about. His grandmother would condition him to act in this way and in all honesty Lisa could hardly blame her. Antony would never know his true history—it had all been written long before his birth.

Adrian was kind and understanding about her son's reaction to her visit but this was a new life, a new world and it became more and more apparent when their daughter Marcia was born in early January.

She was a good and beautiful baby and quickly an ayah was found for her from the family of an Indian soldier. She was sixteen, pretty and gentle, and she loved the baby with ecstatic devotion.

Lisa was glad that she had given birth to a daughter, not a boy who would take the place of Antony and who one day Antony might resent. The bungalow was crowded with flowers from well-wishers, and they came to drool over the baby and swamped them with presents for her.

One evening when their visitors had left Lisa asked plaintively, 'Don't you think you should inform your parents, Adrian? She is after all their grandchild.'

'They'll no doubt hear all about her in due course, darling, as in army life such news soon spreads. Like me many of the officers have friends and families in Delhi; they'll be going there on leave to see them and the story of our daughter will be a sure topic of conversation.'

'What do you think your parents will do? Surely they'll want to acknowledge her existence even if they don't think much of her mother.'

'Darling, if they don't it's their loss. My father is an obstinate, self-opinionated man and my mother invariably gives way to him for the sake of peace and quiet. Shall we wait to see how well she can insist that he changes his views?'

'But you're not hopeful?'

'Lisa, more than anybody, you know how families react—not always in the way we would want them to. Don't you think we should leave it up to them to approach us after all this time?'

Lisa's mother wrote long fulsome letters about the birth of the baby, saying that the vicar and she were delighted, and Lisa wondered how long before her mother could mention her husband as anything but the vicar. The fact that he was no longer a vicar didn't seem to have made any difference.

One letter bearing a Delhi postmark caused the most

disquiet and she sat holding it in her hands for some time before she found the courage to open it.

It contained a pretty card decorated with primroses and simply read: CONGRATULATIONS ON THE BIRTH OF YOUR DAUGHTER. I DO HOPE THAT ALL IS WELL WITH YOU. KINDEST REGARDS. CATHERINE.

When she showed it later to Adrian he said calmly, 'If Catherine knows then my parents must know also. They obviously don't care, but it was nice of Catherine to write.'

'It was magnanimous of her to write, Adrian.'

'I agree, darling. Perhaps she too has moved on; I hope so.'

In the days that followed Catherine's card was looked at long and often and Lisa found herself hoping that one day they might meet, one day when they could be friends with all bitterness and rancour behind them, when perhaps Catherine too had found new love. Surely in all this vast subcontinent there would be a man she could love and who would love her, some man she would not have been conditioned for and who would bring something new and wonderful into her life.

So Lisa reasoned during days that were often lonely, when Adrian was riding out to some distant outpost or living more dangerously near the frontier where so many British soldiers had lost their lives.

He never spoke of the dangers when he arrived home, only of comradeship and how much he had missed her and the baby, and how much he'd been looking forward to playing polo in the next match.

Lisa left Marcia in the care of her ayah, and like all the other wives headed for the Officers' Club and the polo ground. The sun shone gloriously down on pristine lawns and gardens and the women wore their prettiest clothes and hats. A group of them waited for her with warm smiles and one of them asked, 'Isn't the Adjutant's wife with you? I'm sure she intends to come.'

Indeed, watching polo and arranging club matters was the entire pivot of Emily Farnham's life and Lisa was surprised that she hadn't already arrived. Usually she called for Lisa on the way to the club, but when she hadn't done so that morning Lisa thought she should leave without her.

Indeed they were already in the refreshment tent with the match half over when they saw her hurrying from the gates, briefly waving to the ladies before entering to see to the refreshments.

'I wonder what's detained her,' one of them asked, and another said, 'Oh, we'll hear about it in due course; I'm ready for a drink, how about you?'

The match was over and she'd spoken to Adrian briefly, a jubilant Adrian who had played in the winning team; 'I'm going home now,' she informed him. 'I'll see you later, darling.'

'Well, you know I can't get off just yet, Lisa, but I won't be too late.'

She walked the short distance to the bungalow and it was only when she reached the gate that she saw a woman standing in the garden and as their eyes met the older woman came forward to meet her. She had never seen her before, but her heart missed a beat as she gazed into eyes so like Adrian's, and a smile that was his smile with all its charm.

'It is Lisa, isn't it?' the woman said.

Lisa merely smiled, but her heart was racing and after a few moments the other woman said, 'I should have written to tell you I was coming but I thought you might not answer my letter or wish to see me.'

'You're Adrian's mother, aren't you?'

'Yes. He is very like me.'

'Please come into the bungalow. It's very hot out here. Have you been waiting long?'

'No. I went to the Farnhams'. I was sorry to detain Emily but she told me to sit in the garden until the match was over and you were likely to be arriving home. I'm afraid she would be arriving very late. You know Emily, of course?'

'Yes. I find them very nice.'

'They are. He was my husband's Adjutant when we were here.'

Adrian's mother looked round the bungalow appreciatively. 'Oh, this is charming. You must have made quite a lot of alterations.'

'Cushions and curtains, a few rugs but Major Peterson was a bachelor and was happy with the bungalow as it was.'

'Yes, we've met Alan often since he arrived back in Delhi.'

'Please sit down, Lady Lawson, and I'll ask the house-boy to serve tea.'

'You didn't take your daughter to the polo then?'

'No, she is with her ayah. Her name is Marcia.'

'A very pretty name. I had to come, Lisa. You do understand, don't you?'

'I'm not sure quite what you mean. Do I understand about your being here, or the long silences before?'

'You have every right to be angry, my dear.'

'I'm not angry, Lady Lawson. Adrian was angry; I didn't know you but I was disappointed. Please excuse me while I speak to the houseboy and see to my daughter.'

'Please, please may I see her?'

'Of course. I'm sure that is why you are here.'

She could see that the ayah was sitting in the garden under a vast sunshade with the baby asleep beside her, and when she approached them the girl got up with a bright smile and a finger to her lips to tell Lisa that Marcia was asleep.

Her English was minimal, but Lisa indicated that she needed to take the child indoors and she immediately picked the baby up and handed her to her mother.

The boy was serving tea when she arrived back in the bungalow and her visitor looked up with a smile, rising to her feet and coming towards her, hands outstretched.

'Oh please let me see her, let me hold her,' she exclaimed.

Lisa placed the baby in her arms and watched as she looked down at her with tear-filled eyes, before sitting down on the couch with the child in her arms.

Tears rolled slowly down her cheeks and at last she looked up and said tremulously, 'This is our grandchild,

Lisa. I had to see her; nothing on earth would have kept me away.'

'You are welcome to stay with us here, Lady Lawson,' Lisa said. 'We have two other bedrooms, but perhaps you have made other arrangements.'

'Mrs Farnham has invited me to stay with them; she didn't know what sort of reception I would get here. If it was the one I richly deserved then I would be in need of her hospitality.'

'Does your husband know that you are here, Lady Lawson?'

She nodded. 'He knew that I intended to come; nothing he had to say would have deterred me.'

'But he had no wish to come?'

'Lisa, you have never met him. He is a stubborn, proud man who expected to be obeyed. His plans for Adrian went awry and he couldn't come to terms with it. Forgiving doesn't come easy to him, but he is learning very slowly. He knows that his son's marriage has worked, that you are happy and that you have this beautiful daughter, so please, Lisa, be patient with him; help Adrian to forgive him.'

Lisa made no such promise. Her memories were all of connivance and rigidity, pride and intolerance, so how could she ask Adrian to forgive his parents for so many of the evils she had been subjected to? Yet the alternative was insupportable. They all had to move on, put the past behind them, and for the sake of the child become a family she could depend on in the years ahead.

It was some time later that Adrian arrived and looked

at his mother across the room, his eyes wide with astonishment, hers filled with regret. She rose from her chair
and moved towards him; after a few moments he took
her into his arms.

Watching them Lisa began to think that at least there
was hope—surely his father wouldn't throw away all
that had been achieved in one brief afternoon.

CHAPTER TWENTY-NINE

CATHERINE KELSHAW WAS NOT looking forward to the Viceroy's Ball at the governor's palace. Once, years before, she would have been there with Adrian, basking in the approving glances of their respective parents and other officers aware of Adrian's potential and Catherine's suitability. Now she was attending with her parents. She would not lack for partners—her father after all was a general—but would they invite her out of pity or because they had one eye on the main chance?

She surveyed herself in the mirror and saw a tall graceful girl in a white chiffon dress, her blond hair tied back by a hoop of gardenias, her English complexion hardly touched by the hot sun of India. What did it matter that she was beautiful, admired, when the man she had loved for all too long had replaced her with another woman?

Her mother looked at her anxiously as she joined them downstairs and her father said proudly, 'You're looking very beautiful, my dear, there'll be nobody at the ball to hold a candle to you.'

She smiled. 'You would say that, Daddy. I'm not looking forward to it.'

'You'll have a wonderful time. Let the world see that Adrian Lawson is out of your life and you've forgotten him. India is full of handsome young officers simply yearning for a girl like you.'

'And I'm not yearning for them, Daddy, it's too soon. Will General Lawson and his wife be there?'

'I don't know. They've been keeping a low profile recently.'

'Honestly, Daddy, I don't mind if they are. I always liked them, and they were always very kind to me.'

'They wanted you for their daughter-in-law.'

'Well, if we're not waiting for anybody else to join us perhaps we should go,' Catherine said quickly. She wanted no more talk of what might have been.

There had been so many such balls since she was old enough to attend, with British officers in their splendid uniforms accompanied by their wives exquisitely dressed, Indian princes equally splendid, and underneath it all the intrigue and machinations for career moves, coupled with the usual flirtations that were talked about for a short time and then forgotten.

Catherine's partners were friends of her parents, high-up officers, most of them with wives, but all of them determined to see that the General's daughter enjoyed the evening.

She danced the supper dance with the son of one of them, who was rather younger than the others, and as they sat in the conservatory he said, 'I suppose you've been to quite a few of these affairs?'

'Over the years, yes.'

'And they're always the same?'

'Most of the time. People change, they move to other parts of the country, or they go home.'

'Home?'

'England is still home, Nigel.'

'Yes, of course. I've missed a lot of this. I was stationed in Lahore and then Madras. Do you know those places at all?'

'No. I've been to Nepal and Kashmir, but not to those places. Did you like Lahore?'

'I think so. There's a lot going on, whereas here it seems to be all socialising although most of the chaps enjoy that. I say, isn't that Alan Peterson over there? He was in Lahore when I was.'

'I don't know him.'

At that moment the officer standing in the doorway caught sight of them and with a brief smile walked over to join them.

'I didn't know you'd left Lahore. When was that?' Nigel asked.

'A couple of months ago, soon after you moved out to Madras.'

'You prefer it here?'

'Well, I made room for Lieutenant-Colonel Lawson. He took over my bungalow.'

'Was he demoted or something?'

'No, simply that the Garrison was being reinforced.'

He was looking at Catherine closely and she realised that he knew who she was; she was grateful that his reply was short and he was quick to change the subject.

'I'm sorry,' Nigel was saying, 'this is Miss Catherine Kelshaw, the General's daughter. She's been putting up with my dancing but I have to apologise for being out of practice.'

The Major smiled. 'I expect your dance card is already full, Miss Kelshaw.'

'I've been dancing with my parents' friends; I'm sure any one of them wouldn't mind if you took me off their hands, Major Peterson,' she replied. 'Perhaps after supper.'

He filled in his name on her dance card then excused himself on the grounds of getting something to eat.

Nigel Westlake was not the man to let sleeping dogs lie, however.

'Peterson was a nice chap in Lahore,' he said. 'I can't imagine he prefers it here; wonder why they moved him?'

'But isn't that what they do all the time, Nigel? Few officers go where they want to go.'

'Yes, but to change Lahore for Delhi, that needs some explanation.'

'Then you've done remarkably well to exchange Madras for Delhi.'

He grinned. 'I suppose you could say that. Perhaps Uncle Robert had something to do with it; but isn't Lawson a general's son?'

Catherine had had enough of it. 'If you don't mind,

Nigel, I would rather like to speak to some people over there; Martina is an old friend of mine.'

'Of course. Is that the brunette with the cigarette holder?'

'Yes.'

'I say, she's quite something, isn't she? Not as pretty as you, of course, but...' He was blushing furiously and Catherine laughed.

'Martina is quite something, Nigel. I was at school with her; she's set Delhi alight at one time or another—you could easily burn your fingers.'

Martina Jacklin was fun to be with, but undeniably the most outrageous flirt in the whole of Delhi. Married to a captain in a Lancer regiment she did not let her marriage interfere with the fun she was having. Catherine surmised that her partner could very quickly be added to her list.

The conversation now was light-hearted as Martina said airily, 'I'm glad you found a younger man to dance with, Cathy. All those friends of your father's, not one of them under sixty.'

Catherine smiled.

'Except you of course,' Martina went on, smiling at Catherine's escort. 'I haven't seen you around before; just arrived?'

'Not long ago, from Madras.'

'And are you here for some time?'

'I do hope so. Westlake's the name, Nigel.'

'Well, how do you do, Nigel, I hope we'll be seeing a lot more of each other. Catherine can usually be relied

on to pick out some entertaining companion. Things
bucking up for you, darling?'

'Perhaps.'

'Oh well, my advice is to wipe the slate clean and start
again. Look around you, darling, there's one rather nice
specimen at the bar. Major Peterson, just arrived from
Lahore. Bachelor, from a good family I believe, but not
military—gentlemen farmers from North Yorkshire.'

'You have been busy, Martina,' Catherine said.

'Well, anybody new and I have to find out about him.
Why don't I introduce you?'

'Captain Westlake has already introduced us. I believe
I am dancing with him presently.'

'Well, you know he was previously in Lahore and that
Adrian Lawson was sent to replace him; that should really interest you, darling.'

'It doesn't, Martina, they never served together. How
is your husband?'

'Working too hard. He's coming along later so you'll
see him then; in the meantime I'm making the most of
all these handsome, available, young men.'

Martina could be relied upon to be audacious, at the
same time Catherine had always found her to be a good
friend in times of trouble. She was warm-hearted and
amusing, and now as they moved back into the ballroom she pulled Catherine back so that the others could
pass on before her.

'Do you ever hear from Adrian?' she asked.

'No.'

'And his parents?'

'They never hear either. It's so sad, Martina, their one son and now they've lost him.'

'You'll always be their real daughter-in-law, Catherine. I wonder what she's like?'

'Very beautiful, I believe, Italian or Spanish looking.'

'Really. Oh well, that wouldn't have suited.'

'She's probably extremely nice.'

'It's funny, isn't it, but they've both lost out. Adrian's lost you and his parents, she's lost a son and a title; one could say they're starting even.'

'They must have thought it worthwhile. Ah, here is Major Peterson coming to claim his dance, I think.'

The Major bowed his head and took Catherine by the hand before leading her out onto the floor while Martina smiled encouragingly.

'You know Martina Jacklin?' he asked evenly.

'Oh yes, she's an old school friend.'

'Well known amongst the rabble rousers.'

'I believe so; I've always found her generous and kind. Are you going to enjoy Delhi, Major Peterson?' she asked him.

'I think so. I enjoyed Lahore, but it will be different here. Please call me Alan.'

'And I am Catherine.'

'I'm out of practice with this sort of event so I've a lot of catching up to do.'

'Did you see Adrian Lawson before you left?'

'Yes. He took over my bungalow; I hope I didn't leave it in too much of a mess. I had a decent houseboy who was staying on with Lawson.'

'I'm glad. It will be different for him.'

'I know about you and Adrian, Catherine. News travels fast and scandal never loses anything. I served with him for a time in France during the war—he was a good officer, one of the best.'

'Yes, I know he was.'

'I haven't met his wife; she joined him after I had left.'

'I hope they'll be very happy.'

He looked down at her, his expression singularly grave, then with a brief smile he said, 'I'm sure you wish them well, Catherine, you're not the sort of girl to smother them with evil thoughts; better to move on, I think.'

'I'm sure you're right.'

The dance came to an end and he said, 'I suppose the rest of your card is full?'

'I made room for you this time, I'm sure I can find another.'

'In spite of my rotten dancing?'

'It was very good, as good as mine anyway; I'm a little out of practice myself.'

She liked him and he was a new face on the scene. She needed new friends, not always the old crowd who had thought of her and Adrian as a pair. From across the room she saw her parents looking at her in the company of Adrian's parents but she decided not to join them. People still conjectured when they saw them together and she was glad to rejoin Martina, who immediately said, 'Well, and how did you get along with Major Peterson?'

'Very well, he seems very nice.'

'I've never heard anything to the contrary. If you do decide to get involved again, darling, do ask me. I know the low-down on everybody; I'll know if he's suitable.'

Catherine laughed. 'Martina, I wouldn't dare. Everybody would know you were advising me and I'm nearly thirty, you know. I should be able to know my own mind by this time.'

'Not necessarily, darling. Look at Margaret Potts—forty-five and falling for the most dissolute man in the regiment. He's married her for her money and she's still ecstatic about it.'

'Perhaps he makes her happy.'

'He will 'til he's spent all her money.'

'You're too cynical by half, Martina. There's good in everybody.'

'You've got to dig very deep to find it in Tim Potts. Look at the women he's had; gone through all the daughters of the regiment practically and now he's latched on to Margaret ten years his senior. Oh no, my dear, if I see you making any such mistakes I'll be quick to put a dampener on them. Is the Major dancing with you again, the last waltz perhaps?'

'No, I've promised that to Major Redwood.'

'What a pity. He's got a wife in tow, and the last waltz usually means the man gets to escort the lady home.'

'I'm with my parents.'

'So you are, darling, but you could have extricated yourself from that one, I'm sure.'

On a more serious note Catherine said, 'The Major didn't meet Adrian's wife; he'd left before she arrived.'

'I know, darling, he went to meet her in Bombay where they were married. Peter was in Lahore a couple of months ago and the Adjutant's wife told him she'd settled in to the bungalow and was making alterations, cushions and the like. She seemed to be quite happy there.'

'I'm glad.'

'You want to know what she's really like, don't you, Catherine? Are you ready for it, I wonder?'

When Catherine didn't speak she went on, 'She's very beautiful, with unusual green eyes and blue-black hair. Peter says a dead ringer for Cleopatra, but the Adjutant's wife says she's also extremely nice when you get to know her. At first she kept herself very much to herself, but now she's making friends and they seem extremely happy together. I know that can hurt, darling, but isn't it better to face it and move on?'

'I know it is.'

'And can you, do you think?'

'Yes, I know I can.'

'Well, here comes Major Peterson to claim his dance. Cultivate him, Catherine, and see how it works out.'

Catherine merely smiled as she joined the Major on the floor. He was smiling and she said, 'She's so audacious and yet she's funny too; I always wonder how Peter gets along with her.'

'He adores her. He knows all her faults but she's not a girl with a roving eye, even though she knows others who have one. They both come from Essex, she from a little village called Stoke Panton, he from Colchester, and they knew each other as children. Considering that she was a small village girl she's become more sophisticated than Peter, but he's totally wrapped up in her.'

'I'm glad.'

'Well, here he is anyway,' and Catherine watched as they embraced, laughing into each other's eyes before he swept her onto the floor.

'There seems to be so much good humour there,' Catherine remarked. 'Perhaps it's wrong to be too serious. I'm an only child and I was always serious, a bit of a bookworm really. Adrian was such fun, but when he talked to me about Lisa he said she'd bothered him; she'd seemed in a world of her own and was not an easy person to get to know. Perhaps he likes serious women, but why one and not the other?'

'And it still torments you?'

'Not nearly as much as it did.'

'Do you watch polo at all?'

'I always watched polo, but recently I don't seem to have gone there; I should take an interest again.'

'Well, I'm not playing tomorrow but I do intend to watch the others. Can I persuade you to join me?'

'Well, I hadn't exactly made up my mind.'

'It was just a thought, Catherine. I'm going to be there anyway. I've decided when the opportunity presents itself to get back into polo and cricket; it would be good for me.'

'I'm sure it would.'

She was glad he hadn't persuaded her to join him for polo, but at the same time felt aggrieved that he dropped the idea so quickly. It was only later driving home with her parents that her father said, 'I saw you dancing with Peterson, Catherine. You know Adrian replaced him in Lahore?'

'Yes, Father.'

'Did he have anything to say about that?'

'Why should he? He probably thought I knew anyway.'

'He seems a very nice young man,' her mother said.

'Yes, I thought so. You know, Mother, I think I might watch the polo tomorrow; it's so long since I was there. Will you be there?'

'Oh we can't dear, we have the Longworths coming for bridge.'

'I see.'

'But you must go. You have friends there, Martina and the girls you were talking to tonight. Catherine, I do wish you'd go; you'd only be a spare one at the bridge table and you did love polo so much.'

'I'll think about it, Mother.'

She thought about it a great deal while she helped her mother set out the bridge table with its cards and score sheets, but by the time the Longworths had arrived she still hadn't made up her mind.

'We wondered if we were wise to stay in to play bridge when it's such a beautiful day and everybody seemed intent on watching the game, but you've got everything ready.'

'That really doesn't matter if you'd prefer to go to the polo,' Mrs Kelshaw said, but almost immediately Mr Longworth said, 'No polo for me today; I have a very important meeting at the Embassy tomorrow—a few rubbers of bridge suits me better in this heat.'

Catherine sauntered out into the garden where she stood looking towards the polo grounds. People were walking towards them, laughing, chattering, people intent on enjoying every moment of the afternoon; from the gate a voice hailed her, 'Catherine why don't you come with us? We're joining others there.'

Catherine smiled saying, 'I'll join you later; I had half made up my mind to watch anyway.'

They waved, encouraging her to decide quickly, then she went back into the house to tell her parents.

At the ground people were sitting under the trees, on the benches and around the pavilion and as she crossed the paths several people waved to her to join them. It was Major Peterson however who called to her from where he sat with two other people in the shade of a giant jacaranda.

'You decided to come after all,' he greeted her. 'This is Major Allanson and his wife—Catherine Kelshaw,' he said introducing them.

'We're not staying,' Major Allanson said, 'we've left friends over there, so do please sit here.'

As she watched him walking towards the pavilion to order the drinks she tried to analyse her feelings. She wasn't looking for a new man in her life and yet she liked this man more than any other she had met in recent weeks and months.

He was only a little older than herself and was good looking with dark hair and straight blue eyes; but then she nervously thought to herself, he reminds me so much of Adrian, the same height, the same build, and Adrian too had blue eyes and sculptured hair.

She watched him walking back across the lawn and it could have been Adrian walking towards her as he had so often.

CHAPTER THIRTY

ADRIAN'S MOTHER SHOWED NO signs of wanting to return to Delhi. She spent the afternoons sitting with her granddaughter in the garden or visiting friends she had known before they left Lahore. In spite of the fact that her husband bombarded her with telephone requests that she come home, and innumerable letters, she simply remained adamant that she had already wasted too much time and she was enjoying herself.

Adrian was amused. For years his father had been totally dominant and his mother had agreed with whatever he wanted to do; if she had disagreed in her innermost heart she had never said so. Now it would seem she was determined to have her say. It was evident her husband was not going to join her, but he was pulling strings.

Adrian was being recalled to Delhi and in this he saw his father's machinations. He would not come to the mountain, therefore the mountain must go to him.

His mother was complacent as she recognised her husband's hand in his recall, but Lisa asked anxiously,

'Where shall we live in Delhi? Surely not with your parents?'

'No, I'm not prepared to do that. The old man's been difficult for too long. He wants me back, but it's going to be on my terms, Lisa, a new house for us and if bridges are to be rebuilt I think it would be advantageous if we were to build them from a distance.'

It was easier than they had thought. He was informed from headquarters that a bungalow would be available some way from his parents' residence, and it was only then his mother decided it was time for her to return home. General Lawson had for the first time in his life capitulated and Adrian knew that Lisa was not looking forward to her first meeting with her father-in-law. Meeting him would bring back all the trauma of her life with another family, a life she had firmly put behind her. Now it would seem she might have to endure it again. When she voiced her anxiety to Adrian he said, 'Darling, my father can be difficult, but I can handle him, and I think you will find his entire attitude will have changed. Mother will talk to him, and there is another side to him, you know, a very kind and reasonable side.'

She had to be content with that, but at the same time she was not happy to be saying farewell to the friends she had made, although she was very relieved when the ayah's family gave their permission for their daughter to go to Delhi with them. Ashima was a treasure and Lisa only wished they could also be taking the houseboy, but Adrian said he would be needed to care for his replacement.

* * *

She fell in love with Delhi and its broad avenues and white buildings. Even the native part of the city fascinated her with its bazaars and bustling alleyways, and it was in Delhi she discovered the part the British had played in its development, from the parks and gardens to the ambience of its pageantry—and she loved their bungalow with its shaded rooms and beautiful garden.

Adrian's general dealt with his return rather brusquely. 'I'm glad to have you back, Adrian,' he said sharply. 'Why you ever had to move defeats me.'

'I suppose my father had something to do with it, sir?'

'Why do you think that? There's no reason why he should have done.'

'I'm sure you're right, sir.'

He would learn nothing more about his recall so he decided to ask no questions. Life picked up its pattern and Lisa was introduced to Delhi society and all that it promised. She was the topic of conversation, he knew—wherever they went Adrian knew that their marriage was speculated on. This was the woman his parents hadn't approved of, and yet she was charming, incredibly beautiful and the men flocked around her, both married and single alike, speculating on her past as a member of the English aristocracy. Wasn't she supposed to have a son from her first marriage? What sort of affair had prompted her to leave a viscount for a humble army officer?

Gossip came easy to the women sitting at the sporting

club watching their men playing polo or cricket, and sitting with them Catherine Kelshaw was well aware that she too came in for a great deal of criticism and gossip.

Her friend Martina accosted her on her arrival at the club one morning by saying, 'Well, have you met her yet? What is she like?'

'Met who?' Catherine asked innocently.

'You know who I'm talking about, Catherine, Adrian Lawson's wife.'

'You go to as many functions as I do, Martina, haven't you met her?'

'No. You know that Peter and I have been visiting friends in the hill country.'

'I have not been present at any of the functions they have attended.'

'You mean you're afraid of meeting him?'

'No, I mean that Alan Peterson was not available to escort me and I didn't want to go with anybody else.'

'You mean there's really something going on there, Catherine?'

'No, simply that I like his company; he's back now so no doubt I'll be meeting Adrian and his wife in the near future.'

'You should show him that you're well and truly over him, Catherine, and that you've met somebody else.'

'I am over him, Martina. Alan isn't a replacement, he's simply a new friend.'

'Friend?'

'At the moment, yes.'

The women at the club decided it was inopportune to

talk about Adrian's wife, except for Molly Spencer, who was an inveterate gossip.

'Well,' she demanded, 'what do you think of her?'

'Who?' Catherine asked innocently.

'Why, Mrs Lawson, of course. Oh come on Catherine, you know who I'm talking about; we all want to know if you've met her yet.'

'Actually, no I haven't; perhaps at the next function; we have a great many of them so it's inevitable that we shall meet. I believe she's extremely nice; I have it on very good authority.'

'And here is your major,' Martina said, delighted that this was where the conversation ended; looking round, Catherine's eyes lit up at the sight of Alan strolling towards them, and with a brief smile at the other women she went to meet him.

She knew that now that she had left them they would be speculating as to how much she was involved with Alan, but as she didn't have to listen to them she was unconcerned.

'Giving you the third degree, were they?' he asked smiling.

'I'm afraid so, and no I haven't met her, but I'm not afraid to.'

'Good girl. I suggest we sit over there in the shade and I'll get some drinks sent over.'

It was so easy to pick up where they'd left off. They talked about his absence in Madras and his delight at being back in Delhi. At the end of the afternoon she realised that they had had so much to talk about they hadn't needed once to talk about Lisa or Adrian, and as she left him at the gate to the bungalow he said, 'It's the do at the Embassy on Friday, Catherine. Would you like to go?'

'Yes thank you, Alan, I would.'

'In that case I'll pick you up around eight; it'll be well attended, all the glad rags will be out and I have it on good authority that they have some visiting English dignitaries. You know how they like to put on a show.'

'I'll wear my new dress then.'

'You'll look lovely in whatever you wear, Catherine.'

As she let herself into the bungalow she tried to analyse her feelings for Alan Peterson. It had only ever been Adrian, and after him none of the men who had pursued her had meant anything. Alan had never pursued her—he had been kind, a good friend, but she did not know how deeply his feelings were involved. Both her parents were out and she sat outside in the garden thinking about the ball on Friday evening.

They would be watched by all and sundry, particularly her meeting with Adrian and his wife. Alan would be there to support her, so surely she had nothing to fear.

Early the following morning she decided to ride one of the horses around the park, and as she waited for one of the grooms to saddle her favourite mount she went to stand where she could watch a woman riding her horse over the obstacles set out for the horse show the following Saturday. She rode her big black horse with consummate ease over the largest and most difficult jumps and Catherine wondered who she was. She

could not remember having witnessed such horsemanship from any of the women she knew, so it gradually
dawned on her that she was seeing Lisa Lawson for the
first time.

The groom came to stand beside her, a young lancer
in charge of the horses and he said proudly, 'She asked
to ride the lieutenant-colonel's 'orse and 'e isn't the easiest of 'orses to 'andle. She's a fine 'orsewoman and no
mistake; her husband should 'ave bin 'ere to see it.'

'Yes, he would have been impressed.'

'Ah well, she's 'ad enough for this mornin', I'll re-
lieve 'er of the 'orse; I reckon 'e's enjoyed it too.'

She had dismounted and was leading the horse
towards the stables but when the groom took him
away she walked towards Catherine and as they
wished each other good morning Lisa said, 'I did
enjoy that. It seems so long since I did that sort of
riding and on such a perfect horse.'

'You haven't ridden in India?' Catherine asked.

'Once or twice, but not like today. I rode in England
until they took our horses away for the war. Are you riding this morning?'

'I thought I might.'

'My name is Lisa Lawson; I know we haven't met.'

'My name is Catherine Kelshaw.'

She saw the sudden awareness in Lisa's green eyes,
and in turn was acutely aware of her own embarrassment. This was not as it was meant to be, two women
alone in a deserted garden, but it was Lisa who was the
first to break the silence by saying, 'I thought that when

we met it would be at some function, a crowded ball-room or here at the polo, and there would be great speculation—you would feel hurt and embarrassed and I would feel guilty and mortified, but does it have to be like that, Catherine?'

Catherine was momentarily robbed of words. This was not how she had speculated their first conversation would be, and when she didn't immediately answer Lisa said gently, 'Adrian has talked so much about you, Catherine. I would like us to be friends.'

'It would be silly, wouldn't it, to spend the rest of our lives ignoring each other, living in the past, holding on to old resentments when I've been trying so hard to move on.'

'And have you, do you think?'

'Yes. I've made new friends.'

'I'm glad. I too once made someone the centre of my life and there was no room left for anybody else in it; it's so very hard when that one person moves out of it and there's nothing left. I would like us to be friends, Catherine.'

Catherine smiled, and Lisa said, 'Perhaps one morning we could ride together. Were you about to tackle the obstacle course?'

'Gracious no, I simply take out my old hack and ride round the park; you would find riding with me very boring.'

'I don't think so. I rode around there this morning because I was alone; with a friend there'd be so much to talk about.'

'Then perhaps one morning we'll make arrangements

'to meet here,' Catherine agreed, and it was only when Lisa had left her that she began to think back on the way Adrian had described her—the enchantment of her smile and the sadness behind it, her fundamental honesty and her reaching out for love and understanding.

All the time he'd been describing her all she could think about was that he was infatuated, that Lisa was a scheming woman who had taken a lover when her husband was at war, uncaring for her child, disguising her perfidy behind false smiles and expressions of regret; now that she had met her she too found herself believing in her searching need to be understood.

Catherine had been dreading meeting Adrian's wife at the Embassy Ball; now it didn't matter how many inquisitive eyes might watch their meeting, how many people gossiped and speculated; they had met in private and they would be able to greet each other normally in the midst of a crowded room.

Of course there was speculation. Some of the women couldn't understand the warm smiles and civilised greeting, but Catherine had Alan beside her and she could even look up into Adrian's eyes without the feeling of panic she had dreaded.

She rode with Lisa often in the early morning, and it was Lisa who tempted her to jump the smaller fences and ride a more skilful horse.

One morning as they rode back to the stables Catherine seemed in a somewhat pensive mood and Lisa asked doubtfully, 'Is something wrong, Catherine? You seem very preoccupied this morning.'

Catherine smiled. 'Alan Peterson proposed to me last night; it wasn't unexpected and yet I now find myself wishing he hadn't. What will it do to our friendship?'

'You mean you don't want to marry him.'

'I've been so grateful for his friendship and I do like him, but I'm not sure that I'm in love with him. I think perhaps that we're simply used to one another.'

For a long time Lisa was silent then she said slowly, 'How would you feel if he was sent away, into danger perhaps, that you might not see him for many months, perhaps not ever? Would it matter?'

'I'd miss him terribly. But then perhaps after a few weeks, there'd be some other young officer asking me to dance, inviting me out. Would I forget Alan? I don't know, Lisa.'

'Then I can't help you.'

'Perhaps you can, Lisa. You gave up so much for Adrian. What would I be willing to give up for Alan? That's what I keep asking myself.'

'Aren't the circumstances a little different?'

'I suppose so, but you did give up your son, Lisa. How much did it cost to give up your husband?'

'I write every week to my son and he writes back about every six or seven weeks. His letters are factual but hardly affectionate. He writes about cricket and rugger, his pony and his sailing boat, and how much his grandmother spends on him when he goes there on school holidays.'

'You don't understand that, Lisa?'

'I understand it very well. I was hoping he would come to us here, that we would visit him in England, but he doesn't want that. I have systematically been obliterated from his life.'

'By your ex-husband?'

'No, by his grandmother. But this doesn't solve your problem, Catherine. A good man has asked you to marry him, you could refuse and some other man could help you to forget him. Is that what you want, or don't you think that marriage to Alan is right for you? You could refuse him and replace him with somebody else, but would you be replacing the substance for the shadow? I always have the feeling that that is what my son has done.'

'I know what you're saying. I'm thirty, I need to be married and I want a family, my parents like Alan, everybody likes him. What is left if I let him go?'

'I let Adrian go. I thought I'd never see him again but he came back for me because he knew that I loved him. Alan might never come back for you if you refuse him.'

Catherine sighed. 'Never in a million years did I think I'd ever be listening to Adrian's wife helping me out with my problems.'

Lisa laughed. 'No, it does have a certain irony about it, doesn't it? I can't help you out about Alan, Catherine—only you can decide about that.'

'I know. He's coming for his answer this evening. I want my parents to be out, so that the decision is mine and only mine.'

As they reached Lisa's bungalow they could see

Marcia playing in the garden and she ran immediately to her mother, her beautiful face wreathed in smiles as Catherine said, 'Oh but she's so beautiful, Lisa. You must all be very proud of her.'

'Well, Adrian and his mother certainly; I'm not so sure about the General. He would have preferred a son, another future general, another soldier to carry the white man's burden.'

'I know, but he has mellowed surely?'

'We converse now. They come for dinner; he is demanding and dogmatic but yes we try to get along. Perhaps if I ever have a son then he will truly accept me.'

They said their farewells and Lisa stood at the gate watching Catherine walking along the road. She understood what the other woman was going through, the need to be sure, the ever-present uncertainties of life in a land that was not their own however long they lived in it, and the unforeseen hazards that only military life could bring.

When she told Adrian of Alan's proposal he said, 'Surely she's going to accept him; he's a good chap, one of the best, and they're both old enough to know their own minds.'

'Catherine isn't very sure about hers.'

'She'll come round to it, I'm sure. Didn't you encourage her, darling?'

'How could I? It is something only she can decide on.'

Several days later at the polo match everybody was aware that Catherine Kelshaw and Major Alan Peterson were engaged. He was playing polo in Adrian's team and as they emerged from the stables to take their place on the field from all around the park came shouts of congratulation.

Lisa was sitting with her mother-in-law and Mrs Lawson said feelingly, 'Oh I'm so glad, he's such a nice young man, and so right for Catherine. Her parents will be delighted.'

Meeting Lisa's eyes she blushed, saying, 'That sounds awful, doesn't it, but you'll see, my dear, that when Marcia is older you too will want the best for her; there will be some boys you'll dislike and others you'll hope she'll consider.'

'And sometimes it all goes wrong, doesn't it, and your son or daughter brings home the wrong sort, the one you could never have approved of in a thousand years, and then come all the recriminations and the doubts.'

'I know, dear, and we can be so wrong, can't we?'

'Sometimes you can be so right. I hope I can be strong enough never to interfere, to let my children make their own mistakes.'

'You said children, Lisa. You're thinking of having more then?'

'I don't want Marcia to be an only child. I was an only child and got all the love my parents had, but in fact I longed for a brother or a sister, somebody younger who thought as I did and acted as I did. Parents live in a different world somehow, at least the parents I knew did; they want so much for us, and somehow or other it seems to blind them to reality.'

'You're speaking very feelingly, Lisa.'

'Perhaps. My father gave me good advice but he died when I was quite young; my mother was too afraid of circumstances, people; she wanted the best for me, but the best wasn't always right.'

'You've never actually told us anything about your life before you came here, Lisa.'

Lisa was looking out across the park and suddenly she jumped to her feet saying, 'There's Catherine now; I really must go and speak to her. You don't mind do you, Mrs Lawson?'

She was gone, her mother-in-law staring after her rather sadly. It seemed Lisa would tell them nothing of the past—it was locked in her heart forever.

CHAPTER THIRTY-ONE

GENERAL LAWSON WAS ATTIRED in his best uniform for the christening of his grandson Robert Martin, and there was pride written in every line of his face. This was what he had longed for, a grandson to carry on the military tradition his great-great-grandfather had begun and he was now more than willing to forgive his son and daughter-in-law for every transgression they had made.

He greeted them warmly at the church, thinking how beautiful Lisa looked, something he had been reluctant to admit before. The baby was a brave little soul, who hadn't even cried at the splash of water he was subjected to, and as he hosted the banquet that followed those present were finally assured that old rancours and emnities were truly behind them.

Marcia by now was four years old, a beautiful happy child who was already able to twist her grandfather round her finger. Now that he had the grandson he wanted he was prepared to enjoy his granddaughter.

As he moved among his guests Adrian received

Alan Peterson's congratulations with a smile. 'Where is Catherine?' he asked. 'I haven't seen her for some time.'

'The heat was getting too much for her; the baby's due very soon now,' Alan replied with a smile, and Adrian felt a sudden rush of relief that everything had eventually worked out so well. He looked across the room to where his wife sat with Catherine, both of them chatting easily together, no doubt about the joys of motherhood.

How strange it was that there could be joy and trauma, anger and forgiveness, and then in the end there could be peace. Lisa's thoughts too were on the same lines until she looked across the room and found an elderly gentleman looking at her with a strange intensity—in that split second she knew that she had met him before but she could not remember where. When they were joined by one or two others she made her excuse that she needed to circulate and minutes later she stood beside him near one of the windows.

He smiled down at her saying, 'Wonderful party, I'm a visitor here, fortunate to be invited.'

'You say you're a visitor, from England?'

'Yes, I'm staying with Sir Eric Frobisher; I'm in the diplomatic service. We have met before, Mrs Lawson, at a garden party many years ago.'

Lisa's heart began to race. 'Where was that? I felt I'd met you somewhere before but I can't remember your name.'

'Forgive me, Mrs Lawson, my name is Geoffrey Cavendish; we met at Lady Eggleton's garden party in

Worcester. It was a beautiful summer's day and you were there looking very beautiful in pale green.'

'You remember the colour I was wearing?'

'I remember asking who you were and they told me you were Viscountess Lexican. This is the first time I've seen you since then.'

'So you know nothing of the way things have changed.'

'Well yes. People talk, the media get involved with people in high places and because I'd met you, naturally I was interested.'

Lisa remained silent, her thoughts miles away, even when all around her was laughter and conversation, music and people's delight in the occasion. At last he said gently, 'Please don't think I want to bring discord into this happy occasion but I should tell you that Lord Hazelmere died two months ago; perhaps you've been informed, or it could be that anything from the past no longer interests you.'

She stared at him in silence for several seconds. 'I'm sorry, Sir Geoffrey, but no, I didn't know. Was it very sudden?'

'He'd been ill for some time apparently. Would never admit to it, insisting on riding, smoking and doing all the things his doctor had forbidden him to do. He was that sort of man, but I liked Johnny Hazelmere, he was a character and there are few of them about these days.'

'Yes, I liked him too. Did you go to his funeral?'

'Of course. A family and close friends' funeral at the local church.'

'He will be missed for his humour and his audacity. Lady Hazelmere will be very sad. Will she be staying on at Hazelmere?'

'No. Dominic is now Lord Hazelmere so he has moved into the family estate; Lucy has gone to live in the old manor house in the village for the time being.'

'Aunt Jane's house?'

'Was it? I didn't know. She'll perhaps decide to stay there.'

'And Martindale?'

'Of course, I'd forgotten Martindale. That will belong to Lord Lexican when he's old enough to take up residence.'

Of course. But Antony had no right to be called Lord Lexican—Antony's father was a Spanish farmer whom he had never known and was never likely to know.

Wondering why her face was suddenly so unhappy he could only think that she had been truly fond of her father-in-law; he did not know that her thoughts were all for her son, but he was saying, 'The boy is very fond of his grandmother; they spend a lot of time together. She's very fond of travelling on the continent with her cousin, Mrs Jarvison-Noelle; it suits them both as the other lady's husband hates foreign travel. I believe the grandson goes with them during school holidays.'

'Doesn't he see much of his father then?'

'Oh, I'm sure he does. Dominic isn't much like his father, being reserved where Johnny was extrovert; all the same I always liked Dominic. Perhaps I shouldn't be talking to you about people from your past, Mrs Lawson.'

'One of them is my son, Sir Geoffrey and I too liked Dominic; once I even loved him. Sometimes it is better to forget love, although that isn't always easy when there are so many complexities.'

He looked at her sympathetically and she said swiftly, 'Do excuse me, Sir Geoffrey, I'm forgetting my guests, but I am glad to have met you and to learn about Lord Hazelmere's death.'

Much later when all the guests had departed she was able to tell Adrian about Lord Hazelmere's death and he said thoughtfully, 'I liked him, you know. He had character and a wonderful sense of humour. There were times, Lisa, when I saw him looking at you as if he didn't really understand you. Like me he didn't know the circumstances that had shaped your character.

'I always believed that he knew about Dominic and he must have questioned how he came to have fathered Antony. Dominic's mother had no doubt, and I suppose she cautioned him to forget any doubts he had ever had.'

Two weeks after the christening Adrian's father had a minor heart attack and his wife urged him to think about retiring. His doctor proclaimed that he had made an excellent recovery but suddenly Ann Lawson was feeling a desperate urge to go home to England, home to soft lengthy twilights and church spires over the hedgerows, home to English voices and quiet country lanes, so she urged Adrian to persuade his father to look after his health—he'd been a soldier long enough.

At last they departed on the understanding that they were only returning to England to search for a suitable place to end their days—a mellow stone house with a lovely garden, Ann insisted, on the outskirts of a village where there was an ancient church and country inn, somewhere where they would meet similar-minded people and where Adrian's children could stay when they went home to England to be educated.

'They'll spoil them rotten,' Adrian commented with a smile.

They were not surprised when they discovered the sort of house they were looking for in Devonshire, within sound of the sea, and even General Lawson agreed that it was the sort of place where he could live out his days in peaceful tranquillity.

Ann wrote long ecstatic letters about their home, their new friends and the sort of life she'd been yearning for for many years. 'One day it will be yours,' she wrote feelingly. 'One day when like your father you've had enough of foreign places, heat and mosquitoes, endless troubles and the urge to come home will be as great as mine was.'

Neither Adrian nor Lisa had thoughts of going home; they were happy in India in spite of many problems, and they saw no reason for it to change. They went home to England on leave to stay with Adrian's parents in Devonshire and they loved the house; the children spent warm summer days strolling along the beach looking for shell pools or climbing the red cliffs below the house.

Schools were found for the children, a prep school

nearby for their son Martin and a well-known girls' school near Exeter for Marcia. It seemed that everything in their world was perfect and on the morning they visited Lisa's mother in Norfolk she said as much to Mary as they sat in the garden watching the children squabbling on who should use the swing.

'Sometimes I don't think I deserve such happiness, Mother,' she said softly. 'I worry about Antony; I dearly want to see him but I know now that he really doesn't want to see me. I suppose his grandmother has conditioned him to feel that way.'

'Perhaps, dear.'

'Sometimes I think I must write to Dominic and beg him to persuade Antony to visit us but I'm never sure how close he is to Antony.'

'And I can't help you there, Lisa.'

'Have you been happy with the vicar, Mother? Adrian and I smile about the fact that you never give him a name.'

'Yes, we've been happy. He's a good man. His name is Richard.'

'Very appropriate. Was he very upset when he retired from the ministry?'

'He never said so, but I think perhaps he was.'

'Did it have anything to do with me?'

'Oh, I'm sure it didn't. I think that he just thought it was time, after all he was no longer young.'

'I learned in India that Lord Hazelmere had died.'

'Yes. Lucy always complained that he never took care of himself—too many blood sports, too much hunting, mostly on unsuitable horses, too many hot toddies and all he did was grunt and smile. I always liked him. He wasn't always on the same wavelength as Lucy but yes, I did like him. I'm so glad that you're happy, my dear. I worry about you in India; one hears such awful things sometimes about foreign places.'

'Oh Mother, India has so many wonderful things to show people who go there, from its sun-baked plains to its mountain snows. Then there is the pageantry and the beauty of its buildings, not simply the Taj, but so much more. Why don't you come out to visit us there?'

'Darling, Peter would never set foot out of England. He lives for the cricket club and the church where they find him so much to do, even though he's no longer a vicar; and he hates heat, even the sort of heat we get on a good summer's day in England.'

Lisa smiled. 'Then I can see I'm flogging a dead horse. Do you remember Annie, that maid we had at Aunt Jane's house? She always had an answer for everything and I remember once saying to her, "I just want to be happy all my life," and she said, "Ah, love, that isn't possible. If unhappiness doesn't knock on the way out, it knocks on the way in." Is that true, do you think?'

'I think so. We each have so much good and so much bad in our lives, and we can't fight against it, can we? Were you very unhappy with Dominic, darling?'

'With the circumstances, Mother. I shall never speak ill of Dominic—he was my friend then, perhaps he always will be.'

'I doubt if you will ever see him again.'

'No, perhaps not, but we don't forget, do we, Mother?'

'You were very much in love with him once.'

'I know. A long time ago and now I love Adrian so happiness has knocked for me at last.'

She was never very sure if the vicar liked her or not, or if he was still feeling an old resentment and the loss of the work he had loved. He was invariably polite even when their conversation was minimal and she had the distinct impression that he was glad when she decided to return to Devon.

Back in Delhi she missed the children but she received ecstatic letters from Marcia that she loved her school, and from Martin too, in brief childish printing on decorated cards.

Catherine had a daughter called Patricia and she seemed totally happy and contented with her husband and child. They had become good friends and Lisa was relieved that at least where Catherine was concerned old rancour had become a thing of the past.

Her mother's letters were filled with English news, largely concerned with the village in which they lived, but now and again with vague concern about the changing face of Europe with its dictators and rare mention of her cousins Lucy and Sybil.

Lucy had stayed on in Aunt Jane's house where Antony spent a lot of time with her. She never mentioned Dominic, but Helena had two children, a boy and a girl, and Sybil seemed to be more involved with them than she had ever been with her own children.

Adrian's parents wrote of their life in the old manor

house on the cliffs where they entertained friends to bridge evenings and they seemed to have gathered together a group of similarly minded friends. All in all in the summer of 1937 life seemed gentle and uncomplicated, and when Lisa said as much to Adrian he smiled, saying, 'It won't last, darling, there are too many rumblings from too many places.'

When she stared at him in some surprise he merely said, 'It may pass and you can tell me I've been imagining things, but somehow or other I don't think so. We're keeping our eyes open, Lisa.'

One morning Catherine said at the Sports Club that Alan was concerned about the news his parents sent him from home and was trying to persuade his wife to visit them there in the immediate future. When Lisa passed this information on to Adrian she had expected him to dismiss it, but instead he had remained thoughtful and so she pressed him for an answer. 'Perhap's he's worrying unduly,' he said. 'We don't like the look of things, but no doubt he's concerned about his wife and the child.'

'But we're talking about Europe, Adrian, we're miles away.'

'We were miles away at the last scrap, darling, but we were involved. If there's trouble we shall be again.'

'Oh Adrian, surely we're not thinking of another war. Didn't we learn anything from the last one, that nobody really wins.'

'Perhaps not, darling. I have to get down to the Sports Club now, Lisa. I promised to attend the meeting in the cricket pavilion.'

He wanted no more talk about war or similar conflicts, but she remembered vividly the first time she had seen him limping in to Hazelmere in the company of so many badly wounded young men. Surely it wasn't possible that something like that could happen again—twenty years had elapsed, a new generation had grown up, and she thought about those few weeks she had spent in England when life had seemed so normal. Cricket on pristine green lawns, country lanes and white-washed cottages—oh no, surely that gentle peace could never be thrown away.

She was sitting in her garden a year later when the gate opened and a small girl ran across the grass and Catherine was there smiling down at her after gathering Patricia in her arms.

'I thought I'd find you here,' she said with a smile. 'You're not going to the club then?'

'Not today; how about you?'

'No. I've come to tell you that Patricia and I are leaving for England next week. Alan is taking us to Bombay; we're sailing as I don't much fancy the long flight.'

'You're going to stay with Alan's parents. Isn't it rather sudden, Catherine?'

'I suppose it is, but it's Alan; he's convinced there's going to be trouble.'

'But aren't we better here than in England?'

'Well, they're better informed than us, Lisa. Hasn't Adrian said anything?'

'I can tell he's worried—he's often thoughtful and he seems to be miles away. How long will you be away?'

'I'm to stay in England until he feels it's safe for me to come home.'

'I can't understand why he thinks you'll be safer there than here,' Lisa persisted.

When she said as much to Adrian later he said thoughtfully, 'Something is going on, Lisa. I can't say too much about it at this time but we're all thinking it's time we start preparing.'

'Preparing for what?'

'Getting our wives and children home.'

'But nothing is going to happen here. The English newspapers don't even mention trouble in India.'

'We have reason to think that if there is war it will spread; we could have Japan breathing down our necks.'

She knew he would say no more, nor was she surprised that several weeks later he said, 'I've written to my mother, Lisa, and suggested that you join them in England at the beginning of July; you'll have the children during the school holidays and by that time surely we'll all know a little more about events.'

The women talked things over amongst themselves and they knew instinctively that their husbands knew far more than they were telling them. Adrian was adamant that Lisa sailed to England and after a brief stay in Bombay he saw her off on the ship that was to take her to Southampton; when she surveyed her amount of luggage she said ruefully, 'There's so much of it,

Adrian. I'm not expected to be coming back here for some time I take it?'

'Perhaps not, darling.'

'But I need to be with you, Adrian.'

'We shall be together again, Lisa, I promise you, but for the time being I'll be happier to know that you're out of harm's way and I can get on with my job. Darling, you didn't just marry me, you married the Army; it's a hard taskmaster.'

She had to be content with that and in the company of other women sailing on the same ship she quickly realised that they knew no more than she did, only that there were rumblings of troubles ahead and the men could cope better knowing their wives and children were at home in England.

She was hoping that her friend Martina would be with them but she learned that Martina and her husband had left for Singapore the week before, rather hurriedly—so hurriedly that Martina had been unable to say farewell to her friends.

'But why Singapore?' Lisa asked.

'Don't ask me, darling.'

It was several days after her arrival in Devon that the General gave her a long lecture on army life, its demands and allegiances, and although his wife smiled at her apologetically when the outburst was over she said evenly, 'I've listened to him all my married life, Lisa—Army first, everything else second. Fortunately Adrian has never been like that, but he is also well aware of his duty without the need to put it in so many words. At the first sign of trouble he'll be back offering his services and I'm sure he'll have a lot to contribute. That will give you and me more time to get to know one another and get on with our lives.'

Lisa realised that it wasn't that Ann didn't love the General, it was simply that she'd heard it all before.

She was happy taking Martin to his school every morning and meeting him in the afternoon. They spent long happy hours walking along the cliff top or strolling across the beaches, and in the last week of July Marcia came home enthusing about tennis and swimming, unconcerned that her mother was home in England because the future had become dangerously uncertain.

CHAPTER THIRTY-TWO

THE VILLAGERS WERE SAYING IT was the most perfect October they could ever remember as each day the sun shone out of a clear blue sky and the sea rolled in calm and benevolent over the smooth sand.

Lisa watched Martin joining his school friends within the playground, each with his gas mask slung over his shoulder, young children without a care in the world, unmindful of what might be in store, and still enjoying the remnants of a perfect summer. She walked back across the beach, the sand firm and warm under her feet, whilst high above her two tiny planes from the nearby aerodrome circled without any hint of menace. Every day now it seemed there were more of them, and in the village two young men in air force uniform were escorting the village girls to dances, and generally finding much to their liking in this beautiful corner of the West Country.

She had spent one week with Adrian and the children in Scotland before he returned to London and the War Office, but soon he would be rejoining his regiment to go wherever he was needed. Their time together had seemed all too brief, but the days had been precious, creating memories that would sustain them on other days that might prove traumatic and dangerous.

As she climbed up the steep path to the house one of the planes dipped low and she paused to wave her hand, although probably the pilot of the plane was unaware of it.

Mrs Lawson sat in the garden poring over the morning paper and as Lisa joined her she looked up with a smile saying, 'There's nothing, Lisa, they say it's likely the war will be over by Christmas or there'll be no war.'

'Then why have the men gone and why all those air force boys in the village? It hasn't even started yet.'

'No, that's what I think. What had Adrian to say about it? He was very non-committal when I spoke to him.'

'I know that he doesn't like to talk about the war or anything to do with it so I don't ask him.'

'No of course not; I got the message a long time ago. It was silly of me to ask.'

At the weekend Martin sat in the garden his eyes turned on the sky in search of the planes that were ever present, and on one occasion he said longingly, 'Mummy, will the war last long enough for me to become a pilot?'

She stared at him in some surprise, while his grandmother said, 'I hope you don't let Grandpa hear you say that, darling, he'll want you to go into the Army like your Daddy and himself.'

Lisa was glad that Martin didn't labour the subject. Of course that was what they would want; she'd already heard the General going on about his grandfather, father

and a host of relatives who had made the Army their career. It was tradition; she fervently hoped Martin would
keep his ambitions to himself and his intense searching
for the planes passing overhead not so obvious when the
old man came home for brief weekends.

One bright sunlit morning at the beginning of November
two young flying officers in a sports car drove out of the
aerodrome and along the road that followed the cliff
path. It was Sunday and church bells rang out from village churches; they were on weekend leave since as yet
peace reigned supreme, with little hint of the trauma to
come.

'I say, doesn't your mother live somewhere around
here?' Flying Officer Johnny Deptford asked.

'Yes, my father said I should look her up,' the other
young officer replied.

'Why don't you?'

'Not easy. We've lost touch. Oh, she writes to me, particularly when it's my birthday and at Christmas but I
haven't seen her for ages. Granny always had so much
for us to do during school holidays and then somehow
or other there didn't seem much for me to write to her
about.'

'I'm very close to my mother. I couldn't treat her
like that.'

'Well, it was rather different in my case. She married
again after the divorce and they lived in India.'

'Did you never meet her husband?'

'Yes. But I was only very young and he was con-

valescent at Hazelmere; that's where they met. I
haven't seen him since they married. She has two
other children, a girl and a boy. Funny isn't it, I have
siblings and I wouldn't know them if I met them in the
street.'

'Why don't we call?'

'Oh, I don't know. It could be embarrasing for us
both; perhaps it's all too late.'

'Would your grandmother mind?'

'Oh, she'd mind all right. She hasn't had a good word
to say for my mother, but my father wouldn't mind—he
was the one who told me I should call.'

'How does he know she's in England?'

'Some man who has met her told him, and told him
where she was living—with her husband's parents, I believe, for the duration of the war.'

'Your father's never remarried?'

'No. Grandmother's urged him to, but the last time he
told her she'd already arranged one disaster so he wasn't
about to follow her instructions again.'

'They don't get on then?'

'They seldom meet. Now that my father's installed at
Hazelmere I thought they might with Grandmother living in the village, but somehow or other they only seem
to meet at Christmas time and on her birthday. They
don't row or anything, they simply live separate lives.'

'I'm jolly glad my family don't exist like that.'

'I'm used to it. I've never known anything else.'

'But you get along with your father?'

'Oh yes, mostly from a distance, although we did go

fishing together the last time we met; that weekend was pretty good—we talked and we seemed closer than I ever remember.'

Flying Officer Lexican brought the car to a halt at the top of the hill from where they could look down on a mellow stone house surrounded by lawns and gardens and his brother officer said, 'Is that the house?'

'I think so; it's how it was described to me and there isn't another one around here. We'll drive past the gates but I don't think we'll call.'

They paused on the road outside the gates, but a young boy who had been playing in the garden saw them and instantly came running over, excitement in his eyes, his smile warm, this was the closest he had come to his heroes of the moment.

The two men smiled back and Martin cried, 'Are you pilots?'

They agreed that they were indeed pilots and leaving the gate open the boy came to the side of the car to where he could see the wings on the men's uniforms, his face alive with curiosity.

'I want to be a pilot when I grow up,' he said seriously. 'Will the war still be on do you think?'

'I hope not,' Johnny said. 'We'd both be old men.'

The boy laughed, and they they heard a woman's voice calling from inside the garden. Antony said, 'Isn't that your mother calling for you?'

'Yes. Won't you come in and meet her; you could have tea.'

'Perhaps another day,' Antony replied, but they were

too late. Lisa was already at the gate staring into his eyes, and he was climbing out of the car to walk towards her. He had been a child when last they'd met, now he was a man but she would have known him anywhere—he was her son whose dark eyes smiled down into hers and his friend could only reflect on how alike they were and how she was as beautiful as the picture he had seen.

Much to Martin's delight they accepted afternoon tea and sat in the conservatory chatting to Mother and Granny. Johnny talked to him about the Air Force while Antony strolled in the garden with his mother, bridging the gap of too many wasted years.

'Would you have called if Martin hadn't rushed out to meet you?' she asked him.

'Probably not,' he replied. 'I would have wanted to, but I've been pretty awful, haven't I? I never knew what to put in my letters and then there was Grandmother.'

'Of course. She never forgave me; I didn't think she would, but she was wrong to keep you out of my life.'

'Father told me you were living in England; some friend of his told him. He told me as I was so near I should call to see you; the bitterness was all with Grandmother, never with Father.'

'No, I'm sure it wasn't.'

'Your portrait's still on the wall at Martindale. Grandmother was furious and said it should be removed.'

'I'm sure she was, and what did your father say?'

'He said you were Viscountess Lexican and there wasn't likely to be another until I marry. My father's never remarried, you know.'

Lisa decided to say nothing about that statement. Of course Dominic would not remarry, a fact that his mother would deplore.

'How is your father? she asked him.

'Oh he's well. He's thinking of rejoining his old regiment if they'll have him; it's over twenty years on so he's not so sure.'

She smiled. 'How does he spend his time now that he's at Hazelmere?'

'He rides, hunts and goes fishing. I've been fishing with him the last time I was home, trout fishing; we caught quite a few.'

'So you get along well with him?'

'Oh yes. He's reserved and sometimes distant, but perhaps we're closer now than before. Grandmother lives in what she calls Aunt Jane's house in the village; didn't you live there once?'

'Yes, for a time, with my mother. Do you ever see your other grandmother?'

'Only once. They live in Norfolk, don't they? It's some way off.'

'I've been to see her; she's very well.'

'I'm glad. She was always very nice to me. I should see her, just as I should have seen you.'

'Well, you're here now, Antony. You're stationed near here so there's no reason why you can't come often.'

'It's taking so long for things to get moving, we're wondering if the war will ever get started; all we seem to be doing is fly around here waiting for enemy aircraft that don't seem to want to come.'

'But one day they will, Antony. We should treasure these days, make the most of them.'

'I suppose so. Is your husband still in India?'

'No, he's in London at the moment; we've just spent a few days together in Scotland. I have a daughter, you know, Marcia; she's simply itching to join one of the services, but she's still only sixteen so a little too young I'm glad to say.'

He laughed. 'She'll join the ATS of course?'

'I'm not sure; she's talking about the WRENS. Her grandfather will be against it; I'm not sure about her father.'

Back in the conservatory Johnny was entertaining Martin and his grandmother with talk about life in the Air Force and when they joined them he said to Lisa, 'Martin here is itching to join us. I wouldn't like to think we'll be in the RAF quite so long.'

'You'll be an Air Vice Marshall by that time,' Lisa said with a smile, 'or doesn't that appeal to you?'

'Definitely not. It's the flying I like, not sitting around giving orders. It's after four, Antony, we should be getting back.'

They departed with smiles promising to visit again, and Lisa and Martin went to the gate to wave them off. Martin talked about them all through the evening meal but Lisa decided against telling him that Antony was his half-brother—there would be too many questions. Later when he was in bed and she sat with Adrian's mother listening to the war news, or the lack of it, there was time to think of Dominic.

She was glad that he and Antony had found some sort

of companionship and she was grateful that Dominic had persuaded Antony to see her, but looking back on their life together she also remembered the pain and the desolation of loving and being unloved in return.

It was a war far distant from the war people who were old enough remembered. This one was not fought in the trenches of Europe but now throughout Britain towns and cities were being bombarded, and from the garden they could look out at night on flame-coloured skies where Plymouth and other places were being bombed.

Constantly throughout the day and night were the sounds of planes, the droning of bombers and screeching of fighters. Martin could barely conceal his anxiety that the war would be over before he could join in it.

It was weeks since Lisa had heard from Adrian and she did not know if he was still in London or overseas. Every night bombs fell on London and the civilian casualties were mounting.

She heard from her mother who still had contact with the village near Hazelmere that once more the East Wing was acting as a nursing home and that Lord Hazelmere had got his wish and was back with his old regiment. The Dowager Countess was actively concerned with the nursing home and Lisa could well imagine that she would make her presence felt, greeting every new arrival, visiting the wards and organising the villagers to help the wounded in any way possible.

She corresponded with Catherine Peterson, who was living in Sussex with her young daughter. Catherine told her that she too had not seen her husband for many months, and she was not surprised to hear that Martina had joined the ATS and now held a very prestigious commission. Martina could never have been happy sitting and waiting—she needed to be in the centre of things and she had no children to think about.

She saw little of Antony but the constant drone of aircraft overhead told her he had more urgent matters on his mind and all she could do was wait and pray for his return. Marcia was impatient to join the ATS, having now given up on the WRENS since her grandfather had given her every encouragement to join the Army, and Martin was now in Senior School.

It all seemed a very long way from the pomp and show of India, the soirées and the garden parties, the regimental balls and the pageantry of splendid uniforms and parading elephants. She had the strangest feeling that they would never be going back to that life, but what they would get in its place she could never imagine.

On General Lawson's rare visits he was adamant that nothing would change. All right, things were looking bad, but they would win the war; it was inconceivable that they could ever lose it and then they would return to India, to its sunshine and snows, to the glitter of its ambience and the problems that were never very far from the surface.

It was after one of his visits that Lady Lawson said feelingly, 'I never want to go back to India, Lisa. I wouldn't have missed it, it was a wonderful experience but it wasn't home, was it? I used to think about England when the heat was stifling, when the monsoons came and when there were troubles here, there and everywhere. I thought about country lanes and thatched cottages, I thought about village streets and visits to the theatres, and I thought about music, our kind of music, not the strange music of India which we were often subjected to. Now that we are home, in spite of this terrible war, this is where I intend to stay. What will you do, I wonder?'

How could they visualise what the years would do to them? How long would the war last? When it was over she could not think that life would ever be the same. The old way of life might be gone forever; the new way was something yet to be experienced.

Every day now they watched the dogfights in the air above the cliffs and she worried about Antony; he could be any one of those boys in those tiny planes weaving and diving in the sky, one of those boys who never returned.

They kept hearing about planes failing to return, the number that were missing, and when perhaps the next day Antony appeared at the gate she breathed a thankful prayer that he had not been one of them.

She worried too about Adrian's mother as she seemed to have one cold after another, blaming it on the cold damp English weather after the sunshine of India. Much against Lisa's better judgement she decided to go to a meeting at the local church, in spite of the fact that icy sleet was falling and a bitter east wind swept across the cliff top. Lisa drove her to the church, trying all the time to persuade her to return home with her, but to no avail. So she sat in the car and watched as her mother-in-law joined a group of women to walk up the slippery path towards the church.

In mid afternoon the vicar and the sexton brought her home, gasping for breath, a grey pallor suffusing her face. Immediately Lisa sent for the doctor, who diagnosed a viral pneumonia, and although she was whisked off to hospital, three days later she was dead.

Lisa stood with Adrian in the pouring rain at his mother's funeral but it was the General who was giving her most cause to worry. Always a strong, upright man, now he was totally wracked with grief. The woman who had loved and admired him, listened to his commands and proclamations with resignation and forebearance, had gone and in the evening the three of them sat at the dining table uninterested in the meal, trying hard to come to terms with the sudden loss.

'This house will be yours,' the General said, 'After the war you'll live here. You won't want me here; I'll be a nuisance; think about yourselves.'

'This is your house, Father,' Adrian said adamantly. 'This is where you'll live; we shall be going back to India.'

'There'll be no India, son, at least not where the British are concerned. We'll give them back their country and we'll get very few thanks for what we've done for them. Mark my words, the Army will be coming home—oh, not immediately I'll grant you that, but as soon as they can get us off their backs.'

'Like I said, Father, this is your house,' Adrian insisted.

'I shan't be expecting Lisa to look after me; she's got you and the children. No, this will be your house—your mother and I wanted it that way.'

'Father, when we go back to India you will stay on here with a housekeeper. There are several good women in the village who would be glad to work for you; we'll find somebody for you. You like the house, you like the village and you've made friends here, so let us have no talk of turning the house over to us,' Adrian said firmly.

'I've told you, son, you'll be coming home, and I shall move into an officers' club. There's enough of them about, and I'll be with men like myself, men I can talk to about all we've gone through together, play bridge, golf, and in any case the children won't want a crusty old soldier around the place with his demands and censures.'

'We'll talk about it when the time's right,' Adrian said.

Lisa had taken no part in the conversation, but now the General looked at her pointedly to say, 'I notice you've said nothing, Lisa, but I'm right, you have to admit it.'

'We're not talking about tomorrow or the next day either. Perhaps we should wait until we all know what is happening to us.'

'First bit of common sense I've heard all day,'

'I didn't think you credited women with much common sense at all,' Adrian said with a small smile.

'I always said that, didn't I, but underneath I always came around to doing what your mother wanted, and I think this lady here has a great deal of common sense. Don't tell me I didn't always think so. I'm ashamed of all that; now I think we should listen to her, wait and see what is going to happen; we have a war to win first.'

How empty the house felt after the two men had returned to their duties. Lisa took Lady Lawson's place on the church committee where they met several times each week to discuss what could be done to make life a little easier for the men at war; mostly it was concerned with making enough money to provide whatever comforts could be sent to them.

There was no hope of Adrian coming on leave for Christmas but Lisa spent her time trying to make the house look as festive as possible.

Martin helped her to decorate the Christmas tree with whatever baubles they were able to find, but most of the time he was withdrawn and tearful and she knew he was missing his grandmother, but seemed unable to talk about it. He was too young to fully comprehend death, and it was Marcia home from school who was better able to put her sorrow into words.

They went to the carol service at the church and attended the concert in the village hall, but apart from that there seemed little to do beyond making the most of the chocolate ration and the best they could do for a Christmas meal.

'Doesn't Antony come round any more?' Martin asked wistfully.

'Not recently, darling—they have so much to do; you can hear the planes every day going off somewhere.'

'I know. I am going to be one of them one day, Mother.'

'We'll see, darling. We all want the war to be over soon.'

'Not me, Mother,' Marcia said sharply. 'I want to join the ATS; I've written to Daddy to tell him so. Perhaps he'll help me.'

Faced with their enthusiasm Lisa felt there was little she could say.

CHAPTER THIRTY-THREE

IT WAS EARLY JANUARY AND THE entire village was enveloped in thick fog as Martin said dourly, 'The planes won't be going up in this. I hate fog; I can't even go down to the beach.'

He sat morosely staring out of the window, his paintbox unopened, but it was the sudden click of the garden gate that sent his spirits soaring as he rushed out of the house to greet Antony walking up the garden path. He was his usual confident self, a smile on his handsome face as he kissed Lisa's cheek and ruffled Martin's hair; then he was smiling at Marcia who looked up in admiration at the half-brother she had never met.

'I told them you wouldn't be flying today,' Martin said. 'Mother said she hadn't seen you.'

'No, it's been great, up every day, no let-up. I can stay for tea if that's all right.'

'Oh yes, Antony, I've been so worried about you. Do you hear from Hazelmere?'

'From Grandmother, not from Father; he's in London at the moment; he telephoned me.'

'I'm glad.'

'I believe the old lady died. I'm sorry, she was very nice; I liked her.'

'Yes, I miss her terribly. I liked her too.'

'Will the General be living here on his own after the war, or will you be staying on?'

'We don't know. He seems to think we'll soon be out of India, in which case we'll probably come back here.'

'Oh, I can't imagine we'll be out of India. Can they do without us, do you think?'

'Oh yes, Antony, I rather think they can. It appears they want to try.'

'Surely we won't let them.'

'We may not have any option.'

'Let the Jewel in the Crown go, surely not.'

Lisa merely smiled and decided not to labour the subject.

Lisa enjoyed the company of her eldest son, but she was still unable to reconcile him with the child she had chased across the lawns at Hazelmere. So much of his childhood seemed obscure, and now he was a young man she was endeavouring to discover.

She stood at the gate to watch him drive away in his open sports car and as she and Martin walked back to the house Martin said wistfully, 'When the war is over, Mother, will Antony still be able to come to see us?'

'Oh I do hope so, darling; we'll have to ask him.'

'I wish I was old enough to fly one of those planes; Antony says perhaps the war will be over now that America is in.'

'And I'm very glad you're not older, Martin, but you'll soon be back at school and will have so much to do perhaps you'll forget about flying and how long the war's going to last.'

He was so knowledgeable about the planes, he could distinguish the sound of the engines—she had no doubt that Antony had been a very good instructor.

There was so much activity overhead that night she was unable to sleep. She decided to get up instead of lying sleepless listening to the planes, and after making herself a cup of tea she went to stand in the garden where she could see the searchlights raking the sky and the darting and diving lights as far as she could see.

The early morning breeze was warm, the sunrise spectacular and when Martin came down for breakfast he said, 'Did you hear the planes in the night, Mother? There's something going on over there.'

'I know, I couldn't sleep so I got up early and went into the garden.'

'I wish I didn't have to go to school; we're missing so much.'

'Well, you do have to go to school. Is Peter calling for you?'

'I suppose so; his dad tells us off when we talk war all the time.'

'I'm sure he does. Isn't his dad at the Air Ministry offices?'

'Yes, but it's nothing like being a pilot.'

Adrian had been amused at his son's preoccupation

with flying; his grandfather was rather less so and was not averse to giving Martin a lecture on the subject.

'The Army's a tradition in our family, Martin,' he had scolded, 'my grandfather and his grandfather before him. Now you've got me and your father to follow; forget this obsession with this new thing.'

'It's not always going to be a new thing, Grandfather,' Martin had insisted, and in spite of the warning glance his mother had directed at him there had been many times that weekend when she had had to admonish him not to talk about flying in his grandfather's presence.

After Martin left for school with his friend Peter in the staff car his father drove, she spent time in the garden until she could see her daily, Mrs Frisby, walking with another woman in the direction of the house. They had been lucky to have found the services of Mrs Fribsy; her husband was in the Navy and several of their friends had told Lisa she was looking for something to do while he was away.

She was cheerful and practical, that she was also a bit of a gossip kept Lisa entertained since she knew everybody in the village and everything that went on there. This morning was no exception.

'Did you hear all that hullabaloo in the night?' was her greeting. 'I couldn't sleep for it. Looks to me as though they mean business.'

'Yes. It stopped me from sleeping too; oh, I do hope they get back safely.'

'Me too, but there be always one or two that doesn't get back. I'll make a start in the boy's room, Mrs Lawson; it's the one that needs more goin' over.'

They ate lunch together in the kitchen where she listened to Mrs Frisby's account of young Polly Jamieson and her American marine.

'No sooner has she seen 'er boyfriend off to war than she picks up with this young American. Silly girl, he could have a girl back home and Fred Osborne was a nice lad; bin sweet on 'er since school he has.'

'Well, the Americans will be moving out soon, Mrs Frisby, perhaps it won't last.'

'I'm not so sure—together everywhere they are, the local hops and even at the church fete; I don't know what the vicar'll 'ave to say about it.'

'What about Polly's parents? Don't they have something to say?'

'Well 'er father's in the Army and 'er mother's not the sort to say boo to a goose. There'll be trouble, I can see it comin'.'

Mrs Frisby was cleaning in the hall when she called out, 'There's somebody coming in through the gate, Mrs Lawson, an officer I think. I've finished in 'ere so I'll start on the kitchen.'

She clanked her way into the kitchen and Lisa said, 'An officer did you say, Mrs Frisby?'

'Oh yes, ma'am. It's just started to rain and I recognised his light trenchcoat; army I'd say.'

Lisa clutched hold of the chair in front of her and Mrs Frisby said quickly, 'You've gone quite pale, Mrs Lawson. What's to worry about? Perhaps it's somebody bringing a message from your husband. I often get Arthur's mates callin' on me.'

Smoothing her hair, Lisa rushed out into the hall and through the glass-panelled door she could clearly see the tall figure of an army officer wearing his distinctive light trenchcoat. He rang the bell and with a swiftly beating heart she hurried to open the door, staring wide eyed into Dominic's grey eyes and handsome, remote face.

At that moment she couldn't analyse her feelings. His face was grave, unsmiling, and it had been over twenty years since their last meeting. Why had he come now when all they had needed to say to each other had been said a long time ago?

He did smile at that moment, a fleeting gentle smile, and she remembered the charm of it, even when she had wished there might have been so much more.

'Are you going to invite me in?' he asked gently.

'Yes of course. I'm sorry, Dominic, I'm so surprised to see you. Please come in; we'll go into the drawing room.'

He followed her in and as he stood uncertainly unbuttoning his trenchcoat she said, 'Do sit down, Dominic, my daily woman is here. I'll ask if she'll make us tea, or would you prefer something stronger?'

'Tea will do later, Lisa, there is something I have to tell you.'

She stared at him uncertainly, and he said, 'Lisa, I'm sorry but I have some rather bad news for you; it's Antony, I'm afraid—his plane was shot down over France during the night.'

He watched the colour leaving her face, and she sat down weakly staring at him with pain-filled eyes as he said, 'There was no easy way to tell you, Lisa. I heard this morning and decided to bring you the news myself.'

'He was here two days ago; he was so well,' she said lamely.

'There could be hope, Lisa, he could have parachuted to safety. I don't know any more about the actual incident, but I'll do all I can and as soon as I know something more concrete you'll be the first to hear.'

'Oh Dominic, is this something fate intended for him, for us? He has no right to Hazelmere; is this fate telling us he had to be taken?'

'Lisa, every day some young men are being taken; are you telling yourself that they are all imposters? No, my dear, this is what war does to us, not some sinister nemesis singling out people it has haunted for years.'

She nodded slowly, and after a long silence she asked, 'Does your mother know?'

'Not yet; she will have to know, obviously, but I thought you should be told first.'

'Thank you, Dominic. She will be very distressed.'

'Yes, she will be inconsolable. She had built her life around Antony, even more so since Father died. Whatever thoughts you had about her, Lisa, please believe me when I tell you that she truly loved Antony.'

'I believe you. I can't forget however that she did her level best to keep him from me. She blamed me for everything, for leaving him, for leaving you, and we couldn't tell her the truth, Dominic; even so, losing Antony left me with so very little. Now I have a daughter and a son with Adrian but it was those early years that brought me so much pain.'

'I know. I tried to reason with Mother, it wasn't easy; now I have the painful task of telling her that he's gone.'

'When will you tell her?'

'At the weekend—I hope to get home for a couple of days; it won't be the easiest two days.'

'You're with your regiment, Dominic?'

'I'm joining them in Italy very soon. Where is Adrian?'

'I don't know. He came home a few months ago. I never ask him anything about his movements and he never tells me. Everybody seems to think we shall be coming out of India once the war is over.'

'That's probably true, Lisa.'

'You must have tea, Dominic. I'll ask Mrs Frisby to make some.'

'Could I ask you to give my driver a cup? He's been sitting out there in the car all the time I've been talking to you. The day started well, but it's deteriorated I'm afraid.'

Although Mrs Frisby looked at her strangely Lisa was unable to tell her at that moment that the news brought to her had been grave; instead they set about making tea and sandwiches and Mrs Frisby went out to invite Dominic's driver into the kitchen. Lisa pushed the tea trolley into the drawing room and invited Dominic to help himself to sandwiches while she poured the tea.

'You're not eating,' he admonished her.

'I'm not very hungry,' she said softly. 'I'm thinking what I'm going to tell Martin. He liked Antony enormously; he too will be sad tonight.'

She was aware that Dominic made himself eat the

sandwiches she had provided but, like her, food was the last thing he was thinking about. They talked pleasantries and she had to remind herself that once she had been his wife and before that his friend—that she could ever have thought it might have been more than that had been an illusion.

'I'll break the news to my mother tonight,' she told him. 'She was so pleased that we were seeing each other.'

He nodded, and after several attempts at polite conversation Dominic felt the need to leave.

'Please tell my driver I'm ready to leave now, Lisa, and thank you for your hospitality. I'm sorry it couldn't have been in more happier circumstances.'

'The meeting with your mother will be worse.'

'I'm afraid so.'

He smiled down at her, then to her utmost surprise he reached out and for a brief moment held her against him. After he released her she looked up into his face while the tears rolled unchecked down her cheeks.

'You will try to find out everything you can about Antony, Dominic?' she asked tremulously.

'You know I will.'

'But if you're abroad.'

'Whatever I can find out, Lisa, I will see that you are told.'

She stood at the door while he joined his driver at the gate, then after a brief smile and the raising of his hand they were driving away in the wet misery of the day.

Back in the kitchen Mrs Frisby said, 'You've had bad news, Mrs Lawson; you're upset, I know.'

'Yes, I'm just hoping it might not be as bad as I think it is.'

At that moment she didn't want to tell Mrs Frisby any more than was necessary. Mrs Frisby was a gossip and was unaware that she had another son—certainly not the young flying officer who called to see them from time to time.

In the evening Martin received the news with a horrified expression and retired to his room where she had no doubt the tears would come. He was at an age where he felt boys should not cry, whatever the circumstances. He would put on a brave face, but she knew underneath he would be grief stricken at the loss of a young man he had admired, so she left him alone knowing he would prefer it.

She telephoned her mother and even over the telephone she sensed her mother's anguish.

'How terrible for Dominic,' Mary said. 'Antony wasn't just his son, he was the heir to Hazelmere and all it means. What about Lucy? She'll be devastated.'

'Yes, Mother, I know.'

'It must have been very difficult for Dominic to see you; I do admire him for it.'

'Yes, Mother.'

That is what they would all think. For Dominic to tell his erring wife that their son was missing, when she was now happily married to somebody else and had two other children, was a brave thing to do. None of those people would know that Dominic was not Antony's father.

'Oh, I do hope he was able to use his parachute,' Mary cried. 'He could be a prisoner of war; that would be wonderful, at least better than dying.'

When she put the telephone down Lisa thought about Antony sitting out the war as a prisoner of war. He would hate it, listening to the war news, thinking about all those other young men flying over France and Germany, free and unfettered; but yes, her mother was right—to be a prisoner of war was preferable to death.

How strange it was that life should go on in its familiar routine—shopping in the village where she listened to other people's anxieties and kept her own to herself; changing the library books and looking at Martin's face across the dinner table where he sat deep in thought, largely uninterested in the food set before him.

One evening he said, 'Johnny Collinson's uncle's been shot down over Germany, Mother. I told them about Antony.'

'What did you tell them?'

'The same, that his plane was shot down too.'

'And nothing else?'

'No. I didn't tell anybody that he was my half-brother. They would ask questions and it's none of their business.'

Relieved, she favoured him with a gentle smile. 'I'm glad, darling. One day if Antony comes home we'll tell everybody—it won't matter then, nothing will matter then.'

'Why did we never meet him before?'

'Well, we were in India and he was here in England. It's a long story, darling, and it can keep until another day.'

'I'm not sure I understand it.'

'Well, of course not. It's a very long story, and complicated. One day when you're older and better able to understand it I'll tell you more; one day when your father is here and we can tell you together.'

'Does Marcia know?'

'No.'

He sat for a long moment staring in front of him, then as though this was something for another day, and there were more urgent matters to demand his attention, he said, 'I hope I can room with Ponsonby when we move on to public school; he's the only one going to Rugby.'

'You'll make other friends, Martin. Have you been particularly friendly with Ponsonby?'

'Not particularly, it's just that I know him but won't know the others.'

'There'll be a lot of new boys, Martin, and probably they will all be anxious. Take every day as it comes.'

There was the sound of men's voices from outside the house and rushing over to the window Martin said, 'Grandfather's here; did you know he was coming?'

'No I didn't; go outside to meet him and help him carry his bags.'

'He's got a batman carrying the bags, Mother. How will they get on without him? Isn't Grandfather running the war?'

She laughed, the first time in days, and turning round Martin said, 'That's what he thinks, Mother. Oh goodness, he'll be on and on about me joining the Army when I'm old enough, all about his father and his grandfather. I'm sure Dad must have got fed up with it when he was a boy.'

'Perhaps, Martin, but he's an old man now and he's so very proud of the Army and the years he's spent in it. Bear with him, show some interest even if you don't feel it.'

He grinned at her, then sobering suddenly, 'Are you going to tell him about Antony?'

'I'll think about it. At the moment I don't want to talk about it until I'm told he's safe. What do you think?'

'Oh yes, Mother, please let's not tell him. He'll go on and on about my not becoming a pilot, even more so if you tell him about Antony.'

So they greeted the old man with warm smiles and he informed them he'd got several days leave and could think of nowhere better than a few days near the sea.

He spent long hours sitting in the summer house reading the morning papers and then disparaging the comments of innumerable journalists, and in the afternoon he walked along the cliff paths and occasionally went to play chess with the vicar.

In the evening he and Lisa talked about India and what they might expect of the country when the war was over. It never entered the heads of either of them that the Allies might lose the war—only the uncertainties of what peace would bring.

CHAPTER THIRTY-FOUR

DOMINIC HAD DELIVERED THE news of Antony and sat watching his mother's expressions, first of disbelief, then of acute grief and desolation. He had no words to comfort her as she sat with the tears streaming down her face, wringing her hands and asking God what she had ever done to deserve such torment.

'It may not be hopeless,' he said at last. 'Many of the boys are picked up after parachuting from their planes. I'll make every enquiry possible; just keep on hoping, Mother, that he'll be safe.'

'He's already had more than his share of sadness, largely from his mother,' she said bitterly. 'What will she think if she ever hears about this?'

'I have already informed Lisa, Mother.'

'You mean you've told her—before me?'

'I was in Devon on army business not far away from where she lives; she had to know.'

'Why did she have to know? She's not seen Antony since he was a child. She left you to marry somebody else and she has other children; if she'd really cared about

Antony she'd have moved heaven and earth to be with him, but he never saw her, for years he never saw her.'

'She was in India, Mother and she wrote to him, but don't you see that Antony was never available to meet her; you didn't want them to meet.'

'Because she'd never have done what she did if she'd cared for either of you.'

'Antony has seen her in Devon, his aerodrome was close to where she lives. I wanted them to meet and advised him to see her; after the first time he went frequently whenever it was possible. Seeing his mother did not detract from his feelings for you, Mother.'

'I can't believe what you're telling me. If your father was alive he'd be the first to tell you that what you've done was wrong. All those years when I tried to make up for what she should have been to him. I was more than just his grandmother, I was more to him than the two of you, and now he's gone and you've seen fit to involve her. You're still in love with her, aren't you, even after all this time, even when she's probably never given you a second thought.'

Dominic looked at her in pitying silence as she went on angrily, 'All those nice respectable girls you could have married, but you never wanted any of them because you were still in love with her—refusing to take her portrait off the wall at Martindale, finding out where she is living so that you could persuade Antony to visit her. Oh, I can't believe that you've been so devious.'

'Mother, you're overwrought and you're saying things you'll regret. Until the other morning I hadn't seen Lisa for almost twenty years, but she had a right to know that her son was missing, that he had failed to return after being in action. I have promised to let her know if he is safe, a prisoner of war.'

'I can't stay here on my own tonight—I need to be with people, not the servants, family.'

'Then will you drive back to Hazelmere with me?'

'No. I want to go to Sybil's; they'll need to know what's happened, and I wonder what they'll think about you telling Lisa.'

'Mother, I don't care what anybody thinks. I did what was right, and when you've had a chance to calm down I'm sure you'll think so too. This is a time to forget the bitterness you've nurtured all these years; it is something Antony would want.'

She stared at him in disbelief. Didn't he realise that he had lost his only son? After Dominic there would be no next Lord Hazelmere; the title would die out. Didn't he care?

Dominic knew what she was thinking and hated himself for being the sort of man he was—it was he, not Lisa who had brought them to this.

They drove, largely in silence, but he was aware of her sitting next to him, wrapped in her private grief, occasionally dabbing at her eyes and when they arrived at her cousin's house she said sharply, 'I don't want you to come in with me, Dominic. I need to see them on my own; I need them to tell me that I'm right about this.'

'They'll tell you what you want to hear, Mother,' he

answered wearily. 'Do you wish me to come for you this evening?'

'No. Arthur will drive me home, I'm sure. I'll see you when I've had time to recover a little from this morning's trauma.'

The rest of the day stretched ahead and he wished he was back in London. The meeting with his mother had gone exactly as he had expected and he thought about her facing the Jarvison-Noelles—Sybil with her haughty composure and Arthur, incredibly pompous, yet with few original views of his own.

The Jarvison-Noelles listened to Lucy's tearful version of the morning's events, Sybil's face suddenly cold when she spoke of Lisa, as Arthur bumbled on to say, 'Well, I suppose she had to know, Lucy.'

'But not before me surely. Over all these years he's been with me, not with her; he never knew what to put in his letters to her and was always relieved when he didn't have to visit her or meet her in England. She'd gone out of his life and it was better that she stayed out.'

'Is there a chance that Antony could still be alive?' Arthur asked.

'Dominic will make enquiries and let me know. Oh, surely there will be; we hear it every day about young men being picked up somewhere in Europe. He's still in love with her, you know, he must be, otherwise why has he never remarried?'

'Has he admitted to being in love with her?' Sybil asked.

'No. There was a time when I believed he didn't like

women at all, but then when he found Lisa she became all he ever wanted. That's the sort of man he is, a one woman man.'

Sybil's thoughts were on too many occasions when she had witnessed a besotted young girl standing with her head on his breast while he gazed elsewhere, or with her eyes following him yearningly whenever he walked away, a young girl desperately in love, a man who had been charmingly embarrassed but always remote.

Lucy could be blinkered to things she did not want to see, and now she was accusing him of still being in love with Lisa, still festering from an emotion that refused to go away.

Afternoon tea was served to them and Sybil watched Lucy pushing the food around her plate before laying it aside untouched; gently she said, 'Try to hope for Antony's return, Lucy, but remember too that there are so many young men being asked to pay the ultimate price in these awful times.'

Lucy looked at her searchingly before saying, 'Have you forgotten, Sybil, that with Antony's death the last person to bear the title Earl Hazelmere will have died with him. Dominic will never marry again and there are no cousins that can take the title. The Hall will become a museum or some ministry or other will take it over. And Martindale too, will be given to some politician, some man unconcerned with its history, just another title thrown on the scrap heap.'

When Sybil remained silent Lucy said, 'We lost Austin in the First World War, and now Antony. Dominic doesn't seem to care about the title; I doubt if he cares about anything beyond Lisa.'

'And I think that is ridiculous.'

Lucy's eyes snapped haughtily. 'It isn't ridiculous, Sybil, Oh, I'll admit if anybody had told me yesterday that he still cared about her I'd have thought so too, but not anymore, and when I accused him he didn't bother to deny it.'

'When is he going back to London?'

'In the morning.'

'Then he'll start to make enquiries to see if Antony is alive. As soon as he hears anything concrete, you'll know.'

'Another excuse for him to see her, I suppose.'

'Are you staying at Hazelmere tonight?'

'No, I'm going back to the manor. If I see Dominic we shall start arguing again, or at least I shall; he seldom bothers to answer me.'

Sybil was glad to see her driving away with Arthur in the early evening. She was sorry about Antony as she had liked him even when she'd always thought he was too like Lisa and that grandmother who had never been accepted.

It was true that she knew of a great many girls who found his dark, handsome face fascinating. He had the appearance of a Spanish grandee or Italian nobleman, an appearance that most girls found irresistible and Antony had known well how to use that charm. Never as long as she'd known him had she been able to find a single trace of Dominic in him.

They had never seemed close, but she had to admit that lately whenever Antony came on leave they had been together, riding, fishing, even spending time in the garden together. The boy had seemed to have overcome his father's reserve, and even Arthur had remarked on it, a fact that had surprised her as Arthur seldom noticed the behaviour of others.

He had once been astute enough to say, 'The lad's so much like his mother, but he's bound to have a streak of Dominic in him; pretty well hidden, I'd say.'

'Why do you say that?' she'd asked.

And his reply had been, 'Well, the lad's a Lothario, a real heartbreaker. I'd never have described Dominic like that.'

Oh, Antony could have broken some girl's heart because he was a flirt who wasn't ready for marriage; Dominic could only have broken a girl's heart because he didn't care enough.

She found herself trying to think if she had ever seen him with a close friend since Oliver, and once she had asked him if he had a man friend for holidays and such, only to be answered with his brief smile and the remark, 'There's nobody special.'

Dominic telephoned his mother in the evening only to be told by one of her servants that she had retired to bed early as she was feeling unwell.

When he called the following morning on his way to London he was informed she had gone to church and was having lunch with friends. It was obvious she didn't want to see him so there was no recourse for it but to return to London.

He felt no surprise at her behaviour, but at the same

time he was worried that he might have said more, been more gentle, but her remarks about Lisa had made it impossible. That she was in any way to blame for any of it would never enter her head, whereas his mother would always be of the opinion that whatever she had done she had done it for her son and the family name.

Every day Lisa was afraid to go out in case Dominic telephoned, and it was Mrs Frisby who said, 'You can't just lock yourself away 'ere, Mrs Lawson, waiting for the phone to ring. If you're out 'e'll ring again, or maybe 'e'll come to see you.'

If he came to tell her Antony was safe they would find things to talk about; if he told her Antony was dead what would there be to say to each other?

Mrs Frisby didn't altogether understand her anxiety concerning Antony when she had a husband at the war; wasn't his safety of more importance? Nor was she to know that every night Lisa prayed for Adrian to come home now when she needed him most, but she didn't know where he was and she received no letters from him.

It was several days later that she heard the shrill ring of the telephone while she was preparing the evening meal, and as always these days she went to answer it with a feeling of dread in her heart. It was Dominic. She sank into the nearest chair, her heart racing uncontrollably, as he said gently, 'Lisa, it's all right, Antony is safe.'

For several seconds she sat numb with relief, then he was saying, 'He's a prisoner of war somewhere in Germany, Lisa, several of the boys were picked up that morning. I can't tell you exactly where, only that he's alive.'

'Is he hurt?'

'That I can't tell you either, Lisa. I can only tell you that there will be no more war for Antony; he's where he is until it's all over, so let us hope it is sooner rather than later.'

'Have you told your mother?'

'I intend to tell her this morning.'

'Thank you, Dominic, thank you for everything.'

'Lisa, you mustn't worry about Antony; after the war he'll be coming back to England to people who care a great deal for him.'

'People?'

'Yes, whatever you think of my mother her love for Antony is very real; I shall be here hopefully as a good friend and the years will bring us closer. I've watched him grow up, Lisa, and I've liked what I saw in him. I know he'll fill my place very adequately when the time comes.'

'I liked him too, Dominic. I had little contact with him when he was growing up but the man I saw made me very proud. Thank you again.'

'Goodbye, Lisa. I hope Adrian comes home safely and that all goes well with you in India, although I can't think it will be for long.'

'No, that's what Adrian and his father are thinking.'

'And when you return to England you'll see Antony again.'

'Oh yes, that will indeed be something to look forward to. Martin was very fond of him; he'll be delighted to know that he's safe.'

'Goodbye, Lisa.'

'Goodbye.'

For a long time she sat idly, simply thinking about their conversation. But then Martin called to her from the door to say he was hungry, and why wasn't dinner ready.

She laughed and looking at her in surprise Martin said, 'You're laughing, Mother, you've been so sad lately.'

'I know, darling. Antony's safe; he parachuted out of his plane and was picked up. He's a prisoner of war somewhere in Germany.'

'That's great, how do you know?'

'His father rang to tell me.'

'That means he'll have to stay there until the war's over, doesn't it? He'll not be flying any more.'

'No, that's right.'

'Mother, he'll hate that—sitting in some prison while other men are flying. What will he do all the time?'

'I don't know, Martin, but at least he's alive. Isn't that wonderful?'

'I suppose not being able to fly is better than being dead; perhaps I'll be flying by the time he gets home.'

'And perhaps you'll be still at school, studying and growing up.'

Martin grinned. 'Would you be so tetchy if I said I wanted to join the Army, or would that be all right?'

'You're still a schoolboy, Martin, but I've told you before not to talk about the Air Force in front of your grandfather—you know how angry he gets.'

Over their evening meal Lisa reflected that from now on their life would go on as it had before Antony made his appearance. Martin would be away at school, Marcia would come home on leave from the ATS with stories of so many escapades, and probably some young man with her to back her up; but when would Adrian come home?

The news was better, the tide was turning but there were still atrocities in the Far East and on the rare occasions that the General managed a long weekend with them she complained bitterly that she had had no news from Adrian.

'He'll write when he can,' the old man said. 'No news is good news.'

'But not to know where he is; other women get letters from Europe, so why not us?'

'He may not be in Europe, Lisa. Like I said, he'll write when it's possible.'

Lucy sat alone in the Hazelmere pew during the evening service but afterwards as she walked out into the spring sunshine she was surrounded by people smiling their delight that her grandson had been rescued even though he was now a prisoner of war.

She accepted their good wishes with a delighted smile, happy for the first time in weeks. She didn't care that Antony was a prisoner of war—at least he wasn't putting his life in danger every single day; now he would sit it out until it was all over, then he would come home.

One day he would bring his bride home to Martindale and his mother's portrait could be removed from the head of the stairs. She might not be as beautiful as Lisa, but she would no doubt be a more worthy ambassador to bear the name. They would have children, children who she could indulge and educate into so much promise, and perhaps she'd try to get along with Dominic.

She had no doubt that Dominic would not allow her to have a free rein with Antony or with Antony's children, but she could do it surreptitiously; she'd managed it with Johnny, she'd manage it with Dominic.

Over the teacups Lucy and Sybil planned and plotted for their children and grandchildren, but it was Sybil who said, 'I doubt you'll get all your own way with Antony, Lucy. Dominic doesn't say very much but there have been times over the years when he's gone his own way.'

'Well, of course, but he's always come round to my way of thinking in the end.'

Sybil remained silent. Let Lucy think what she liked, she knew that she was right. Take that portrait at Martindale—Dominic had adamantly refused to have it removed, and there'd been other times too when he'd gone his own way, not his mother's.

'How are Helena and her children?' Lucy asked innocently, knowing full well that Helena and her mother did not get on.

Sybil replied shortly, 'They're well enough, although I see them very seldom since they live at the other end of the country. Helena's always been stubborn and her husband indulges her far too much.'

'You see far more of the other two girls, and you see little of your son.'

'Well, he's married. When a son acquires a wife it becomes more difficult; you'll find that out when Antony marries.'

Lucy decided to change the subject.

'Dominic must have spoken to Lisa again to tell her about Antony—when I asked him he simply said he'd informed her, and that was that.'

'What did you want him to say?'

'Well, obviously they must have had some sort of conversation; I'm surprised he wants to talk to her at all.'

'Well, if you think he's still in love with her then obviously he'll want to talk to her.'

'What about? She's married to somebody else and they've got children. She's made a new life for herself, surely Dominic doesn't want to hear about that.'

'I wasn't sure that he was ever in love with her.'

Lucy looked at her askance. 'Well of course he was in love with her, he still is. How can you even think that, Sybil?'

'Well, you have to admit you did have doubts about him, and you did encourage him to be friends with Lisa, even to letting Mary and Lisa have Aunt Jane's house so that they'd be nearby. I thought she loved him, but I was never sure about him.'

'I never heard such nonsense in my life. He adored her; they had a child together. Martindale reeks of her; he still cares for her.'

'You say Martindale reeks of her, but she spent very little time there.'

'Well the war was on; Martindale was given over as

a nursing home, but she did spend time there and they went there after their marriage. No, Sybil, I won't have it. We did not push Dominic into a marriage he didn't want; if we did why is he still smarting from it?'

'Only you seem to think that, Lucy.'

'And I'm his mother; shouldn't I know more than anybody?'

Sybil thought about her argument with Lucy all the way home. She knew she couldn't win—Lucy would be adamant—and when had she ever been able to win an argument against her? All the same she'd given her cousin something to think about.

CHAPTER THIRTY-FIVE

IT WAS OVER, THE POMP AND the pageantry; the last viceroy had given his last ball, entertained and been entertained by the princes who had both revered and hated him, paraded their gorgeously clad elephants and pristine horses in front of him for the last time. Now the streets were quiet—wide empty streets lined by government buildings the British had built, edged by gardens and parks the British had enjoyed; now the British were going home.

Lisa had finished packing and the rooms were filled with trunks containing gowns she had worn for garden parties and soirées at the Sports Club. When would she ever wear them again? They were probably too grand for English ballrooms and as she put the last one away she reflected sadly that it had been admired by so many of their friends at the Viceroy's Ball.

It was too grand for the ship taking them home, too grand for any occasion she could think of, but Adrian had said with a smile, 'There'll be another occasion, darling. We're going home, but we're not giving up on life.'

His father would be proud of him since he had attained the rank his father had achieved and as she sat in the garden waiting for his return she could only think that these last few days he had seemed withdrawn and not a little sad.

The houseboy came out with fruit juice, placing it on the table near her chair and favouring her with his usual deferential smile.

'Would you like biscuits, Memsahib?' he asked courteously.

'No thank you, Mehza, we'll have lunch when General Lawson returns.'

How much did he mind that they were leaving? she wondered. She thought that the boys had liked them, considered they were kind and reasonable employers, but underneath it all was there a feeling of resentment that they were servants to the British in their own country?

She thought about the stone house on the cliffs overlooking the sea in distant Devon, the winds that swept through the trees in the winter, the biting north-easters that sent the sea tumbling over the rocks filling the air with spray and spume, and the gentle summers that came after.

She would miss the sunshine of India, even when the heat was often unbearable, and then she would remember the shuttered rooms and the wicker furniture, the garden under the trees and the ambience of wealth in a land burned with poverty.

She could see Adrian walking towards the house in the company of another officer; they seemed to have a lot to talk about but when they parted at the gate he looked up and smiled, and it was like that first time when she had looked into his eyes at Hazelmere.

He was wearing his officer's cap although she knew that underneath it there were streaks of silver in his dark hair; his grey eyes were still the same, his mouth still firm until he smiled, that slow gentle smile that made a slave of her heart.

He stood looking down at her, saying, 'All packed, darling?'

'Just about. There's so much of it, Adrian.'

'I know, it's the same for everybody. Are we having lunch out here, or would you prefer to go inside?'

'Oh no, Adrian, out here please. Let us enjoy the sunshine as long as we may; even in the summer England is not going to be to be like this.'

As always the houseboy anticipated their wishes—it was almost as though he could read their thoughts, what they wanted, where they would be, what time they would arrive home, and always with that same respectful bow and gentle smile. Lisa said softly, 'Do you think he minds that we're leaving?'

'I doubt it, they're pretty inscrutable; but then again perhaps he will mind; what will he do when we've gone? Serving some British family is all he's ever known.'

'But it's what they want, Adrian.'

'Of course, but will the result be anything like the anticipation?'

'If we came back in ten years' time I wonder what it would be like,' she said softly. 'Who will be living here and what sort of government will they have? How much will it have changed and will it be for the best?'

'I think we'd hardly recognise it, Lisa. Oh, we'll recognise the buildings, some of the old India will be the same, but there'll be Pakistan in the north run by the Moslems and India—India too will be different. I don't want to come back in ten years' time, I want to be able to remember the India we helped to create. You know, Lisa, you can do your best, think you're doing people one hell of a good turn, but they have to want it, want you, and we haven't always been right.'

'What do you mean?'

'Well, England didn't always send the right people. The Army did a good job—we tried—but so many people were intent on treating the people as "natives," lesser people, and the resentment grew and festered. We have to learn, Lisa, that other lands breed other men, and it doesn't necessarily mean they are less than us—they're just different, that's all.'

'I wonder if your father would agree with those sentiments.'

He laughed. 'We used to argue like mad about it. My father's the old school, pompous and blinkered. I'll admit he's mellowed considerably, but if he'd stayed on here I'm not sure that he would have.'

'He's hoping Martin will make the Army his career. Is it what you want?'

'I want him to please himself, at least that's what I tell myself, but it is a tradition, darling, in our family; perhaps secretly it's what I hope he'll choose.'

'He's leaning that way.'

'How do you know?'

'From his letters. Have you never thought so?'

'Perhaps.'

She had to be content with that. Now that she knew for certain that their days in India were numbered she wanted to get home quickly, to meet Marcia and the young man she never stopped writing about, another army officer, and she thought wistfully that whether she liked it or not this was where destiny was leading.

She had no doubt that Martin would follow in his father's footsteps, but these days she was thinking more and more more of Antony. He had started to write to her frequently now, although he told her very little of his experiences as a prisoner of war. She was sure he was anxious to forget that period in his life, but now he wrote about Martindale, where he intended to spend time.

He wrote about race meetings and cricket matches, house parties and the sort of social events she had once looked forward to, and occasionally he wrote about the girls he had met—one of them in particular.

She was a Miss Heather Blackstock and her father was an air vice marshal. He had introduced her to his father and to his grandmother—his father approved of her, his grandmother rather less so, and reading that information Lisa smiled to herself.

His grandmother would want him to marry, to produce the next Hazelmere, but not yet—a girl would take him away, she'd see less of him, and Lisa hoped that Antony would please himself. One day, he'd written, he'd like her to meet Heather; he was so sure she would like her.

It all seemed so long ago and far away, those times at Hazelmere, but Antony's letters brought them to life. After reading his letters she could think that she was a girl again, riding her horse across the hills behind the house, taking tea with her mother in Aunt Jane's drawing room with its preponderance of china figurines and gentle watercolour paintings, or listening to Lucy and Sybil vying with each other over some social event.

What sort of life would she be returning to? A life far removed from the affluence of Hazelmere and the glamour of India, but a life she could relate to, the gentleness of an English village and a world at peace.

It was hard to part with friends she had known well in this land of pageantry, pomp and potency, but they assured each other that they would keep in touch wherever they were; it was all she could hope for. The men were going home but they were still Army, they would still obey the rules, go wherever they were sent; she simply hoped that for a little while at least they could live as a family, enjoy the English summer.

Adrian's father greeted them on their arrival in Devon, stating almost immediately on their arrival that he intended to move out to an officers' club where several of his friends had taken up residence. 'All widowers they are,' he said. 'Enjoying the things on offer there; I'm looking forward to it.'

'There's really no need to move out, Father,' Adrian was quick to assure him. 'Lisa and I have talked about it, we'd rather you stayed on with us.'

'And I don't believe a word of it. You want the house to yourselves; you don't want on old man like me with his likes and dislikes spoiling things for you. No, I've made up my mind, I'm going to stay at the club. You're very welcome to visit me there whenever you feel like it, and I might even decide to spend Christmas with you, but that's the sum of it.'

They didn't attempt to dissuade him simply because they knew it would be no use. Adrian drove him with his pile of luggage to the home situated in the middle of vast parkland, complete with nine-hole golf course and tennis courts, and the old man proudly showed his son around the comfortable rooms and his bedroom overlooking the gardens.

'I'll be happy here,' he said firmly. 'I know a good many of the chaps and we'll find plenty to talk about. Now I want you to promise me that you'll talk to young Martin and encourage him to join the regiment, I think he's got the Air Force out of his system at last.'

'We'll talk about it, Father.'

'You need to do more than talk about it. You need to insist, Adrian.'

'Well, it's early days. We're just settling in; when we've had an opportunity to talk I'll keep you informed.'

'It's what I want for him, Adrian, and it's what you should want too. I'm glad to see young Marcia's got herself a nice young officer, glad he's Army—she could have brought anybody home.'

'Of course, father, he could have been Navy or RAF, then what?'

'It's all right for you to be facetious about it, but girls are not like they used to be; they've had too much freedom. Why, your mother was a sweet pliable little creature who knew how to behave; nowadays the girls are making the decisions, running wild.'

When later Adrian repeated the conversation to Lisa she saw at once the advantages of the General's departure, and Adrian laughed. 'We get along better now than we ever did,' he said. 'All the same he'll never change. I tolerated it but a younger generation might not. I'd rather not take that chance.'

* * *

It was a warm day at the end of summer when a car pulled up at the gate and a man and woman got out to stand for a few moments looking up at the house, then with a smile he took hold of her hand and drew her into the garden.

Lisa had watched their arrival and with a warm smile she went out to meet them, kissing Antony before he brought the girl forward, a pale blonde girl with bright blue eyes, her smile warm and friendly.

'This is Heather, Mother,' he said. 'I've told her all about you; we're staying over at her aunt's place near Sidmouth and it seemed such a good opportunity to drive over to see you.'

'I'm glad that you did. Martin's visiting friends in London but Adrian is here; he'll be so glad to meet you and Marcia will be home later.'

Lunch was a happy affair while the two men talked about India and Antony said, 'I can't believe we came out, why they wanted it.'

'It's only the beginning,' Adrian said. 'Other parts of the empire will follow suit; the sun is finally setting.'

Lisa and Heather left them talking while they strolled along the cliff top and down to the beach. There were so many question Lisa needed to ask but she allowed the girl to talk and she needed little encouragement.

'I met Antony years ago at a party,' she said with a

smile. 'I was ten years old and he was there with some girls older then me. I thought he was the most handsome man I'd ever seen but I was very young and he didn't even notice me.'

'But he has now, Heather.'

'Yes. I couldn't believe my luck when he asked me to marry him.'

'And when will that be?'

'Next spring, we hope. There's so much to do at Martindale. It became a nursing home during the war and it hasn't entirely been put to rights. There are workmen there now; Antony's very enthusiastic about us living there.'

'I remember it as a lovely house.'

'Oh, of course, you lived there too. I saw your portrait on the wall and thought you were very beautiful, so much like Antony. I did so want to meet you.'

Lisa stared at her curiously, before saying, 'You say my portrait is on the wall at Martindale?'

'Why yes, at the head of the stairs, where they divide. You're wearing a pale-green ball gown and emeralds. There are so many portraits on the walls at Hazelmere and Martindale, but I thought yours was the most beautiful of the lot.'

'I didn't realise it was still there.'

'Well, Antony's grandmother has said mine will replace it, although Antony doesn't agree with her; he says there's room for both of us.'

'And what does his father say?'

'That his mother is right; your portrait will go to Hazelmere.'

'Why should it go anywhere at all?'

'That's what Antony's grandmother says, but I rather think Lord Hazelmere will have his way. They don't really get along too well.'

'I think perhaps she's right; it has no place at Hazelmere.'

'He'll find a place for it, I feel sure.'

For some time they walked along the beach in silence and when they turned to go back they found Antony walking towards them, a smile on his face, and as he took hold of Heather's hand he said, 'I'm glad you've been getting to know one another. I've really come to invite you to our wedding, Mother. Has Heather told you it's to be next spring, April we think?'

Seriously Lisa said, 'Darling, I don't think it will be possible.'

'Why not? Mother, times are changing. We've stopped shutting people out now because of things that mattered once and which are no longer important. I told my father I was going to ask you—he didn't think it was a bad idea.'

'Did he say as much?'

'Well no, but he didn't disagree either.'

'And your grandmother?'

'It's our wedding, Mother, surely we should be able to invite the people we want to it.'

'In normal circumstances, yes, but surely you want peace and harmony on your wedding day, not the bitterness and resentment my presence would create.'

'Why should you care, Mother, you'll have Adrian beside you, and you are my mother after all. We've been to dos recently where there's been all sorts of past scandals but for one day at least they've been forgotten.'

'Antony, I grew up with the sort of resentment and bitterness a family was capable of showing. There were times when I wished Mother and I had been left alone to live our own lives but the very people who decided we'd had enough were capable of adopting the same bitterness later. It's too late, darling, I don't think I could watch you getting married and knowing that all around me there would be people thinking I shouldn't be there.'

'I'd want you there, Mother.'

'And I'd be there in spirit, Antony. I'll be thinking about you all day and wishing you well.'

'Can't we see what Adrian thinks about it?'

'We can, but I rather think he'll be on my side.'

'Perhaps my father can persuade you.'

'I'd much rather you didn't ask him to try.'

'You know, Mother, whenever I disagree with Grandmother she always says there's a lot of you in me, that I can be stubborn and go my own way. It's the Spanish in me.'

Lisa didn't reply but for the first time in a great many years she thought about that young Spaniard who had loved her at a time when she was hurt and vulnerable. He had had no say in Antony's life, never knew of his existence and had probably long since forgotten her as she had forgotten him, but in the end perhaps Lady Hazelmere was right—there was something in both of them that was alien and discordant.

They left in the early evening after Marcia had arrived home with her fiancé and there had been much laughter and cheerful farewells as they stood in the garden to watch them drive away. Antony's last words were, 'We'll see you at the wedding, Mother, if we don't see you before.'

It was much later that Adrian said, 'What was all that about seeing you at the wedding?'

'He wants us to be there, Adrian, I've told him it's impossible.'

'Does Dominic know he intends to invite you?'

'I believe so; his grandmother would be horrified. It is impossible, isn't it, Adrian? You would hate it and so would I. Think about it, darling. Only Dominic and us know the real truth; the rest of them regard us as the sinners. It was all so long ago and should be forgotten even though it can never be forgiven.'

He smiled gently and taking her into his arms he said, 'If that's how you see it then I'm sure you're right, darling. I really can't see us watching the ceremony in the church while all around us there'd be so much antagonism and local curiosity.'

'No, it would be terrible. We should not be asked to face that even for Antony.'

At the beginning of May she sat overlooking the garden with the pictures of Antony's wedding spread out before her and she smiled gently at his handsome face looking down at his beautiful young bride. The family pictures brought a smile of bitterness to her face.

Dominic stood beside his new daughter-in-law, tall, unsmiling, but proudly handsome. His mother took pride of place in a great many of the pictures, a handsome woman still, and Sybil, so very much older than Lisa remembered her but bringing back old memories of those winter mornings when she had tramped along the icy drive on the way to the lessons she had hated—perhaps not the lessons themselves but why they should ever have been thought to be necessary.

Adrian found her sitting with the pictures spread out before her and picking one of them up he said with a smile, 'They make a handsome couple, Lisa. I can't think we would have fitted in anywhere amongst that lot.'

'No. I wonder what Dominic was thinking. It was always hard to tell what he thought about things.'

'I couldn't even begin to hazard a guess about what Dominic might have been thinking but I'm pretty sure that his mother would have been thinking that the family name is safe, that the line will continue. Isn't that what she always wanted most?'

Of course he was right. People's feelings, beliefs, even heartbreak had never been as important to Lucy Hazelmere as the continuance of the family name, and looking down at Lisa with a gentle smile he said softly, 'You were the lucky one, darling. You escaped from her domination a long time ago; you never need concern yourself with it again.'

Enjoy the dazzling glamour of Vienna on the eve of the First World War…

Rebellious Alex Faversham dreams of escaping her stifling upper-class Victorian background. She yearns to be like her long-lost Aunt Alicia, the beautiful black sheep of the family who lives a glamorous life abroad.

Inspired, Alex is soon drawn to the city her aunt calls home – Vienna. Its heady glitter and seemingly everlasting round of balls and parties in the years before WW1 is as alluring as she had imagined, and Alex finds romance at last with Karl von Winkler, a hussar in the Emperor's guard. But, like the Hapsburg Empire, her fledgling love affair cannot last. Away from home and on the brink of war, will Alex ever see England or her family again?

As the Battle of Britain rages over the Essex coast, two teenagers fall in love…

On the bleak family farm on the Essex marshlands, Annie Cross slaves all day for her cruel father. The one thing that keeps her going is her secret meetings with Tom Featherstone.

But war steals Tom from her when he joins the RAF. Annie would love to do her bit but, stuck on the farm, she lives for Tom's letters – until they stop coming.

When, against the odds, her beloved Tom returns, he finds a different, stronger Annie to the one he left behind. But he also finds the girl he loved is carrying another man's child…

Available from 21st March 2008

MIRA

A collection of short, period regional sagas – especially for Christmas

Bride at Bellfield Mill
by Penny Jordan

A Family for Hawthorn Farm
by Helen Brooks

Tilly of Tap House
by Carol Wood

M&B

A compelling North-East saga in the bestselling tradition of Catherine Cookson

Born the day of the great mining disaster at Jane Pit, Merry Trent is brought up by her only surviving relative, her feisty grandmother Peggy, and lives in stricken poverty. Times are hard, and when an unwelcome visit from the ruthless mining agent, Miles Gallagher, leaves her pregnant, she tells no-one.

When Merry begins training as an apprentice nurse she attracts the attention of dashing young doctor Tom Gallagher, Miles' son, and Merry falls pregnant again. She loses her job and accommodation at the hospital, and her future looks bleak as she faces a tough choice: a marriage of convenience, or destitution and the workhouse…

M&B

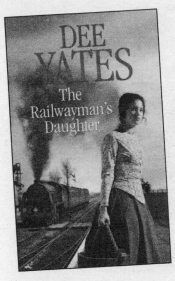

In 1875, a row of tiny cottages stands by the tracks of the newly built York – Doncaster railway…

Railwayman Tom Swales, with his wife and five daughters, takes the end cottage. But with no room to spare in the loving Swales household, eldest daughter Mary accepts a position as housemaid to the nearby stationmaster. There she battles the daily grime from the passing trains – and the stationmaster's brutal, lustful nature. In the end, it's a fight she cannot win.

In shame and despair, Mary flees to York. But the pious couple who take her in know nothing of true Christian charity. They work Mary like a slave – despite her heavy pregnancy. Can she find the strength to return home to her family? Will they accept her? And what of her first love, farmer's son Nathaniel? Mary hopes with all her heart that he will still be waiting…

www.millsandboon.co.uk

M&B

Set in 1940s London during the Blitz, this is a moving tale about family, love and courage

Queenie McLaren and her daughter Laura have long had to protect each other from Jock Mclaren's violent temper. In 1940, the evacuation of women and children from their homeland in Gibraltar is the perfect chance to escape, and Queenie and Laura eventually find themselves in London during the height of the Blitz.

During the darkest of war years, mother and daughter find courage in friendships formed in hardship, and the joy of new romances. But neither of them has yet heard that Jock is in England – and he won't rest until he's found them…

www.millsandboon.co.uk